Implacable Resentment

by

Jann Rowland

One Good Sonnet Publishing

This is a work of fiction, based on the works of Jane Austen. All of the characters and events portrayed in this novel are products of Jane Austen's original novel, the author's imagination, or are used fictitiously.

IMPLACABLE RESENTMENT

Copyright © 2015 Jann Rowland

Published by One Good Sonnet Publishing

All rights reserved.

ISBN: 0993797768
ISBN-13: 978-0993797767

No part of this book may be reproduced or transmitted in any form or by any means, electronic, digital, or mechanical, including photocopying, recording, or by any information storage and retrieval system, without permission in writing from the publisher.

To all those who continue to show love, and support, patience, trust, kindness and belief.

ACKNOWLEDGEMENTS

Ever writing,
Little sleeping,
It can hide a,
Zest for living.
A thanks to all who,
Bless and lift me.
Especially to,
Tomoko, Lelia,
Helpers, supporters.

Chapter I

*I*t is an inescapable truth that a gentleman, when confronted with a set of untenable circumstances, must take it upon himself to ease the situation when the principals involved in said situation are unable — or unwilling — to resolve matters for themselves.

Edward Gardiner was painfully aware of that fact as he walked the corridors of his brother's house one fateful morning, determined that something must be done to ease the situation before something tragic happened.

He stepped up to the door of his brother's bookroom, and after a staccato rap on the door, he heard the command to enter, a prompt with which Gardiner lost no time in complying.

The bookroom was his brother's sole consolation in a house where the boisterous concerns of a wife and five daughters were paramount, and although Gardiner was not precisely forbidden from going inside the room (unlike his female relations), he was not precisely welcomed in Mr. Bennet's sanctum either. The room was not overly large, but every available wall space was covered with bookshelves, and although there was still space left on the shelves for further purchases, Gardiner could tell Bennet had not been remiss in adding to his collection over the years since they had first become acquainted.

Seating himself in the chair opposite the desk, Gardiner studied his brother, comparing himself to the older man seated across from him. Gardiner had been taught from an early age the importance of industry; his father had instilled in him a sense of responsibility, not only to himself, but also to his family, those with whom he worked, and society in general. By contrast, his brother Bennet rarely felt the need to stir from his bookroom, preferring to shut himself away from the world, ignore his family, and comfort himself with his books. Gardiner was not certain how the work of the estate was ever accomplished, as he had rarely seen Bennet exert himself in any manner for the betterment of the estate or his children. Circumstances being what they were, Gardiner knew it was imperative that his brother start planning for the future of his family should no heir be produced.

He was greeted shortly and offered a glass of port. Mr. Bennet seemed curious as to what brought his brother into his bookroom and, after a moment, posed the question.

Mr. Gardiner began the conversation thus:

"I have come to speak to you today about a matter of some concern."

Mr. Bennet regarded his brother through narrowed eyes. "Well, then, speak your mind."

"It is regarding Elizabeth, brother."

Mr. Bennet nodded his head, as if his suspicions were confirmed. "What has that child done now? Surely this is something you could have taken up with your sister; I am certain she will see to the girl's punishment if she has misbehaved."

Gardiner had to smother his inclination to exclaim in disbelief. "From what I have seen of Elizabeth, she is far too timid and emotionally fragile to misbehave as you suggest."

Much to Gardiner's dismay, his brother chose to ignore his words about the girl's emotional state. "Then why have you interrupted my solitude? Whatever you have to say about the child could certainly have been said at dinner or when the family is gathered together in the parlor."

Gardiner forbore mentioning that the opportunity to have any kind of discussion while the family was gathered together was unlikely due to Bennet's propensity for spending every waking moment with his books. Instead, Gardiner came right to the point.

"I would like to know what has happened to her, brother. While I have not seen her in some time now due to being preoccupied with my business, I am startled at the change that has come over her. When I last saw the child, she was a bright and precocious girl of two, and now at nine, she can hardly be recognized as the same child."

"And what of it? All children change substantially in six years' time."

Gardiner was not to be put off. "Please do not insult my intelligence, brother. Sarah and I can both see what is happening here, and neither of us is comfortable with the way Elizabeth is being treated by this family."

A dangerous glint appeared in Bennet's eye, and for a moment, Gardiner considered whether his brother was a little mad. The thought was brief and barely flickered across Gardiner's consciousness. However, the anger on Bennet's face was evident.

"What are you suggesting, Gardiner?" demanded he. "Do you think I abuse my daughter?"

"Calm yourself, Bennet. I was suggesting nothing of the kind. Anyone with eyes in their head can see the child bears no marks of physical abuse. I was speaking of emotional scars, not physical ones."

Bennet's response was to bluster. "I have no idea of what you are speaking. Now, if we are finished, I would very much appreciate the use of my bookroom."

"No, Bennet, we are not finished. Do not sit there and try to tell me you cannot see what is happening in your house under your very nose—and with your tacit approval, I might add!"

The two men glared at each other over the desk, the tension in the room no less than Gardiner would have expected for a discussion of this nature. He reflected grimly that there had been a time when he would have been hesitant to challenge a man who was not only his elder brother by marriage, but who was also his superior in the eyes of society. It was a fortunate thing, indeed, that his dealings and experience with the world had done away with his youthful reticence when speaking those of the upper classes.

"I am sorry to bring you pain, brother, but I fear I must speak clearly. Sarah and I are very concerned for the emotional wellbeing of your second daughter. She wears the dullest, most threadbare dresses I have ever seen on a young girl—dresses I would not expect to see worn by the lowest of urchins on the back streets of London. No one in this family, outside of Jane, has a kind word to say to her, and even then, if Jane speaks kindly to Elizabeth in the company of her mother, she is immediately scolded and told not to waste her . . . *breath* on . . . well, let us just say I shall not repeat my sister's words. Furthermore, *your wife* treats her as a being worthy of only contempt, as if she is something less than human, and it may have escaped your notice, but the younger girls, Lydia in particular, have begun to emulate their mother, and they treat her with the utmost in disdain and cruelty. And unless I am very much mistaken, I suspect the child's education has been all but nonexistent; indeed, I would hazard a guess that at the age of nine, she is still unable to read. Need I go on?"

Throughout Gardiner's recital, he could see the defiance and anger drain from his brother's countenance, to be replaced with a profound sorrow, the likes of which he had only seen once on Bennet's face. "You would be correct. To the best of my knowledge, she has had no education and is illiterate."

"Can you not even say her name, brother?"

Bennet's countenance darkened once again, but he did not deign to respond to the charge.

"Robert, as a brother and a friend, I feel it is my place to intervene on Elizabeth's behalf. She is desperately unhappy, and spends every spare minute of her time out of doors, going as far from the house as she can and still be on the grounds, obviously wishing to be as far removed from her family as she can contrive. At the dinner table, she rarely forces more than a few mouthfuls of food past her lips. She is so thin as to be almost emaciated, and soon, you are likely to lose a daughter; she will no doubt starve herself to death—if the unhappiness of her situation does not make her do something desperate before then."

Mr. Bennet let out a long sigh and stared at the book sitting on his desk, refusing to meet his brother's eyes. "Believe me, Edward; I know all of this."

"Then why have you not done something about it?" demanded Gardiner.

"Because I . . . cannot. I fully understand the situation with Elizabeth and have berated myself on my inability to do anything about it many times. I cannot even begin to relate the number of times I have sat here, listening my wife mistreating her, steeling myself to have a word with Maggie over it, only to find myself powerless to move from my desk. Your sister has treated her cruelly, the other girls have been encouraged to speak to her with contempt, and I have allowed all of this to happen. I simply cannot . . . Every time I see the child, I *remember*."

"Robert, I understand your pain. Is it not time to let go of the past?"

Gardiner's statement brought the fire back into his brother's eyes. "How can you possibly understand? *You* who are childless," spat

Bennet as he rose to his feet and began pacing the room.

Gardiner never felt more in need of guidance than at that moment, and he said a quick prayer to the Lord above for patience and understanding. "Then let us say that I can empathize, brother."

"Empathize!" Bennet's tone was cloaked in bitterness. "I should like to see your reaction to similar circumstances. I should like to see you witness . . ." Bennet's voice faltered, and he sat down in his chair again heavily, desperately fighting to gain control over his emotions.

Gardiner regarded him for several moments. He suspected his appeals would amount to naught, but there was no other option but to try. It seemed as though his brother and sister were still trapped on that fateful day more than six years before, and nothing could convince them to let the past go and move on. If Gardiner could not make his brother see reason and take action for Elizabeth's welfare, then he would have no recourse but to fall back on the other option he and his wife had discussed.

"Robert, I understand that it has been hard for you—the births of the younger girls must have made it doubly difficult—but have you never considered the fact that as a child of two, Elizabeth should not have been held responsible for what happened? Indeed, I am inclined to think that negligence was more the cause than willful disobedience."

Bennet barked a short, mirthless burst of laughter. "You certainly think highly of your sister! Negligence indeed!"

"Can you deny it?"

"I cannot," said Bennet after a moment's pause. "The circumstances . . . let us simply say I have tried to tell myself this more often than I can relate."

"Can you not exert yourself for her welfare, Robert? As I recall, she was once the apple of your eye."

His countenance cast in a morose expression, Mr. Bennet stared at his desk for several moments. "I am sorry, Edward, but I can do nothing. I told you—every time I think to do something, the mere sight of her causes me to remember . . . Ah! I cannot even speak of it! She is the cause of our family's distress; she is the instrument of this family's eventual downfall. I cannot forgive her for this."

Gardiner sighed and leaned back in his seat, unhappy that his conjectures regarding the result of his appeal should prove so prophetically correct. There was only one thing left to do, and he hoped most fervently that his brother would be amenable to the proposition.

"In that case, brother, I fear it is up to me to resolve the situation."

Bennet peered at him, his gaze sharp and penetrating. "What do you mean?"

"Let us take Elizabeth with us to London."

"You, a newlywed man, wish to take a girl of nine to live with you and your wife? What will Mrs. Gardiner have to say about this?"

"It was her suggestion, Robert. The plight of your second daughter has touched us both, and we cannot, in good conscience, allow the situation to continue as it has. I wish to God I had paid more attention to your family and visited Longbourn a few years ago. If I had, I would have intervened long ago. I fear the damage to Elizabeth will not be easily overcome, as it has been six years in the making."

Bennet hung his head in shame at the pronouncement, allowing Gardiner to feel some measure of hope.

"I am not attempting to place any blame," said Gardiner. "But something must be done, and although I would prefer that you take up your daughter's cause so that she may stay with her family, I fear this is impossible. Allow us to take her to London with us. We will care for her, provide her with an education, and love her as you and Maggie are unable to do. Think of her welfare, Robert."

The silence in the room was deafening, and as it wore on, Gardiner began to feel fear that his offer would be rejected. What would he do if it was? Could he, in defiance of all that was proper, remove Elizabeth from his brother's house forcibly? Yet could he in good conscience leave her in a situation which was crushing her? At the very least, he did not suppose his brother would stop him if he did decide to take so drastic a measure—surely he could not be roused from his bookroom for such an effort.

Finally, Bennet's eyes rose from where they have been fixed at some spot on his desk, and he tried one last feeble protest. "Your sister will not approve. She will be most put out that you would take her least deserving daughter to enjoy the delights of London."

"Bennet, to be perfectly frank, Maggie's opinion does not concern me in the slightest. I have always known my sister was not blessed with the greatest of sense, and although I knew she was capable of spiteful behavior, I never would have imagined it would be directed in such a vindictive manner at one of her own children. I am quite determined that something must be done. You and Maggie are destroying that poor girl, and I cannot stand idly by and do nothing. If you will give me your consent, I will readily deal with my sister."

With a sigh, Bennet extended his hand. "It is settled then, Edward. Take the girl with you to London. It is for the best."

Gardiner shook his brother's hand, feeling no small measure of relief. "Thank you, Robert. Believe me when I say we shall treat her as our very own."

"She will be far better off with you, I am certain. I advise you to keep this development to yourself until it is time for you to leave—you will hear no end of nervous suffering and complaints of ill-usage once Maggie becomes aware of your plans."

"I am well aware of my sister's disposition. Be that as it may, it is of little import, as we intend to leave today."

"So soon?" asked Bennet, the surprise clearly evident on his face.

"I believe it to be necessary. We must remove Elizabeth from this house as soon as possible for her own good, and Sarah has been preparing all morning for such an eventuality. We will celebrate Christmas in town with Elizabeth."

Bennet winced as the implications of what he had just been told entered his consciousness. Nevertheless, he nodded curtly to his brother, indicating his consent. "I hope you understand what I am doing for the girl, Edward. Maggie will be upset that you are leaving so soon after you arrived, and that is not even taking into account the objections she will raise over your plans to take her daughter with you. *You* will only have to put up with her nerves until you close the carriage door behind you, while *I* will likely have to deal with them for months to come."

Gardiner inclined his head in understanding. "Consider it the least you can do in light of the situation. If you had been able to control your wife's behavior toward your daughter, we would not be in this situation."

Bennet said nothing in response, merely waving his brother from the room, his hand already reaching for the book that had been discarding. Expecting no less, Gardiner nodded in response and strode to the door, pausing to turn and regard his brother, knowing it could be some years again before they met.

"Brother, if I make a suggestion. Now that you are ceding guardianship of Elizabeth to me, it would behoove you to think of your other daughters. Hiding yourself away in your bookroom will not provide for your children once you are gone, especially if there is to be no heir. I strongly suggest you curb Maggie's spending and put some money aside for their eventual care."

Bennet scowled but did not deign to look up from his book. Sighing with regret, Gardiner turned his back on his brother and left to inform his wife of their impending departure.

And so it was that—not more than an hour later—the Gardiners took their leave of the Bennets, ensconced themselves in their carriage, and settled down for the half-day trip to their house in town, feeling drained and emotionally sick due to the events of the morning.

As Bennet had predicted, Mrs. Bennet was aghast at the change in arrangements and had been vocal in her disapproval of the scheme, railing at her brother for his ill-judged and blatant interfering in the workings of her family. Surely, if he meant to take one of her daughters back with him to town for a visit, he should take Jane, the sweetest and most beautiful child in the world. Needless to say, her fury reached new heights when she learned that Elizabeth's sojourn in town was to be a permanent arrangement. She had berated and cajoled, demanding that the scheme be given up, and when that had failed, she had turned her venom on her daughter, making it abundantly clear she wanted nothing more to do with such a worthless child. Elizabeth had listened to her mother's diatribe with what Gardiner had come to understand was her customary stoic and emotionless mask. Yet the single teardrop trickling down the side of Elizabeth's face at her mother's words had not escaped his attention.

Elizabeth's distress being the final straw, Gardiner had immediately risen and ordered the coach, instructing his wife to take Elizabeth outside to await the carriage and mentally thanking his foresight to have everything prepared for a quick departure. He had delayed telling his sister of their plans until the last possible moment, expecting just such an outcome. Once Sarah and Elizabeth were out of the room, Gardiner proceeded to tell his sister *exactly* what he thought of her behavior, and then he had taken his leave of the house with all possible haste.

The carriage had been ready in moments, and quickly stowing their possessions—as well as the few meager possessions Elizabeth owned—they made to leave Longbourn behind them. During the entire period of uproar, Mr. Bennet had not once removed himself from his bookroom to take leave of the daughter he would likely not see for many years—a good many years if Gardiner had anything to say in the matter.

On his way out the door, Gardiner had seen his sister go directly to her husband's bookroom, and almost immediately the sound of raised voices had reached him, causing him to be even more firmly resolved to quit the house. The only member of Elizabeth's family to follow them out to take leave of Elizabeth had been sweet Jane, who, being the eldest and the only one of her siblings to understand—or care—that her younger sister was to quit the house permanently, had pulled Elizabeth into a firm embrace and admonished her to be happy in her new home. Elizabeth had merely nodded in her heartbreaking emotionless fashion and had then climbed up into the coach at Sarah's urging.

Looking back on the sad state of affairs in his sister's home, Gardiner could not help but feel sorry at the way it had all turned out. His brother Bennet had been correct—taking a young girl into his home was not the most ideal of circumstances for a newly married young man. But Elizabeth's reaction to the morning's drama had put to rest any lingering doubts—if Gardiner had indeed had any—over the necessity of her removal from her parents' home. For the first part of the journey, Elizabeth huddled in the corner of the carriage and resisted all attempts to be coaxed to sit nearer to her relations. It was only after they left the vicinity of Meryton that she was finally persuaded to sit beside her aunt. After a moment of Sarah's tender ministrations, the dam burst, and Elizabeth buried her head in her aunt's lap, her body shaking with wracking sobs, as if her heart would break into pieces. Gardiner could feel his heart breaking along with hers.

Once she finally cried herself to sleep, the rest of the journey passed swiftly, with husband and wife spending the time in earnest conversation over how to reclaim their niece from the unhappy circumstances of her childhood. It was clear that the damage to her self-esteem was extensive, and her recovery would be long and arduous.

Chapter II

Ten years later

It is said that still waters run deep, and in the case of Jane Bennet, that maxim was certainly not without foundation. The eldest of a family wholly comprised of daughters, she was a gentle soul, and most of those with whom she interacted considered her to be lovely and amiable, yet one who was not in the habit of feeling deeply. Nothing could be further from the truth.

On a particular day in late September, Jane stepped into the carriage bound for Netherfield, eager to be away from her home for a short time. She loved her family, and she generally thought well of them, little though some of them seemed to deserve it at times. Escaping the chaos which was so prevalent in the home was a boon, and never did she feel it more than at that moment. The author of the morning's excitement had been, of course, Mrs. Bennet.

In truth, Jane's feelings for her mother were complex. On the one hand, the dutiful daughter in Jane insisted that Mrs. Bennet was owed her allegiance and respect. The woman had given birth to her, after all—surely she deserved Jane's gratitude for that fact alone!

But it was so very difficult at times. Mrs. Bennet was a silly woman, with no true understanding of proper behavior in gentle families, herself having been the neglected daughter of a tradesman. Therefore, her behavior was often a trial for Jane, and Mr. Bennet had never seen fit to take his wife in hand and curb her ways. In fact, her father rarely bestirred himself from his library, preferring the company of his books to that of his family. Other than family meals and the occasional social event, only rare occasions could cause him to emerge at all.

That morning, her father had not even been present at the breakfast table when Jane received an invitation to join Mr. Bingley's sisters for dinner. Never had Jane been so happy that the day was warm and fair, for if rain had threatened, Jane was certain that Mrs. Bennet would have insisted that she go on Nelly—the old horse her father kept for the rare occasions when he could actually be induced to ride around the estate—and thereby necessitate her stay overnight. Of course, such a stratagem could have easily been foiled should the sisters have offered to send her home in their carriage.

Regardless of the circumstances, Jane was happy to be going to Netherfield. She was quickly becoming close confidantes with the two ladies of Netherfield and enjoyed her time with them. Caroline Bingley and Louisa Hurst had been quite kind to her, declaring her to be their particular friend within days of arriving in Hertfordshire. And then there was Mr. Bingley, the man with whom, even after so short an acquaintance, she was beginning to feel an attachment unlike any she had ever felt before . . . .

Jane shied away from such thoughts. There were many reasons for her to esteem Mr. Bingley—his amiable nature, his friendly discourse, and his handsome mien among the most prevalent—and there were many reasons why she sincerely hoped that her relationship with Mr. Bingley would lead to a more permanent arrangement. But Jane had known disappointment in her life, and she was not about to allow her fancy to get the better of her. Not when she had only known the man for less than a full month.

The Bennet carriage entered the drive at Netherfield a short time later, and when it stopped in front of the large manor, Jane stepped out with the assistance of a footman.

"Dear Jane!" exclaimed Miss Bingley as she alighted. "How good of you to come!"

By her side, Mrs. Hurst greeted her, though she did so with less enthusiasm than her sister, which Jane had come to understand was in line with Mrs. Hurst's character.

"Thank you very much for your kind invitation," said Jane.

"You are very welcome," said Miss Bingley. "In fact, I believe it is you who do us a favor. You would not wish for my sister and me to quarrel, would you?"

"No, indeed," replied Jane.

"Then it is well that you have come," said Mrs. Hurst. "With the gentlemen away from the house, only a disagreement can result. Now, let us go into the sitting room."

When they were settled in the aforementioned room, they began to converse in a pleasant fashion, much as old friends would. However, as they were new acquaintances, there was a certain probing quality to some of the questions, no doubt due to the fact that Jane's new friends wished to know her better.

When they adjourned to the dining room, the conversation continued, and the talk turned to extended family and friends. Jane soon learned that the Bingleys had two aunts and an uncle, all of whom lived in the York area, from whence they had originated. As Mr. Bingley was the son of the eldest sibling, he had inherited the family business, though his uncle still owned part of it and was very much involved in its daily operations. These connections were somewhat quickly passed over, and Miss Bingley took care to ensure Jane understood that it had been their father's wish that Mr. Bingley would rise above his roots in trade and enter the ranks of landed gentlemen.

Soon thereafter, the conversation turned to Jane's relations, and it was at that point that she became a little uncomfortable, though she did her best to hide the fact from her hosts.

"You are the eldest of four sisters, is that correct?" asked Louisa Hurst.

The truthful person in Jane could only hesitate a moment before replying, "Actually, there are five of us."

"Five?" asked Miss Bingley with a raised eyebrow. "I am sure that I have only seen three sisters at any of the gatherings in the area which we have attended."

"My next youngest sister is away from home, living with my aunt and uncle in London."

An interested expression came over Miss Bingley's face. "Living with her aunt and uncle, is she?"

"Yes," replied Jane, not wishing to discuss the situation any further.

Unfortunately, the subject seemed to have caught the sisters' attention, and neither seemed willing to allow it to drop.

"That must be difficult," said Mrs. Hurst in a commiserating tone. "My sister and I quarrel on occasion, but I should not wish to be separated from her for long periods."

"But it must make the reunions all that much sweeter," added Miss Bingley.

"Indeed, it does," replied Jane in a quiet tone. "I very much miss Elizabeth, and I look forward to seeing her again."

The sisters seemed to understand that she did not wish to speak of the matter any further, and they turned the conversation slightly.

"It is very hard indeed when a sibling must be sent away for reasons of economy," said Miss Bingley. "Members our set are rarely required to do such things."

"Oh, Elizabeth is not with my aunt and uncle because my father cannot keep her," said Jane, though she immediately wished that she had kept her own counsel. "Rather, Elizabeth lives with my uncle in order that she may take advantage of the opportunity for education in London."

After so many years, the lie came easily to her lips. Jane had only been a young girl when Elizabeth had left Longbourn, but she still remembered the whispers of gossip which had plagued them. Her father had soon decreed that to protect the family, they would spread the word that Elizabeth had gone to live with Mrs. Bennet's brother in London due to a desire for more education, particularly in the field of music. Of course, it had not escaped the gossips' attention that Elizabeth had not visited her family once since she had quit the neighborhood, but talk had died down to the point where it was now mentioned by only the most determined.

That did not make the necessity of lying about why Elizabeth no longer lived at home any easier. Jane was a truthful person, and the subject had always left a sour taste in her mouth. Kitty and Lydia did not seem to mind, heedless and wild as they were, and Jane was not sure what Mary thought, as she rarely voiced any opinion which did not originate from the Bible or Fordyce. The subject always brought out the worst in her mother, though it could just as easily be a cold and disdainful huff as an attack of her infamous fluttering nerves. And as for Mr. Bennet . . . Well, Jane had never been close to her father—not that *anyone* in her family was—so she could not say precisely what he thought of the matter.

"Your sister has had access to music masters, has she?" asked Mrs. Hurst seeming impressed. "Is she very talented?"

"By all accounts, she is," prevaricated Jane. "You understand that I have not heard her play in some time."

"It is very pleasing when a young lady attends to such things," said Mrs. Hurst quickly, when her sister appeared about to interject something into the conversation. "Are you able to play, Miss Bennet?"

"I do play," said Jane. "I enjoy it very much and it has been my solace for many years." It *had* been her solace for some time, given the trials she endured with her family. "I do not claim to be a true proficient, as my access to masters has been limited, but I do enjoy it."

The conversation turned to talk of music thereafter, and Jane had to force herself not to breathe a heavy sign of relief. Talk of Elizabeth made her uncomfortable, especially as it always caused her to think of what Elizabeth had endured before her departure.

Recently, Jane had discovered that Elizabeth was soon to return. It would certainly be uncomfortable for her, as the prejudice within the family was as violent as it had been before she left. But Jane remembered the happy times they had had, and she recalled the bright, happy child who had followed her and loved her. They had been close when they were very young, and Jane wished to recapture that closeness. Furthermore, Jane was determined to make Elizabeth feel as welcome as possible, though she knew she could be the only member of the family would do so.

When Jane Bennet departed, Caroline Bingley turned to her sister with a raised eyebrow. "Well?"

"I am excessively fond of Jane Bennet, as you well know," replied Louisa.

Caroline waved her off before she turned and led the way back toward the sitting room. "Yes, yes, we have already canvassed that fact. She is a dear, sweet girl. That much is indisputable."

"If you are asking whether I consider her to be a suitable prospective wife for our brother, the answer is, as you well know, that though Miss Bennet is the daughter of a gentleman, Charles can do much better."

Caroline entered the room after stopping to order a tea service from a nearby footman. She knew that she could always count on Louisa to support her.

It was too bad, she thought with some regret. Miss Bennet was indeed a wonderful girl, and under other circumstances, Caroline would have been happy to accept her into the family. In addition to her sweetness, she also possessed an extremely self-effacing and modest disposition, and she would likely be susceptible to suggestion. Caroline's control over the family would remain uncontested.

Unfortunately, the more pertinent concern was the possession of a substantial dowry and, even more importantly, connections to assist in the Bingley family's continued acceptance in the highest levels of society. Louisa had married Hurst, and though he was a drunkard of little intelligence and horrible manners, he *was* a gentleman and possessed an acceptable measure of wealth and connections. By marrying him, the Bingleys had taken the first step into higher society. It was now up to Caroline and her brother to further raise the family's fortune by marrying well. And she had just such a gentleman in mind for herself . . . .

"I wish Mr. Darcy were here," mused Caroline.

Louisa shook her head. "You always wish for Mr. Darcy's presence, so *that* is not a surprise."

"He would be able to dissuade our brother from showing Miss Bennet too much attention."

"I believe that you credit Mr. Darcy with more influence over our brother than he actually possesses."

Louisa was prompted to further explain by Caroline's dubiously raised eyebrow. "I believe that Charles's own actions have led to our being able to persuade him from further pursuit of his previous interests. Should he show any true interest in a young woman, I am not certain we would be able to persuade him to change his interest to another."

"All the more reason for Mr. Darcy to intervene before Charles begins to become seriously attached to Miss Bennet," replied Caroline in a firm tone which invited no dispute.

Silenced reigned between the sisters for several moments, and when the tea service arrived, they served themselves and sat drinking in silence for some time. At length, Caroline broke the silence to address a matter which had been on her mind since earlier that evening.

"What did you think of this talk of the banished sister?"

Louisa blinked with surprise. "Banished sister?"

This time, it was Caroline's turn to feel exasperation with her sister; Louisa never had been able to read between the lines.

"The sister in London?" prompted Caroline.

A blank stare was Louisa's response, and Caroline had to suppress a sigh.

"Miss Bennet mentioned nothing about a banishment," said Louisa.

"Do you truly think that she would speak so openly about it to us?" demanded Caroline. "And did you also miss the way she became uncomfortable discussing the subject?"

"I noticed no deception."

"Nor did I, though there most definitely were signs that all is not as it appears." Caroline was silent for several moments, considering the matter. At length, she mused, "I wonder if the truth of the matter is something which we could use should Charles become seriously attached to Miss Bennet."

Louisa fixed her with a stern glare, and for a brief moment, Caroline almost felt like a child being scolded by her elder sister. Almost. Those days were long gone, after all.

"Take care, Caroline," chided Louisa. "These are good people, regardless of whether you feel they are beneath us. I am certain that the situation with the second Bennet sister cannot be anything out of the common way, and even if there is something to your suspicion, it is none of our concern."

"I was not speaking of spreading rumors or ruining the Bennets," protested Caroline. Inside, however, she knew that should the situation become dire enough, there was not much she would *not* do to safeguard her family's position in society. "I was merely suggesting that we might use the circumstance with Miss Bennet's sister to convince Charles to pursue someone else."

"I suggest you forget about the matter entirely," said Louisa, her voice infused with an uncharacteristic firmness.

Though annoyed that Louisa would show resolve about so critical a matter, Caroline decided that now was not the time to press the issue. There would be time enough to bring Louisa to her point of view should Charles's interest in Jane Bennet become a problem.

Caroline was confident that Louisa would see things her way. Louisa had always been open to persuasion before.

Chapter III

Throwing the offensive letter down on his desk, Edward Gardiner sat back in his chair and rubbed his eyes. As a man of business, Gardiner was well accustomed to receiving unwelcome news, and though he was now a very successful businessman, he had suffered his share of setbacks and disappointments. If only this letter brought news which was so innocuous as the failure of a ship to arrive or a fire at one of his warehouses. *Those* things he could deal with.

Knowing that nothing could be gained from delay, he rang the bell to summon the butler and gave instructions to have Sarah join him as soon as was convenient. His wife would not like this any more than Edward did himself.

Sarah joined him before he had an opportunity to brood much longer, which was just as well. She had a calming influence on him and was a true partner rather than a typical society wife.

"I was about to go fetch Elizabeth and the children from the park," said Sarah as she entered the room.

Crossing the room, she approached him and bent over to allow him to kiss her on the cheek. Edward smiled at her and indicated that she should take a nearby seat. As she did so, he could not help but reflect that he had been immeasurably fortunate that she had entered his life.

The death of his father during Edward's first year at school had left the young man in possession of a modest yet prosperous business. Following his father's wishes, he had completed the schooling for which his father had scrimped and saved since his birth. The elder Mr. Gardiner had hoped that his industrious son would use what he had learned to make a better life for himself and his future children. Understanding his father's wishes and sacrifices, Edward Gardiner had determined from a very young age to honor that sacrifice, a resolution which had not suffered in the slightest due to his father's untimely death.

Thus, when he had completed school three years later, Mr. Gardiner had set out to fulfill those wishes, throwing himself into the building of the business to the exception of all other concerns. He had spent years building up his contacts, engaging suppliers, and traveling throughout the continent and even overseas to the new world. In that time, he had seen little of his family, for he had largely been away from London.

When he had finally felt secure enough in his business's position to settle down, Mr. Gardiner had allowed his thoughts to turn to having a family of his own. Hiring a few good men to do the travelling and contracting in his stead, Mr. Gardiner had, at the age of two and thirty, purchased a modest yet comfortable home. While the house was located in one of London's less fashionable districts, it had the benefit of being very close to his warehouses. At last he had allowed himself the leisure of looking for a wife.

Edward had the very great fortune to soon meet a young lady who not only captivated him, but who also had the distinction of being the only child of a prosperous businessman. Knowing that his daughter and her suitor were to be married for the greatest of affection and feeling relieved that his precious daughter would be cared for by an industrious and intelligent man of business like himself, Sarah's father had consented to their marriage with alacrity and had immediately begun the effort of merging his business with that of his new son-in-law, increasing their joint holdings immeasurably. As glad as he was of the increase in his fortune, Mr. Gardiner was even more delighted with his wife, and he still doted on her as much as he did when they first married.

"Now, Edward, what was so important that it could not wait?"

"I think you will understand if you read that letter," said Edward, gesturing at the piece of paper adorning his desk.

With some curiosity, Sarah retrieved the letter and began to read. Almost immediately, a frown creased her brow; the expression soon turned to concern and then anger as she proceeded through the letter. The letter was brief—rather succinct, Edward thought, which was unsurprising considering who had written it—and it was not long before Sarah finished reading and turned to him with a glare mixed with sadness. The letter she discarded back to its place on the desk, as though it were nothing more than some offensive piece of offal, better consigned to the rubbish heap.

"So, it has finally happened," said Sarah, her voice flat and emotionless.

"Indeed, it has," replied Gardiner in a quiet voice.

Sarah was not impressed by his seeming apathy. "The question is: what do we do about it?"

"You know the situation as well as I," said Edward. "If Bennet wishes for Elizabeth to return, then legally, it is his right to do so as her guardian."

Sarah regarded him as if he had grown another head. "Edward, he allowed Elizabeth to be treated by her family as an inferior, *abused* her for six years, and left her so fragile that it took us years to rebuild her confidence, and all you can do is sit there and say *he has the right?* From where I stand, he has no right whatsoever in anything to do with that precious girl's life!"

"I do not disagree with you, Sarah," said Gardiner in a conciliatory tone. "But the law is clear. As Elizabeth is only nineteen years of age, her father still has authority over her."

"I will not allow Elizabeth to return to a house where her confidence will once again be destroyed!"

"And what of Elizabeth's opinion?" asked Gardiner in a quiet tone.

Almost instantly, Sarah deflated, and her anger bled away. It was one of the things he loved most about the woman he had married; she was a warm and caring person, fiercely protective of her children. And she counted Elizabeth as one of those children, providing her with the love and support of a mother, though in reality they were more of age to be sisters than mother and daughter. Regardless, it was clear to all who knew them that Elizabeth was as much Sarah's child as any of the four children born to her and her husband.

But though Sarah and Elizabeth were close, Sarah had never been able to persuade Elizabeth to take her side regarding what should be done if Bennet should recall Elizabeth to Longbourn. Elizabeth had always been adamant that should it happen, she would return with her head held high; the Gardiners, on the other hand, had always assured her that they would fight such a summons should it be issued.

Now, Gardiner was well aware of his brother's financial situation, and though they had not spoken since Elizabeth left Longbourn, Gardiner had kept up with his brother's business over the years. By all reports, Bennet had not made any effort to improve his estate, and his income was now, in all likelihood, less than what it had been ten years before. By contrast, Gardiner himself had been industrious in improving his own income, and it was now in excess of three times what Bennet's had previously been.

Thus, Gardiner doubted that Bennet had the resources to bring a suit against him should he refuse to comply. And if Bennet should be willing to sue him, Gardiner was confident that he possessed the resources to crush the other man and see his suit dismissed in shame.

But Elizabeth, displaying a stubbornness which she had inherited from her mother, was firm in saying that she would not impose upon the Gardiners any longer. No amount of cajoling, pleading, or loving encouragement had induced her to change her mind on the subject. She was truly an exceptional young woman, and she was not intimidated by anything, least of all by a father she had not seen in years.

But in Gardiner's mind, though he recognized Elizabeth's growth and her exceptional qualities, he could not forget the frightened, emotionally broken child she had been when she had come into his care. Perhaps she truly was as strong as the front she put up for others, but he was afraid that when confronted with her tormentors, that strength would crumble like so much kindling in a stiff breeze. He feared for her.

"She is still underage," said Sarah, exhibiting her own brand of stubbornness. "We will fight this. She does not even need to know that her father asked for her return."

"We cannot act in such a fashion," said Gardiner softly. He leaned forward and grasped her hand, holding fast when she would have withdrawn. "I know you love Elizabeth, Sarah. I love her also, and I have no more desire to see her return to that house than you do.

"But we have agreed that we would not treat her as her parents have. Elizabeth deserves the right to choose her own path in life, and regardless of our love for her, our fear for her well-being, or our own opinions of what she should do, we cannot stop her."

Sarah seemed to deflate slightly, but when she spoke, defiance was still evident in her tone. "And if she is mistreated again?"

Gardiner smiled at his wife, knowing that she would be reassured by his fierce expression. "Then we will remove her again, regardless of what my sister or Bennet should say on the matter."

Silence fell over the room as Sarah considered his words. But it was short lived, as she soon spoke.

"You understand that I will still try to convince her to stay."

"I would expect nothing less. She will have my full support should she choose to ignore her father's summons."

"Very well," said Sarah, but through her stern demeanor, a hint of a smile shone through. "But you had best we aware, Mr. Gardiner, that I shall hold you to it."

Gardiner reached out his hand and pulled his wife to him, situating her comfortably on his lap. "I love Lizzy as much as you do, Sarah. She will be protected, no matter what the cost."

At that moment, Elizabeth Bennet was just entering the house with her young cousins after a walk in the nearby park. The late September weather carried a hint of the warmer weather of the summer gone by, but it had become cool enough that the party had been required to don light jackets to keep warm. Her younger cousins—boys aged six and five—might well have done without jackets, as their rambunctiousness more than made up for any chill in the air. Their elder sister, who was eight and well on the way to considering herself to be quite the lady, was having none of that. Holding Elizabeth's hand, she walked into the house with a certain demure gravity, and after she kissed Elizabeth's cheek, she left with the governess to return upstairs with her brothers. The youngest Gardiner, a child of three, was already in the nursery, waiting for her siblings to return.

After depositing her spencer, gloves, and bonnet into the hands of a waiting servant, Elizabeth climbed the stairs to her room, making use of the chilly water in the basin in her room to refresh herself. After she had finished these tasks, she climbed up on her bed and sat back against the headboard, thinking about her life and situation.

Her cousins were dear children, well-behaved and intelligent, and Elizabeth counted every moment spent with them a joy. In fact, she was blessed to live with her uncle and his family, especially . . .

On instinct, Elizabeth shied away from thoughts of her family, knowing it would do no good to dwell on such thoughts. The fact of the matter was that the Gardiners *were* her family in every way that mattered. And they would continue to be so, she was certain.

In an effort to dispel such thoughts from her mind, Elizabeth stood and approached the vanity mirror along the wall of her room. The image that stared back at her was a young woman, vibrant and full of life, a little petite, perhaps, but with a fair complexion and a wealth of luxurious brown hair swept up in the typical style of a young woman of her station. Her finest feature was perhaps her eyes, which were a deep brown and were framed by long, beautiful lashes. Or so she had been told by several admirers attempting to impress her and gain her favor.

Elizabeth shook her head in exasperation. She had come out in society at the beginning of the previous season, and although the Gardiners did not inhabit a circle in which the finest of England's society moved, they at least were able to introduce her to many who were of quite comfortable situations. Among their acquaintances, there numbered not a few of the gentry in addition to the men of business with whom her uncle associated. There were a number of men who attempted to flatter her with pretty words and happy manners.

And Elizabeth was well aware that her uncle had hoped that she would manage to catch the attention of a good man who would marry her and provide her with the protection of a husband. But though Elizabeth knew that his worries were well-founded and his hopes understandable, she was simply not ready for such a step. She had never met a man who had interested her as she had always thought a prospective husband should, and she was determined that she would have the kind of relationship with her husband that the Gardiners shared. She was determined to never marry if she could not find such a man. It was perhaps a foolish sentiment, but she was not willing to relinquish it.

Of a far more practical concern was her current age, as she was still more than a year and a half from reaching her majority. If a man were to become attached to her, he would still be required to apply to her father for permission to marry, and Elizabeth was not about to subject a man to such an application. She had no real reason to believe that her father would deny his permission, but it seemed best to avoid the situation altogether.

Thus, she was determined to bide her time, living with her aunt and uncle and assisting by caring for their children as much as she was able. In time, she would think further on her desires for her future. But the subject could wait until she had attained the age of one and twenty, as her life up until that point depended on her father's whims.

The fact that she barely remembered the man was irrelevant. Considering what her life had been like at Longbourn, she felt that she had ample reason to fear what he would do if he should decide that her life was too easy and happy.

A knock on the door startled Elizabeth, and after she gave permission to enter, a maid delivered a summons from her uncle to join him in his study. Smiling, Elizabeth advised that she would be down directly, and then she gave her image a final inspection in the mirror before she quit the room.

The study had always been a favorite room in the Gardiners' house. Not long after she had arrived in London, she had discovered a voracious appetite for the written word. She had arrived unable to read anything except what she had taught herself of her letters through her own infrequent opportunities and the clandestine assistance of the housekeeper at Longbourn. But she had quickly learned, and now she considered herself well-read, for her uncle—a lover of books himself—had laughingly indulged her love of books by buying as many as she could read. He had told her more than once that he was truly happy that she read more than novels, as he had never acquired much of a taste for what he considered to be such frivolous material. Elizabeth had no dislike novels herself, but she tended to prefer histories and some of the classical writers, which neatly meshed with his own preferences. They had spent many an hour discussing and debating the various texts they had both read. It was an activity which they both cherished.

Elizabeth stepped into the study, to the smiles of her aunt and uncle, who welcomed her to take a seat, and though they appeared to be cheerful, Elizabeth was able to detect a certain counterfeit quality to their cheer. Something was troubling them, and given the matter which was almost never discussed between them, Elizabeth was certain she knew what it was.

They talked of inconsequential things for several moments before her uncle finally leaned forward and addressed her:

"I am certain you are aware that I have not called you in here to talk of such things, Lizzy. In fact, I have received a letter today which concerns you. It seems that my brother has called for your return to Longbourn."

Elizabeth nodded her head with a calmness she did not feel. Inside, she was a mass of roiling emotions, most of which she herself could not even identify. Amidst the maelstrom, however, she could detect uncertainty, resignation, a little anger, and even some fear. She forced these feelings aside with a ruthless determination and acknowledged her uncle's words.

"I see. Does my father state exactly why he has seen fit to recall me after all these years of silence?"

"Perhaps you would like to read his letter yourself," said her uncle, leaning forward to hand her a single sheet of paper.

For a moment, Elizabeth searched her uncle's eyes, but when she found nothing, she turned her attention to the sheet in her hands. Unfortunately, the letter did not tell her much more than she already knew. Elizabeth's memories of her father were somewhat disjointed, and her uncle had told her little other than what he thought she needed to know. This, she suspected, was due to his desire not to speak ill of another person rather than due to any affection or loyalty to the man. But what memories Elizabeth still possessed suggested that her father was not a man of many words, so perhaps the letter was not out of the ordinary.

"It does not say much," said Elizabeth at last.

"Your father was ever thus," replied Uncle Gardiner. "He is an especially indifferent correspondent."

Elizabeth's mind was awhirl with conjectures of why her father would want her to return now after ten years. She had always known, however, that this was possible, and she had prepared herself for the eventuality. But it did not make this moment any easier, especially since she could not determine *why* she had been summoned.

"Then I shall prepare to depart," said Elizabeth in a quiet voice, moving to rise.

"Elizabeth," her aunt said as she rose with her and took her hand, "you do not need to go."

Elizabeth regarded her aunt with affection. "You know I must. Regardless of whatever history we share, he is still my father, and they are still my family."

The words sounded hollow to her own ears—the only family she possessed lived in this house, though Elizabeth did maintain some fond memories of her eldest sister. Still, by the definition of the word, she knew that her words were true. It could not be so very bad to live at Longbourn again, she told herself. She was not the frightened child she had been then.

"We will fight this if you will just give us the word," said her uncle.

Elizabeth smiled at him. "I will not have this discussion again. You know I do not wish to be any more of a burden than I already am."

"You have never been a burden, Lizzy," said Mrs. Gardiner.

"And I love you for all you have done for me. But this is something I must do." Elizabeth gazed at her beloved relations, silently pleading with them to understand.

He aunt and uncle both regarded her for a long moment, and though their features were soft and affectionate toward her, she almost thought that they would continue to protest. But no matter what they said, Elizabeth would not yield. She needed to do this for her own peace of mind and for the purpose of showing her family that she could meet them again with her head held high.

"Neither your aunt nor I are happy with your decision," replied her uncle at length. "But we will respect it.

"However, should your family act in a reprehensible manner, as I suspect they will, and if you should wish it, then you must always remember that you will have a home with us."

Tears moistening the corners of her eyes, Elizabeth moved forward to embrace her aunt and uncle. "I am so fortunate that I have you both as relations. I love you both and will always be thankful for what you have done for me."

"And we are thankful for the joy you have brought into our lives, dear girl," said Mrs. Gardiner, her voice as thick with emotion as Elizabeth's.

Smiling, though inside she was a trembling mass of nerves, Elizabeth excused herself from her uncle's study and returned to her room to begin the task of packing for her imminent journey. She was determined to return to her childhood home without the slightest appearance of meekness. In doing so, she hoped to show them that she would not be intimidated. And maybe she would also make her aunt and uncle proud.

In the study she had just left, her aunt and uncle watched as the door closed behind her, neither saying anything for a long moment after their niece departed. A sense of foreboding had fallen over Gardiner, as he doubted that Maggie had grown in either sense or compassion. Elizabeth would almost certainly face severe censure from her mother when she returned, and Gardiner did not think that Maggie would be temperate in either her words or her behavior. It seemed equally unlikely that Bennet would rouse himself to temper his wife's behavior.

Elizabeth was a strong woman, and she had grown into everything that Gardiner and his wife had hoped she would when they had removed her from Longbourn. He only prayed that she would be strong enough to weather this storm and emerge stronger for the experience.

"I worry for her," said Sarah in so soft a tone that Gardiner had difficulty hearing her.

"As do I," said Gardiner, drawing his wife close to him.

"She will have to keep us informed," insisted Sarah as she pulled away and regarded him with a fierce expression which he had always associated with a lioness protecting her cubs. "If Bennet so much as puts one foot out of line . . ."

". . . Then we shall retrieve her and file suit to become her guardians," finished Gardiner. "We will simply have to trust Elizabeth and hope for the best."

Gardiner could tell that Sarah liked it as little as he did himself. But for the moment, there was no other choice. But heaven help Bennet if he gave them any cause to act against him.

Chapter IV

"It is not that I do not enjoy your company, but I assure you that I am fully capable of doing this myself."

Uncle Gardiner smiled at Elizabeth and nodded. "I am certain you are, dear girl," said he, an enigmatic smile adorning his features.

But Elizabeth was not fooled in the slightest. Raising an eyebrow, she regarded her uncle, saying, "Are you certain you can spare an entire day away from your business?"

"For you, I can spare much more," said Uncle Gardiner with a pointed look. "Lizzy, as I have been your guardian for the past ten years, it is fitting that I should deliver you to your father in person."

He turned and looked out the window for a brief moment before he once again fixed his gaze on Elizabeth. "I know that I am in no way deceiving you, and I would not even attempt to do so. I shall have a discussion with your father and make him aware of the reality of the situation."

Shaking her head, Elizabeth was nevertheless forced to smile at her uncle. She was fortunate that such a conscientious guardian had watched over her for the past ten years. If only she could have counted on her father to do the same.

"I thank you, uncle," said Elizabeth in a warm and affectionate tone.

"It is the least I can do, Lizzy." Mr. Gardiner's expression became serious once again, and he gazed at her pointedly. "Just remember, dear girl, should anything happen which distresses you—anything at all!—you have only to send word, and I will immediately return you to London."

The sincere concern displayed by her uncle caused Elizabeth to become misty-eyed, and she had to fight to choke back a sob. Once she had mastered herself, she directed a brilliant smile at him and said, "Thank you, uncle. But I assure you that I shall be well."

"Let us hope so," said Mr. Gardiner, his voice so quiet that Elizabeth could hardly make out his words.

In truth, Elizabeth was not nearly as confident as she had assured her aunt and uncle. The thought of seeing her family had caused a nervousness such as she had not felt for years to well up within her, and she was certain the return to Longbourn would be the longest she had ever undertaken.

They had traveled for two hours when her uncle suggested that they make a stop at an inn. Elizabeth readily acquiesced, not only due to the fatigue of the journey, but also due to the desire to delay the inevitable a little longer. They entered the inn and ordered some refreshments to wash down the dust of the road, and as they were readying themselves to leave once again, Elizabeth indicated her desire to stroll outside for a moment while her uncle settled the bill for their brief stay.

Stepping outside into the bright sunshine, Elizabeth closed her eyes and tilted her head upward, reveling in the warmth of the day. She stood in that attitude for several moments before the clearing of a throat startled her from her reverie. Elizabeth's eyes snapped open, and she saw a young gentleman regarding her with a suspicious curve tilting the corners of his mouth. He was tall and handsome, and he was impeccably dressed, wearing well-tailored clothes which were made of what appeared to be costly material. Clearly, he was a man of fashion and of some influence in society, and he no doubt inhabited a level of society far above any that Elizabeth or her relations could boast.

"Pardon me!" exclaimed Elizabeth, mortified at the picture she must have presented to such a man.

"It is no trouble at all, Miss . . ."

The man's voice trailed off, and he watched her in earnest. Elizabeth, realizing that they had not been introduced, blushed and was about to demure when the door behind her opened and her uncle stepped out of the inn.

"Elizabeth?" asked Mr. Gardiner with some confusion.

"My apologies," said the man, turning to Mr. Gardiner. "Your daughter and I encountered one another as she was exiting the inn."

"No harm done, it appears," said Mr. Gardiner, looking at the man curiously. "Unfortunately, this wonderful young lady is not my daughter. She is my niece."

"Fitzwilliam Darcy," said the young man, introducing himself with a bow.

"Edward Gardiner," responded Mr. Gardiner. "And this is my niece, Elizabeth Bennet." Then he regarded Mr. Darcy with a tilted head. "If I may, are you Mr. Darcy of Pemberley in Derbyshire?"

Though the young man had been congenial up to that point, a shroud seemed to come over his countenance, and his expression grew guarded. "Yes, I am."

Mr. Gardiner appeared to sense that he had somehow offended the young man. "My apologies for the impertinence, Mr. Darcy. My wife hails from Lambton, a town with which you must certainly be familiar."

"Indeed, I am, Mr. Gardiner," said Mr. Darcy, apparently mollified. "Lambton is a delightful town."

"My wife considers it the dearest place in the world, and she has often spoken of the Darcy family's reputation in the area and the benevolence of your parents in particular."

"I thank you, Mr. Gardiner. My parents were indeed well regarded."

Mr. Gardiner smiled. "I believe that you are as well regarded as your parents were." He then turned to Elizabeth and said, "Unfortunately, I believe that it is time for us to depart, Elizabeth.

"Mr. Darcy, it has been a pleasure to make your acquaintance," said Mr. Gardiner, turning to the other man.

"The pleasure is all mine," replied Mr. Darcy.

With a final nod of farewell, Elizabeth allowed herself to be led to their waiting carriage. As her uncle handed her up into the equipage, she turned and caught a glimpse of Mr. Darcy watching them; then the driver was given the order, and the carriage departed.

"Well, I never would have expected such notice from a man of Mr. Darcy's stature," said Mr. Gardiner.

"Mr. Darcy's stature?" echoed Elizabeth.

"You have heard your aunt speak of her childhood home in Lambton?" Elizabeth nodded and smiled, as her aunt had often spoken of the area with great fondness. "Mr. Darcy owns the nearest estate,

Pemberley. It is a great estate, with a park which is ten miles around at least, and its annual yield is a clear ten thousand pounds, if it is a shilling. Most men of his stature are unapproachably proud and will not deign to speak with anyone not of their sphere."

"But surely Mr. Darcy could not have known that you are in trade," said Elizabeth. "You certainly do not act like a man in trade."

Mr. Gardiner laughed. "I thank you, Lizzy, for that bit of flattery."

Then her uncle suddenly sobered and regarded her with regret. "If only I could have seen you well settled with a man of even half of Mr. Darcy's consequence long ere now. I would have been well pleased to see you thus protected."

Moved by his continued care, Elizabeth leaned forward and placed her hand on his arm. "I shall be well, uncle. Truly, I shall."

"I hope that is so," replied her uncle in a quiet voice.

And Elizabeth, in the confines of her own mind, agreed fervently with the sentiment. Hopefully, she *would* be well in the home of her father, though that was by no means certain.

The carriage pulled up to Longbourn, and Gardiner noted with annoyance that neither his sister nor her husband had seen fit to exit the house to greet their long-estranged daughter. It appeared that the only person present was one of her sisters—Jane, unless Gardiner missed his guess. The other sisters would have been too young to remember much about Elizabeth, and Jane had always been a gentle soul, eager to please all. Gardiner doubted that she had changed in the interim.

Gardiner turned to Elizabeth and almost attempted to persuade her to give up this madness and return to London. But a glance at her told him that he could not convince her to return. The stubborn and courageous young woman who had emerged from the shattered child of yesteryear was not to be intimidated by anyone.

The coach stopped, and Gardiner stepped out, handing Elizabeth down before turning to regard his eldest niece. The years had been kind to Jane; when he had last seen her, she had been a pretty child full of promise, and that promise had been fulfilled in the beautiful woman who now stood before him. She also appeared to be as sweet-tempered as Gardiner remembered, for she bore a welcoming smile for them both and evinced a hint of eagerness which he attributed to a desire to again know the sister whose company she had been denied all these years.

"Welcome to Longbourn, uncle," said she in a low but almost joyous tone. Then she turned to her younger sister and greeted her with a hesitant, almost diffident embrace. But her tone was not less welcoming as she whispered, "Welcome home, Elizabeth."

For her part, Elizabeth's eyes were suspiciously misty, and she met her sister's embrace with one of her own. "Thank you, Jane. I am very happy to see you again."

"And I you. I hope that we shall once again be as close as we were when . . ." Jane trailed off, clearly embarrassed and not wishing to once again bring up unhappy times or reopen old wounds.

But Elizabeth merely smiled in that indomitable way of hers and, pulling away from her elder sister, grasped Jane's arms and favored her with a brilliant smile. "I hope to regain that closeness, too, Jane."

Jane nodded. It was at that moment that a manservant exited the house to unload the carriage. Behind him was a stout woman of middle years who approached the two Bennet girls. "Miss Elizabeth?" said the woman, her smile and her shining eyes belying the question implied in her tone.

"Mrs. Hill," said Elizabeth. An indefinable emotion seemed to well up within Elizabeth, and Gardiner, knowing that the elderly housekeep had been Elizabeth's protector to her limited ability, could see that his niece had been assaulted by memories of the woman's support and kindness. For that matter, Gardiner was grateful to Mrs. Hill as well—there was no telling what might have happened to Elizabeth if she had not had at least one adult to look after her.

But now was not the time for such thoughts. Though he had acquiesced to Elizabeth's wishes, it did not follow that he would leave her behind without assuring himself as well as he was able that she would be well looked after.

"You should go inside and get settled," said Gardiner to Elizabeth. "I will speak with you again before I leave."

"Thank you, uncle," said Elizabeth. After she had kissed him lightly on the cheek, she allowed her sister to lead her into the house.

Gardiner watched her go, a lump forming in his throat. He truly did not wish to leave her here.

"Do not concern yourself with the young miss, Mr. Gardiner," sounded a voice behind him.

Gardiner turned and noted the housekeeper regarding him with compassion evident in her eyes.

"I will watch her as if she was my own daughter," said she.

"Thank you," said Gardiner with a bow. "She has become very precious to us. We will miss her dearly."

"As it should be, sir."

"Has anything been said as to why now, after all these years, she has been recalled?"

The housekeeper pursed her lips for a moment, and after a surreptitious glance about the area, she leaned forward and said in a soft voice:

"Nothing within my hearing, sir. For many years after her daughter's departure, Mrs. Bennet would not even allow the girl's name to be spoken in the house. But the master decided a fortnight ago that Miss Elizabeth's presence was required again, and though the mistress made quite a fuss about it, the master would not be moved."

"And he has not given any reason for this sudden determination?" asked Mr. Gardiner with a frown.

"I do not believe he has, Mr. Gardiner. The mistress still has her nose out of joint over the matter, though she appears to be resigned to it now."

"How will she behave toward Elizabeth now?"

Mrs. Hill shook her head sadly. "Not well, I am afraid. She still blames the young miss, you understand."

Gardiner scowled. "Of that, I am not surprised." Then he smiled at her. "I thank you for this intelligence. I believe that I shall have a brief word with my brother before I say farewell to my niece."

"Should I announce you, sir?"

"I know the way," said Mr. Gardiner. It was difficult to avoid making a comment about taking his brother to task about his behavior. He had already been too open with the woman as it was, though he was grateful for her insight.

Entering through the open front door, Gardiner handed his coat and hat to a maid who was standing nearby, and then he proceeded down the hall to Bennet's study. A moment later, he had knocked, and when no answer was forthcoming, he opened the door and entered.

The first thing that Gardiner noticed was the fact that his brother had not been idle in the intervening years—or perhaps it was more correct to say he had not been idle when it came to the purchase of new books. The shelves were fairly groaning with the bounty of books which would make even the most dedicated book lover croon with delight. The second thing he noticed was that the years had not been kind to Bennet. Though the man was only fifty, his skin hung off his face, and his eyes appeared haunted and sunken. The gaze he fixed on Gardiner was anything but welcoming.

Unfortunately for Bennet, Gardiner was not particularly concerned for his brother's opinion. "Good day, Bennet," said he in a congenial tone.

The only reply he received was a grunt, which was not unexpected, given the circumstances.

"I believe we need to have a serious conversation, brother."

"Much like you felt necessary ten years ago," said Bennet. His tone was hard and cold and not at all in keeping with the lackadaisical man that Gardiner remembered. "I am afraid that I do not have anything to say to you."

"Then you shall listen," said Gardiner in a firm tone, "for I have something to say to you. I have delivered Elizabeth to you as you have demanded. But I must tell you that I have done so against my better judgment."

Bennet leaned back in his chair and he sighed. "I assure you that Elizabeth will come to no harm in this house."

"It is not *physical* harm which concerns me," replied Gardiner, directing a pointed glare at the other man. "I am sure you remember the state Elizabeth was in when she left you." Gardiner paused and regarded his brother, who was watching him with an air of impatience. "If you had only taken the time to nurture your daughter, you might have found an intellectual equal, which I suspect you do not have among your other daughters."

This seemed to reach Bennet, and he leaned forward. "Elizabeth is intelligent?"

"Very much so," returned Gardiner. "I know you are well read. Speak to her of Milton or Shakespeare when you have the opportunity. I believe you will be surprised at some of her insights."

For the briefest of moments, the lines around Bennet's face softened, and his eyes lost their focus. Gardiner had always known that his brother-in-law craved someone with whom he could speak on an equal basis, and though Jane was intelligent in her own right, her interests would not likely mesh with those of her father. And given some of the reports Gardiner had received over the years—though there had been nothing from the Bennets themselves, Gardiner's sister Phillips had kept him informed—Mary was interested in nothing more than moral texts, and the younger girls were a lost cause. Bennet had tired of his wife's lack of intelligent conversation years earlier.

But the moment lasted only an instant before the hard look came over his brother's eyes yet again. He nodded in a sharp manner and said: "I shall speak with her."

Gardiner regarded him with skepticism, but he chose not to address his brother's curt demeanor.

"I would have you understand the true situation, Bennet. As I said, I have no concerns for Elizabeth's *physical* welfare under you care. But I will not hide from you the fact that I am very concerned for her state of mind."

"And you should not be," said Bennet in a gruff tone. He fixed a baleful glare on Gardiner and continued: "I shall remind you that regardless of how Elizabeth has lived with you these past ten years, *I* am still her father and still her guardian."

To say that Gardiner was unimpressed by this show of force was an understatement. "Yes, but you are a father who has not acted as one."

Bennet glared at him, but Gardiner would not be intimidated. "I challenge you to refute this, Bennet. I told you ten years ago that if you would only take your wife in hand, I would not have to take Elizabeth into my home. You declaimed any ability or inclination to do so, which is why I acted as I did.

"But you must also understand that I will not allow Elizabeth to be returned to the state she was when she left your care. You and I have not had any direct contact since we left, but you should know that my annual income is now substantially more than what you receive from Longbourn. I am also aware that your estate is your *only* source of income."

"Are you threatening me?" snarled Bennet. *This* was a side of his brother that Gardiner had never seen before—it was an impressive head of steam, but it still did not make Gardiner quail. He had seen similar displeasure from men of much more social clout and intimidating demeanors than his brother possessed.

"I do not threaten," said Gardiner, though his tone was hard. "I am telling you to treat her as a valued member of your family. I should tell you that it was the opinion of both Sarah and myself that your summons should be ignored. The only reason we are here at all is at *Elizabeth's* insistence."

"And what would you have done when I brought a suit against you?"

"Defended Elizabeth to the best of my ability," replied Gardiner, his relentless gaze never wavering. "I would not have enjoyed bankrupting you for Elizabeth's sake, but I would have done it if required."

Bennet did not even bat an eye. "The courts favor keeping children with their parents."

"That preference can be overturned, and I would not have spared any mention of your behavior—or even that of my sister, for that matter. I have *many* contacts, Bennet. I would not be telling you of this if I was not confident of my success."

The glare did not lessen for some time, and Gardiner met his brother's fierce look in every respect.

Eventually, the war of wills subsided, and Bennet sat back in his chair. "This discussion is pointless, as I have no intention of mistreating the girl."

"Why did you call her home after all this time?" asked Gardiner. "She has been happy with us and has largely known no other life. Why now?"

"Because it is time for her to learn her true place in society," was Bennet's reply. "She is the daughter of a gentleman. She needs to learn what that means as she prepares herself to find a husband."

Gardiner regarded the other man with great skepticism. "I was not aware that you were at all concerned about your daughter's prospects." Bennet did nothing more than scowl, so Gardiner continued: "I am aware that you can give your daughters very little, Bennet. Though I would like to think that their charms are enough to find them respectable husbands, you cannot expect them to make exceptional matches."

"On the contrary," replied Bennet in a gruff tone, "there is a new arrival of some fortune who has been paying considerable attention to Jane, and we have high hopes that this will lead to an engagement."

"Oh? And who is this man?"

"His name is Bingley. He comes from a background in trade, but he is seeking to purchase an estate and is leasing Netherfield in order to gain some experience."

"And have you checked into this man's background?"

A blank look met Gardiner's query. "Should I have?"

Gardiner sighed. His brother had always been indolent, but this particular failure suggested a lack of care which was far out of the common way. "Yes, you should have. There are many men of society who are not what they claim to be."

Bennet waved his hand with impatience. "As you have so ably pointed out, my girls have nothing to tempt a fortune hunter, so there is little danger."

It was not as if Bennet was stupid or deficient in any way other than his unfortunate tendency to ignore anything which would cause him to have to exert himself, but Gardiner was almost unable to believe what he was hearing. Discussion with the man was futile, so Gardiner decided that he would have this Mr. Bingley investigated himself.

"Very well. As for Elizabeth, see that she is well taken care of. I will not hesitate to intervene."

And then, before Bennet could once again state his displeasure with Gardiner's treatment of him, Gardiner said: "You should also know that I have settled a dowry on your daughter. It is perhaps not as much as I would have liked, but as I have two daughters of my own to consider, it is the best that I could do for the moment."

At this intelligence, Bennet actually appeared to be affronted. "Was that not a little presumptuous?"

"Until a few days ago, we thought that Elizabeth would remain with us until she left for her own home," replied Gardiner pointedly. "You have given us no indication over the past ten years that you ever wished to have her back. I wished to give her every advantage in finding a husband or being able to support herself should she remain unmarried."

Bennet grunted. "How much?"

"Ten thousand pounds," said Gardiner, watching for his brother's reaction. It was slightly heartening that Bennet's eyes only widened in response. Gardiner saw nothing else to give him concern.

"It seems you have done well for yourself after all."

Shrugging, Gardiner replied, "Well enough.

"Now, I will take my leave of you after I have said my farewell to Elizabeth. Would my sister welcome me if I paid my respects to her before I leave?"

Bennet grimaced. "You may wish to spare yourself the trouble. As I told you when you spirited Elizabeth from this house, I have had to bear the brunt of your sister's ill humor, and she has still not desisted to this day. She particularly blames *you*."

Nodding, Gardiner rose to his feet. "In that case, I shall not brave her displeasure. I am no more eager to exchange 'pleasantries' than she is." He turned, but as he opened the door, he faced his brother once again. Bennet's expression had not softened in the slightest. If anything, it had gotten harder, and Gardiner wondered just what game he was playing. He was concerned that Bennet had something specific in mind for his summons, but Gardiner was not able to discern what it was.

"Just remember, Bennet—treat her well, or I shall remove her from this house again, with or without your approval. Do not test me."

Then, without another word, Gardiner turned and left the bookroom.

Elizabeth said farewell to her uncle amid admonishments to correspond regularly and whispered instructions to contact him at once if anything untoward happened. Elizabeth appreciated his concern, but she was certain that whatever the reason her father had for summoning her home, it must have been a benign one. Regardless, she was not one to be intimidated, and she would meet her fate cheerfully.

Jane was much as Elizabeth remembered—sweet, pleasant, and intelligent, yet reticent and placid and seemingly very adept at hiding her thoughts. Elizabeth was certain that they would eventually be as close as sisters could be when they were given enough time in one another's company. Elizabeth had spent a very agreeable half hour with her sister before her uncle had departed, and they were about to return to the room which had been assigned to Elizabeth when a summons arrived through a maid for them to present themselves before their mother in the parlor.

Suddenly tense and knowing that this was at the very least likely to be awkward, Elizabeth nevertheless straightened her shoulders and motioned for Jane to precede her.

"Do not worry, Elizabeth," whispered Jane. "I believe that all shall be well."

Though Elizabeth thought her sister was being more than a little too optimistic, she said nothing and allowed herself to be led into the parlor where her mother waited.

The room was much as Elizabeth remembered. Her changed perspective and the ravages of time did account for some of the differences that were present. The furnishings were comfortable and well appointed, if somewhat shabbier than she remembered; the wallpaper was a little more faded, and in general, the room simply felt . . . somehow *smaller*, though she suspected that it was merely that she had grown in the interim. It was a good room and very handsome for a family of the Bennets' status. But it did not feel like *home*—unfortunately, there was too much time and distance involved for her to feel that way about it. And besides, it was not her uncle and aunt's place of residence, which had been home to her for the past ten years.

All of these thoughts passed through Elizabeth's mind in an instant, for her attention was captured immediately by the occupants of the room. An older woman sat with three younger girls, and Elizabeth knew they were her other sisters. Mary was easy to identify, as she was dressed in a most conservative fashion and had her hair tied up in a tight and conservative bun; even as a girl of seven, Mary had always been a serious child. The two younger girls were Catherine and Lydia, though as they were both of a size of one another and possessed robust, womanly figures, it was difficult to determine which was the elder and which the younger. Elizabeth's memories of those two girls was largely unpleasant, as they had both picked up on their mother's antipathy for her at a young age and had begun to tease her before she had left.

The woman who sat in their midst was still youthful-appearing and spry, and Elizabeth thought that the passage of time had been kind to her. Mrs. Bennet appeared to be regarding Elizabeth as if she were some particularly repulsive wild animal which must be watched carefully.

"Step closer, child," commanded Mrs. Bennet when Elizabeth hesitated in the doorway. "I would prefer not to strain my neck by looking up at you."

"Yes, mother," replied Elizabeth. In truth, she was not certain how exactly to refer to her mother. Their long estrangement made 'mama' seem too familiar, not to mention the fact that her memories of unkindness at the hands of this woman rendered her little inclined to pay the compliment of the respect such an appellation would suggest. The more formal 'mother' was outwardly respectful enough while still allowing Elizabeth to think of Mrs. Gardiner as her true 'mama,' even though Elizabeth had never addressed her as such.

"Well, it appears my brother has kept you well fed and cared for," said Mrs. Bennet after inspecting Elizabeth for several moments. "And I can see that he has provided you with clothes of ample quality, though my sister Gardiner is obviously not my equal in choosing the proper style, regardless of her knowledge of what is currently in fashion."

"Yes, mother," replied Elizabeth. "I am very grateful to the Gardiners."

Mrs. Bennet stared at her very hard, evidently unhappy with the thought that she had been well cared for.

"You have participated in a season in London, I presume?"

"Yes, mother."

"And you are not yet attached?"

"No, mother."

"My Lydia would not have allowed such an opportunity to pass her by," said Mrs. Bennet, gesturing toward the taller of Elizabeth's two younger sisters. Elizabeth was surprised, having thought that Catherine would be the taller sister, if for no other reason than the fact that she was two years older.

But Elizabeth was given no further opportunity to think on the matter, as Mrs. Bennet had continued speaking: "Perhaps you were given no instruction concerning the best way to capture a husband."

Though Elizabeth did not really care for this talk of "capturing" a husband, she ignored it. "I did not find a man whom I thought would suit me."

Mrs. Bennet's nose wrinkled with displeasure. "Perhaps you should think of the more practical things in life. Once your father passes on, I shall not be able to keep you, so you should take thought for your future. I have to think of these things due to the circumstances, you understand."

Although Elizabeth understood the thrust of her mother's words very well indeed, she refused to rise to the bait. Instead, she replied with a barely audible, "I shall."

Mrs. Bennet sniffed with disdain. "I am not certain whether you remember your sisters. This is Mary, and here are your youngest sisters, Kitty and Lydia," said Mrs. Bennet, pointing at each girl in turn.

Mary greeted Elizabeth in a mild fashion, but the two youngest, who had been whispering and giggling between them, only giggled harder, causing Elizabeth to suppress a frown. Theirs did not suggest proper behavior, though Elizabeth knew not to point that out.

"Very well," said Mrs. Bennet once the introductions had been completed. "You may go and settle in to your room. Your sisters will see that you arrive to the dinner table at the proper time, I am sure."

Nodding, Elizabeth dropped a very shallow curtsey and turned to follow her elder sister from the room. Before they left, however, they were arrested by the sound of Mrs. Bennet's voice:

"Though you have lived in London, partaken in the season, and wear finer clothes than the rest of my girls, you must not think that you are any better than they are."

Aghast at the mere suggestion, Elizabeth turned to regard her mother. Mrs. Bennet was glaring at her with a hard and unfriendly expression, and she appeared to be daring Elizabeth to contradict her words. Elizabeth had no thought of disagreeing, though she wondered why the woman could think such a thing of her.

"I assure you that I do not," said Elizabeth.

Mrs. Bennet grunted in response, and Elizabeth, sensing that she was dismissed, turned and left the room, all the time wondering what sort of situation she had gotten herself into.

Chapter V

The first few days after Elizabeth's return to Longbourn passed, and though she did not truly feel at ease in her old home, at least she did not precisely feel *unwelcome*. She still had no knowledge of why she had been summoned back to her father's house, but at this point, she supposed it truly did not matter.

Of her family, she was still uncertain as to each of their characters, though some definite trends had emerged quickly. Of course, the easiest to determine were her two youngest sisters. The giggles that Elizabeth had witnessed the first time she had met her mother and younger sisters in the parlor were only the prelude to the true depth of their poor behavior. They were loud, rude, fought with one another constantly, and showed very little knowledge of—or interest in—the proper sort of behavior expected of young ladies. And though there were no social engagements those first few days, Elizabeth felt certain that her two youngest sisters would acquit themselves with even less distinction out in society.

Unfortunately, they were also much as she remembered them in their treatment of herself specifically. That very evening before dinner, the two girls had burst into her room while she was talking with Jane and began to pepper her with questions of London, the season, and everything else which came into their flighty minds.

The true unpleasantness came near the end of the conversation. Elizabeth answered all their questions with as much composure as she could muster, and when their questions died down, Elizabeth chanced to say:

"London is perhaps not all that you imagine, Kitty. But maybe someday you shall be able to go and experience it for yourself."

Kitty had smiled hesitantly and thanked her, but she was immediately overshadowed by her younger sister's glare.

"I do not think that people such as you should be on so intimate terms as to use Kitty's nickname," said she in a rather prim manner. "Kitty, I think that you should insist on Elizabeth calling you 'Catherine.'"

Though Elizabeth was rather shocked at the young girl's forthrightness, she peered back at Kitty, only to see a rather uncomfortable frown on her face. Deciding that it was much better to not antagonize her sisters on her first day in the house, Elizabeth had nodded and replied:

"Of course, if that it is what you prefer."

Though still looking uncomfortable, Kitty replied that it was, and she immediately became Catherine in Elizabeth's eyes. The incident also illustrated another important fact of the relationship between the two youngest Bennets. Simply put, though Catherine was the elder of the two sisters by two years, she was also a follower and orbited around Lydia's determined and forthright nature, emulating her in the hope, or so Elizabeth suspected, of gaining her mother's approval.

By contrast, Mary was serious, rarely laughed or even spoke, and generally seemed ill at ease with everyone. She appeared to enjoy playing the pianoforte. But Elizabeth was grateful that Mary did not seem inclined to sing, as the one time Elizabeth heard her do so, she displayed a rather weak voice and an affected manner. Her playing was competent but evinced little feeling for the music. Elizabeth, who had spent many an hour practicing, fancied that she was much more proficient and had a much prettier voice, though she was not vain enough to think herself a superior performer. The other pastime which Mary indulged in to excess was the reading of moral texts and religious treatises of all kinds. Of course, this was accompanied by a tendency to inject banal platitudes into conversation which always seemed forced and which generally concerned proper behavior. With such sisters as Catherine and Lydia, Elizabeth could only understand Mary's preoccupation and agree with her assessment.

In addition, Mary was the plainest of the four girls, though in reality she was not at all unattractive. It did not help that Mrs. Bennet frequently bemoaned her daughter's appearance and suggested that Mary would find it difficult to ever find a husband. The first time Mrs. Bennet had said something disparaging her daughter's beauty, Elizabeth had hardly been able to believe it. To do such in front of her daughter displayed a lack of sensitivity which was reprehensible.

Mary's behavior was often tiresome, though Elizabeth vastly preferred it to Catherine and Lydia's wildness. In truth, Elizabeth pitied Mary. The girl was ignored by her father and her mother—except when her mother bemoaned her lack of beauty—and held in contempt by her younger sisters. While Jane was kind to Mary, they were very dissimilar in both their character and interests. Elizabeth was certain that Mary had it within her to be a pleasant girl, but one would have to make their way through Mary's moralistic tendencies to discover that side of her. And though Elizabeth made overtures in those first few days, Mary firmly, but politely, rebuffed her.

Jane was everything that Elizabeth remembered. She was kind to all, was often cheerful when Elizabeth felt that she had no right to be, and possessed such a serene disposition that Elizabeth felt her incapable of offending anyone. Unfortunately, she was also very reticent, rarely betraying a reaction to anything, and she seemed almost incapable of thinking poorly of anyone. But after considering the issue further, Elizabeth realized that rather than not thinking poorly of others, Jane was in actuality disposed to attributing the best possible motives to everyone she met. Though it was an admirable character trait, it was somewhat dangerous in a woman who was also very beautiful.

Still, Elizabeth could find little to criticize in her elder sister. In a family which appeared to be connected by name only—and with the examples of three younger sisters who displayed less than proper behavior—it was no less than astonishing that Jane was so unaffected and sincere. And that did not even take into account the behavior of her parents.

The very thought of her parents always caused Elizabeth to feel the need to suppress a sigh. She was aware of the fact that she should look up to her parents and afford them a measure of respect due to the simple fact that they had brought her into the world. Unfortunately, Elizabeth knew that neither deserved such respect.

Mrs. Bennet's present behavior was undoubtedly the easier to understand. She was a simple woman, delighting in gossip and possessing little discernment and less intelligence. It was clear that her youngest, Lydia, was her favorite, likely because Lydia was most like her in both face and character. Indeed, Mrs. Bennet could be as silly as her youngest daughters, laughing and gossiping with them as if she were a young girl herself. The news that a company of the militia was to winter in Meryton induced the three of them to squeal in delight, all convinced that the girls could not fail to capture the eye of some handsome major or perhaps even a colonel. Mrs. Bennet was also engaged fervently in the business of seeing her daughters married off as soon as could be, and it did not seem to matter to whom, as long as the man was eligible and could support a wife. Elizabeth herself was excluded from this all-consuming desire, though she did not repine the fact.

Of course, the first meeting between Elizabeth and her mother had told Elizabeth that Mrs. Bennet had not let go of her resentment despite the passing of a decade. Indeed, Elizabeth suspected that her mother could remember and hold a grudge for millennia if required. Thus far, Mrs. Bennet had taken the simple expedient of ignoring Elizabeth whenever possible, though she was certainly not above making the occasional veiled remark at her daughter's expense. Elizabeth let all this pass, knowing that her mother's opinion was of little consequence.

The one member of the family who she could not make out, however, was her father. Mr. Bennet was an odd mix of traits, she supposed, and though her memories of her father were not at all unhappy, neither were they happy. Mr. Bennet had never been cruel to her himself before she had left with the Gardiners, but he had never stopped Mrs. Bennet's emotional cruelty.

Now, however, Elizabeth found herself wary of the man. The first night when the family had gathered for dinner, she had entered the dining room with Jane, not knowing quite what to expect. Jane immediately sat to her father's right, as was her privilege, but at her father's left, which was where Elizabeth should have sat if she had had a happier family situation, Mary was already seated, as she would have done during the years of Elizabeth's absence.

"If you will sit, we can begin," said Mr. Bennet when Elizabeth hesitated.

Elizabeth, knowing that it would be best for her to immediately obey and avoid bringing attention upon herself, sat in the only location where there was an unoccupied place setting—in the middle between Mary and Lydia.

"Yes, sir," murmured she, taking her seat.

On her one side, Lydia merely snorted at her, while Mary took no notice of her at all, and Elizabeth immediately understood that she had been placed there to bring her both the greatest humiliation and to deny her the benefit of sitting where she would be able to easily converse with Jane, who was the only one who had attempted to make her feel welcome.

Though Elizabeth would not have dreamed of saying anything concerning the arrangements, she was unnerved to see her father's eyes upon her only a moment after the family had begun to serve themselves.

"I see you have arrived," said Mr. Bennet as he availed himself of some of the potatoes.

"I have, sir," replied Elizabeth in a quiet tone.

He appeared to be waiting for her to say something further—she fancied that he expected her to complain about the seating arrangements—but she had determined that would not give them the satisfaction of her questioning their motives and kept her silence. She felt his cold gaze upon her for several moments, but she took no notice and affected a concentration on her meal.

Thus began her custom of sitting between Mary and Lydia at mealtimes, generally saying very little unless addressed directly (which happened infrequently), and leaving as soon as she could after the meal was finished. She became grateful for the fact that she *was not* seated next to her father, as the man made her feel particularly uncomfortable. It was nothing he said or did. In fact, he rarely addressed her at all. It was more the fact that she could often feel his eyes upon her, and they were not friendly in the slightest. In fact, if Elizabeth was to describe his gaze, she would have said his eyes were cold and almost lifeless. Yet at the same time, his eyes almost appeared to bore right through her, piercing her with their sharpness. Elizabeth attempted to ignore the discomfort his stares engendered. She sensed that whatever else he was, he was not violent, and she decided that she had nothing to fear from him on that front.

The first night in the parlor, Elizabeth sat by herself reading a book, distancing herself even from Jane, who was working on some embroidery. She wished to know her sister better, but she knew instinctively that Mrs. Bennet would not look kindly on any overt overtures of friendship between her two eldest daughters.

That evening was the first time Elizabeth found her father watching her in a disconcerting manner. She thought that he almost seemed on the verge of speaking to her several times, but whether it was her fancy or he decided otherwise, he did not engage her in conversation, and on the following nights, he never appeared close to speaking her again.

But his eyes followed her, always watching in that same lifeless fashion. It was almost as if the man was contemplating a wall rather than a daughter he had not seen in ten years.

Elizabeth's first experience with Meryton society came a few days after her arrival. The Lucases had invited the Bennets and several other prominent families of the area to their estate. Once she arrived there, Elizabeth was to discover that the evening at Lucas Lodge was not simply a typical evening engaged with country society.

The manor house itself was similar to most other country estates Elizabeth had seen. It was built on a smaller scale than Longbourn, made of red brick and sprawling over one floor, though that floor appeared to be quite extensive. It was obvious by looking at it that the estate had undergone construction several times to add additional rooms, so that when one entered into the house, the manor was a rambling maze of hallways and rooms which would undoubtedly be confusing to one who was not familiar with it.

It was equally evident that the Bennets were comfortable here and that the families were well acquainted with one another. Lucas Lodge was the closest estate to Longbourn, and as such, it made sense that the families were on good terms with one another. The Lucas family had just moved to the lodge when Elizabeth had left for London, so she really had no memories at all of them.

"Mr. Bennet," greeted a heavyset but jovial man upon their entrance into the room where the family awaited their arrival. "How good of you to join us this fine evening."

A veritable sea of faces met Elizabeth's eyes, and none of them were familiar. The little information that she had been given suggested that the evening's festivities would be limited to the Bennets, the Lucases, and another family or two. Staring back at her—with no little curiosity, she noticed—were such numbers that it must have been almost every prominent family in the area, and they all paused in their various conversations to watch the Bennets as they entered the room, staring at the mysterious daughter who had been away for so many years. Squaring her shoulders, Elizabeth gazed back over the assemblage, determined to show them all that she had nothing to hide.

"And this must be Miss Elizabeth!" enthused the man as he stepped forward to greet her. "But I forget my manners," continued he, though his joviality never faded a jot. "Jane, perhaps you could do the honors?"

It was a good thing that she had not been standing by any other member of her family, Elizabeth reflected as she glanced at Jane. Though the rest of her family obviously understood that they needed to act in a manner that would not invite scandal, she did not trust several of them to not blurt something out thoughtlessly.

Jane—dear, sweet Jane, who was already becoming a favorite to Elizabeth—smiled with pleasure. "Of course, Sir William. Sir William Lucas, this is my younger sister Elizabeth Bennet, returned to us from my uncle's house in London. Elizabeth, this is Sir William Lucas, the master of Lucas Lodge and our closest neighbor."

"How do you do?" inquired Elizabeth as she sank into a curtsey.

"Very well indeed," said Sir William with an enthusiasm which was far from the common sort. "And I am very happy to see you again. I see that you have grown into a very beautiful woman. I am very sure that your return shall bring great pleasure to all. We have lived here long enough that I do recall a few escapades of yours from when you were a girl."

Elizabeth blushed. "I am certain I have outgrown such antics, Sir William."

"I am sure you have," said the man with a gentle laugh.

"Yes, indeed, she is here now, Lucas," said her father, interrupting their conversation and startling Elizabeth in the process. "I believe that we would prefer that you did not make such a fuss over Elizabeth's return."

His words were spoken with a stern glare at Elizabeth out of the corner of his eye. Contrary to what he might be thinking, Elizabeth would much rather that her return be commented on as little as possible, so she kept silent.

But Sir William was not to be deterred. "Nonsense, Bennet!" cried he. "It is indeed a reason for celebration, which is why we have invited you all here this evening. Besides, I believe your daughter needs to become reacquainted with the members of our little society. I shall be happy to perform that office, I assure you."

There was nothing indeed that Mr. Bennet could say to that, but though he did not betray it in his countenance, Elizabeth got the distinct impression that he was not happy with Sir William's insistence. The whole matter perplexed Elizabeth. If he did not wish for her to become acquainted with the local families, then why had he called her back? But she was given no time to ponder such a question, as Sir William was at that moment guiding her away from her family.

What followed was a confusing array of introductions, banal pleasantries, and names which she could not hope to remember during the course of one evening. In short order, she was introduced to a succession of Longs, Gouldings, Kings, Robinsons, and others, most of whom she would forget by the end of the evening.

Most of these went by in a blur, but there were two particular introductions which stood out in her mind once the evening had been completed. One of the first groups Sir William approached to perform the introductions was his own family, and Elizabeth was greeted warmly. Lady Lucas was all that was agreeable and obliging, though she appeared to be very similar to Mrs. Bennet in essentials.

But it was Sir William's eldest daughter who was most prominent in Elizabeth's mind. She was a dark-haired yet handsome woman, and she stood a little taller than Elizabeth and was likely several years older. She was also friendly and kind, though a little quiet, and she spoke to Elizabeth with affection.

"It is wonderful to see you again, Miss Elizabeth," said she.

"Again?" asked Elizabeth, searching her memory for some hint of the other woman.

Miss Lucas smiled kindly. "It is not surprising you would not remember me, as you were still so very young when you left. You were a little scamp as a child. The first time I met you, I had left the house for a walk not long after we arrived at Lucas Lodge, and I spotted you high in the branches of a tree."

Memories assaulted Elizabeth, and she suddenly remembered the meeting very well indeed. It had been a particularly trying morning after listening to her mother berate her yet again for some imagined mischief, and she had escaped the house and wandered near Longbourn's border with Lucas Lodge. To attempt to elude anyone in her family returning her to the house, Elizabeth had climbed a tree and had sat there with tears running down her cheeks.

"I remember now," said Elizabeth, smiling at Miss Lucas. "You shared some of your sweets with me that morning and helped cheer me up."

"Well, it helped somewhat," replied Miss Lucas, peering at Elizabeth strangely.

Elizabeth was not certain how much Miss Lucas knew or suspected of her absence, but she decided to ignore the issue for now.   Elizabeth was not certain how much Miss Lucas knew or suspected of her absence, but she decided to ignore the issue for now.

"I thank you again for the sweets, Miss Lucas," said Elizabeth in a light-hearted tone. "I was very happy to have a friend that morning."

"It was my pleasure," replied Miss Lucas. "But I do feel like we would have been great friends if you had remained in the area. I would be pleased of you would call me 'Charlotte.'"

"And you must call me 'Elizabeth,'" replied Elizabeth with a grateful smile.

Soon thereafter, she was led away by Sir Lucas and forced to partake in the seemingly never-ending succession of introductions.

It was near the end of her time with Sir William that the second memorable introduction was made. She and her host had approached a small group comprised of three gentlemen and three ladies—one of whom was her sister Jane—and Sir William began speaking in his ever ebullient tone.

"And here are the newest additions to our little neighborhood," said he, "though I am certain you are already acquainted with your eldest sister."

Elizabeth smiled at Jane before turning her attention to the rest of the group.

"Miss Elizabeth," said Sir William, "please allow me to introduce Mr. Bingley, who is currently leasing Netherfield Park. With him are his eldest sister and her husband, Mr. and Mrs. Hurst, and his youngest sister, Miss Caroline Bingley."

Elizabeth looked at the two ladies and two gentlemen as they were introduced, noting in the back of her mind that Sir William did not seem to be acquainted with the third gentleman in the group.

Mr. Bingley smiled in an animated fashion which betrayed an artless and open character. "Miss Elizabeth, how do you do? I am glad to finally meet you. Your sister has spoken of you."

The way that he looked at Jane told Elizabeth that he admired her sister, and though Elizabeth could not discern her sister's feelings with any certainty, she felt confident that Jane was not opposed to his attentions. Indeed, she wondered why she had not heard any mention of such a thing in the time since she had arrived. She could hardly imagine her mother being circumspect about potential nuptials, after all.

"And I am very happy to meet you, sir," said Elizabeth.

"Indeed!" enthused Mr. Bingley. "I understand from your sister that you have been in London studying music at the home of your aunt and uncle. Shall we hear you display your talents this evening?"

It was not an unusual request, and it was one which Elizabeth had been expecting. But though she was well aware of her competence, she was bashful at the thought of playing in front of so many people.

Still, she gathered her courage and said: "If Sir William wishes for some music, I shall be happy to oblige the company."

"Then we shall consider it settled," said Sir William. "Mr. Bingley, would you be so kind as to introduce us to your friend?"

"Of course," said Mr. Bingley, turning to the member of the party who as of yet had not been introduced.

And Elizabeth turned and looked into a pair of startling blue eyes. And she realized she had seen those blue eyes before.

Chapter VI

Elizabeth was more than a little surprised to see Mr. Darcy present at a gathering at Lucas Lodge, but she controlled her reaction carefully. The man in question was watching her, seemingly unsurprised to see her, and Elizabeth knew that even though he appeared to be of an inscrutable disposition, her entrance into the room had occurred some time ago, therefore allowing him time to compose himself for their meeting.

Elizabeth curtseyed to Mr. Darcy, who returned her gesture with a bow, and said, "Mr. Darcy."

"Miss Bennet," returned he. "I was not aware that you lived in the area."

"I have just returned after a long absence, sir."

"You are acquainted with Miss Elizabeth, Darcy?" asked Mr. Bingley with some surprise.

At once, Elizabeth became aware of a number of eyes watching their exchange, and she realized her mistake. She had much rather avoid any scrutiny, and the fact that she had been seemingly acquainted with such an important man was surely to be remarked upon.

"Only a very little," said Elizabeth quickly.

"We met briefly at a rest stop the day I came to Netherfield, Bingley," added Mr. Darcy.

"The day you returned to Longbourn," said Jane.

Elizabeth nodded and smiled. "So if Mr. Bingley will do the honors, then perhaps we can be introduced properly."

Mr. Bingley grinned at her and performed the office with what Elizabeth was certain was his typical cheer, and the group settled into conversation. As she had expected, Mr. Bingley was happy and talkative, but he was also intelligent and truly amiable. By contrast, Mr. Darcy was serious and quiet, only adding a few words to the conversation, though when he did venture to say anything, he did so with authority, speaking words of substance rather than the usual banalities.

Of the rest of Mr. Bingley's party, Elizabeth was unable to obtain more than the barest of impressions. Mr. Bingley's sisters were dressed fashionably and expensively, but they added relatively little to the conversation, instead, standing together and whispering to one another the whole time Elizabeth was with their party. Elizabeth could not state so with a certainty, but she rather fancied that she could see in their manners what she had sometimes seen in company in London—a superciliousness and a determination to be displeased with everything they saw. This fact amused her, as she quickly learned that Mr. Bingley's money had come from trade, which made his sisters the daughters of a tradesman. The other member of their party, Mr. Hurst, said nothing, concentrating his attention on his glass of punch and some delicacies which were situated nearby. He was obviously a dullard and a drunkard, and Elizabeth had no desire to further an acquaintance with him.

When Sir William began to lead her on to another introduction a few moments later, Mr. Darcy again bowed to her, saying:

"I has been a pleasure, Miss Bennet. I am certain your family is happy to have you returned to them."

Elizabeth curtseyed and allowed herself to be taken away by Sir William. But though she continued to greet others with perfect composure, her mind—and her eyes—kept straying back to the enigmatic man who watched her from across the room.

In a rustic gathering such as this, it was difficult for Darcy to feel comfortable, though privately he was forced to acknowledge that it was not so much different than gatherings he would have attended at some of the smaller estates near his home in Derbyshire. But though the manners of these people would not stand up to the scrutiny of London society, they did seem to be good at heart. And besides,

Bingley was his closest friend, and Darcy would not embarrass his friend by displaying anything less than completely proper behavior.

The one member of the party who was different was, of course, the second eldest Bennet daughter, and Darcy supposed that was unsurprising, as she had spent much of her formative years in London. Mr. Gardiner, her uncle, had appeared to be a proper sort of gentleman, and he had obviously done well in raising her to be a proper young lady. Her elder sister was also genteel and elegant.

Miss Elizabeth was obviously very well read and intelligent, genteel, kind, witty, and in possession of seemingly every virtue. However, she also seemed to carry some sorrow about her; it was something with which Darcy was certainly familiar. There was nothing that Darcy could put his finger on, and he doubted that most would have recognized it, but something in her eyes told Darcy that she had experienced great disappointment in her life. Yet he could not help but think that she had emerged from whatever trials life had dealt her all that much stronger for the experience.

As for the rest of her family . . . Well, the less said about *them*, the better. The father was silent and grave, and his eyes followed his second eldest as if he expected her to do something to embarrass him. In reality, he should have been watching his youngest daughters, who were loud and rude and appeared to have no thought for propriety. The mother was no better. In many ways, she was worse—a woman of her years and position in local society should have known to exhibit better behavior.

"I say, Darcy," said Bingley by his side, "you are full of surprises. I had not expected to hear that you had met the mysterious missing Bennet daughter before any of the rest of us."

Darcy turned a glare on his friend. "Have a care, Bingley. She has lived with her uncle, which is not unusual, you know."

"It is not," chimed in another voice, and Darcy turned to acknowledge the presence of Bingley's youngest sister. "But to be away from her home for so long without any communication is strange, you must agree."

"And where did you hear that, Caroline?" asked Bingley with a frown.

"From her eldest sister," replied Miss Bingley.

Darcy looked around surreptitiously and noticed that the eldest Miss Bennet had moved and was now once more in company with her sister. No one else appeared to be close enough to overhear their conversation, but it was still not a proper one to be having in company regardless.

"Miss Bennet told you that she had not heard from her sister?" said Bingley, skepticism lacing his voice,

"Not in so many words, of course," replied Miss Bingley airily. "But I am well able to read between the lines, and it was clear that she did not wish to discuss the matter."

"That is a rather extraordinary assumption, Miss Bingley," replied Darcy. "I might note that the middle of a gathering where anyone can overhear what you say is not the place to be having such a conversation."

Though she could not have missed the censure in Darcy's voice, Miss Bingley merely smiled and said, "Of course, Mr. Darcy," and then she moved away to speak with Mrs. Hurst.

Darcy watched her go, knowing that she would do almost anything to garner his approval. Unfortunately for her, Darcy was not disposed to give her what she wanted. He had counseled his friend many times since making her acquaintance that Bingley had best curb her behavior, lest she embarrass him, but thus far, all of his words had fallen on deaf ears. She was not unintelligent, but she was so fixed upon her own desires that it made her somewhat blind.

"I apologize for Caroline, Darcy," said Bingley, disrupting Darcy's thoughts. "She should have held her tongue."

"Yes, she should have."

Bingley returned Darcy's bland stare with a look of exasperation. "I *have* listened to your lectures regarding my sister. Unfortunately, she has seen fit to ignore my instructions."

The only response Darcy allowed himself was a raised eyebrow. At the sight of it, Bingley gave him a rueful grin. "Darcy, if Caroline makes your stay uncomfortable, you need only to say so, and I shall send her to my aunt in Scarborough."

"That is not necessary, I assure you," replied Darcy. "I can handle your sister."

Bingley favored his friend with a knowing look, and then he left to put himself once again within the influence of his angel. Darcy watched him as he went to speak with Miss Jane Bennet and reflected on how Bingley had once again found a lady to adore. What appeared to make this situation different from all the previous times was that Bingley seemed to be much more serious in his pursuit than Darcy had ever seen before. Whether the lady in question returned that sentiment remained to be seen, though from what Darcy had been able to observe through the course if that evening, she was not averse to Bingley's attentions.

But it was for Bingley to determine the state of her affections and his own. Darcy would not involve himself in the matter, though Miss Bingley had already made certain hints which suggested that she would appreciate his assistance in saving her brother from a "most imprudent match."

Turning his attention away from thoughts of Bingley and his sister, Darcy focused his attention on the other person who had attracted his interest. Miss Elizabeth Bennet was currently on the other side of the room speaking with Miss Lucas and some other ladies of the area, obviously becoming acquainted with all and sundry. There was something about the woman's situation which struck Darcy as odd, though he could not quite put his finger on it.

Still, Mr. Gardiner had been a genteel and seemingly intelligent man, and it was not unheard of for children to live with relatives of their parents. Whatever the reason, it was not Darcy's business, so he left off all of those thoughts in order to concentrate on the pleasure that a pair of fine eyes had to bestow.

Throughout the course of the evening, Darcy watched Miss Bennet as she moved about the room, and he even spoke to her on two separate occasions, though only briefly. During those conversations, Darcy found that his initial impression of her had indeed been correct. She was intelligent and engaging in her conversation, and her opinions betrayed a knowledge of the world about her which was far from the common sort in a woman of her background.

But it was when she played later in the evening that Darcy found himself truly enchanted. As had been agreed on, the pianoforte was opened, and the ladies took turns playing for the company. Miss Mary Bennet was technically proficient, though there was something deficient in her interpretation of the music, and while Miss Jane Bennet was much less competent, her playing was light and unaffected and pleasing to hear. Miss Bingley, of course, feeling the need to assert her supposed superiority, played in her affected manner after several of the other ladies had taken their turns. Darcy had always taken her mannerisms as her attempt to show herself to be a virtuoso, but he had considered them to be false, much as the woman who displayed them.

But when Miss Elizabeth sat before the instrument, the entire room quieted, no doubt due to the interest in the return of the young lady to the area. As the first strains of her playing wafted over the assembled, the exquisite tones told Darcy that here was a young woman who was truly a proficient. And she displayed more than just technical proficiency. She possessed an innate feel for the music, and her joy and love for it shone through in her playing. Though he had heard more proficient ladies in the past, Darcy had to acknowledge that he had never before been so truly moved. It was at this point that Darcy realized that he found this young slip of a girl intriguing, and he did not scruple to tell himself that he wished to know her better.

One person in particular noticed how Mr. Darcy's attention kept returning to the recently arrived Miss Elizabeth Bennet, and to say that she was displeased with such a development was rather an understatement.

The Bennets were beneath the Netherfield party, pure and simple, and though Charles had a tendency to make himself appear the fool with any pretty young woman he came across, Caroline Bingley was not about to allow their family to be pulled down by such reprehensible connections. She had spent too much time and effort ensuring that her family rose to the heights of society to let them lose it all to such a family.

And there was something . . . odd about the situation with Elizabeth Bennet, though the reason remained beyond Caroline's grasp. But though the young woman *did* play well as Caroline, she was forced to acknowledge, this whole story about her living in London did not ring true. Add to that the fact that Mrs. Bennet—a woman who had always seemed to be incapable of holding her tongue about *anything*—had remained stubbornly tightlipped about her second eldest daughter, and it was vexing to say the least.

Regardless, Caroline was not blind. In fact, she fancied herself to be a keen observer, particularly when it was her family's respectability and advancement in society at stake. And what she saw that night suggested that Mrs. Bennet held her daughter in barely concealed contempt, and only a few quelling looks from Mr. Bennet had kept her opinions from being poured out upon the company.

This suggested to Caroline that the reason for Miss Elizabeth's absence was not so benign. At this juncture, Caroline had no concept of what the actual reason was, but she was certain that she would be able to discover it. She had the highest motivation to do so, after all.

Chapter VII

The morning after the gathering at Lucas Lodge, Elizabeth appeared in the dining room, though she would have much preferred to avoid the meal altogether. Though Mrs. Bennet had not said anything, Elizabeth had the distinct impression that her mother was not at all happy with Elizabeth's success the previous night. Indeed, Elizabeth had hardly had a moment's respite at Lucas Lodge, as everyone present had been intensely interested in meeting her.

The breakfast room held only her mother, her father, and Jane that morning, and though Elizabeth could not say with a certainty just yet, she suspected that the younger Bennets were not early risers, particularly on the morning after a social engagement. Jane smiled in greeting, and Mrs. Bennet did not even deign to grace her with a look. Mr. Bennet, true to form, gave her one of those piercing looks she had come to expect from him.

Hoping to eat quickly and escape from the room, Elizabeth settled into her seat and dished some food onto her plate. Unfortunately, the food was not exactly to her taste; while breakfast at the Bennets' generally consisted of eggs, sausages, bacon, and other such fare, the Gardiners had always preferred much lighter foods in the morning, and Elizabeth was therefore accustomed to foods such as scones and muffins early in the day. Still, it would not do to criticize, so she took a little of the hot foods and some toast. For some time, the only sounds in the room were the clinking of utensils on plates.

When Elizabeth had almost completed her repast, she made to withdraw from the room, only to pause when her mother addressed her:

"You seem to have made something of an impression last night."

Far from being an innocuous comment, the statement seemed to indicate that Mrs. Bennet had something specific to say. Thus, Elizabeth decided on a bland reply.

"I have been away for some time. It is only natural that our neighbors should be curious."

Mrs. Bennet sniffed with disdain. "I suppose that must be the case. You appeared to be rather successful in turning back their inquiries."

"I have no idea of what you speak, mother," replied Elizabeth. "I spoke with those who wished to speak and returned courtesy with courtesy."

"That is well, for we cannot have any scandal attached to your return."

Elizabeth resisted pointing out that if any scandal were to erupt, it would be because of her parents' actions, *not* because of Elizabeth's behavior or her loose tongue.

"Regardless, I must warn you to stay away from Mr. Bingley and Mr. Darcy. We cannot have you interfering with Jane's chances with Mr. Bingley."

A retort almost sprang to Elizabeth's lips, but she held it back with a supreme effort. Instead, she contented herself with saying: "I dare say that Mr. Bingley appears to be quite besotted with Jane. I doubt there is anything I could do to prevent him, even should I be inclined to make the attempt."

"But we must not make a poor impression upon him," insisted Mrs. Bennet. "And his friend, who I believe holds great influence with him, would not hesitate to warn him away from our family should we be anything but proper." Mrs. Bennet's expression changed to an ugly sneer. "And it is not as if Mr. Darcy would be interested in such a plain girl as you."

Elizabeth would have liked nothing better than to give a biting comment on the behavior of certain members of the family, but she once again kept her composure, instead settling for a mischievous response.

"Mother, you must know that if I should marry Mr. Darcy, then you need not worry for my welfare upon my father's death." Smiling insincerely, Elizabeth rose and directed one final barb at her mother. "That is what you wanted, is it not?"

With a nod of her head, Elizabeth quit the room. Truly, a very little time in her parents' presence more than sufficed for meeting her duty as their daughter.

That day, Elizabeth began a custom of walking out into the surrounding countryside as frequently as she could. Not only did it afford her less time in the company of her family, but she also found that she enjoyed it greatly. While the walks in the park near the Gardiners' home had been a welcome respite at times, she soon found that rambling through nature in the vicinity of her father's estate far outstripped the city in the sheer joy and contentment that the activity imparted to her sometimes troubled mind. There was something about viewing the calmness and tranquility of the country which set her mind at ease, no matter how petty her mother, silly her youngest sisters, and unsettling her father's scrutiny were. For the first time, she began to repine what she had potentially lost with her removal to her uncle's home.

In those first few days in her father's house, Elizabeth exchanged several letters with her uncle and aunt, and it was not difficult to read between the lines. Both were understandably concerned for her welfare, and Elizabeth loved them dearly for it. She did her best to calm their fears, but it was difficult due to the lack of welcome she had received from her family.

But several days later, Elizabeth received a letter from her uncle which proved to be upsetting. It was a short letter which contained little of the normal pleasantries and affectionate words which were the hallmark of her communications with her uncle. What it did contain was the news that the Gardiners would be departing shortly for Ireland due to some of her uncle's business concerns.

Reading the offending words, Elizabeth was forced to dash an errant tear from the corner of her eye. Though she had returned to her home with her head held high, she had been comforted by the knowledge that her uncle and aunt were a short journey away and therefore able to come quickly should anything untoward happen. Now, her peace of mind would be removed, and she would be forced to deal with whatever happened on her own. What made it even worse was that she had always wished to see more of the world; if she had not been called home, then she would undoubtedly have been going to

Ireland with them.

At once, Elizabeth straightened and chastised herself for her moment of self-pity. She had always prided herself on her courage, and this news would not affect her.

Therefore, she wrote back to her uncle that night, assuring him that she was well and telling them she wished they had a good journey.

"Are you well, Miss Elizabeth?"

The young lady in question started and peered at Darcy, seemingly a little confused; then she attempted a tentative smile. "I am very well, Mr. Darcy. I thank you for asking. My apologies for not attending."

Smiling, Darcy assured her that he was not offended, and then he said, "I hope there is nothing distressing you at present."

"No, sir," said Elizabeth with a smile. "I am merely thinking about a letter I received from my uncle this morning."

"And how is your uncle?"

For the first time during his visit that morning to Longbourn, Darcy saw her face light up with a true smile. "My uncle and his family are all very well, I thank you. I just received word this morning that he will be traveling to Ireland to deal with some business concerns."

That received Darcy's full attention, and he felt surprised, though he endeavored to hide the fact from his conversation companion. "Mr. Gardiner is a man of business?"

By Miss Elizabeth's reaction, Darcy could immediately determine that he had made a mistake with his inelegantly phrased question, but the young woman spoke before he could clarify his statement:

"Yes, he is. But a better man would be difficult to find."

Her tone was frosty, and Darcy almost winced at how tactless his query had sounded. He endeavored to put her at ease with his reply.

"I beg your pardon, Miss Elizabeth, but I did not mean to cast aspersions on your uncle. He seemed a most gentlemanlike man indeed. I was merely surprised, as I had assumed he was a gentleman."

Though she appeared to be somewhat mollified, she still regarded him warily, prompting Darcy to say, "Bingley is my closest friend, Miss Elizabeth. I do not look down on another man because he works for a living, I assure you. I judge people on their merits."

Seeming uncomfortable, she looked down and paused for a moment before she spoke again. "My uncle tells me that my impetuosity is my greatest failing, Mr. Darcy."

"It is no failing to protect a beloved relative, Miss Bennet."

Miss Bennet finally raised her eyes, a delightfully arch smile directed at him. "I hardly think my uncle Gardiner requires my protection."

"Perhaps not," said Darcy with a laugh, feeling enchanted by this young woman's manner. "But I assure you that the most powerful of men appreciate the support of a beloved family member."

"Elizabeth!" rang out a shrill voice at that moment.

Though the young woman hid it well, Darcy could almost see her suppress a cringe.

"Come here, Elizabeth!"

When the voice sounded again, Miss Bennet drew in a deep breath and smiled tentatively. "If you will excuse me, Mr. Darcy, I believe that my mother has need of me."

"I have enjoyed our conversation, Miss Bennet. I hope we will have a chance to speak again very soon."

"As do I, Mr. Darcy," replied she before she curtseyed and left him.

Watching her as she strode away, Darcy could not help but fancy that she was girding herself for battle as she approached her mother, who had, of course, been the one who had called her. Her mother's voice, which was scarcely ever modulated, hit Darcy with the force of a bull horn.

"Elizabeth!" the woman's voice once again rang out. Then in a slightly quieter tone—though claiming that was akin to saying that a rifle shot was quieter than a cannon blast—she said, "I directed you to stay away from Mr. Darcy. You must not jeopardize Jane's chances with Mr. Bingley, and you know that Mr. Darcy could never have any proper interest in someone like you!"

An intense feeling of affront and disdain for Mrs. Bennet swept over Darcy, and he had to look away in order to avoid glaring at her with contempt. Darcy was uncertain which offended him more—her inelegant statement regarding Bingley and her eldest daughter, her belief that Miss Elizabeth could not tempt him, or her insinuation that the early acquaintance between Darcy and Miss Elizabeth portended any underhanded intensions on the young lady's part.

"Do you still believe that there is not something strange happening in the Bennet family, Mr. Darcy?"

Stiffening, Darcy turned his gaze upon Caroline Bingley, who was watching him with an expression akin to a smirk plastered upon her face. Darcy kept his own expression bland. He had learned the disadvantage of agreeing with anything this woman said and of saying anything which she could even remotely construe as criticism of another person, and he would not give her a new target upon whom to vent her spleen.

"Have you ever heard a mother berate her daughter in public in such a fashion?" continued Miss Bingley, ignoring the fact that he had not responded to her first question. "Miss Elizabeth hardly seems as if she is being welcomed like a daughter who has been away from home for an extended period."

"Mrs. Bennet is not the most circumspect of women, I grant you," replied Darcy. "Beyond that, we know nothing of the family's situation, and I suggest we do not indulge in speculation or innuendo when it is none of our concern."

With that statement — which he accompanied with a pointed glare — Darcy excused himself and strode away from Bingley's youngest sister. Miss Bingley could try the patience of a saint, and he would much rather contemplate someone much more agreeable. And one who had eyes as fine as any he had ever seen.

Though she had been avoiding it since her arrival, Elizabeth still had one place to visit, and she was not looking forward to the experience in the slightest. But it needed to be done, for though her family had never forgiven her for what had happened when she was two years of age, there was someone else in particular she believed would have granted her absolution.

The trees were swaying gently in the autumn breeze that day, and the air was crisp but warm enough that the exertion of the walk kept her comfortable. Near the back of Longbourn's park, Elizabeth had found a pretty patch of wildflowers, and knowing that she did not wish for anyone to learn of her errand, she stopped there to pick a few which she tied into a small posy, and then she made her way from the park.

Her destination was only a short distance from the house, and it was an area she had come to know well. The steeple of Longbourn's small church could be seen from the window of her bedroom, and it was there that she made her way. Outside the church, she waved a greeting to the church's elderly parson, but she did not stop to talk to him, so intent was she on her mission that morning.

Behind the small church was a small graveyard in which generations of Bennets had been interred, their memories kept alive by stories of the family and headstones which were meticulously carved and placed with care. Of course, Elizabeth did not know much of her family's history. This place had always scared her a little as a child, though after her fall from grace within the family, she had often taken to visiting it at odd times, almost daring goblins and ghosts to accost her. Perhaps she had wished they would end the misery of her life. She could no longer recall.

She wended her way through the headstones with ease, remembering the location of the one she was looking for as precisely as she would have had she visited only the day before, and when she arrived, she looked down at the stone. It was exactly as she remembered it, the elements having done no discernable damage. The plot was well maintained and clean, as if someone came here regularly to clean away the detritus.

It was more difficult than she remembered, visiting this place, and she sank to her knees, tears pricking the corners of her eyes as she stared at the inscription on the stone. And for a moment, she thought she heard an echo of childish laughter, though she knew it was impossible. Had that laughter been hers? Or had it been that of the one who slept below the stone in front of her?

Angrily, Elizabeth dashed away her tears, willing such fanciful thoughts to leave her in peace. The past could not be changed.

She leaned down and gently laid the posy in her hands next to the gravestone, and after touching it reverently, she rose again to say a silent prayer, though whether she was praying for peace, for forgiveness, or for something else entirely, she could not say.

There was no answer, though she felt a little lightness enter her heart. And with one final glance at the stone, she turned and left the graveyard.

Chapter VIII

Several days later, Elizabeth was told that there was to be an assembly at the gathering hall in Meryton and that her attendance would be required. In truth, Elizabeth was of two minds about the affair. On the one hand, any opportunity to leave the stifling atmosphere of her family home was to be considered a source of good fortune. On the other hand, she was not in a mood to socialize, and an evening spent pretending that everything was well seemed almost hypocritical, not to mention draining. But the demands of society were not to be ignored, so she girded herself up to once again play her part, all the while wishing that she was somewhere else.

As she was preparing herself for the evening, Elizabeth thought of her aunt, missing her more now than she ever had previously. Elizabeth knew by now that she would be the last to enjoy the services of Longbourn's maid and that her mother and younger sisters would take quite a bit of time before they were ready.

The Gardiners were well able to afford the services of a maid for both Elizabeth and her aunt, but the two ladies had long assisted each other with their toilette, so her uncle had never seen fit to add to the single ladies' maid he employed. Elizabeth was well aware of what most in London would think of such an arrangement, but she and her aunt had always enjoyed their time together, and her husband had indulged the small idiosyncrasy which brought the ladies of his house such joy. Thus, Elizabeth had some experience performing the tasks which needed to be performed, and she was therefore able to ready herself to a large degree.

The thought of her aunt and the times they had shared caused Elizabeth to ache with longing for her presence. She truly wished that the situation was such that she could leave this house behind and accompany her family to Ireland.

Before she could indulge further in such thoughts, a knock sounded at her door, and Elizabeth, though she would almost prefer to be left in peace, called out permission to enter.

The door opened, and Jane stuck her head into the room with the diffidence Elizabeth would have expected of her.

"May I come in, Elizabeth?"

"Of course, Jane," replied Elizabeth, feeling rather grateful that it was not her mother. Of course, she should have known already that it could not have been her mother, as the few times Mrs. Bennet had entered Elizabeth's room, she had certainly not deigned to knock in such a polite manner.

"I was hoping," said Jane, "that we could perhaps assist each other in readying ourselves for this evening? Kitty and Lydia have a tendency to require the maid's attentions for an inordinate length of time."

Elizabeth smiled, her heart melting at her sister's painfully awkward attempts to come to know her better. From what Elizabeth had seen, Jane was always given the first attention by Longbourn's maid, no doubt because Mrs. Bennet was in such a rage to marry her eldest off as soon as she could. Indeed, Jane looked as if she was already prepared for the evening, as her hair was perfectly coiffed, and she appeared to be as radiant as Elizabeth had ever seen.

But the incident highlighted another facet of life at Longbourn that Elizabeth had not previously understood. Simply put, Jane had not had another sister upon whom to rely since Elizabeth had fallen out of favor with her parents. Mary and Jane were far too dissimilar, and Catherine and Lydia were confidantes, leaving Jane to become more reticent than she might otherwise have been.

Therefore, Elizabeth accepted the gesture in the way she was certain it was meant, saying: "What a perfectly wonderful idea, Jane. My hair is often unruly, and though my aunt and her maid are adept at wrestling it into submission, I am afraid that it is difficult to manage by myself."

Smiling, Jane stepped into the room. She picked up a brush and began to pull it through Elizabeth's hair, a contented smile settling over her features. The motions and feelings of the brush running through her tresses had a calming effect on Elizabeth, and soon she found herself concentrating on her sister rather than worrying about her situation.

"My aunt used to do this every night," said Elizabeth quietly. "We cherished our time together in the evenings. Even my uncle, who is everything one could wish in a man, could never take the place of those quiet times with my aunt."

Jane seemed to study Elizabeth while she continued to pull a brush through her hair, and for a moment, she was silent. But Elizabeth could see that she was attempting to gather her thoughts and struggling to find the words for what she wished to say.

Finally, after a few moments, she sighed and fixed her gaze upon Elizabeth. "You have been happy with my aunt and uncle."

Though her question had all the appearance of a statement, there was a pleading quality to Jane's words which took Elizabeth back to those horrible days. Elizabeth remembered Jane's heartfelt "Be happy in your new home" as she had been led to her uncle's carriage the day she had left Longbourn all those years before.

"Very happy indeed," stated Elizabeth, wishing to ease Jane's anxiety. "My aunt and uncle have treated me like one of their own children. I could not have wished for anything more."

A relieved smile bloomed on Jane's face, and she said, "Then I am grateful to them for their care and attention." She then ducked her head in embarrassment. "I always knew that you would blossom with the right encouragement. I am very happy to see that I was correct in believing in you."

Elizabeth felt a lump settle in her throat, and she was forced to blink tears from her eyes. Had the situation been different, she and Jane would have been the closest of confidantes. And they would be now, she decided. All they required was a little time, and Elizabeth was certain they could attain the closeness they had been denied.

The budding moment between the two sisters was not to last, as the door opened and Elizabeth's mother entered the room. She took in the situation, and her lip curled with disgust, though an instant later she concealed that expression with an exasperated look at Jane.

"Jane, whatever are you doing, child? I have been looking everywhere for you."

"I was speaking with Elizabeth, Mama," replied Jane.

Elizabeth thought that her sister would say more, but she apparently realized that her mother would likely not appreciate whatever she had to say, so she held her tongue. Elizabeth was careful not to release a sigh of relief—apparently, Jane's penchant for looking for the best possible motives in others did not extend to the situation between her parents and her younger sister.

Mrs. Bennet's sniff of disdain clearly illustrated her thoughts concerning Jane's response, however, and she exclaimed, "Now is not the time for such things. You must hasten to finish making yourself ready. We must arrive early so that you may make a good impression upon Mr. Bingley."

Though Jane was clearly ready to depart, she allowed herself to be guided from the room and put into the care of Longbourn's maid. But Mrs. Bennet did not leave the room with her eldest daughter. Instead, after watching Jane leave, she turned back to Elizabeth and regarded her with an expression of distaste for several moments. Elizabeth kept her expression carefully neutral, not wishing to incite any further censure.

"Jane is not your maid," said she after a pause of a few moments, confirming Elizabeth's suspicions concerning her mother's thoughts. "I know not how your aunt manages her household, but at Longbourn, my daughters do not do the work of the maids."

Ignoring the implication that she was *not* recognized as Mrs. Bennet's daughter, Elizabeth could only reply, "I did not ask for my sister's help; she offered it."

Mrs. Bennet waved her hand impatiently. "How Jane came to be in this room is irrelevant. In the future, should she offer her assistance, you shall refuse it. The maid shall be made available to you before we leave for an evening and in the morning after we rise. You will avail yourself of her services."

"Yes, mother," replied Elizabeth, knowing that it was pointless to argue.

Nodding her head, Mrs. Bennet turned and left the room, leaving Elizabeth alone and wishing that she might leave this house and never see it again.

For Darcy, an evening spent in an assembly hall attending a country dance was torture in its purest sense.

Being blessed—or cursed, depending on how one viewed the matter—with a reticent disposition made such affairs utterly drab and tedious. Add to that the fact that everyone in the vicinity of this tiny hamlet had known Darcy's estimated income within hours of his arrival—and that every unattached young lady hoped to become *Mrs. Darcy*—did not improve his mood in the slightest.

He had attempted to be open and approachable with Bingley's neighbors since his arrival for the purpose of reflecting well on his friend, but thus far, he had only been required to speak with people in the setting of a drawing room. An assembly hall was a completely different matter. In a drawing room, he could always fall back on the subject of estate management with the local men, completely eschewing conversation with the young ladies if none interested him. In an assembly room, he was expected to actually *dance* with them, and unless he was particularly acquainted with them, it was a punishment rather than a pleasure. Those batted eyelashes, the breathy sighs which pushed bosoms into his sight, the false flattery—they all grated on his nerves. There were times when he wished he was married so that he would not have to deal with it any longer.

The worst example of such behavior was the Bennet matron. For some reason, the silly woman seemed to have taken it into her head that her youngest daughter—a silly, vapid, ignorant girl of only fifteen years—was particularly suited to be his bride.

"It is very obliging of Mr. Bingley to single out my Jane for a dance the moment he entered the room," squealed Mrs. Bennet when the couple in question moved away for a cup of punch before the first dance. "They are such a handsome couple, are they not, Mr. Darcy?"

"Indeed," was all Darcy could bring himself to say.

Other than contempt for this woman, his primary thought was that she need not bother attempting to push them together—Bingley seemed well on his way to being besotted already. And if Mrs. Bennet was attempting to gain Darcy as an ally in a quest to secure Bingley for her daughter, that effort was doomed to failure. Though Darcy had reservations about Bingley connecting himself to such a family, he desired only his friend's happiness, and if that happiness was tied up in Jane Bennet, then Darcy would support him. What he would not do was promote her to his friend—Bingley was capable of making his own decisions and determining the state of her affection without Darcy's interference.

"Mr. Bingley is so good. I consider him to be almost part of the family already."

Darcy attempted to ignore her. It was the height of crassness to suggest such things even before a courtship had been acknowledged—particularly to one of Bingley's party.

"But Mr. Darcy, you have not secured a dance for the opening set yourself," cried Mrs. Bennet.

"Thank you, madam, but I rarely dance," said Darcy with a short bow, intending for that to be the end of the conversation.

But Mrs. Bennet was not to be deterred. "Come now, Mr. Darcy. My Lydia is lively and handsome. I assure you that you could not find a better partner should you search high and low throughout the length and breadth of the kingdom."

Almost on cue, the youngest Bennet batted her eyelashes in what he supposed was intended to be a provocative manner. Of course, the effect—had it not already been completely ludicrous—was ruined by the girl's simpering giggle.

Darcy decided then and there that friendship to Bingley and being a good reflection on his friend only went so far. He could not abide another minute in Mrs. Bennet's company, much less a half hour with her silliest daughter. Therefore, he bent in a perfunctory bow and said, "Excuse me, madam," before he turned and stalked off to another part of the room.

As he left, he could hear Mrs. Bennet's voice rising behind him, saying, "Well, I never . . ."

But Darcy could not repine his behavior. He had no ties to the Bennets, so he had no need to care for their good opinion. Besides, if his actions offended Mrs. Bennet, perhaps she might be less likely to importune him with offers for her daughters' hands.

Thus began the evening for Darcy. He danced once each with Bingley's sisters, and then, mindful of his intention to support his friend, he danced once with Sir William's eldest daughter, who was a steady and intelligent woman, if a trifle plain, and once with the object of Bingley's affections. During the course of that last dance, he noted with some amusement the fact that Mrs. Bennet looked upon him with displeasure, whereas only a short time earlier she had been throwing her youngest daughter at him. It appeared that he had fallen out of favor with Mrs. Bennet indeed.

Once his dance with Miss Lucas ended, Darcy decided that he had done his duty to Bingley, and he relegated himself to the fringes of the room, wandering around and watching the proceedings with more than a little boredom while occasionally speaking with some of the other men. A number of them were tiresome—such as Sir William, who, though a good sort of fellow, was a little too impressed with his knighthood—and some were incomprehensible—such as Mr. Bennet, who seemed to see the world as some sort of vast satire—but others were truly good men, and Darcy did not consider it an imposition to converse with them. They were, none of them, very well educated, and many of the topics Darcy would have liked to pursue were simply not an option, but these men were also no different from many of the lower level of landowners with whom Darcy had associated in the past.

But throughout the course of the evening, Darcy's eyes repeatedly wandered back to the aforementioned Miss Elizabeth Bennet. She was by far the best dressed woman in attendance, and Darcy also believed that her clothes were also the most recent in fashion. Darcy could not say for certain why the other Bennet girls did not have some clothes of a newer fashion, for their sister had been living a relatively short distance away, which must have necessitated at least occasional visits. It seemed to hint at that mystery which Miss Bingley kept speaking of. But having formed a favorable opinion of Mr. Gardiner, Darcy was determined that it was none of his business.

He would like to get to know Miss Elizabeth better, and the opportunity appeared to be available, but he needed to figure out a way to begin. She danced less frequently than her sisters, though Darcy was not certain why, for she was as handsome of any of them. But though he wished to approach her, something indefinable held him back. But he watched her. Almost as much as her father watched her.

Sighing, Elizabeth sat down on one of the chairs along the side of the assembly hall, wishing that this interminable night would come to a close. Elizabeth had never been of an overly social disposition, though she had certainly learned to enjoy the events that her aunt and uncle often escorted her to. But she fancied that when attending an assembly, she had rarely suffered from a lack of dance partners. Unfortunately, this assembly was nothing like she was accustomed to.

Whether her mother had said something impolitic which had worked its way through the neighborhood, whether the neighborhood men still did not know her and were therefore unsure of her, or whether something else was at work, Elizabeth was not certain. But regardless of the reason, she found herself sitting out at least half of the dances, though Jane and her two youngest sisters stood up for almost all of them. Mary only danced a few, but then again, she almost seemed put out to be dancing at all and did not appear to repine her lack of partners. Add to that Mrs. Bennet's barely concealed glares when Elizabeth *did* stand up, and Elizabeth heartily wished for the solitude of her room.

Her relief came from an entirely welcome, though somewhat

unexpected, source. She had noticed that in addition to her father's constant scrutiny, she also appeared to have attracted the attention of Mr. Darcy, though his looks had more of a searching quality inherent in them. She knew already that she interested him—and she could not say that the feeling was not mutual—but for what reason, she could not say. Elizabeth was well aware of the fact that men of Mr. Darcy's importance did not pursue young ladies of her station unless they had something decidedly less . . . proper in mind, and Elizabeth could not believe that of Mr. Darcy.

After standing up for a dance with Charlotte Lucas's younger brother, Elizabeth was forced to sit for two, and she began to despair of being asked to dance again. It was then that she noticed that Mr. Darcy was standing very close to her, though his back was away from her as he watched the dancers as they progressed across the floor. He did not appear to be aware of her presence.

The dance came to a close, and the dancers made their way across the floor. Mr. Bingley approached Mr. Darcy, and as they were near Elizabeth, she could hear their conversation quite clearly.

"Well, Darcy," said Mr. Bingley in a tone which conveyed a sense of amusement, "you began the evening well enough, but you are back to stalking around the dance floor in your usual stupid manner."

Though Elizabeth could not see Mr. Darcy's face, she thought she caught the curve of the side of his lips, and his response belied any anger which such a statement might have produced. "Yes, I suppose I am—by your estimation, of course. But you are aware of the fact that I take little pleasure in a dance unless I am intimately acquainted with my partner."

"So you have informed me. I am happy to see that you have at least performed the basic necessities attached to polite behavior. I will say that I was somewhat surprised to see you single out Miss Bennet for a dance, though your dance with Miss Lucas was quite proper, as she is the daughter of the man who welcomed us to Hertfordshire."

"Why should you be surprised?" asked Darcy. "Miss Bennet is the handsomest woman in the room, as you have so often pointed out yourself."

"I would never presume to disagree with such a sentiment. But I would have thought that a pretty face alone would not be enough to tempt your fastidiousness."

"I rather think that you overestimate my 'fastidiousness,' as you call it. I am as susceptible to a pretty face as the next man."

"Oh?" It was clear from Mr. Bingley's tone that he was skeptical, though his beaming countenance suggested that he was enjoying their banter very much.

"Yes, well, Miss Bennet *is* very handsome, and she also seems to be an intelligent sort of girl, though very reticent."

"Much like you, old boy."

Darcy nodded and turned his attention away from his friend, which brought his face into profile, allowing Elizabeth to better make out his features. It was a very handsome face, which Elizabeth had already acknowledged, but it was made even more uncommonly so by the intelligence alight in his eyes and the slight smile which his friend's teasing had provoked. There was much to appreciate about Mr. Darcy, Elizabeth decided yet again, and she would very much like to know him better.

"But you must own, Darcy, that Miss Bennet is not the only handsome woman in the room."

Mr. Darcy did not answer, as he was searching the room and appeared to be looking for someone in particular.

"In fact," continued Mr. Bingley, "I dare say the Bennet girls are all quite handsome in their own ways, though the younger girls are clearly not the equal of their two eldest sisters."

"You shall receive no argument from me on that score," said Mr. Darcy, though his air was still distracted.

"Then perhaps you should ask Miss Elizabeth to dance. She has been sitting behind you for this last quarter hour or more without a partner."

Elizabeth's gaze dropped to her lap in mortification. Mr. Bingley had known of her presence the entire time, and he was undoubtedly aware that she could hear their conversation! How she wished to be swallowed up in a hole at that very moment!

It was thus with great astonishment that she heard Mr. Darcy's next words, as he said, "Thank you for the suggestion, Bingley. I believe I shall."

Not daring to look up, Elizabeth nonetheless noted Mr. Darcy's approaching footsteps and listened with wonder as his smooth baritone voice sounded in her ears.

"Miss Bennet," said he.

Though still embarrassed at being caught out in such a fashion, Elizabeth knew that she had no choice. So she gathered her courage and looked up, murmuring, "Mr. Darcy."

"I believe the next set will begin soon," said he. "Will you do me the honor of standing up with me?"

"Of course, sir," replied Elizabeth with as much composure as she could muster.

Mr. Darcy smiled at her with what appeared to be a true and sincere affection, and then he gestured to the refreshment tables. "Would you care for some punch before the next dance begins?"

Smiling, Elizabeth rose and grasped his offered arm, making her way with him to the tables and accepting the offered glass of punch.

They drank in companionable silence for several moments, and then Mr. Darcy, looking around them, leaned closer and said in a quiet voice: "I assume you heard my conversation with Bingley?"

Coloring, Elizabeth cast her gaze down toward the floor. "I confess I did, Mr. Darcy. I apologize for such a breach of decorum."

"I believe that you were already sitting there when we began to speak within your hearing," was Mr. Darcy's compassionate reply. "No fault can be found in you."

Elizabeth gazed up at him gratefully, relieved that he did not think poorly of her.

"I would not have you think that I consider myself to be above my company. It is simply that I do not easily converse with strangers, and I find it difficult to dance with young ladies whom I am not especially acquainted with."

"I understand, Mr. Darcy," said Elizabeth. "Indeed, I find these occasions to be somewhat trying myself."

Mr. Darcy regarded her with some disbelief. "Truly? I would have thought you to be completely comfortable in social situations, Miss Bennet. I fear I have misunderstood your character most grievously."

With a laugh, Elizabeth replied, "It is not that I am *uncomfortable* in social situations. It is merely that I do not, as a rule, enjoy them, though I will grant you that being in the company of close acquaintances is much more tolerable."

"You certainly have fooled me," replied Mr. Darcy. "I would have thought you to be completely at ease in any situation in which I have previously seen you."

Elizabeth directed an impish smile at him. "Is that not the very art of moving in society? Interacting with one and all as if it is the one thing you most want to do in all the world, though in reality you would much rather be at home, curled up in a chair in front of the fire with a good book?"

Mr. Darcy laughed. "It appears to be a talent for subterfuge which you possess and I lack. I dare say if I attempted to project such a complaisant demeanor, I should merely convince those around me that

I am constipated."

The delighted sound of their joint laughter brought several glances in their direction, and one of the young men of the area apparently decided that it might be the time to come to know her better, as he approached to ask for the next dance.

"I am sorry," said Elizabeth, "but I am engaged to dance the next with Mr. Darcy. The set after that is yours if you should want it."

It was agreed upon, and the young man—who she had likely already met, though she could not remember his name—left them alone.

Mr. Darcy was watching her closely, all mirth forgotten in the interim. "I must own that I am curious as to why you dislike society. You give all the appearance of being a bright light which shines in such forums rather than the reverse."

Elizabeth sighed. She had hoped to be able to avoid such a conversation with him. "It is merely that society seems so . . . artful, I suppose. Fortune hunters try to get in a woman's good graces because they covet her dowry, those of lower station affect awe and interest toward those higher than them in an attempt to ingratiate themselves, and there is an overall sense of artificiality to most interactions which I am certain you must have seen for yourself."

"I quite agree, Miss Bennet," said Mr. Darcy with a nod. "I assure you that I am well aware that when I enter a room, not five minutes pass before rumors of my situation are heard by every young lady in the room, not to mention their mothers."

"Then we shall have to be completely genuine with one another," said Elizabeth, directing a hopeful smile at him.

"An excellent idea, Miss Bennet," responded he in like fashion.

At that moment, the music started, and Mr. Darcy led Elizabeth out onto the dance floor. It was perhaps the most enjoyable dance she had ever participated in. Mr. Darcy was light on his feet, graceful in his movements, and seemed to have some occult sense as to her location at all times. While they danced, their conversation flowed effortlessly on a number of topics, all made interesting by the insights ad intelligence of her partner.

Elizabeth was sorry to have it come to an end, and she reluctantly followed her newest partner to the next dance when he arrived to claim her hand. But for the rest of the evening, she found her eyes seeking out Mr. Darcy with great frequency. And she was gratified to know that when she did, he was often looking back at her.

Chapter IX

Unfortunately, the magic of the evening—at least, what there *was* of it—completely dissipated during the carriage ride home. The moment the door of the carriage closed behind them, Mrs. Bennet began speaking of the assembly, and though it might be supposed that the subject of her discourse might perhaps be the success of her eldest in attracting the attention of the young man from the north, no such thing seemed important enough to focus her attention. Instead, she began a diatribe about Elizabeth's behavior which lasted the entire journey back to Longbourn.

In short, she was displeased with everything that Elizabeth had done that evening. Elizabeth was too impertinent, she had used her wiles to attract men when she should have been demure and silent, and she had generally behaved badly. Interspersed with this were comments about how Elizabeth had not danced every dance and how she should have done more to attract the attention of the men in attendance. It was the contradictions in her long-winded diatribe which removed any feelings of hurt which Elizabeth might otherwise have felt. Such nonsense could never result in pain.

And her mother did not cease her comments once they had arrived back at the house.

"And where do you think you are going?" asked her mother's voice, arresting her escape.

"To my room, mother. It has been a long night, and I find that I am fatigued."

"Not yet, if you please. I believe that we should have some further discussion regarding your behavior."

So Elizabeth found herself in the parlor in the company of her mother, her two youngest sisters, a worried-looking Jane, and her father, who must have heard Mrs. Bennet's words, though he had been riding with the driver due to the crowded interior of their small carriage. Mary had not deigned to join in the criticism, which was something at least to be thankful for.

Once they were situated in the parlor, Mrs. Bennet cast her steely gaze upon Elizabeth. "Well?" demanded she. "What have you to say for yourself?"

"I have not the slightest idea of what you speak, mother," replied Elizabeth. She was determined not to simply take her mother's abuse without defending herself.

"I refer, of course, to your disgraceful behavior this evening!" said Mrs. Bennet.

"What specifically do you object to, mother?"

"You know perfectly well," cried Mrs. Bennet. "I have told you several times to stay away from Mr. Darcy and to not importune him, lest you ruin your sister's chances with Mr. Bingley."

"Exactly how would I ruin Jane's chances?" snapped Elizabeth. "Not only does Mr. Bingley not even notice me when Jane is nearby, but Mr. Darcy approached me tonight at Mr. Bingley's suggestion. I do not believe that either man views me as an impediment to Jane's chances with Mr. Bingley."

"Do not speak to you mother in such a tone, Elizabeth," interjected her father.

Elizabeth looked at him, expecting to find some censure in his voice or expression, but there was none. He was as unreadable as ever, and his rebuke was delivered with as much emotion as he might have displayed while swatting a gnat. Mrs. Bennet, however, looked positively smug that she had provoked her husband to deliver a reprimand.

Almost grounding her teeth in frustration, Elizabeth fought for control of her temper, and in a voice as even as she could manage, she replied, "I shall remind you, mother, that as a woman, I have no control of who asks me to dance. Mr. Darcy asked me to dance and then suggested I drink some punch while we waited for the dance to begin. Do you believe I should have refused him and perhaps offended him? Or should I have simply ignored him, showing for all to see how improper and ill-mannered we Bennets are?"

Mrs. Bennet pursed her lips, and after a moment's thought, she said: "I believe it *would* be best if you did refuse him. In fact, in the future, perhaps you should not dance at all. That way, you will not risk affecting this family any more than you already have."

Now truly angry, Elizabeth shook her head and glared at her mother, ignoring the giggles which issued from her youngest sisters. "I shall not. It would be remarked upon and would reflect poorly upon us all. And furthermore, I shall not allow you to take away something which brings me pleasure."

Mrs. Bennet's eyes nearly bulged out of their sockets at Elizabeth's direct refusal. "You *will* oblige me!" Her words were nearly a shriek.

"I will not," replied Elizabeth in an unbending tone. "If you have brought me here for such silliness, then I wonder why I was summoned home at all. The Gardiners will be passing through shortly on their way to Ireland. Perhaps it is best that I accompany them, as I am obviously not welcome here."

Mrs. Bennet's eyes narrowed, though it was likely more because Elizabeth might receive pleasure from such a trip than due to any desire on Mrs. Bennet's part for Elizabeth to stay at Longbourn. Indeed, the Bennet matron had made it very clear that she did not wish to have Elizabeth in the house at all.

"There is no need for you to leave," rumbled Mr. Bennet, though he did not say anything further.

Mrs. Bennet shot Elizabeth a triumphant glare. She then said, "You will oblige me and refrain from dancing."

"I shall not," said Elizabeth.

"I believe that it is time for us all to retire," said Mr. Bennet.

With that, Mr. Bennet rose, and though Mrs. Bennet appeared unwilling to let the matter go, he directed a quelling glare at her, and she subsided with a huff. Elizabeth was therefore left with the satisfaction of not allowing herself to be bullied by her mother. What exactly her father intended was a matter for conjecture—that he did not wish for her to leave was evident, though his reasons were still a mystery. At least he had not sided with her mother and forbidden her from dancing.

By the next morning, everything returned to normal in the Bennet household. Mrs. Bennet seemed affronted by the fact that she had not been able to impose her will on Elizabeth and had taken to once again ignoring her. Being ignored, Elizabeth decided with somewhat of a philosophical bent, was far preferable to cutting remarks, and thus she found that she truly had little cause to repine. Not that she saw her mother until late afternoon that day—Elizabeth had risen with the sun and walked out, ranging further than she ever had before, and had not returned to the house until well after luncheon. It was while she was on that walk that Elizabeth met someone unexpected, but not unwelcome.

It was a path which Elizabeth had quickly come to consider her favorite, though she had only discovered it in the past week. It started behind Longbourn's church and wended its way through woodlands, past streams, and through valleys and up the sides of small hills, and at its furthest point from Longbourn, the trees to one side fell away and yielded up a fine view of the surrounding countryside. In particular, at the end of a long series of fields, Netherfield could be seen rising from the surrounding countryside, dominating the area like some ancient monolith. It was an impressive sight.

As she approached the location where Netherfield became visible in the distance, Elizabeth heard the sound of horse's hooves. Then the rider came around a bend in the path, and Mr. Darcy emerged astride his black stallion.

"Miss Bennet," greeted he as he swung down from his horse. "How do you do?"

"Very well, indeed, Mr. Darcy," said Elizabeth.

Mr. Darcy stepped nearer, holding his horse's reins, and executed a short bow, which Elizabeth returned with a curtsey. The horse ambled closer, and Elizabeth reached forward and patted his nose, eliciting a snorting sound in response and a gentle nuzzling of her hand.

"And who is this friendly fellow?"

"This is Shadow," said Mr. Darcy, introducing his horse with a smile. Shadow simply continued to nuzzle Elizabeth's hand, no doubt hoping for some tasty morsels.

Elizabeth laughed. "I am sorry, my fine fellow. I have not a carrot or anything to gift to you this morning. Should we meet again, I shall be sure to have something for you."

"I believe you have charmed him, Miss Bennet."

"He is quite friendly."

"That he is. He is eager to be pleased with everyone he meets, and I have never had a finer mount."

Presently, Shadow became more interested in some nearby hardy grass which was still defying the cooler temperatures brought on by the advancing stages of the year, and he began to graze.

"Do you ride, Miss Bennet?"

"I have not had the opportunity to learn, living these past years in London as I have," said Elizabeth. "But I do love horses. They are such majestic creatures."

Mr. Darcy nodded and motioned toward the path. "Shall we continue on together?"

Acquiescing, Elizabeth took his proffered arm and walked by his side, with his horse trailing behind.

"I see you have discovered some of the more delightful paths in the area."

"As have you," replied Elizabeth with a laugh. "The only walks available to me in London were in the nearby park. But I believe that the greater variety that the country affords suits me very well indeed. I believe I have missed my time in the country."

"I am partial to the country myself," said Mr. Darcy, his words snapping her back from the introspection into which she had fallen. "If not for the demands of society and the thought of preparing for my sister's coming out, I should be happy to live in the country forever."

Smiling, Elizabeth looked up at her companion. "You speak of her in an affectionate manner, Mr. Darcy."

"She is my only close family. But as she has been my ward for these years since my father passed, our relationship has been more that of a father to a daughter."

"How old is she?"

"Just sixteen. Yet she is womanly and handsome, though still somewhat shy and lacking in confidence."

Thinking of Lydia and her brash nature, Elizabeth replied, "Sometimes a little shyness is not a bad thing, Mr. Darcy. I rather think it helps to keep her from trouble."

Mr. Darcy laughed. "It might at that. I have never had to concern myself that she would stray. She is compliant and easy to care for, though I have been attempting to build her confidence in recent years."

"I am sure she is everything delightful."

The subject of Miss Darcy seemed to loosen Mr. Darcy's tongue, and they spoke of her for some moments, Mr. Darcy telling her several stories of his sister's exploits as a girl. His devotion and affection for the girl shone in his words, and Elizabeth was struck with the fact that he had, willingly and seemingly without complaint, taken on the guardianship of a much younger sister at a time in life when he should have been enjoying the life that a man of his station would normally lead at the tender age of two and twenty. Most young men did not come into their inheritance until they themselves had a wife and family. It spoke to Mr. Darcy's constancy and sense of duty, but also his love for his sister.

As Elizabeth and Mr. Darcy walked, the topics of discussion turned to many different things, and Elizabeth felt that she was gaining a good impression of her walking partner. She was happy—it was a pleasure to be able to converse with an amiable and intelligent man. She could not imagine anything wanting in the gentleman by her side.

When they parted, Elizabeth returned back to her family home, her thoughts full of her interactions with Mr. Darcy. Some part of her mind turned to the fancy of being the sole focus of his attentions, but she dashed that thought to the side as soon as it occurred to her. He inhabited a sphere high above hers, after all, and it would not do to indulge in thoughts which were very unlikely to ever come to pass.

When Elizabeth returned to Longbourn, Jane, sweet sister that she was, met her at the door with expressions of concern, but Elizabeth assured her sister that she had felt the need for solitude and gone out walking that morning. Being the soul of discretion that she was, Jane allowed the matter to drop, though not without urging Elizabeth to let her know when she left the house so that she would not worry. Then Elizabeth returned to her room, still loath to deal with her mother and sisters, and there she began reading a book which was part of a small cache she had brought from London.

After reading in her room for some time, Elizabeth sighed and put her book down. She had no desire whatsoever to be in the same room as her mother, but she felt that it would be remarked upon if she did not show herself at least once. So she gathered the threads of her determination and descended the stairs. But as she was about to enter the parlor, the sound of a voice interrupted her.

"I understand you went walking today."

Surprised, Elizabeth turned to behold her father. He was standing in the open door to his bookroom watching her and wearing that infuriating emotionless mask.

"I did, sir," replied Elizabeth, instantly wary.

"How far?"

"Some miles, I suppose," replied Elizabeth. She did not want him to know that she had met Mr. Darcy, so she prevaricated slightly. "I do not yet have a feel for the distances involved, but I went north and ended climbing a hill of some prominence."

That seemed to get a response from him, though in truth it was nothing more than a raised eyebrow. "North, you say?" When Elizabeth nodded, he rubbed his chin. "You climbed Oakham Mount then, which is easily two miles distant from Longbourn. More, in fact."

Elizabeth nodded. She had taken that path before, so she had an idea of the distance involved.

Mr. Bennet seemed to struggle with indecision for a moment before he forced out in a gruff tone, "You must take care. You are still unfamiliar with the area, and we would not want you to become lost."

With those words, he disappeared again into his bookroom, and the door closed behind him. Elizabeth stood there for some minutes, wondering at the exchange she had just had with her father. Could it be that the man was beginning to soften toward her? Elizabeth could only hope so. It would make her stay in this house so much more bearable if she had her father as an ally rather than . . . well, whatever he was right now.

While Elizabeth did not see a profound change in her relationship with her father, she was heartened by the fact that he seemed to look upon her with a little less disfavor than was his previous wont. Still, though she was marginally easier in his company, his silent stares never diminished, though to Elizabeth they seemed to take on an almost wistful quality. It was better than her mother's overt hostility, however, and Elizabeth was forced to be content with the improvement, no matter how small.

The next week also brought another change to the local community, as the long-awaited company of militia finally arrived in the area. Elizabeth's two younger sisters particularly greeted the arrival of the regiment with an unbounded enthusiasm which was just bordering on impropriety. But they were not to be censured, for her mother was as excited as the two girls were themselves, notwithstanding her long marriage to Mr. Bennet and the fact that she was no longer a young girl. On the day of the militia's arrival, Catherine and Lydia insisted upon walking to Meryton and greeting the company with all the enthusiasm that young teenaged girls could muster. Of course, though Elizabeth accompanied them, more due to a desire to leave the house then any desire to see the company of soldiers, she quickly discovered that Catherine and Lydia's behavior mortified her in the extreme.

The other unfortunate event which took place that week was the arrival of her aunt and uncle as they passed through on their way to Ireland. Unfortunately, Mr. and Mrs. Gardiner were not welcome at Longbourn; Elizabeth's mother refused to exit the house to greet them, and the Gardiners did not enter the house themselves, though Mr. Gardiner did express his desire to speak with his brother-in-law after he greeted Elizabeth.

"Is there any need for you to do so?" said Elizabeth.

Her uncle looked at her, an intense expression upon his face, and Elizabeth felt as if she were once again a young child attempting—and failing—to get away with some mischief.

"I merely wish to ensure that you are being treated well," replied Mr. Gardiner.

"How have you been here?" asked Mrs. Gardiner.

"Well enough," said Elizabeth. "My family has perhaps not been as welcoming as I would have wished, but I find that I am content. You need not speak with my father."

Her aunt and uncle looked at her with a skeptical eye, but Elizabeth regarded them calmly. She doubted that she would ever be completely happy or comfortable with her family, but they *were* her family, and at present, she had little choice but to make the best of her situation.

"Truly, I am well. I pray you do not worry for me at all."

The Gardiners shared a look before Mr. Gardiner addressed Elizabeth again. "I am sure you understand that is impossible. Your aunt and I will never cease to worry for you so long as you are residing in this house."

"And I thank you for it," said Elizabeth. "But I am quite comfortable, I assure you."

Mrs. Gardiner stepped forward and put her hands on Elizabeth's shoulders, searching her eyes intently. "Are you certain it is not merely your desire to avoid inconveniencing us?"

Privately, Elizabeth was aware that this was exactly what she desired, and Mrs. Gardiner had hit upon the crux of the matter without any effort at all. But she refused to impose upon her aunt and uncle any longer. The situation at Longbourn was not the best, but she was not as uncomfortable now as she had been when she had arrived. She could handle her family, and she was determined to do so. Her aunt and uncle had done so much for her, but now it was time for them to let her go.

Thus, she stoically met her aunt's concerned gaze, trying to put her at ease. "I shall not attempt to convince you that the situation is perfect. But I *am* well, I assure you. There is no cause for concern."

Elizabeth was subjected to the searching looks of her aunt and uncle, as she would have expected, but in the end, they gave way, though it was as much due to their trust in her judgment as to any faith in the Bennets. But it was what it was, and Elizabeth had already decided that she would continue with her family at Longbourn. The seeming improvement in her relationship with her father gave her hope that things would only get better.

Mr. Gardiner exchanged a look with his wife, and Elizabeth recognized from his expression that she had not convinced them of the wisdom of her continued residence at Longbourn.

"Excuse me, Miss Elizabeth," said a voice, causing Elizabeth to turn in the direction of the door.

The elderly housekeeper of Longbourn, Mrs. Hill, stood there, looking distinctly uncomfortable.

"Your mother requires your presence in the parlor."

As Elizabeth was about to respond, she was arrested by the voice of her uncle, who replied in a cold tone, "You may tell my sister that we are still speaking with Elizabeth. She will return to the house once our conversation is completed."

Mrs. Hill bobbed a quick curtsey, and though Elizabeth was not completely certain, she thought she saw a hint of an amused smile appear on the woman's face as she turned away and entered the house once again. Bemused, Elizabeth turned to her uncle and regarded him with a raised eyebrow.

"Have you managed to turn Mrs. Hill against my family?"

"I rather think *you* have managed that, my dear," replied Aunt Gardiner. "She was ever your protector, was she not?"

"As much as she was able," confirmed Elizabeth with a sigh. "I am very grateful to her."

"And so she shall be again," said Mr. Gardiner. There was a firmness to his voice which Elizabeth had not heard often. When she *had* heard it in the past, it was usually in conjunction with some sort of conversation regarding her family.

"We shall expect you to write us often, Lizzy," continued Mr. Gardiner. "We wish to know that you are well. Should anything untoward happen—anything at all!—you are to write to us immediately. I will do everything I am able to remove you from this house posthaste, should it be required."

"And do not hesitate to go to Gracechurch Street on your own if it is necessary," added Mrs. Gardiner. "The senior staff has been kept on in anticipation of our return, likely sometime early in the New Year."

"But it would be highly improper for me to stay there alone in your absence."

"That is true," conceded Mr. Gardiner. "But I should like you to know that you will be able to retreat to our home should it be required. The staff there has instructions to notify us immediately should you arrive, and arrangements will be made for you to join us should you leave this house."

"Thank you," replied Elizabeth, fighting back the emotions welling up within her. "I shall be very relieved to have a safe haven to go to should the situation here become unbearable."

"I truly wish you would quit being so stubborn and simply accompany us to Ireland," said Mrs. Gardiner, her tone soft and her sentiment heartfelt.

"I would certainly enjoy it," replied Elizabeth, though she was attempting to show a brave face to her relations. "But I shall be well. And you shall hear from me often—more often than you should ever wish, I assure you!"

The Gardiners looked at her with great fondness. "Now that is simply impossible," said her uncle.

They continued speaking for a few more moments before the Gardiners entered the carriage, and after a loving farewell with the children, Elizabeth watched the carriage depart. Though she attempted to put such thoughts behind her, she could not help but wonder if she had made a grave error. She did not think that her time with her family would be anything more than unpleasant, but there was a little voice whispering in the back of her mind which suggested that she still was no closer to understanding the true reason why she had been called home than she had been previously.

Chapter X

As time wore on, the doings at Longbourn began to be dominated by the recently arrived company of militia. Within days of their arrival, the officers of the regiment were invited to the gatherings of the area, with little thought given to whether they were even worthy of such an honor. It appeared as if the entire town—or at least the female half—had nothing else of which to speak than the officers. Even the married ladies seemed to be no exception.

Elizabeth herself was much more reserved with the members of the militia than most of those around her, though she noticed with some satisfaction that Jane also paid them little mind. Elizabeth did, however, interact with some of them, and she was able get a sense of what kind of men they were. The commanding officer, a Colonel Forster, was a bluff yet kindly man who seemed well chosen for his position. He was, perhaps, not the most stimulating conversationalist, but he was much more interesting than most of the men under his command.

Of the other officers, there were a few who seemed to be a cut above the others. Captain Carter was friendly and agreeable, while there were several of the other officers who were also congenial and fairly discerning, though many were still rather boyish.

There were a few who Elizabeth avoided, particularly Lieutenants

Sanderson, Pratt, and Denny, who were favorites of Lydia and Catherine. They seemed to watch her with an interest which was more than friendly, and they encouraged the younger Bennets in their poor behavior whenever possible. How her father could allow them to carry on in such a manner, Elizabeth could not understand. But knowing that she could do nothing concerning the matter, she gave the men to understand in a polite but firm manner that she was not interested in their flattery. They soon took the hint and confined their attentions to Elizabeth's youngest sisters and the other young ladies in the neighborhood.

On a day about a week after the departure of the Gardiners, Lydia contrived a reason for them all to walk to town. Elizabeth was not taken in by her subterfuge—Lydia's one and only reason for walking into town that day was to take the opportunity to once again flirt with any of the officers who were to be found in Meryton. Though she would normally avoid her youngest sisters, not wishing to be mortified by their behavior, Elizabeth decided to accompany them on this occasion, as they intended to call upon their Aunt Phillips in advance of the card party that the woman had planned for that evening.

Of Mrs. Phillips, Elizabeth had relatively few memories, but since she had returned to Longbourn, she had met the woman twice and had discerned that she was much like Mrs. Bennet. Mrs. Phillips was a social woman, delighting in hosting company, gossiping, and doting over her nieces. She was a simple woman, but at least she was not unkind, which heightened Elizabeth's desire to know her better.

Thus, the five Bennet girls departed their home early that afternoon, following the narrow road which led to Meryton about a mile distant. Catherine and Lydia walked on ahead of the rest of their sisters, chattering happily about the officers and who they expected meet that day, while Mary followed behind them. Elizabeth and Jane brought up the rear of the company, neither initially saying much. The silence, however, was companionable, and Elizabeth was content.

It was about halfway to Meryton when Jane spoke up, saying: "Elizabeth, your playing is truly beautiful. I understand you had access to masters in London?"

Elizabeth smiled at her sister. "I did indeed, Jane, and I availed myself of the opportunity to practice frequently. The Gardiners' pianoforte is a fine instrument, and I often lost myself in the music.

"But I cannot claim to be accomplished," continued Elizabeth. "I do love to play, but I do not think that I have as much talent as many."

"I cannot understand how anyone who has had the privilege of hearing you could find anything wanting," said Jane without a trace of hesitation.

"I thank you," replied Elizabeth with a laugh. "But I am afraid that I must put your opinion down to sisterly bias. I assure you that I am not so talented as you would suggest.

"You also play very well, Jane," said Elizabeth, forestalling what she suspected would be another heartfelt comment on Elizabeth's skill.

Jane turned away, a blush spreading crimson over her cheeks. "I do not play very well at all, for I have not had much instruction. I am nothing to your talent, I am afraid."

"I believe you have done very well for yourself," replied Elizabeth.

"Thank you," said Jane, favoring Elizabeth with a sweet smile. "But I would very much like . . ."

Elizabeth looked at her with a quizzical expression as Jane trailed off. "Yes? What is it, Jane?"

"I was just thinking . . ." Again, Jane trailed off, clearly fighting to find the words for whatever she wished to say.

"I would very much like it if we could play together," Jane was finally able to force out. "I would love to see some of your technique so that I may imitate it."

Throwing her head back, Elizabeth laughed, though she remembered just in time to stay quiet so that she would not invite the censure of her sisters.

"In that, you may be disappointed," replied Elizabeth at length. "Any masters who taught me quickly began to complain of the fact that I rarely followed their directives. According to Mr. Fleming, who was the last master to teach me, I shall never be truly proficient, as I have too many poor habits that I have no desire to break."

"I cannot find anything wanting," was Jane's quiet reply.

"And yet there certainly is something wanting," replied Elizabeth with good humor. "But be that as it may, I would be very happy to play the pianoforte with you."

Jane beamed at Elizabeth, but as they had arrived in Meryton, their conversation ended in favor of the goings on in the town. At first glance, there was no indication that any members of the militia were present, which caused no end of pouting for the youngest Bennets. Elizabeth, on the other hand, was relieved, knowing that her sisters would embarrass her if given the chance.

They busied themselves with visiting the shops Meryton had to offer, and Elizabeth, who had not truly had an opportunity to shop in Meryton, was especially pleased with the small bookstore. She spent some time there, looking at the varied texts and purchasing some few with the money she had brought with her from Gracechurch Street. Lydia, of course, was much more interested in the milliner's and other such shops, but the sisters were quite happy to allow each other to shop according to their own interests.

When the sisters again met along the main street in Meryton, intending to go to their aunt's, across the street two soldiers appeared with another man at their side. Lydia squealed and called to them from across the street:

"Denny! Sanderson!"

This breach of propriety prompted more than one look in response, but neither of her youngest sisters appeared to notice. They had caught the attention of the two soldiers, and that was all that concerned them.

The two men turned and made their way toward the Bennet sisters, and with them, they brought a third gentleman who quickly caught the attention of them all. He was tall and fair-haired, with a handsome mien and a gentlemanly bearing, and Elizabeth was not unaware of the looks he was receiving from most of the ladies nearby. As she watched him, she marked the frequent glances he made to those watching him and the way he tipped his hat as he walked, and she could immediately see he enjoyed the attention he was receiving. It spoke to this man's opinion of himself, which was quite obviously high. It also suggested that she should be wary of him.

The three men stopped in front of the five sisters, and the customary greetings were exchanged, though they were not completed without the giggles of the youngest sisters. Then Lieutenant Denny turned to the gentleman who had accompanied them and introduced him.

"Ladies, please allow me to introduce my friend, Mr. Wickham." He then turned to the ladies and with an exaggerated bow said, "Wickham, these are the Bennet sisters. Please allow me to introduce Miss Jane Bennet and her sisters, Miss Elizabeth, Miss Mary, Miss Catherine, and Miss Lydia."

Each of the sisters curtseyed as they were introduced to the gentleman, and though Elizabeth could not know what her sisters thought of the man, she had to suppress a shudder as his eyes raked over her form. She had seen that look enough times in society to know exactly what it meant. This was not a man to be trusted.

"I never imagined I would meet such an abundance of lovely ladies from the same family. I hope that we shall become the best of friends."

"Oh, are you to stay in Meryton?" asked Lydia with a flirtatious flutter of her eyelashes.

"I am to take a commission in Colonel Forster's regiment," said Mr. Wickham. "The next time you see me, I will undoubtedly be dressed in regimentals."

Catherine clapped her hands with excitement. "I am sure they will be pleased to have you."

"I do not doubt you will lend the uniform much distinction," said Denny with a grin.

"I am sure he will!" chimed in Lydia. From Elizabeth's perspective, Lydia appeared to almost be devouring the future soldier with her eyes. "I hope you will attend the parties and balls with your fellow officers."

"There is nothing I like better than the society of good people. I am sure I would be very happy to attend any such gatherings."

"Then you should attend our aunt's card party this evening," enthused Lydia. "It is only supper and cards, but it shall be a merry time for us all."

"Lydia," admonished Elizabeth, deciding that someone needed to take the girl in hand, "perhaps you should apply to Aunt Phillips before you issue invitations to a gathering at her house."

Lydia speared Elizabeth with a glare laced with contempt. "As I am far better acquainted with our aunt than *you*, I am certain that she would be pleased to accept anyone I invite."

"That is enough, Lydia," said Jane, an uncharacteristic hint of steel in her tone.

Though he was clearly interested in what was passing between the sisters at that moment, Mr. Wickham nevertheless appeared obliged to speak up. "It is true that I have not been invited. But if Mrs. Phillips is kind enough to extend the invitation to include me, I should be very happy to attend."

"Then you may consider yourself invited, Mr. Wickham," said Lydia. "I am certain that my aunt will be very pleased to make a new acquaintance. And the rest of the officers are invited, after all."

Mr. Wickham bowed and thanked her. They stood there for several more moments speaking, and while Mr. Wickham seemed to accept Lydia's fawning as if it was only his due, he soon edged toward Jane and attempted to strike up a conversation with her. To Elizabeth, this simply meant that he had sized up the Bennet sisters and targeted Jane for his attentions due to her great beauty. But Elizabeth was heartened to see that while Jane answered his queries with her typical serenity, his flattery did not induce any further reaction from her than that, and he appeared to be slightly put out. It was clear that his winning manners had rarely failed him in the past.

They were about to part ways when a pair of riders trotted up to the group and dismounted, revealing themselves to be Mr. Bingley and Mr. Darcy.

"Miss Bennet," said Mr. Bingley in his usually jovial tone. "It is very good to see you today. How do you do?"

"Very well, Mr. Bingley," replied Jane, a light blush appearing on her features.

"Excellent! I should have liked to call on you this morning, but unfortunately, a problem arose with one of the tenants of Netherfield which required immediate attention. Perhaps instead I might call on you tomorrow?"

"I should be very happy to receive you."

While they were thus speaking, Elizabeth was watching Mr. Wickham, and the expression on his face was one that was akin to a young child being denied a favorite toy. Though he had only been acquainted with her for a few moments, it was clear that Mr. Wickham had wished to make himself agreeable to Longbourn's most beautiful young lady. Elizabeth was simply glad that Jane was not nearly as senseless as Lydia.

Apparently deciding that pursuing Jane was not worth his time, Mr. Wickham cast his eyes around until they fixed upon Elizabeth. But before he could say anything to her, she moved her attention to the second gentleman who had just joined their party.

"Good day, Miss Elizabeth," said Mr. Darcy, stepping forward and bowing over her hand.

He then turned to Wickham and, in a voice thick with frost, said, "Wickham."

Instantly, Mr. Wickham's countenance lost all color, and he stammered a greeting to Mr. Darcy. Curious, Elizabeth glanced over at Mr. Darcy, and she saw nothing there to interest a casual observer—his mien was as empty of any emotion as Elizabeth had ever seen it. But underneath it all, Mr. Darcy's air seemed to suggest disapproval. And armed with the suspicion that Mr. Darcy and Mr. Wickham were not friends, Elizabeth vowed to stay clear of the latter man.

"I—I had not thought to see you here," managed Mr. Wickham at last.

"Evidently," was Mr. Darcy's clipped reply.

Then Mr. Darcy turned away from Wickham as if he was worthy of no notice at all. "I am sorry to interrupt your reunion with Miss Bennet, Bingley, but we should continue on."

"Of course, Darcy."

While Mr. Bingley was saying his farewells to Jane, Mr. Darcy looked at Mr. Wickham with such an expression of severe displeasure that the man backed away in some discomfort; then, once Mr. Darcy appeared satisfied that he and Elizabeth had a modicum of privacy, he directed a concerned look at her.

"Are you well, Miss Elizabeth?"

The solicitousness in his voice was unmistakable, and though Elizabeth was afire with curiosity over what she had witnessed between the two men, she knew enough to hold her tongue.

"I am, Mr. Darcy," said she.

"Mr. Wickham did not importune you improperly?"

"No, but he seemed eager to know Jane better." Elizabeth laughed. "He received nothing more than the short shrift from her, much to his own chagrin."

Mr. Darcy's answering smile was slight, and it in no way reached his eyes. "As you have likely already apprehended, Mr. Wickham is not a man to be trusted. Please take care when you are in his company. He would consider a pretty young gentlewoman such as yourself fair game."

Though she was taken aback for a moment over his words of admiration, Elizabeth quickly recovered and let him know that she would indeed be on her guard.

Mr. Bingley finally managed to tear himself away from Jane, and the two gentlemen departed after saying their farewells, though Elizabeth noted that Mr. Darcy sent Mr. Wickham a warning glare.

"I believe that it is also time for us to depart," said Mr. Denny as the gentlemen were riding out of sight. "We need to deliver Wickham here to our commanding officer and see that he is outfitted in regimentals."

"And we are all looking forward to seeing Mr. Wickham in his new scarlet coat," said Lydia. She leaned toward the man, and in a voice which was obviously meant to be seductive, she said, "I hope that you will favor us with your attention, sir. I for one cannot wait to become . . . better acquainted."

Elizabeth could hardly believe her ears—for a girl of Lydia's age to be speaking in such a manner to a man was completely beyond the pale. She was unable to stop herself from voicing a harsh reprimand:

"Lydia! That is enough!"

Spinning around with a harsh glare, Lydia almost shouted, "Be silent, Elizabeth! Someone with your past should never speak to someone else about proper behavior."

Her fists clenching and unclenching, Elizabeth's first instinct was to slap Lydia senseless. But she was interrupted by Jane's loud:

"That is enough, Lydia! Do not speak of matters you know nothing about!"

Silence fell over the group, and though Elizabeth was still fuming at her ignorant sister, she was surprised at the sternness in Jane's voice and at the fact that Lydia actually listened to Jane and subsided, though she was still glaring hatefully at Elizabeth. Catherine was glancing at both her sisters with wide eyes, the impropriety of their confrontation in a public place seeming to penetrate her thoughts, and Mary just looked at Lydia with disapproval, mumbling under her breath about the loss of virtue in a female.

As for the men, the two officers were shuffling their feet back and forth, clearly trying to look anywhere but at the scene which had played out before them, while Mr. Wickham, glanced back and forth between Lydia and Elizabeth. When his gaze rested on Elizabeth, however, she thought she detected a hint of interest in his manner. What he could be interested in, she was not certain, but she was resolved that she would never even speak to him if she could manage it.

"I believe it is best for us to be on our way," said Lieutenant Denny. After a subdued farewell, the three men bowed and went their way.

But as they were retreating, Elizabeth thought that she could see a quiet yet animated conversation spring up between them, and she noted several times when they glanced back at her and her sisters.

Stupid, stupid mistake! She should never have called Lydia out, especially when she was well aware of the fact that Lydia could never hold her tongue. They would be lucky if rumors of the confrontation had not begun to make their way around Meryton before nightfall.

Disheartened, Elizabeth followed her sisters down the street and to her aunt's house.

Chapter XI

"Elizabeth Bennet!"

The piercing shriek reverberated through the parlor, and Elizabeth thought for a brief moment that it would almost be easier if she were deaf—at least then she would not be subjected to her mother's bellows.

They had arrived home after spending some time with their aunt, and as Elizabeth had not felt equal to speaking with anyone, she had immediately retired to her room to rest until it was time to return to her aunt's home for the card party. The situation that Lydia might have inadvertently created was weighing heavily on her mind.

Of course, it had not been made any better by Lydia's furious glares and the demeaning comments which she had frequently made at Elizabeth's expense. Not that Elizabeth paid any attention whatsoever to the spiteful girl; Lydia's opinion was not precisely of any concern, especially when the girl had not an ounce of understanding of propriety.

But Elizabeth was not allowed to rest for long. Lydia had no doubt wasted no time in relating to Mrs. Bennet what had occurred in Meryton, though Lydia's version of events likely only bore cursory resemblance to the truth. Mrs. Bennet's shrieks had soon proclaimed her knowledge of the confrontation, however, and her screaming demands for Elizabeth's presence forced Elizabeth from her room and down to the parlor where she could be called to account for what had happened.

"Let me make myself rightly understood, Elizabeth!" Her mother's voice was in full force, and it grated on Elizabeth's nerves and her ears. "You are never to speak to Lydia that way again!"

All the while, Lydia sat to her mother's side, an insufferable smirk directed at Elizabeth. How Elizabeth longed to wipe it from her face!

"I am waiting, Elizabeth!" snapped Mrs. Bennet. "You *will* oblige me."

"I would not have to say anything to her if you would do so yourself!" retorted Elizabeth, her anger getting the upper hand over her better judgment.

Mrs. Bennet's eyes bulged out, and she screamed, "There is nothing wrong with my Lydia's behavior! She is high-spirited, which is just the kind of behavior that attracts the officers!"

"The kind of behavior which attracts all the *wrong sort* of officers," said Elizabeth. "Her behavior is more suited to a girl from a house of ill repute than to a young lady of gentle breeding."

If Elizabeth thought her mother was furious before, it was nothing compared to the rage which now showed in the redness of her face and the whiteness of her knuckles as she clutched the arms of the chair in which she sat. For a moment, Elizabeth was certain that the woman would either strike her or fall over dead of apoplexy.

At length, however, Mrs. Bennet turned to her husband and demanded, "Are you going to allow her to speak of your youngest daughter in such an infamous manner?"

"It is nothing more than the truth, is it not?" was Mr. Bennet's reply.

Mrs. Bennet stared at her husband, aghast at what she was hearing. "How can you say such a thing, Mr. Bennet?"

"I say it because Elizabeth is correct. Your youngest daughter is silly and ignorant, and she has not the first inkling of proper behavior. I suppose that someday she will expose us all to ridicule with her behavior. I merely hope that it is in some forum which does not come back to reflect poorly on her family and that it will teach her of her own insignificance."

Mrs. Bennet was stunned to silence by her husband's denunciation of her favorite daughter's behavior. But in reality, it was not truly a denunciation—in fact, Mr. Bennet might have been speaking of nothing more than the weather for all the emotion of his words.

Clearly, he was well aware of the fact that his daughter was on the road to ruination, and he could not be bothered to rouse himself enough to check her behavior. Elizabeth gazed sadly at him. But Mr. Bennet merely caught her gaze and regarded her with that same empty expression which he always wore.

At that moment, Lydia huffed and quit the room, but not before she favored Elizabeth with an angry look which clearly suggested that the matter was not closed. Though the girl's behavior was all that was detestable, Elizabeth pitied her. She was indulged by her mother in her every whim and ignored by her father, and she would undoubtedly discover one day, to her great detriment, that her behavior would bring her nothing but ruin. Hopefully, she would discover it in a manner which would not disgrace her sisters, for Elizabeth had little hope for the girl herself.

Mrs. Bennet gazed at her husband in horror, completely unable to respond to such brutal honesty. Mr. Bennet merely ignored her.

"But regardless of whether it is the truth," said he, looking at Elizabeth, "you will not speak to your mother in such a fashion."

In searching his face and the inflection of his voice, Elizabeth attempted to divine his thoughts on the matter, but he was as inscrutable as always. That in itself told Elizabeth that he was just as indifferent to this matter as he was to almost everything. His directive seemed to be nothing more than a show, but Elizabeth was not certain of the reason for it. To exert his authority? But why would he exert his authority over Elizabeth when he did not do so over the rest of the family? Elizabeth felt a frisson of unease pass through her.

But she could do none other than agree with his directive and ask that she be dismissed, which he allowed. Needless to say, Elizabeth spent the time before her aunt's card party alone in her room, as she did not wish to speak with anyone in her family.

Darcy entered the bookroom, and his first impression was that this was a room which had seen extensive use. The sturdy desk dominated the room , yet it showed unmistakable signs of age. Books of every sort lined the bookshelves and spilled out onto the floor, and even the chair in which Mr. Bennet sat creaked and groaned alarmingly when the man shifted his weight in it.

Darcy could see that the weathered nature of the room was a reflection of the man in front of him. Mr. Bennet could be no more than perhaps fifty, Darcy thought, but his sunken cheeks, the extensive grey in his hair, and the way his hands shook slightly—these all seemed to suggest a greater age than he actually possessed. It was a mystery, as

Mr. Bennet did not have the appearance of a man who indulged in excessive drink, and as for other vices, it was said that he rarely emerged from this room, so the more common of those seemed out of the question.

"You have requested my attention, Mr. Darcy," said Mr. Bennet without any attempt to engage in the typical pleasantries. "What would you like to discuss?"

Suppressing a grimace, Darcy decided that it was best to oblige him by going straight to the point. "I have come today because something happened in Meryton which excited my concern."

Mr. Bennet merely looked bored. "Has one of my daughters offended you, Mr. Darcy?"

"No, indeed, sir. Rather, I met in the village a man by the name of Mr. Wickham who has joined the militia."

"And meeting this man is a cause for concern?"

"If you knew George Wickham like I do, you would find cause to be concerned, too, Mr. Bennet." Darcy watched the other man for any indication of his thoughts, but when he received no response, he continued. "I have long been acquainted with Mr. Wickham, as he grew up at my estate and was the son of my father's steward."

"And his descent offends you?"

"No," snapped Mr. Darcy, his annoyance beginning to be piqued. "But his fondness for the gaming tables, his propensity toward leaving debts wherever he goes, and his penchant for ruining young ladies—gentlewomen and servants alike—definitely offends me."

Mr. Bennet regarded him evenly. "Those are serious accusations, Mr. Darcy. Am I to suppose that you have proof of these claims?"

The insinuation was, of course, that Darcy expected to be believed based on nothing more than his standing in society, which would betray an arrogance far from the common sort. But Darcy refused to rise to the bait.

"If required, I do," confirmed Darcy. "I have kept the receipts from his debts at both Cambridge and Lambton, a small town near my estate in Derbyshire, and I can call on the testimony of more than a few regarding his other activities. If these are insufficient, I suggest that you wait a week or so and then canvass the shopkeepers in Meryton and his fellow officers. I doubt he has reformed since I last saw him."

"I will take your information under advisement," said Mr. Bennet.

Aghast, Darcy glared back at the other man. "I do not think that you understand the gravity of the situation, sir. When I came across Wickham, he was being introduced to your daughters and appeared to be making quite an impression on them. From Miss Elizabeth, I had the impression that he had attempted to make himself agreeable to your eldest in particular, though I witnessed his interested glances at Miss Elizabeth as well."

"Elizabeth and Jane you say? In that case, I believe all is well. I do not doubt he will have no success with either of them. And my other daughters have not the means to attract a fortune hunter."

"And if his purpose is seduction?"

Mr. Bennet waved his hand. "Again, I doubt he will receive any attention from Jane or Elizabeth, and my younger girls are so silly that I should think they would drive him away long before he could try anything underhanded."

Whatever Darcy had expected upon coming here, *this* was certainly not it. He had known from his observation that Bennet was indolent and an indifferent father, but this was beyond any comprehension.

"And what of the merchants?"

"Do not worry, Mr. Darcy. I shall take care of the matter."

Though he doubted that Mr. Bennet would take any action at all, Darcy decided at that point that it was fruitless to argue the matter any further. He had done his duty in bringing Wickham's proclivities to the man's attention, and if Mr. Bennet chose to ignore his warning, then there was nothing further that he could do.

With nothing further to discuss, Darcy rose and bid the other man farewell, noting that he was not afforded the same courtesy in response. His horse had not been stabled at his instruction, so he was soon mounted and riding away from Longbourn, seething at the treatment he had received and the lack of any kind of response from Mr. Bennet.

Wickham was a problem. He wreaked havoc wherever he went, leaving behind ruined lives and debts unpaid. He had intruded far too often in Darcy's life, and Darcy had just about had enough of repairing the damage Wickham left in his wake.

Perhaps it was time Wickham learned the true measure of his own importance, Darcy mused. His cousin the colonel was highly placed in the army and had recently received a promotion which had resulted in his addition to Wellesley's staff. A quick letter to Fitzwilliam would likely see Wickham transferred to the front lines in the battle against the tyrant on the Spanish Peninsula. Darcy could not imagine such a fate handed to a more deserving recipient than George Wickham. He decided to send a letter to his cousin immediately.

And as for Miss Elizabeth—for Darcy had witnessed the man's

interest in her—if her father was not about to exert himself in her defense, then Darcy supposed that he must take the office upon himself. He thought much too highly of her to allow her to fall prey to such a libertine.

Elizabeth walked into the parlor of her aunt's home that evening feeling an emotional ambivalence. She would almost have preferred to avoid the event, though it would take her from her father's house for a time. But even that benefit was muted by the disgust she felt for her mother and youngest sister. She was already wishing that she had accepted her uncle's offer to accompany them to Ireland.

But she had made the decision to stay at her family home, and as she was not disposed to worry over past decisions, Elizabeth firmly put the matter from her mind.

The home of Mr. and Mrs. Phillips was not a large one, and since they had apparently invited a number of acquaintances, the crowd appeared larger than it actually was due to the close quarters. But as the Mr. and Mrs. Phillips were not of the gentry themselves, regardless of their connection to the Bennets, most of those invited were acquaintances of theirs, and there were relatively few people present who Elizabeth already knew.

Mr. Phillips was a kind enough man, but he was also a little dull and bluff. He readily performed the office required, introducing Elizabeth to those she whom had not already met. The card tables had already been placed, and refreshments were sitting on several side tables. There were more people present than positions at the card tables, so many people were in conversation about the room, and Lydia had gathered a number of officers and acquaintances about her to play lottery. Among them were several of the officers, including Wickham, so Elizabeth was cheerfully able to avoid that particular entertainment. Unfortunately, she underestimated Mr. Wickham's resolve.

Elizabeth and Jane sat on a sofa conversing amiably for some time before Jane excused herself to go speak with another acquaintance. Elizabeth was about to rise when the seat which had been vacated by her sister was taken by Mr. Wickham.

"Miss Elizabeth," said he with animated smile which did nothing to hide his calculating expression. "I have wished to speak with you this evening, but you seem to be quite popular."

"On the contrary, Mr. Wickham," replied Elizabeth, "I have not been the focus of any unusual attention."

"I am certain you are much too modest. I have heard it said that you have been from home for quite some time."

"I lived with my aunt and uncle in London."

"Ah, then you must be happy to be home."

"Quite."

He paused and regarded her for several moments, clearly thinking over his next words, and though Elizabeth would have preferred to quit his presence entirely, her innate sense of politeness kept her from leaving. Surely if she was noncommittal and added little to the conversation, he would tire of it and move on.

"I must say that society here in Meryton exceeds my expectations," said he after a moment. "This is a quaint little town, and I am certain that I shall be quite happy here as long as the militia is in residence."

"That is fortunate indeed," said Elizabeth.

"Yes, indeed," was his pleasant reply. "But while the great majority of the town is obliging and kind, I suppose even Meryton cannot be perfect. For you see, though I like what I see of the area and the people I have met, the presence of one gentleman forced me to consider leaving without joining the regiment as I had intended."

Privately, Elizabeth wished that he had followed through with that inclination, as it would have spared her his words now. And though it was obvious to whom he referred, she was quickly tiring of the conversation, and she wished she knew how to end it.

"Miss Elizabeth, I noted that you were speaking with Darcy earlier in a somewhat intimate manner. Since you obviously cannot know exactly what Mr. Darcy is, I had thought to illuminate you so that you might be on your guard."

"I am already on my guard," replied Elizabeth a little sharply. "I think you had best desist from this improper conversation, Mr. Wickham."

"Please indulge me, Miss Bennet," said he, forestalling her departure. "I shall only take a moment.

"You see, I have long been acquainted with the Darcy family, and his father was among the best men of my acquaintance. I was nothing more than the son of his steward, yet Mr. Darcy loved me as his own. I received my education at Cambridge due to his largesse and was treated with affection the entire course of his life.

"Unfortunately, the son was not cut from the same cloth as the father. After his father's death, Darcy refused to honor his father's wishes and present me with the family living which had been designated in his will. That is why I am now a member of the militia, having been left to fend for myself when I should have been provided for by my godfather. Had his son been honorable, I might already have been married." Here, he paused and directed a handsome smile at Elizabeth which she could only see as false. "Of course, though I would be set up and provided for, I likely would not have met as enchanting a lady as yourself, so I suppose that I have no real cause to repine."

Ignoring his empty flattery, Elizabeth turned a baleful glare on the man. "Why are you telling me this, Mr. Wickham? What can it possibly have to do with me?"

"I speak due to sincere concern for your wellbeing," said that man with a false earnestness. "Darcy is not what he portrays himself to be to the world at large. Not only does he feel himself high and mighty and above all those he meets, but he also misrepresents himself to those with whom he comes in contact. In actuality he is engaged to his cousin and will unite two great estates upon that marriage. However, he often woos young ladies such as yourself, leading them to believe that he intends to make an offer to them. Then, when he has obtained what he wants, he departs, leaving blasted hopes and ruined ladies in his wake."

"He does," said Elizabeth, allowing a healthy measure of skepticism to lace her voice. "And you have proof of Mr. Darcy's unchristian tendencies to prove your assertions."

"I would hope that you would accept my warning in the manner in which it was offered. There is no reason not to take care in your dealings with him, is there?"

"So you have no proof."

An injured expression came over Mr. Wickham's face. "I am afraid that Mr. Darcy's position in society makes him nigh unassailable, and to those with wealth and consequence, his situation renders him impervious to claims that one such as I might make."

"Mr. Wickham," said Elizabeth, deciding it was time to disabuse him of the notion that she would give credence to anything he said, "I suggest you cease this improper slander at once."

"Is it slander to tell the truth?" objected Mr. Wickham. His manner was all offense, but Elizabeth was certain that it was feigned.

"It is when you have not the means to prove your assertions. Now, please leave the subject and do not importune me again in the future."

It was at that moment that a truly ugly sneer came over Mr. Wickham's face, and he leaned forward, prompting Elizabeth to lean back in response.

"Tell me, Miss Bennet, are your sister's words about you true?"

"I have not the faintest idea of what you speak, sir," snapped

Elizabeth. She rose from her chair, intending to leave him behind altogether.

He rose with her, towering above her as he glared downward, his face twisted with rage.

"I refer to her comments about your *past*. What secrets are you hiding, Miss Bennet?"

"I fear you seem to have this false impression that Darcy has any interest in you at all, though we both know that he considers you to be beneath his notice." Mr. Wickham paused, and a truly unpleasant leer came over his countenance. "Or perhaps what your sister said was true. If it is, then you and I should find a secluded place to become better . . . acquainted. You will find me to be more of a man than that spineless milksop Darcy."

Elizabeth gasped in shock. However, outrage quickly took its place, and her hand rose. The sound of her slap to his cheek echoed throughout the room.

"Why, you—" snarled Mr. Wickham, his hand darting out to grasp her wrist.

"What is the meaning of this?" demanded Mr. Phillips as he rushed up to Mr. Wickham. "Unhand my niece at once!"

For the first time, Mr. Wickham appeared to remember that they were not alone in the room, and he paled slightly. He readily let go of her hand, however, and stepped back, as if trying to give the impression that he was not a danger to her.

Elizabeth rubbed her wrist, grateful that her uncle had intervened when he had. Jane rushed over to her, and Elizabeth accepted her embrace gratefully.

"I asked you what you meant by taking hold of my niece, sir," repeated Mr. Phillips.

"We were merely engaged in a discussion which became a trifle animated."

It was an obvious attempt to obfuscate, and to say that it had no effect on her uncle was a large understatement. Unfortunately for Mr. Wickham, there was one other in the room who was less than pleased to see what had happened.

"I believe that since Wickham is my officer, I should be the one to take him to task for what has happened." Colonel Forster stepped forward and motioned to two other officers in the room. "It is your first day in the militia, and already you have a poor start of it. I suppose that what I have heard concerning your dissolute ways is nothing more than the truth after all.

"Jones, Tilney, escort Lieutenant Wickham to the camp, where he is to be confined to quarters. I will speak with him later and determine what to do with him."

The two officers in question nodded to their commanding officer and escorted Mr. Wickham from the room. Before he left, however, he directed an expression of such poison at Elizabeth that she feared for her safety should he ever catch her alone and unaware.

"Miss Bennet," said the colonel as he turned toward her with a bow. "Please accept my apologies for the behavior of my officer. You may rest assured that this matter is not closed. When I am finished with Mr. Wickham, he will wish he had never laid eyes upon you. I will also make it clear that he is never to approach you in the future."

"Thank you, Colonel Forster," replied Elizabeth with some feeling. "You have always been perfectly gentlemanly, and Mr. Wickham's actions are not your fault."

"Perhaps not, Miss Bennet, but he *is* an officer under my command. The conduct of the men in my regiment reflects on their fellow officers and on me in particular, and I take my responsibilities very seriously, I assure you."

"Thank you," was Elizabeth's quiet reply.

The party broke up soon after that, and Elizabeth stepped into the carriage for the return to Longbourn. She now wished more than ever that she had accepted the Gardiners' invitation.

The next morning brought Colonel Forster to Longbourn at the earliest visiting hour which could be considered polite. It was only happenstance that Elizabeth was present at all, for she had made it a habit to walk out in the morning. On this morning, however, she had been defeated by a broken bootstrap and had reluctantly given up on her morning constitutional.

The colonel entered the room slowly, his gait uncertain, and it was clear that he was nervous of the reception he was to receive. It bespoke to his good character and the seriousness with which he approached his duties.

In this case, Elizabeth knew his apprehension to be completely unfounded. Even if Elizabeth had not seen the indifference with which the matter had been received by her parents the previous evening—the entire event had been gleefully imparted to them by Lydia upon their arrival home—she knew that she did not rank high enough with her parents to warrant even a small measure of outrage, let alone any decisive action in her defense.

"Mr. Bennet, Mrs. Bennet," said he as he sat on the edge of a chair in the parlor. "I have come this morning to offer my sincerest apologies to you and Miss Elizabeth," he nodded in her direction, "for the regrettable incident involving one of my officers last night."

"Yes, we did hear something happened last night," replied Mr. Bennet. He sat in his own chair, seemingly relaxed and without any care.

His carefree behavior startled the colonel, and for a moment, the officer was silent with confusion. It could not be said that he was without fortitude, however, as he spoke again a moment later.

"If you have heard, then you know of the appalling nature of Lieutenant Wickham's behavior last night. To have importuned Miss Elizabeth so improperly was disgraceful and a mark upon the entire regiment. I most humbly beg your pardon for this grievous breach of conduct. I assure you that it will not happen again."

Deciding that it would be best for her to take charge of the situation, lest her parents completely embarrass her or betray the family's dysfunction, Elizabeth said, "I thank you, colonel. I must own that his behavior on our first meeting did not inspire confidence, which was only confirmed last evening. I am grateful that you have taken such decisive action to punish him for his misdeeds."

The colonel smiled at her. "There was nothing else to be done, Miss Bennet. As I indicated last night, I must have discipline, and behavior such as that which you were subjected to cannot be tolerated." The colonel paused and smiled at the entire family. "The regiment does not receive nearly so warm a welcome everywhere as we have received here, and the actions of a rogue officer may cause that welcome to be rescinded."

"And we thank you, Colonel Forster," said Mr. Bennet, speaking up finally. He was watching the colonel closely, but unless Elizabeth was mistaken, he appeared to be focused on her rather than the colonel. "We cannot have such a man preying on ladies of the area, especially our daughters."

The colonel replied that it was no trouble, but while he appeared to accept Mr. Bennet's words at face value, he seemed to be confused by Mr. Bennet's sudden interest in the conversation. Elizabeth was confused herself, but she decided that it was just another example of her father's contradictory behavior and put it from her mind.

After only a few more moments, Colonel Forster departed, though not before promising Elizabeth yet again that Mr. Wickham would not be allowed to importune her again. Unfortunately, the inanities of her family only continued from there.

"I am certain that this must all be Elizabeth's fault," said Lydia almost as soon as the colonel had left the room. "Mr. Wickham is so charming and obliging; I am certain that he could never have behaved in such a manner without provocation."

"And you know him well enough to state that after two very short meetings?" challenged Elizabeth in disgust.

"Of course," said the stupid girl. "Mr. Wickham is far too handsome and congenial to be the miscreant that you seem to be eager to brand him as."

Elizabeth regarded her sister with no little disdain. "I will have you know, Lydia, that *Mr. Wickham suggested* that I accompany him to a more *secluded* location so that we may become better acquainted. And do you know why he made such a heinous suggestion? It is because of your ill-advised comment in the middle of Meryton's busiest street concerning *my past*. He seemed to think that I have loose morals based on one stupid comment you made for all to hear. You attempt to portray yourself as a knowledgeable and discerning girl, but it is obvious to anyone with a lick of sense that you are nothing more than a silly little flirt with nothing but fluff in your head!"

All pandemonium broke loose as both Lydia and Mrs. Bennet shot to their feet and simultaneously cried: "How dare you!" and "Do not speak to Lydia that way!"

Elizabeth rose to her own feet to meet them. "I would not have to if you would do your duty and take her in hand yourself!"

"You can have nothing to say to me!" cried her mother. "You are a disobedient and disobliging daughter, and I wish you had never been born!"

"And I wish I had never been born *to you*!" spat Elizabeth. "You place a great deal of responsibility on my shoulders, mother. I was two years old!"

"Old enough to already be the most disobedient girl who was ever born! Do you take great pleasure in the ruin you have wrought on this family?"

"I hardly think that I have ruined my family through nothing more than my own actions." Elizabeth paused and gazed at her mother with more contempt than she had ever felt for any other. "I would remind you that whatever is said about *me* affects all of your other daughters by association. If you do not wish for your precious Lydia's reputation to ruined, then I suggest you muzzle her, for she cannot seem to hold her tongue on her own. Of course, this presupposes that she will not ruin us all with her wild and willful behavior first."

Surprisingly, it was not Mrs. Bennet who reacted first. Rather, it was Lydia who let out a screech and flew at Elizabeth with her fingers extended like talons.

"Stop it, all of you!" thundered Mr. Bennet. And with more quickness than Elizabeth would have credited him with, he was on his feet, catching Lydia before she could reach Elizabeth.

"Silence!" shouted he when Lydia kept screaming and trying to reach Elizabeth. Elizabeth just looked on her youngest sister with contempt.

Once a modicum of order had been restored, Mrs. Bennet rounded on her husband, crying, "She is impertinent and rude, Mr. Bennet! And it is because you will not censure her yourself."

Mr. Bennet merely ignored her inanities as usual and focused his attention on all of them. "I care not what you say to or about each other within the confines of Longbourn—insult each other to your heart's content. But physical confrontations are forbidden."

A completely incongruous sternness evident in his demeanor, Mr. Bennet glared at Lydia. "Am I very clear?"

"Yes, sir," said Lydia sulkily.

"Good. And there is another thing, Lydia," continued he, a frown of severe displeasure directed at his youngest daughter. "I believe I made it very clear that *no one* was to speak of Elizabeth or our family's situation. Is that not so?"

At first, Lydia appeared as if she would refuse to answer, but it was not long before her father's glare cowed her into allowing that it was so.

"And yet, in your silliness and idiocy, you have blurted out something about which you should have kept silent in the middle of the street where anyone may hear. Regardless of Elizabeth's past or her position in this family, she is correct about one thing: you are silly and ignorant, and you have not the sense that God gave a sow."

Lydia gasped and made to defend herself, but Mr. Bennet would not allow her to begin. "From this time forward, *nothing* is to be said on the subject, and *none* of our neighbors will be given any reason to gossip about the Bennets. Am I clear?"

For once, Lydia appeared to be listening, and she agreed with her father's demands with alacrity, as did the rest of her sisters in the room.

"Good. You do not have the sense to understand, so I shall not be explicit about my reasons, but I assure you that much rests upon this. There must be nothing for our neighbors to gossip about. If I hear another word concerning anything which will give anyone to doubt our family's respectability, you shall be returned to the nursery and will not be allowed back into society until you are thirty."

Lydia was stricken at her father's words, but he regarded with a pitiless glare, and she meekly lowered her head.

"Very well. You may now go to your room and regain your composure."

Without another word, Lydia stalked off, followed closely by Catherine.

Jane, who had been watching the confrontation with an expression of shock and disbelief, turned to Elizabeth, but Elizabeth was too busy watching her father to pay her sister any mind. She was in agreement with her father that the family's troubles should be kept from society to prevent tongues from wagging, but the words "much rests upon this" confused her. Quite frankly, in all the time she had been at Longbourn, she had not had the impression that Mr. Bennet particularly cared about the state of his family's reputation.

Unless, of course, he knew something of the talk or gossip in the neighborhood which told him that Elizabeth's situation was already being spoken of. But that did not make much sense either, as Elizabeth fancied that she would have seen signs of it. People had a way of betraying when they were speaking of a certain person, not only in their judgmental expressions, but also in the way they would suddenly stop speaking when the person drew near. And she had seen none of that behavior.

Thus, her father must have had something else in mind. Unfortunately, Elizabeth could not fathom what it might be, and she decided that she would not concern herself about the matter any longer.

Her father excused himself to go to his study, and Elizabeth went to her room, her mind and heart full of thoughts of her family. In particular, she was absolutely disgusted with her father. Mr. Bennet had taken his improper daughter in hand, but he had unfortunately only done so to the minimum degree required, and he had accomplished it in a most insulting manner. In truth, she pitied Lydia. The child had never been taught proper behavior, and she was on a road to ruination that she did not even understand.

Chapter XII

After the most recent argument, an uneasy peace settled over Longbourn. Though the situation was not comfortable in any sense of the word, Elizabeth thought it to be much better than outright hostility between herself and the rest of the family.

That was not to say that the rest of her family ignored her outright. In fact, Elizabeth would have preferred to have been ignored rather than to receive the treatment she was given. The chief instigators were, of course, her mother and her youngest sister. They both took every opportunity to belittle her and make comments designed to provoke and demean her. But since they were both equally careful to say nothing when they were in company—and it was easy to tell when they found it necessary to restrain themselves, as their mouths would often snap shut as they gave a slightly apprehensive glance to Mr. Bennet—Elizabeth decided against any kind of response. Her mother had long made her opinion known, after all, while Lydia's opinions were so absurd and ill-considered as to make them worth nothing. And while Catherine ostensibly followed her younger sister, as was her wont, there often seem to be a slight uneasiness underneath Catherine's actions, as though she did not always agree with her more forceful sibling's opinions.

In those days, Elizabeth began to feel as if she was making a true sisterly connection with Jane, and she tried to speak with her eldest sister whenever possible. These efforts were complicated by her mother's insistence that Jane have nothing to do with her, but as Jane seemed less and less inclined to follow her mother's directives as time wore on, Elizabeth often found opportunities to speak with Jane alone. Her impressions of Jane were quickly proving themselves true, and Elizabeth came to understand that her sister was even more angelic than she had initially thought.

But more and more as the days passed, Elizabeth became aware of her attraction to the gentleman from Derbyshire, and as they interacted, she began to believe that the gentleman was not unaffected by her either. Their meetings were not infrequent; Mr. Bingley was a regular visitor to Longbourn and spent an inordinate amount of time in the company of Longbourn's eldest daughter, and he was often accompanied by his friend. And it was evident that when Mr. Darcy visited, he preferred Elizabeth's company to that of anyone else. That he had relatively little to say to anyone else offended no one other than Mrs. Bennet, who waxed long and eloquent in her denunciation of the man's manners.

Elizabeth attempted to tell herself that she should not excite her own expectations. She reminded herself over and over that gentlemen of Mr. Darcy's standing in the world did not consider young women of her station as prospective brides. But while she was aware of this fact, her heart proved traitorous, and she began to feel that it would be something indeed to be the sole focus of Mr. Darcy's attentions. He was circumspect in all his interactions, though Elizabeth could detect a certain disinclination for Miss Bingley's company, but if he and Elizabeth were together in any gathering, he almost always sought out her company, and their conversations spanned a wide range of subjects of interest to both of them.

He was intelligent and knowledgeable about many things, and though she would scarcely have imagined it, their opinions coincided more often than not. And though perhaps she would have thought that he might have replied with a patronizing air to a slip of a girl who dared to disagree with him, he did nothing of the sort. Instead, he would listen to her intently while she explained her reasoning and would then state his own opinion in an intelligent manner. In a few circumstances, Elizabeth actually felt the pleasure of persuading him to her own point of view, which surprised her greatly. He was certainly not proud enough to dismiss her opinion out of hand without even listening, unlike some other men she had met whom were only a fraction of his consequence.

The incident where Mrs. Bennet had tried to keep Elizabeth from speaking with Mr. Darcy was not repeated. Mr. Darcy's pointed look the first time Mrs. Bennet had attempted to call Elizabeth away had induced the Bennet matron to desist all such similar efforts. This did not stop the woman from complaining outside of Mr. Darcy's hearing, and she quite loudly proclaimed ill use and reprimanded Elizabeth for purposefully seeking to ruin Jane's courtship with Mr. Bingley. But since Mr. Bingley remained as assiduous as ever in his attentions to Jane, Elizabeth chose the simple expedient of ignoring her mother.

The other development in those weeks was that Mr. Wickham was transferred away from the regiment in Meryton, though Elizabeth's youngest sister railed at the injustice of it. As the officers were instructed to be silent on the matter, not much was known of his departure or where he went, but if the rumors were to be believed, he was headed for Spain and a new commission in the regulars. It was just as well, Elizabeth thought—though she was in no danger whatsoever of falling prey to the man, Lydia and Catherine could well have been ruined by him. As long as he was gone, Elizabeth did not particularly care where he had been shipped off to.

In this fashion, the rest of October passed away, and the first weeks of November slipped by. Then one day, near the middle of the month, a note arrived from Netherfield, inviting to the two eldest Bennet sisters to dinner.

"An invitation to dinner at Netherfield!" exclaimed Mrs. Bennet with an excited squeal. She stood and snatched the letter from Jane's hands, and then she sat back down to read it more carefully.

"This is a clear sign of Mr. Bingley's favor, Jane. Of course you must go, and you must dress carefully so as to use his fascination with you to its best advantage."

"Really, mother," said Elizabeth, "I would think that Mr. Bingley would still consider Jane to be the loveliest woman he has ever seen even if she were dressed in nothing more than sackcloth."

Mrs. Bennet directed a contemptuous glare at Elizabeth before she once again turned to Jane. "You must go up to your room and choose a dress carefully, Jane. It would not do to show up wearing nothing more than an everyday dress."

Though she was obviously not in agreement with her mother concerning her wardrobe, Jane clearly decided that it was not worth the argument which would ensue should she demur. Instead, she turned to Elizabeth and said:

"Let us prepare together, Elizabeth."

As Elizabeth was not averse to the prospect of being in company with the mysterious Mr. Darcy, she readily agreed, and the two rose to return to their rooms to prepare.

But Mrs. Bennet had other ideas. "Elizabeth does not need to accompany you."

Jane turned and regarded her mother quite calmly. "The invitation includes Elizabeth, Mama."

Sniffing with disdain, Mrs. Bennet did not even deign to look at her second eldest. "You may tell Mr. Bingley that your sister is indisposed."

"No, Mama." Jane's voice was surprisingly firm. "I wish to have Elizabeth with me today. We shall go together."

Angrily, Mrs. Bennet turned and glared at her eldest daughters, but instead of railing against them, she turned to Mr. Bennet in mute appeal. But as Mr. Bennet took no notice of the conversation and was not inclined to forbid Elizabeth from going, Mrs. Bennet desisted and merely waved them both from the room. In truth, she had given in far more quickly than Elizabeth would have expected. Perhaps she had actually learned something about Mr. Bennet's indifference.

Thus, Elizabeth and Jane made their way to Netherfield early that afternoon in Mr. Bingley's carriage, which had been dispatched to collect them.

"Our mother is certainly correct about Mr. Bingley's intentions," said Elizabeth once they were ensconced in the conveyance. "I cannot imagine that it will take the man much longer to come to the point."

"Lizzy!" exclaimed Jane, though she was giggling and blushing at the same time.

Elizabeth felt a warmth well up inside her at the sound of her sister using a shortened form of her name, glad that they had managed to gain a measure of closeness between them despite her mother's attempted interference. Elizabeth thought that she would like having a close sister very well indeed!

"In fact," said Elizabeth, "I very much wonder whether he will even bother with a courtship. He seems eager to move directly to engagement and marriage, as long as both are of a short duration, of course."

Though her countenance was still bright crimson, Jane managed to turn an arch look on Elizabeth. "And Mr. Darcy is courting you less assiduously, I suppose?"

All levity departed from Elizabeth at that moment, and she looked away from her sister in embarrassment. "Mr. Darcy is indeed an excellent man," said she in a quiet voice. "Your Mr. Bingley is, too, of course. But men of Mr. Darcy's stature do not look among penniless young gentlewomen who have been dispossessed from their homes for marriage partners."

"Elizabeth," said Jane, the compassion in her voice bringing Elizabeth around to face her sister, "I doubt Mr. Darcy knows much of our troubles."

"Perhaps he *knows* little, but I am certain he *suspects* much."

"If that is so, it has not seemed to cool his ardor. Surely you have noticed that he speaks to no one at Longbourn other than you and, occasionally, me. The man can hardly take his eyes away from you. It is part of the reason that my mother is so critical of him, though his refusal to dance with Lydia was the genesis of her dislike. I suspect that he is just as lost to you as you suspect Mr. Bingley is lost to me."

"Please do not raise my hopes, Jane," said Elizabeth, fighting against the tears that seemed destined to well up. "I could not bear it if my hopes were raised, only to be dashed to pieces should he go away."

"I shall not," said Jane, though she reached forward and grasped Elizabeth's hands between her own. At length, Elizabeth looked up into the eyes of her sister, and she was mesmerized by the compassion she saw there. There, within their depths, she could see the love that her sister already felt for her, and she began to feel the tears of quiet joy rolling down her cheeks.

"I would urge you, however, to watch Mr. Darcy," said Jane. "Truly watch him, Lizzy. He is not an inconstant man. I have only spoken with him a handful of times, but I can already be certain of that. Given the attention he pays you, I cannot think of any explanation other than that he is considering you as a potential companion in life. He might not even truly know what he is considering at this time, but his interest is plain for all to see."

Jane paused for a moment before she smiled and said, "Do not send him away for the mere suspicion that what society deems acceptable will rule his actions. And remember: a man needs some encouragement from a woman before he will find himself in love. Give him that encouragement."

It was through watery eyes that Elizabeth smiled, and when Jane moved to her side of the carriage and gently held her to her breast, Elizabeth allowed herself to rest against her sister. Elizabeth sighed in contentment. Aunt Gardiner had often provided this comfort to Elizabeth in the time she had lived at Gracechurch Street, particularly in the early years of Elizabeth's sojourn there, when the pain of memories become too great for her to bear. To have such comfort now provided by her dearest sister was almost beyond Elizabeth's capacity to understand.

"I will not send him away, Jane," said Elizabeth at last in a tremulous voice.

"And you will make him fall in love with you?" asked Jane in an arch tone.

Elizabeth laughed. "As much as I am able, I will see that Mr. Darcy falls in love with me."

The rest of the ride was spent with Elizabeth ensconced in her sister's embrace, relishing the help and support which she had not found for the past six weeks in her father's house, but which she now realized that she had missed desperately. And as their sisterly moment had occurred early in the journey to Netherfield, it was some minutes before they arrived at the estate. Thus, Elizabeth was able to compose herself so that when they disembarked at the entrance to the estate, she felt tolerably able to greet their hosts.

They exited the carriage with the assistance of Mr. Bingley, who was there with his ever-cheerful smile etched upon his face, and for a moment, Elizabeth wondered if the expression were a permanent fixture. Elizabeth smiled at the two of them, noting that as soon as Jane's feet touched the ground, she and Mr. Bingley had all but forgotten Elizabeth; if anyone deserved the happiness of being courted by a good man, it was dear Jane.

Content with the knowledge that everything was proceeding as it should, she turned her attention to the other man who had been there to greet them, and her breath caught in her throat. Mr. Darcy was not an open man like his friend; rather, he kept his own counsel. If she had to choose one word to describe him, that word would be "inscrutable." But at that moment, he was watching her with such intensity and such utter *warmth* that his feelings were clear to see for anyone who cared to look.

Regarding him with wonder, Elizabeth approached him, aware of the fact that they were essentially alone, as Jane and Mr. Bingley were so focused on each other that they could not spare any attention for anything else. Mr. Darcy watched her approach, a hint of a smile tugging at the corners of his lips. When she had arrived within arm's length of where he was standing, Elizabeth stopped and waited for him to speak.

"Miss Elizabeth," said he, taking her hand and bowing over it. "Are you well?"

"I have never been better, Mr. Darcy," replied Elizabeth breathlessly. The emotion she put behind her voice seemed to pierce Mr. Darcy's demeanor, and all at once, his face was suffused with the widest smile she had ever seen upon it. And in that instant, all of her questions seemed to be answered. Jane was correct; Mr. Darcy not only held her in high regard, but he also appeared to be well on his way to falling in love with her.

As she was with him, she realized in an instant.

"I am glad to hear it," murmured he. "You are very welcome here. Though the invitation specified that both you and your sister were invited, I was afraid you would not come."

"How could I not?" asked Elizabeth. She cocked her head to the side and gazed up at him, wondering if he would say anything else. Not that it mattered, she supposed—it was not as if there was anything holding her back. Except for perhaps her father's recalcitrance.

The thought sobered her, and she felt a little of the joy of the moment bleed from her heart. If her father should be obstinate and refuse his consent, then what would she do? She was more than eighteen months away from her twenty-first birthday, and the thought of continuing to live in her father's house was quickly becoming intolerable.

"Is something wrong, Miss Elizabeth?"

Elizabeth blinked, and her eyes refocused on Mr. Darcy, who was watching her. His smile had left, and now he appeared to be somewhat apprehensive.

"Not at all, Mr. Darcy," said Elizabeth, forcing away the errant thought. There was nothing she could do about the situation with her parents, and she was determined not to waste another moment concerning herself with such matters during her time at Netherfield.

"Then let us enter the house. I believe that Bingley's family is waiting for us in the music room."

Elizabeth allowed herself to roll her eyes in an exaggerated fashion, and Mr. Darcy chuckled at the sight.

"To own the truth, I believe I would much rather walk about the grounds in the company of a certain lady than brave Bingley's sisters in their den."

Mr. Darcy's voice was quiet, so as to avoid being heard by Mr. Bingley, but Elizabeth giggled at the thought and allowed herself to be led into the house, where they were followed by Mr. Bingley and Jane.

"I do not disagree, Mr. Darcy. But we should observe the social niceties. After all, did we not address that subject previously?"

"Indeed we did, Miss Elizabeth," said Mr. Darcy, leading them into the sitting room, where the sisters stood to greet them. Mentally, Elizabeth prepared herself for what would almost certainly be a trying time.

By the end of the first quarter hour in the sitting room, Darcy was already longing to be away and alone in the company of the bewitching Miss Elizabeth Bennet. By the end of the first half hour, he was wishing Bingley's sisters were residents of bedlam, although India would be equally acceptable.

Their every statement was filled with such condescension toward the Bennet sisters—ladies who were above them in social status, to say nothing of their deportment and manners—that he wondered that the Bennet sisters did not take offense to their thinly veiled attacks. Actually, to be truthful, Miss Bingley's statements were the offensive ones; Darcy had to acknowledge that Mrs. Hurst did not wholly take part, though she was generally engaged in supporting her sister. After some time, even her patience appeared to begin to wear thin.

The Bennet sisters, to their credit, withstood all Miss Bingley's poor manners with good-natured responses, holding her at bay and turning her attacks back on her without giving offense. Miss Bennet was every bit the angel which Bingley had always described her as, and though she responded calmly when necessary, Darcy had the distinct impression that she understood the thrust of whatever Miss Bingley said. He quickly realized that she was the perfect woman for Bingley. She was steady and calm, whereas Bingley tended to be rather excitable; she would bring stability to his somewhat frenetic life; and though she kept her emotions under good regulation at all times, she appeared to feel for Darcy's friend deeply. He determined then and there that he would support Bingley against whatever machinations Miss Bingley devised and would see him obtain his heart's desire, assuming Miss Bennet was that desire.

But the bulk of Darcy's amazement was reserved for the object of his own affections. Miss Elizabeth was, in a word, masterful. While she was more outgoing and vocal than her sister, she never stepped beyond the boundaries of propriety in responding to Miss Bingley's impertinent comments. Her replies were given with such a mixture of sweetness and archness that one could not take offense, even if one happened to be the recipient of her clever barbs. If Darcy had not already been well on his way to being enamored with her, he fancied that evening would have cemented the matter in his mind once and for all.

Only once did he note anything other than her usual spirit in her demeanor. Hurst had chosen that evening to be more active in company, and he took a lull in the conversation to regale Darcy with tales of his latest acquisition of a hunting rifle, going over the piece in exquisite detail to the disinterested Darcy. Miss Elizabeth listened to the long-winded monologue for some minutes before she fixed Darcy with an arched eyebrow, indicating quite clearly that she would not suffer the buffoon any longer. Then she excused herself to go speak with her sister and Bingley. The part of Darcy that was in love was tempted to follow her and ignore the fact that Hurst was almost certain to become offended by his desertion. The gentleman in him, however, could not bring himself to act in such a rude manner, even to such a colossal bore as Reginald Hurst.

But Miss Elizabeth had not gone more than twenty steps before she was waylaid by Miss Bingley, and though Hurst continued to drone on about his rifle and the sport at the estate, the two women were close enough that Darcy could hear much of what was being said between them.

"Miss Eliza!" cried Miss Bingley with false friendliness. "I see you have tired of the gentlemen's conversation. Mr. Hurst can be ever so tiresome when he speaks of his guns, his hounds, and his hunts."

Smiling, Miss Elizabeth replied, "You shall find no argument from me. I am afraid I do not know one end of a rifle from the other."

Privately, Darcy had to own that he completely agreed with both ladies as to the boring nature of such a subject. A rifle was a tool to be used, and though he could afford to purchase the best, he could not imagine rhapsodizing over one, as Hurst was prone to do.

"But if you please, Miss Bingley," continued Elizabeth, "I would appreciate it if you would refrain from calling me 'Eliza,' as I have never before answered to it."

Miss Bingley's eyes narrowed, as if annoyed at the thought that she would be denied anything, even the use of what was, to Darcy's mind, a rather unlovely moniker. Now, "Elizabeth," on the other hand, was a dignified and pretty sort of name, and he wholeheartedly approved of her parents bestowing it on such a lovely example of feminine charms.

"It must be wonderful for you to have returned to your family home," said Miss Bingley, ignoring Miss Elizabeth's previous words. "But settling in must be difficult after so long an absence. Are you quite comfortable in your home?"

"I have been back for almost six weeks complete, Miss Bingley," replied Miss Elizabeth. "I am quite well settled, I thank you."

"I must own that we were all surprised to meet you," continued Miss Bingley, who appeared to have not heard a single word that Miss Elizabeth had spoken. "The first time we heard of a mysterious missing Bennet sister was when dear Jane dined with us in September. I was astonished, as I had only met your younger sisters and had heard nothing of you."

"It is not at all mysterious, Miss Bingley, nor have I been 'missing.' It is not uncommon for children to live with relations, particularly when there is some benefit in education or circumstances to be had."

Miss Bingley smiled, but even from his seat, Darcy could tell that the expression was in no way reflected in her eyes, which were as hard and dark as coal. "Miss Eliza, you must understand how it appears from our perspective, particularly since we have not lived in the area for long and could not have known your family before.

"First, there was nothing said of you by any of your family; then, to my surprise, dear Jane mentioned the fact that she had another sister during dinner; and finally, if you will forgive me for being so bold, I received the distinct impression from her words that it had been many years since she had seen you. How do you account for this seeming distance?"

Darcy was about to rise from his seat to intervene, but then he noted, upon looking at Miss Elizabeth, that while her color was a little higher than usual, she gazed at Miss Bingley with an expression which was censorious but not intimidated in the least.

"I know not where you might have received such an impression, Miss Bingley, but I assure you that I am as close to my sister as I ever was."

"Yes, that does seem to be the case." Miss Bingley's saccharine smile became even more overtly—and falsely—solicitous. "But what of the rest of your family? Your dear mother has at times appeared overly . . . critical of you."

"What child can go through life without occasional reprimands from a parent?" said Elizabeth rhetorically. And though Darcy could see that outwardly she remained as calm as she ever was, he fancied he knew her well enough to recognize that only her innate good manners were preventing her from giving Miss Bingley a well-deserved dressing-down.

"I suppose," said Miss Bingley in a doubtful tone. "I cannot empathize with you, as I always enjoyed the best of relationships with my mother."

A snort from Hurst drew Darcy's attention, and he turned to the man, noting the glare which Darcy could tell was directed at his sister-in-law.

"Caroline despised her mother," said Hurst in a low tone meant only for Darcy. "Caroline disliked her low origins and her attempts to bring her children up in a way which would credit the family. The fact that Caroline has become the shrew she is today is a testament that the woman failed, though I would certainly not place the blame on her."

Darcy gazed at Hurst with unfeigned astonishment.

Hurst only raised an eyebrow at him. "Come now, Darcy. Considering how observant you are, I would have thought that you were aware of my opinion of my *dear sister*. It is one which closely resembles your own, I believe."

"It quite escaped my notice," said Darcy at last.

"You thought I was nothing more than a drunk, interested in only my meal and my spirits, did you?" Hurst chuckled at his own words. "I am all of that, I assure you. But I was a little livelier before we met." He directed a surreptitious glance at Miss Bingley, who was still interrogating Miss Elizabeth, though Mrs. Hurst had now joined them. "I thought the woman I was marrying was more than simply an adjunct of her younger sister. My life would be much more pleasurable if Caroline was not a part of it."

"Surely it is not that bad."

"Perhaps not. Louisa has recently begun to develop more of a backbone when it comes to her sister, and I must own that I have encouraged it. But Caroline is still the leader and Louisa the follower, and for now, I bide my time until that dynamic changes."

There was nothing Darcy could say to that, though he understood Hurst's feelings quite well indeed. "So your tendency to keep to yourself and sleep in the drawing room . . . This is all brought on by Miss Bingley?"

"Oh, not all of it," said Hurst with a snort. "I *am* a rather indolent fellow, after all. But yes, I find it much easier to avoid Caroline altogether. And I am not always sleeping, you know."

A sly smile came across Hurst's face. "At one point, I was hopeful that you would solve my problem and take Caroline off my hands."

Darcy suspected that his eyes were fairly bulging out of his head at the mere suggestion. He had *never* considered Miss Bingley as the successor to his dear mother, and he never would. Though his family would applaud him for having no designs on the daughter of a tradeswoman, Darcy was not a typical man of his set. His parents had enjoyed a loving relationship which had almost undoubtedly led in part to his father's early demise once his mother had passed on. Though the chances for heartbreak were much greater with a love match, he had determined long ago that he would accept nothing less. And Caroline Bingley would never meet his requirements for that very reason.

"I knew within moments of seeing you both in company that it would never happen, of course," said Hurst. "It was clear to me, even if she is blind of it to this day, that you tolerated her only because of your friendship with Bingley."

"You could have informed me of your true character ere now," said Darcy. But he was only slightly piqued at Hurst's revelations. More than that, he was amused—Hurst was *indeed* too indolent for Darcy's tastes, but he suspected that the man was of a sardonic bent, which Darcy would find amusing, provided it was not shown too frequently.

"And how would that provide amusement for me?" asked Hurst.

Darcy was forced to chuckle. "How, indeed?"

"Now, I suspect that my sister is becoming much more impertinent with her questions, little though you can imagine it, given the way she began. You had best go and rescue your Miss Elizabeth before she has cause to reprimand Caroline severely."

Looking up, Darcy could see that Hurst's prediction was indeed being borne out, and he rose to go to Miss Elizabeth. But before he could walk away, Hurst spoke again, though in a very quiet tone which Darcy could only just make out.

"Darcy, a word of advice, if you will. You had best mute your admiration for Miss Elizabeth as well as your attentions toward her unless you actually intend to do something about it. Caroline has noticed, and I expect this is what has caused her to unsheathe her claws."

With a nod, Hurst leaned back against the couch and closed his eyes. Darcy could only stare at the man before turning and making his way to Miss Elizabeth's side.

"I thank you for the offer, Miss Bingley," said Miss Elizabeth at that moment. "I can assure you that if I ever require your assistance, I shall ask."

"Ah, Mr. Darcy!" said Miss Bingley with a smile. "I have offered to introduce Miss Eliza to our friends in town when next we are there. She would be such a . . . sensation, do you not think?"

Her tone led Darcy to understand that she expected that Elizabeth would not be accepted by his circle. Whether she would be accepted by Miss Bingley's circle was of no concern to Darcy, as he did not like the women with whom Miss Bingley socialized.

"I dare say she would be indeed," said Darcy. "But come, Miss Elizabeth—I believe that your sister was trying to catch your eye a moment ago. Shall we?"

Smiling, Miss Elizabeth put her hand on his arm. But before they could move away, she directed one final parting comment at Miss Bingley.

"I thank you for this illuminating conversation, Miss Bingley. I dare say we shall have many more such opportunities to speak in the future."

A significant glance at her sister and Mr. Bingley left no doubt as to her meaning, but Elizabeth and Darcy turned away from Miss Bingley before the woman could form a response.

Feeling admiration for her courage and tenacity, Darcy escorted Miss Elizabeth to her sister, and the four of them fell into conversation as easily as if they had been acquainted for years.

In the back of his mind, however, Darcy was replaying his conversation with Hurst. He *was* attracted to Miss Elizabeth, and he found himself becoming increasingly loath to conceal it. But had he seen enough of her to leave him confident of proceeding? As a sober and serious man, Darcy was deliberate in his decision-making, which could be both a blessing and a curse. The thought of Miss Elizabeth's reaction to seeing him upon her arrival that afternoon filled him with a sense of peace, as he now knew that she was not indifferent to him.

With that in mind, what was holding him back? Was that not what a courtship was for? To see if his interest was enough to proceed to marriage? Perhaps it was time to make that next step, but Darcy was disposed to be extra careful. This would be one of the most important decisions of his life, after all, and he wanted to be certain before he moved forward.

In the back of his mind, however, he knew that he was already certain. He was enamored of Miss Elizabeth Bennet, and his feelings would only become that much stronger the longer he revolved in orbit about her.

"Caroline!" hissed Louisa.

The fact that Caroline simply huffed and glared at her sent Louisa into further heights of fury. Her sister had always been blind about certain things, and Mr. Darcy happened to be the one thing about which she was most mistaken. Caroline was almost delusional, Louisa thought, and she risked being ostracized from society herself if she did not desist.

Louisa took her sister by the arm and led her to a nearby sofa which was out of earshot of the Bennet sisters and Mr. Hurst, whom Louisa suspected was not nearly as insensible as he tried to portray.

"You should be extremely careful about what you say to Miss Elizabeth, Caroline," said Louisa once they had seated themselves on the sofa.

Her sister's only response was an unpleasant sneer. "And why should I be? She is nothing more than a country bumpkin, even if she has lived with her *tradesman uncle* in London these past years."

The scathing contempt in Caroline's voice was easy to detect, but then again, it nearly always was. Louisa resisted the urge to roll her eyes. How Caroline could believe Miss Elizabeth to be unintelligent was beyond her.

"I am not certain whether you and I are speaking of the same woman, Caroline," said Louisa with exaggerated patience, "but you are a simpleton if you truly believe that."

Caroline's eyes narrowed, but she did not speak. Louisa had so rarely spoken to her in such a manner that she was likely nearly insensible with rage.

"You must give up this fascination. Mr. Darcy has never paid you any notice, and furthermore, he is aware of everything which happens with Miss Elizabeth. You run the risk of angering him."

"Eliza Bennet could never hold his interest for long," snapped Caroline. "If he is interested in her, then his interest will wane as soon as I expose her secret."

This time, Louisa could not refrain from rolling her eyes. "Whatever this 'secret' is, you had best forget it. Perhaps you did not notice, but when Mr. Darcy approached you and Miss Elizabeth, he was fixed upon your conversation rather than my husband's."

"Obviously, he was paying attention to me."

Louisa shook her head. "Do what you will, Caroline, but tread softly. You shall proceed without my sanction and without my assistance. I will not risk turning Mr. Darcy against my husband. I would never hear the end of it were his friendship to be withdrawn."

"Fine!" spat Caroline. "Just know that you shall not be invited to be my guest once I become mistress of Pemberley!"

Standing, Caroline fixed her sights upon the two couples animatedly conversing on the other side of the room. "Now, I shall go and ensure that Mr. Darcy escorts me to dinner. You will see that I am right."

And with that, she stalked off. It was no surprise, therefore, that when Mr. Darcy *did* actually escort Caroline to the dinner table, he had Miss Elizabeth on the other arm. And once he had seated Caroline in her chair at the head of the table, he left her and proceeded with Miss Elizabeth to sit next to Charles.

Louisa did not need any great insight into Caroline's character to see the rage burned into her features. Louisa only hoped that Caroline managed to restrain herself and not put a strain on Charles's friendship with the gentleman.

Chapter XIII

The night after Elizabeth and Jane had dined at Netherfield, an event of a slightly different nature occurred, though Elizabeth supposed that it was more of an announcement than an actual event. But though it did not truly concern Elizabeth, she thought it interesting for the reactions it provoked in her family. In herself, it resurrected a hint of the old guilt which still made its presence known on occasion, though Elizabeth was able to shrug it off.

It started as a typical evening meal in the company of her family. Elizabeth was by now so accustomed to the way that such meals usually proceeded that she tended to fall into her own thoughts almost as soon as she had served herself from the platters on the table. Generally, if anyone spoke—and conversation was always abundant at the Bennet table—their words were not directed at her, or if they were, she could usually ignore them with little effort.

On this night, however, they had only just sat down to their meal when Mr. Bennet cleared his throat and called for the attention of his family.

"You had best prepare for a visitor, Mrs. Bennet, as we shall be entertaining one on the morrow," said Mr. Bennet, his voice gruff and his tone short.

"Mr. Bennet!" screeched his wife. "How can you wait to inform me of such a thing? I must have more time to prepare for a visitor!"

"A single night should be more than sufficient to have our spare bedchamber refreshed with new linens."

"But the menu must altered, entertainments devised . . . It is more than just preparing a single chamber, Mr. Bennet."

"Before you decide to welcome our visitor with open arms, Mrs. Bennet, do you not wish to know exactly whom we will be welcoming?"

There was an edge to his voice which Elizabeth had heard on occasion, and she did not like it in the slightest. Mr. Bennet truly sounded as if he held his wife in contempt. Elizabeth presumed that he had married her with his eyes wide open, so why should he now treat her as if she was the cause of all his misery?

Mrs. Bennet stifled back a retort, likely knowing that he would merely say something equally rude and likely even somewhat humiliating. She gave him an expectant look and said: "I have no objection to hearing his name, Mr. Bennet."

"I am happy to hear it, Mrs. Bennet, given how often you have vilified the gentleman, even though you have never met him. He is Mr. Collins, my cousin and heir to Longbourn."

Mrs. Bennet's eyes grew wide, and for a moment, Elizabeth felt certain that her mother would faint. Unfortunately, it was not to be, as after directing a glance of utter poison at Elizabeth, she fairly screamed:

"How could you invite that odious man here, Mr. Bennet? How can you countenance him approaching any nearer than fifty miles of this estate? That he should pass through the door with his greedy eyes falling upon all of our possessions is more than I can bear!"

"And yet he will arrive on the morrow," said Mr. Bennet. "You should also know, Mrs. Bennet, that Mr. Collins wrote me a letter in which he requested the opportunity to heal the breach in the family. So before you brand him as the worst of men for committing the capital sin of inheriting Longbourn, you may wish to hear him speak for himself."

Mrs. Bennet rounded on Elizabeth. "This is all *your* fault! Had you behaved as you ought, this could never have happened!"

Though the accusation stung, even after all these years, Elizabeth was almost inured to her mother's diatribes and accusations, and as a result, she found it no trial to ignore her. There was no sense in arguing with the woman, as she would never see sense anyway.

Mrs. Bennet quickly turned back to Mr. Bennet, saying: "No, this is no good at all, Mr. Bennet. You must write an express to Mr. Collins at once, telling him that he is not welcome at Longbourn and will not be as long as you live!"

"I shall do no such thing," said Mr. Bennet coolly. "The invitation has been dispatched and accepted, and Mr. Collins shall arrive before dinner tomorrow evening."

When Mrs. Bennet appeared about to descend into paroxysms yet again, her husband glared at her contemptuously and said: "Mrs. Bennet, I suggest you accept the matter and welcome Mr. Collins as generously as you are able. He shall be our guest for a few days, and nothing you say can change that fact.

"I might remind you that once I am dead, you will be entirely dependent upon my cousin's mercy. You know that your sister has not the means to keep you, and as for your brother . . ." Mr. Bennet paused and looked over at Elizabeth. "Well, let us just say that Mr. Gardiner might not be so generous with his assistance in light of the events of recent years."

Rising, Mr. Bennet made to quit the dining room. But before he did, he turned and looked at Mrs. Bennet, who was regarding him with fear. His own expression was fixed and unreadable, but to Elizabeth, who thought she knew his ways well enough to understand him to a degree, it almost appeared as if he looked on his wife with hatred.

"There is another thing you may wish to consider, Mrs. Bennet. I am more than a decade your senior. The time of your removal to the hedgerows may be upon you sooner than you would have thought possible. Think on that when you consider how you will receive my heir on the morrow."

And with that, the man was gone, the door closing quietly behind him.

For a moment, there was no sound at all in the dining room, as the occupants were too shocked to speak. Of course, such a fortunate circumstance could not continue for long, as soon Mrs. Bennet began to speak of how ill-used she was and how cruel it was of Mr. Bennet to betray her so.

Before Mrs. Bennet could begin to berate her for her own role in the debacle, Elizabeth decided that she had no need of any further sustenance and rose to excuse herself.

"I have not given you permission to leave the table, Elizabeth," said Mrs. Bennet, her tone all that was insolent and petulant.

But Elizabeth was not of a mind to pay any heed to her mother. "And yet I will return to my room, mother. I believe that I should prefer to eschew my supper altogether than to sit here and listen to you berate me for something I cannot even remember."

"You will sit!" shrieked Mrs. Bennet.

"I suggest you prevail upon my father to make me return, as otherwise, I shall not."

And with that, Elizabeth left the room and climbed the stairs. Unsurprisingly, her mother, though she screamed after her, did not take the matter to her husband. Elizabeth had to credit her with some small measure of insight, for she could not imagine any situation in which Mr. Bennet would force Elizabeth to bend to his will. She doubted he gave three straws as to whether she stayed in the dining room that evening, particularly when he had not done so himself.

The more pressing problem, Elizabeth thought when she had reached the sanctuary of her room, was divining the meaning of her father's words. It was almost as if he was giving them all notice of his imminent passing, though Elizabeth could not detect anything which suggested that he was ill or about to expire. It could merely be another of the games he often played with his wife; it would be just like him to tweak her nose.

Elizabeth was tempted to attribute the matter to simple teasing, but she could not be certain. It was a fine kettle of fish, and though Elizabeth willed it to be otherwise, she could not completely suppress that old feeling of guilt which crept its way up into her breast.

She had a long night ahead of her with nothing but her own thoughts to keep her company, as even Jane did not risk her mother's displeasure by joining her in her room.

By the next morning, things had calmed down considerably in the Bennet household. Though Mrs. Bennet was every bit as fearful of the words her husband had spoken the previous night, it seemed as if sleep had allowed her to view the matter with a kind of fatalistic acceptance. She still bemoaned her fate, but she also spoke of ensuring that the visiting man would be given every possible courtesy, all in the hopes of inducing him to be merciful on her when the time came that he should become the master of the estate.

Wishing to escape from the house, Elizabeth readily acquiesced when Jane suggested that they walk into Meryton that morning, as did the rest of her sisters. It seemed that even Lydia and Catherine had grown tired of their mother's never-ceasing discussion of the topic of Mr. Collins. Of course, Elizabeth suspected that the opportunity to see and be seen by the officers, who were still a fixture in Meryton, played no small part in their eagerness to accede to the scheme.

By the time they reached Meryton, Elizabeth had grown tired of their constant chatter, and mindful of the previous scene which had ensued when she had tried to check their behavior, she allowed Catherine and Lydia to go their own way at the first sign of a red coat. Mary also left on her own errand, leaving Jane and Elizabeth together in the street.

"Is there a particular shop you would like to visit, Lizzy?" asked Jane as soon as their sisters had departed.

"The bookstore perhaps," replied Elizabeth, smiling at her elder sister. "And perhaps also the milliners and the confectioners?"

Jane laughed, by now understanding Elizabeth's penchant for the written word. "I shall not allow you to bury yourself in the bookstore while I wait for you, sister," said she, though her stern tone was belied by the grin suffusing her face.

"I promise you that I shall not," replied Elizabeth in like manner. "But you must allow me some time to look through Mr. Clarke's wares. I am very much in need of new reading material."

"And I shall certainly let you have the opportunity," said Jane. She began walking, tugging Elizabeth's hand and leading her forward. "But the milliner's is closer. Let us visit there first, and then we may proceed to the bookstore."

They spent an enjoyable time together, looking at ribbons and bonnets and fabrics in the milliners' shop. When they left with a few ribbons each, Elizabeth thought privately that the time they had spent together was worth more than any number of ribbons.

As they stepped from the milliner's, Elizabeth and Jane were about to proceed to the bookshop when they were hailed.

"Miss Bennet! Miss Elizabeth!"

As one, they turned and noted the smiling visage of Mr. Bingley and the darker, more mysterious one of Mr. Darcy approaching them.

"How fortunate we are to come across you," said the irrepressible man as he stepped forward and bowed over Jane's hand. Elizabeth, however, was distracted by his companion, as Mr. Darcy did the same to her.

After the pleasantries had been exchanged, Mr. Bingley looked between them and said, "Were you about to depart once again for Longbourn? If so, Darcy and I would be happy to escort you."

"Indeed," was Mr. Darcy's quiet reply.

"We are not yet ready to return," said Elizabeth.

"Yes," said Jane, though she gave Elizabeth an amused glance. "But I must own that I do find my sister's ability to peruse the bookshop endlessly a little intimidating. I have been with her but once, and even that once was far longer than I have ever spent there!"

"Jane!" said Elizabeth, her cheeks blooming with embarrassment.

Mr. Bingley only grinned. "I must own that Darcy's capacity for the written word is much greater than my own, and by our mutual agreement, we never visit such a shop together. He wishes to examine the shelves to his heart's content, while I am continually asking if he is finished so that we may depart."

The sister's laughed at Mr. Bingley's portrayal, but Mr. Darcy, after chuckling for a moment, addressed them all. "It would seem, then, that we have an opportunity here. I shall escort Miss Elizabeth to the bookstore, and Bingley shall accompany Miss Bennet to the confectioner's. Then we can meet for the return to Longbourn."

"Capital idea!" cried Mr. Bingley. "What say you, Miss Bennet?"

Though Jane beamed at him, no doubt relishing the continued favor he showed for her, she seemed reluctant. And Elizabeth was certain she knew the reason for her hesitancy—Jane had been enjoying having Elizabeth in her company, and though she wished for Mr. Bingley's attentions, she also wished to know Elizabeth better.

"I believe that is an excellent idea," said Elizabeth, catching her sister's eye and giving her a smile. "That way, Mr. Darcy and I may browse to our heart's content."

Jane smiled, immediately understanding what Elizabeth was saying. The sisters exchanged a brief embrace before they turned to their escorts and parted ways amid laughter and admonitions that if Mr. Darcy and Elizabeth took too long at the bookstore, then Jane and Mr. Bingley should return to Longbourn ahead of them. When at last they left the nearly acknowledged lovers, Mr. Darcy and Elizabeth shared a commiserating smile.

"Shall we, Miss Bennet?" asked Mr. Darcy.

With pleasure and a little embarrassment, Elizabeth grasped the gentleman's arm, and they began the short walk to their chosen shop.

"To be honest, I am most happy to exchange Bingley's company for yours, Miss Bennet," said Mr. Darcy as they walked. "Though he spoke in jest about my love of books, his words were not far from the truth. And since I have been here for more than a month, I have nearly exhausted the collection I brought with me."

Delighted with his openness, Elizabeth arched an eyebrow in his direction. "And there is nothing suitable in Mr. Bingley's library to satisfy your taste, Mr. Darcy?"

"Bingley would actually have to possess a library, Miss Bennet.

Although there is certainly a room at Netherfield which has been set aside for the storage of books, Bingley is not a great reader, and he has made little use of it. I have sampled those few texts which interested me, but it is not exaggeration that there were less than twenty altogether."

Elizabeth laughed delightedly. "I am unable to account for this lapse on Mr. Bingley's part. He studied at Cambridge, did he not?"

"Indeed, he did," said Mr. Darcy. "But there are times when you would never know it. His correspondence—whenever he can be bothered to actually write a letter, that is—is filled with blots and half-formed thoughts, and any receivers invariably wish that he had not bothered when they are forced to try to decipher them."

"Surely he cannot be that bad," exclaimed Elizabeth.

"I assure you that he can be," said Mr. Darcy. "Should I ever have the chance, I shall show you. I have the advantage, so to speak, of having received several letters from him, and I suspect that I am as skilled at interpreting his words as any other. But that does not make it a joy."

By this time, Elizabeth was laughing so hard that tears were rolling down her cheeks, though she attempted to keep her decorum about her. Unfortunately, Mr. Darcy did not appear to be inclined to take pity upon her.

"I believe that our army should simply use Bingley to pass information to our commanders in the field. They will have a difficult enough time making out his letters. I am convinced that should the French ever intercept them, then they will be completely at sea. It is a method guaranteed to keep our communiqués secret from our enemies."

"Surely not!" she finally gasped, attempting to rein in her mirth.

"Perhaps not," allowed Mr. Darcy with a smile. "But I assure you that it is not much of an exaggeration."

As they neared the bookshop, Elizabeth was able to bring her laughter under control, and she looked up at Mr. Darcy askance as something occurred to her. He caught her look and asked what she was thinking.

Blushing at being caught looking at the gentleman in such a frank manner, Elizabeth attempted to demur, but Mr. Darcy was having none of it.

"Miss Bennet, clearly you wished to say something. I shall not be offended, even if your words contain more of your delightful impertinence, I assure you."

"You should not encourage me so, Mr. Darcy," said Elizabeth, her mirth once again returning.

"I merely wished to say," she said after a moment's thought, "that I was not expecting to see this side of you. My first impression was that you are a serious gentleman, and subsequent meetings have not taught me that I was incorrect."

Mr. Darcy sobered, and he looked down at her thoughtfully. Elizabeth attempted to apologize, but again, Mr. Darcy would not hear of it.

"Miss Bennet, one of the things that I find the most refreshing about you is your delightful tendency to speak as you find. I assure you that I am not offended. On the contrary, I find that young ladies who only speak to agree with me or to put down their perceived rivals, all with the intent to curry favor, are the ones who offend me. You are assuredly not of their ilk."

Elizabeth could not help but smile, though it was obvious that he was speaking of Miss Bingley, at least indirectly. Given his fortune and position in society, Elizabeth did not doubt that there were far more Miss Bingleys in London than young ladies he could speak to without fear that they would take it as a sign of favor.

"I can assure you that I will never treat you thus, Mr. Darcy," said Elizabeth sincerely.

"I already have enough of a measure of you to know the truth of that statement, Miss Bennet," replied Mr. Darcy. "But come, let us go inside. I should not wish for your sister to accuse me of taking you from her under false pretenses."

The couple entered the bookshop, where they were met by Mr. Clarke, the jovial proprietor. He greeted both with pleasure, proving that he had seen Mr. Darcy in his store previously.

For the next thirty minutes, Elizabeth and Mr. Darcy examined the small shop in great detail. They kept to one another's company, discussing this or that text which they had both read or making recommendations when they discovered one had not read a favorite of the other. Mr. Darcy, Elizabeth soon determined, possessed rather eclectic tastes when it came to literature. He had read many classic works, and from what she was able to glean in a short period of time, he possessed intelligent and insightful opinions of them all. On the other hand, he had also read many newer works and enjoyed a wide variety of different styles of literature, from poetry to philosophies, and he even acknowledged that he had read a few novels, though, he assured her with a smile, he had only done so to ensure that the material was suitable for his much younger sister.

It was clear in the way he spoke to her that he considered her an equal. He listened to whatever she had to say with great interest and was even able to discover a few texts he had not read which Elizabeth had found in her uncle's library. In all, it was the most enjoyable time that Elizabeth had ever spent conversing with a young man, and she was sad when it came time to depart.

"I would like to thank you for this most enjoyable time, Miss Bennet," said Mr. Darcy after they had exited the shop. They each carried some books they had purchased, and Elizabeth was greatly anticipating the opportunity to read a few of the selections he had recommended for her.

"No more than I would wish to thank you," said Elizabeth. She forced herself to meet his eyes instead of succumbing to a sudden bout of bashfulness at his praise. "I thank you for your recommendations. We must discuss them at our earliest opportunity."

"I assure you that we shall," replied he in a quiet voice.

"Here, Darcy!" the voice of Mr. Bingley cut off their interlude. "I must own that I expected you to be ensconced in the confines of Mr. Clarke's shop for some time to come!"

Jane, who was holding Mr. Bingley's arm, laughed and greeted her sister and her suitor's friend. The four stood on the side of the road conversing for some time until Jane reluctantly noted that it was time to return home. Elizabeth wondered what had become of Lydia and Catherine, but she decided that it was of no moment. They could obviously find their way back to Longbourn on their own.

The gentlemen gallantly offered to walk with them, and after fetching their horses, which had been tied up by the side of the road, the group began to walk the mile back to Longbourn. And though there was not much conversation between Elizabeth and Mr. Darcy—Jane and Bingley spoke between themselves almost the entire duration of the walk—Elizabeth felt within her heart that much was said nonetheless.

Mr. Darcy watched her as they walked, and he was solicitous of her comfort and her well-being. Furthermore, his eyes seemed to contain some sort of unidentifiable emotion within their depths, and though Elizabeth could not state such with a surety, she fancied that she could see his heart within his eyes. She felt certain that it was directed at her.

As is often the case in such situations, Elizabeth felt a measure of confusion. She had come to Hertfordshire at the behest of her father, and she would never have imagined that she would attract the attention of a gentleman such as Mr. Darcy, particularly under such circumstances as existed in her life at present. But it seemed indisputable that Jane was correct: Mr. Darcy seemed to admire her.

Elizabeth's sole problem at present was to determine the state of her own heart. She was not indifferent to him; such a thing was inconceivable. But though her aunt and uncle had showered her with love and support from the moment they had taken her in, she was still the product of her upbringing as a young gentlewoman, and as such, she was sheltered and inexperienced in the ways of the world. She simply did not feel as if she had the knowledge to understand how she felt—how she *should* feel—at this moment.

But there was one thing she did know without any hint of doubt. She knew that should Mr. Darcy ask anything at all of her, she would be unable to deny it of him. She trusted that his attentions were honorable; the idea that such an exceptional gentleman could harbor any untoward intentions beggared belief! She did not know that she was in love with him, but she felt sure that given the opportunity and the necessary experience, she would find herself deeply in his thrall. And though the mere thought should have been terrifying, Elizabeth in fact felt nothing but peace and safety.

Mr. Darcy did not speak much more that day. Beyond the typical—though somewhat sparse—conversation exchanged between them, he spoke no words of true substance, and certainly he did not speak the words which Elizabeth was quickly becoming convinced that she longed to hear.

The gentlemen did not stay long. Indeed, they did not even enter the house, citing a need to return to Netherfield, as they were engaged at one of the neighborhood families for dinner that evening. But as they were leaving, Mr. Darcy gave Elizabeth a look of such intensity and utter *regard* that Elizabeth became certain that some time or another those words would be spoken. And then he kissed her hand for the first time as he went away, and for Elizabeth, it was like a jolt of lightning which pierced her very soul.

Yes, she thought, as he was riding away, if he asked her that all important question, she would accept with alacrity. To do otherwise would be beyond comprehension.

Later that afternoon brought the arrival of the man whose coming was silently dreaded by most of the Bennets. What Elizabeth herself thought of the man's arrival, she could not truly say. He was the heir to the property, but his ultimate inheritance was a matter of extreme indifference to her. Though she would not always wish to be a burden and longed to eventually have a home of her own, Elizabeth knew that she would always be able to stay with the Gardiners if required.

When the man himself was shown into the parlor for the first time, he was announced by Mrs. Hill, and soon he had greeted the entire family. He was tall, standing taller than Mr. Bennet, though not nearly so tall as Mr. Darcy. He was also dressed all in black, wearing the garb befitting a parson, which was a bit of intelligence that Mr. Bennet had not seen fit to impart to the rest of his family. Mr. Collins was also portly and seemed to constantly perspire from his forehead, even in the coolness of the late autumn air. His head was plastered with a mop of greasy dark hair, and his face, which was not pleasant to look upon, was made even less attractive by the look of self-importance and pompousness affixed to it. His first words made clear his unqualified lack of intelligence for anyone paying any attention whatsoever.

"Mr. Bennet, Mrs. Bennet," said he in a grave and ponderous tone, "I thank you for the kind welcome you have bestowed upon me and for your gracious indulgence in accepting this proffered olive branch. Truly, you are to be praised, for it is the personal testimony of my patroness, the honorable Lady Catherine de Bourgh, that strife within a family is unseemly and must be rectified with alacrity to keep calamity from falling upon the heads of all. I thank you, from the bottom of my heart, for heeding the wisdom of these words and for accepting me to your comfortable and convenient abode. You are much to be praised!"

The Bennets regarded him with varying levels of shock; whatever they had been expecting, Elizabeth was certain that none of them could have expected a man such as this.

A moment later, Elizabeth was forced to revise this opinion, for she caught her father's expression as he regarded his cousin. Mr. Bennet was watching the man with a dark smirk and an air of satisfaction etched upon his features. As he was the only one who had previously corresponded with Mr. Collins, he must have had some indication as to the man's character, and it appeared that all his conjectures were turning out to be correct.

For a moment, Elizabeth wondered at exactly what sort of man her father was to actually enjoy the abject stupidity of another. Did he take great pride in the fact that Mr. Collins would not be a good steward of the land and that the estate would, in all likelihood, fall into disrepair after his death?

"I must commend you, Mrs. Bennet, on the elegance of the arrangements of this room," Mr. Collins was saying at that moment. "I had not known what to expect, but it is clear that the estate is prosperous, and the comfort and quality of the house is only matched by the handsomeness of you and your daughters."

It seemed that Mr. Collins was blind to the impropriety of his statements concerning the estate, and even if he could not see how his words would be construed, it appeared as if Mrs. Bennet was at that moment envisioning the very moment when Mr. Collins arrived and personally removed her from the house. Or so it seemed to Elizabeth, given the sudden pallor of her mother's countenance.

Surprisingly, Mrs. Bennet did not descend into vapors. Instead, she took a deep breath to compose herself and returned Mr. Collins's ridiculous civility with her own brand of politeness.

"I think you, Mr. Collins. You are certainly . . . welcome, at Longbourn. It is . . . so good of you to call."

Mrs. Bennet fell silent after her halting welcome, and though it had been lukewarm and forced, Mr. Collins accepted it as if he had been welcomed as an old friend by the queen herself.

The parson's arrival was only the beginning of the absurdities. Elizabeth quickly understood that Mr. Collins had only two things that he deemed worthy of conversation: Longbourn (and the compliments upon it which he seemed to think were necessary) and his patroness (of whom it seemed he could drone on endlessly). Of the first, any intelligent person would conclude that before long, such continuous flattery would begin to appear empty, but Mr. Collins remarked on anything which came into his head, no matter how small. Of the second, well, Elizabeth soon came to the conclusion that not only was his patroness a colossal bore, but she was also a meddling busybody.

"You appear to be rather . . . fortunate in your position, Mr. Collins," observed Mr. Bennet at one point.

"Indeed, I am," replied Mr. Collins, a rapturous expression of otherworldly ecstasy settling over his ugly face. "But I would not have you believe that the position is of itself the reason for my good fortune. No, that privilege is reserved for my gracious and condescending patroness, Lady Catherine de Bourgh, she who has preferred me for the appointment to the position as rector of Hunsford."

Mr. Collins leaned toward Elizabeth, who had been sitting quietly in a nearby chair, and said, "You must understand that my humble abode is so near to her ladyship's estate of Rosings that I may walk there in as little as fifteen minutes. Indeed, the great estate is even visible from my upstairs chambers; the chimneys of Rosings rise majestically above the trees bordering her estate like the very heights of Olympus."

"I believe you suggested that this Lady Catherine is the reason why Hunsford is such a sought-after parish, sir," said Mr. Bennet.

"Yes, indeed, Cousin Bennet," replied Mr. Collins. "Quite frankly, her ladyship is of such a splendid lineage and august position in society—and her understanding is so profound—that I doubt there is another position in all of England which can compare with Hunsford. And as it is situated in the very center of the garden of England, there can be no place on earth so blessed."

Again, Mr. Collins leaned toward Elizabeth, and with an unctuous smile, he said: "You must understand that the mistress of Hunsford will reside in so desirable a position that she may only consider herself extremely fortunate."

Elizabeth regarded the parson with a raised brow. "Then you are engaged, Mr. Collins?"

If anything, the parson's unpleasant smile became all that much more pronounced, and he verily simpered at her. "I am indeed, Miss Elizabeth. She is a most fortunate woman, and I must say that I am extremely fortunate as well. Ours shall be a union of felicity and common purpose. I can scarcely wait for the nuptials so that I may spirit her back to Hunsford, where she may glory in the excellence of our position and give thanks and praise to Lady Catherine for the magnificence of her beneficence."

Elizabeth could not imagine *anyone* giving praise for being tied to such a rank dullard. The way Mr. Collins spoke of his patroness, one might almost think the woman was deity made flesh.

Regardless, it seemed as if the man already had a fiancée, and that was something to be celebrated. Elizabeth could well imagine such an insensible man descending on his newly restored relations, intent upon gaining a wife from among his cousin's daughters, congratulating himself on the magnanimous gesture of making amends to them for being the means for dispossessing them from their home. She was thankful that she did not have to worry about him fixing his attentions upon her.

That night at dinner saw a change in the usual seating arrangements. As they had a guest at dinner, he was seated at her father's right hand. That this was not in the position of honor by the mistress a guest would usually occupy seemed to go unnoticed by the man in question, and though Elizabeth could not be certain, she suspected that Mrs. Bennet felt that her civility in welcoming the man did not extend to being seated next to him for dinner. To accommodate this change, Jane had been placed in Mary's place, and though

Elizabeth would have thought that she would have been left in her usual place, instead she was moved across the table and seated on the right of the ridiculous parson. It was not a place that she relished, but since he was primarily engaged in conversation with her father—though to be correct, he spoke almost continuously, whereas Mr. Bennet merely inserted a few comments which seemed to be designed to encourage his silliness—Elizabeth found herself able to bear his company.

But though most of his attention was on her father, he glanced over at her and flashed his oily smile too often for Elizabeth's comfort. Several times, she had to force herself to suppress a shudder. She could not help but pity the woman who had agreed to become the man's life partner. Elizabeth could not imagine anyone who could tolerate him!

Chapter XIV

The next day was uncomfortable for Elizabeth. After the previous night's activities, she had retired, determined to suffer Mr. Collins's company as little as she was able to manage. Thus, it was disconcerting that Mr. Collins seemed to be intent upon paying her attention above anyone else in the family. Why this was so perplexed Elizabeth, as the man had a fiancée by his own admission. She could think of no possible reason for him to single her out for his exclusive attention, but it seemed as if he had.

It started at breakfast that morning. As was her wont, Elizabeth was at the table before anyone else in her family except for her father, who made no comment when she entered the room. It was much to her surprise, then, when Mr. Collins appeared in the breakfast room soon after Elizabeth had arrived. He was obviously tired and somewhat unkempt, and Elizabeth had the distinct impression that his appearance that morning had been made a good deal earlier than he was accustomed to.

His stupid countenance brightened upon seeing them, and he immediately went on a long monologue on the delight of family relations and the felicity in which he was eager to partake as an extended member of the Bennet family. Elizabeth sat and proceeded to allow her attention to wander, knowing that the parson rarely required a response and would not notice that she was paying him no heed whatsoever.

Her thoughts went back to a letter to the Gardiners that she had posted that morning, assuring them that everything was well at Longbourn. Elizabeth still wished that she had been at liberty to accompany them on their journey, but in an odd sort of way, she had become accustomed to the situation at Longbourn and her place within its walls. She knew that she would never be happy or truly comfortable there, but it was better than it had been when she arrived.

"I understand that you are a great walker and are very fond of nature, Miss Elizabeth."

For a moment, Elizabeth was confused by the voice which brought her from her ruminations, but she was quickly able to discern that the parson expected a response from her.

Gathering her wits about her, Elizabeth was able to respond, "Indeed, I am quite fond of the outdoors, Mr. Collins."

"Then perhaps when you depart for your constitutional today, you might show me some of your favorite vistas."

Though she disliked the thought of walking about the countryside with Mr. Collins, Elizabeth caught a glimpse of Mr. Bennet's stony countenance, and she immediately understood that the man did not wish to antagonize his cousin, perhaps due to some belated sense of duty toward his family. And realizing that it would be impolite to demur, Elizabeth consented, albeit reluctantly, to the parson's request.

"Excellent!" cried Mr. Collins. "I shall anticipate our constitutional with much pleasure."

After eating breakfast, Elizabeth retreated to her room with a certain sense of dark glee. After her stated intention to return to her room, Mr. Collins had latched onto Mr. Bennet as his companion for the morning, following him to his bookroom, where Elizabeth believed he stayed. She felt a certain level of satisfaction at the action; as her father had seen fit to encourage the parson to be in her company, she thought it only fitting that he should be extended the same consideration.

It was some time later that morning when Elizabeth finally emerged, knowing that she could not delay her walk any longer without inviting her father's censure. And after gathering her outer wear, she departed the house in the company of the detested Mr. Collins.

It quickly became apparent that despite Mr. Collins's stated appreciation for nature and his suggestions that he liked nothing better than a stroll about the environs of his home, he was actually quite ill-suited for the activity. He was portly and ponderous, and it was not long before Elizabeth's brisk pace rendered him breathless. But unfortunately, much like a fly buzzing about one's head, he seemed determined not to free Elizabeth from his odious presence.

As they walked, though Mr. Collins often seemed incapable of even drawing breath, he kept up a monologue of conversation designed to praise his situation and his patroness.

"The parsonage is eminently suitable to a clergyman in my situation," said he, "for it is not so large that its governance would keep me from my duties in the neighborhood, and it is not so small that it would fail to provide adequate comfort to a man of my influence."

It was clear that the parson considered himself to be some sort of exalted personage by virtue of his entirely accidental position. And accidental, Elizabeth was certain it was—no one could employ such a man unless they were either insensible themselves or so convinced of their own importance that they required someone to praise them at all hours of the day and night.

On another occasion, he rhapsodized about his coming nuptials, declaring that his future wife would find herself in the most fortunate of circumstances. "Indeed, Lady Catherine is of such a generous and virtuous nature that my wife will no doubt benefit from her opinions and knowledge. For one cannot be allowed to stand before her august presence and emerge unscathed."

Privately Elizabeth agreed with him; she doubted that any young woman could leave the lady's presence without very strongly needing to purge herself of all the unwanted meddling that the old crone was almost certain to engage in.

The parson's words were so abundant and his conversation all-encompassing that Elizabeth was quite unable to fit a word in of her own. It was not long before she began to consider how she could affect her escape. Unfortunately, the man resisted all attempts to separate from him, claiming that he was enjoying himself far too much for them to return to the house. And though Elizabeth continued to increase her pace, he gamely matched her, though the exertion soon began to affect even his ability to talk.

Finally, Elizabeth saw the spire of Longbourn church in the distance, and an idea entered her mind.

"I do not believe that you have met with Mr. Jones, the parson of Longbourn church. Would it not be polite for you to extend your greeting as a courtesy, Mr. Collins?"

Though Mr. Collins at first appeared to be somewhat affronted by her interruption of his monologue, his expression soon softened. He bowed low to her and said, "Your sense of duty does you credit, my dear cousin. I believe that this Mr. Jones would only benefit by the wisdom I bring. Please, lead me to him."

Saying a silent prayer for her deliverance—and suppressing a snicker at the thought of Mr. Collins's brand of *wisdom*—Elizabeth led the way to the church. Therein, they found Longbourn's parson, a man who, though decrepit and likely senile, was a kindly old soul who performed his duties with a cheerfulness which could only be pleasing.

"Mr. Jones," said Elizabeth as they stepped forward, "Mr. Collins has requested the honor of making your acquaintance. Mr. Collins is my father's cousin and is visiting us for a few days."

Of course, Mr. Jones was quite happy to be introduced to his patron's cousin. But within moments, Mr. Collins had begun speaking with his distinct brand of civility, and soon thereafter, Mr. Jones was staring at him with unaffected incredulity. For an instant, Elizabeth felt guilty for leaving Mr. Collins with him, but she comforted herself in the knowledge that Mr. Jones, in addition to being a little senile, was more than a little deaf and would thus only actually hear one word in three.

While Mr. Collins was thus engaged, Elizabeth made her escape, edging from the room and then fairly running from the church. It was some time before she felt able to slacken her pace, relieved in the knowledge that she had managed to elude the parson.

For the next quarter hour, Elizabeth wandered, reveling in the freedom from the man's rambling. And though she knew that she would eventually be required to return to Longbourn, she decided not to concern herself with such eventualities for now.

It was thus that she came upon Mr. Darcy. In truth, his sudden appearance startled Elizabeth, for she was rounding a bend on the narrow path she was traversing when suddenly he was there, sitting astride his great stallion. A moment later, he dismounted from his horse and greeted her with unfeigned pleasure, holding the reins in hand.

"How do you do, Miss Bennet?"

"I am very well, Mr. Darcy," replied Elizabeth. "At least, I am very well now."

Clearly confused, Mr. Darcy looked at her askance, and Elizabeth could not quite suppress a giggle.

"If you are at liberty, shall we walk as I tell you of the calamity which has befallen our family since you left me at Longbourn yesterday?"

This time, the corners of Mr. Darcy's mouth rose with pleasure at her obvious jest. "I should like nothing better than to talk with you, Miss Bennet. Please lead the way."

They began to walk, Elizabeth's hand ensconced in the crook of Mr. Darcy's arm, his horse trailing behind them. Not much was said for those few moments, and the few words which did pass between them concerned inconsequential subjects. Elizabeth marveled at the ease of their interactions, which was such that even the most mundane of subjects could be made into the most interesting simply because it was Mr. Darcy with whom she spoke.

"I believe you promised me an explanation for the 'calamity,' as I believe you called it, which has befallen you."

Elizabeth laughed. "It is not so much a calamity as it is a great imposition, sir. Yesterday evening, my father's cousin, a Mr. Collins, arrived at Longbourn for a visit. He is, you must understand, my father's heir due to the entailment upon the estate."

Mr. Darcy frowned. "And the gentleman's arrival is an imposition?"

"You would not question me so had you ever made the gentleman's acquaintance, Mr. Darcy," said Elizabeth. "Mr. Collins is a rank dullard of the first order, not to mention a fawning toady unlike any I have ever seen. The man talks incessantly and without requiring even a hint of a response, and he quotes his patroness as though her words were the very words of God himself."

By this time, Mr. Darcy was chuckling at Elizabeth's words. "Surely you exaggerate, Miss Bennet."

"If you were to be introduced to the gentleman, I am sure you would take my side of the matter, Mr. Darcy," replied Elizabeth. "I am certain that should I ever be introduced to Lady Catherine de Bourgh, I should not know whether to laugh or be offended the first time she offered her *wisdom* to me."

Mr. Darcy stopped with an abruptness that startled Elizabeth, and she turned to look at him with confusion.

"Mr. Collins is your relation?" asked he. There was a certain incredulous quality to his voice which Elizabeth could not quite understand. "Mr. Collins of Hunsford in Kent, the rector to Lady Catherine de Bourgh of Rosings Park?"

A slight frisson of unease worked its way up Elizabeth's spine. Was the lady known to Mr. Darcy?

"That is what we have been led to believe, sir."

A broad grin broke out on Mr. Darcy's face. "In that case, I believe you will agree that we have been beset by the most absurd coincidence, Miss Bennet, for Lady Catherine is my late mother's eldest sister and, therefore, my own aunt."

"Oh, Mr. Darcy," cried Elizabeth, feeling embarrassed for having insulted the woman, "I must beg your pardon for speaking of your relation in so irreverent terms. I had not the slightest notion that such a connection existed."

"Nor should you have," said Mr. Darcy in a gentle tone. "We have never spoken of our extended family, after all."

"But I should not have spoken with such sarcastic disregard for another person," said Elizabeth. "My uncle has always said that my unguarded tongue would one day cause me no end of trouble, and it appears that he was right."

More than anything, Elizabeth feared the end of Mr. Darcy's approbation. His opinion of her had become *that* important.

"Perhaps it is as you say," agreed he, though his lips still twitched as though he were trying to suppress a smile, "but if you actually knew the lady, then you would understand that your supposition is actually not far short of the truth. Lady Catherine is as overbearing as she is convinced of her own infallibility. My cousin Fitzwilliam and I visit her every spring, but it is due to family duty and the need to curb her extravagant ways rather than due to any affection, I assure you. She is tyrannical to everyone within reach of her influence, and her family is not immune from her controlling ways. At least, she likes to *believe* that she can dominate us all. To keep the peace within the family, the rest of us simply allow her to have her say.

"And as for Mr. Collins, I met the man the last time my cousin and I visited Kent. He was newly installed as the cleric in Hunsford and seemed exceedingly grateful to have been so noticed, I assure you."

This time, it was Elizabeth's turn to laugh. "I suppose that it is every family's lot to have at least one relation who is a less than admirable one. Mine is silly, while yours is a gorgon."

"I would never dispute that," replied Mr. Darcy. "Lady Catherine fits that description so well that I wonder if you have not actually made the lady's acquaintance ere now."

"I assure you that I feel as if I have," said Elizabeth, "for Mr. Collins has spoken almost incessantly of the lady since his arrival, and I believe I know more of the lady's preferences than she does herself!"

Together, they laughed and then fell into a companionable silence, and Elizabeth was forced to consider how much more agreeable the intelligent and gentlemanly Mr. Darcy was than the absurd Mr. Collins.

They walked on for some time, and though Elizabeth occasionally made a few comments, Mr. Darcy's replies were brief. He appeared to have something important on his mind, and though Elizabeth sensed that he was not upset with her or their conversation, she wished that the amiable Mr. Darcy would make another appearance.

Just as Elizabeth had decided that she needed to return to Longbourn, Mr. Darcy halted and turned to regard her. Elizabeth stopped and looked at him, and her breath caught in her throat. Mr. Darcy was looking at her with such seriousness, with such affectionate intensity, that Elizabeth fancied she could see his heart in his scrutiny. And what she saw there did not displease her; in fact, she was in that instance convinced that Jane was about to be proven correct in her estimation of Mr. Darcy's intentions toward her.

"Miss Bennet, I have debated with myself, trying to understand my feelings and having little luck deciphering them. I have always thought that regard—true, deep, abiding regard—was the work of many months in which those involved grew to understand one another, learned each other's preferences, and developed the kind of love which would sustain them throughout the entirety of their lives.

"You have completely upset a lifetime of such sureties, Miss Bennet, and you did it so effortlessly that I found myself wondering how it could have come to pass."

Elizabeth knew that she should be embarrassed at his words of admiration, but in reality, she found that she was anticipating his words so much that there was no room left for embarrassment. Their acquaintance *had* been of short duration, but she knew that her feelings for this tall, handsome man were in no way anything less than a perfect match for the feelings he possessed for her. It was a heady feeling, and she almost felt as if she could fly.

"I think I have found the answer." Mr. Darcy paused and smiled. "Or perhaps it is correct to say that I have found *an* answer. The answer I have found is that it truly does not matter. I have come to feel for you such a strong regard and respect that I can no longer question how it has come to be.

"All my life, I have striven to live up to my parents' examples, and one of those was their example of matrimony. They had the closest of relationships, Miss Bennet, and when my mother passed away after a long illness, my father was left a shell of a man. Until that time, Pemberley's halls were filled with love and devotion, and I believe that if we should wed, they will be filled with such again.

"May I have the great honor of a courtship with you, so that we might become further acquainted? I assure you that my intentions are most honorable. I mean to follow this through to its natural conclusion, a fact which I shall make clear to your father when I ask his permission to court you."

His mention of her father was like a bucket of cold water poured over her head. Mr. Bennet did not appear to care one way or another what happened to her, but a little niggling fear suggested that he would not be happy with such a development.

But surely he would not think to refuse a man such as Mr. Darcy! Indeed, he would be foolish if he did. Furthermore, Elizabeth could not but imagine that her parents would be glad to be rid of her and to know that Mr. Darcy, being a creature of duty, would be in a position to ensure that Mrs. Bennet was cared for after Mr. Bennet's death. Certainly there was much benefit in her making such an alliance.

That her mother would disdain her and be angry that she could attract such a man to offer for her, Elizabeth did not doubt. But the woman would not scorn a connection which would be of such a boon to her own situation.

Still, Mr. Darcy could not be allowed to approach her father without any inclination of the truth of the matter of her past. To allow him to do so would be unconscionable, and any affection he felt for her could potentially be killed when he inevitably learned the truth. And though she was fearful for his reaction, Elizabeth made the decision in that instant to explain the matter to him in full.

"I thank you for your heartfelt statements, and I accept them and your offer with pleasure, sir." Elizabeth smiled at him, a gesture which he returned with equal fervor. "I cannot explain what has occurred between us any more than you can. But I have felt drawn to you from the time of our first meeting outside the inn. I am more than sensible of the great honor you do me, and I wish to inform you that I, too, wish to have a marriage based on true respect, affection, and love. I will endeavor to learn these things with you, sir, and I give you my word that I will strive to make you proud of me as your life partner, should such an event come to pass."

"I wish for nothing more, Miss Bennet," said Mr. Darcy, reaching down to take her hand within his. His hands were large and callused in places, but soft and gentle, and she immediately felt as if her hand was the most precious item he had ever held.

"Thank you, sir," said Elizabeth, her cheeks feeling as though they would burst. "But I feel that I must inform you, sir, that my father's blessing may not be easy to obtain."

"He would refuse me?" asked Mr. Darcy. Though his tone was even, Elizabeth could sense a hint of incredulous disbelief. It was an echo of a trace of arrogance which Elizabeth knew was part of his character, though it was by no means a defining characteristic. She smiled, thinking that if such a minor defect were the price to pay for such incandescent happiness, then she would gladly pay it a thousand times over.

"I do not believe he would," replied Elizabeth. "Yet he may not be happy about it."

Elizabeth struggled for a moment, uncertain how to phrase what she knew she must tell him. After a moment, she gave up trying to make it sound like anything other than what it was.

"I am certain you must have noticed that the situation in my family is . . . difficult."

"I would have had to have been blind not to notice," was Mr. Darcy's wry reply.

"There is a reason for it. You must understand, Mr. Darcy, that I am not close to any of my family members. There was a reason for my living in London these past ten years."

"Miss Bennet," said Mr. Darcy, interrupting her and drawing her eyes to his compassionate face. "Is this something which would in any way prevent our coming to an understanding?"

"I . . . I do not think so, Mr. Darcy," said Elizabeth. "But it might affect your understanding of me."

"You make it sound so ominous," teased Mr. Darcy. He smiled for a moment before her distress appeared to sober him.

"Unless there is some very dark secret of your past, I doubt there is anything which could affect my opinion of you, Miss Bennet. But for now, I believe that the hour is getting late, and you had best be returning to your home. Shall we leave such grave discussions for some other time? Perhaps the morrow, after I speak to your father, would be a more appropriate time?"

Elizabeth looked at him with wonder. She imagined that most men would immediately demand an accounting upon hearing of the existence of such an ominous secret regarding her family, yet Mr. Darcy seemed to shrug it off. It seemed as if his regard for her trumped all other considerations, even that of an event he had, as yet, no knowledge of. A warmth filled Elizabeth—this man was truly the best of men.

"Then let us speak of it then."

They turned and began to make their way back to Longbourn,

making easy conversation about nothing in particular. Later, when the storms overtook Elizabeth's life, she would look back on this time as that of an idyllic interlude, one to be cherished and stored up against the adversity which was to come. When they finally came within close proximity of the estate, Mr. Darcy halted their progress and turned to Elizabeth.

"I shall call on you tomorrow and speak with your father. I believe it best that your family does not learn that we were alone together without a chaperone. May I call during normal visiting hours?"

"You may, Mr. Darcy," replied Elizabeth. "And I thank you for your care and attention to my reputation."

"It is only proper, Miss Bennet," said he, "loath though I am to part from you."

He then took her hand tenderly in his own and bestowed a kiss upon its back, his lips lingering against her gloved hand for some time. He then pulled away and favored her with an easy smile.

"Until tomorrow, Miss Bennet."

And all at once, he mounted his horse and departed, but not before looking at her with such longing and devotion that Elizabeth's heart almost stopped beating. In a daze, Elizabeth turned and began to make her way to the house, her mind and heart full of Mr. Darcy.

Unfortunately, Elizabeth's euphoria could not survive the return to her childhood home. From her family, nothing was said about her extended absence from the house, though Jane looked at her askance and Mr. Bennet with a raised brow. Elizabeth, however, acknowledged none of this—except for Jane, everyone in Elizabeth's family had such a disregard for her feelings and well-being that she did not feel obliged to account for her actions or to apologize for causing worry, if such was even possible.

Mr. Collins was another story. After she refreshed herself in her room and entered the parlor, the parson had approached her, an expression of reproach etched across his countenance.

"That was poorly done, Miss Elizabeth," said he without preamble. "I would expect a recalcitrant child to go off without regard to their elders, but I would not have thought it of a young lady of almost twenty years. And to have caused your dear family to worry so acutely for your well-being . . . Well, let us just say that such behavior will not be tolerated."

"Mr. Collins," said Elizabeth, who was in no humor to listen to his reprimands, "I believe that you have no say over my behavior."

"No say over your behavior?" sputtered Mr. Collins. "How can you say such a thing?"

"I believe that as I am living under my father's roof, he is the one who holds the responsibility for me. You are nothing more than a cousin, Mr. Collins. You had best remember that."

Outrage bloomed in his eyes, and Elizabeth wondered at his reaction. What could the man possibly be thinking? Bewildered, Elizabeth watched as he turned to Mr. Bennet and said: "What have you to say about such impertinence, cousin?"

"Elizabeth, I will speak to you in my bookroom," said Mr. Bennet, ignoring the parson. "Now."

"Mr. Bennet—" began Mr. Collins, but he was cut off by a harsh glare from the Bennet patriarch and subsided, albeit somewhat sulkily.

Elizabeth did not know what to think. She had not been called into her father's study since her return to Longbourn. As Mr. Bennet departed the room, Elizabeth glanced at the parson, only to see him flop into a chair and regard her with some peevishness.

All at once, an unpleasant suspicion welled up in Elizabeth's mind, and she stared at the parson with chagrin. Her father could not possibly be thinking of betrothing her to the imbecilic Mr. Collins, could he? The very notion that she would consent to wasting herself on such an odious man was in every way unthinkable! Besides, he was already betrothed!

"Now, Elizabeth!" her father's stern command echoed through the open door.

With great reluctance, Elizabeth stood and made her way from the room, but not before she caught a glimpse of Mr. Collins's insufferable smile, which was fairly dripping with smugness. Praying that her father would merely reprimand her for speaking so to his cousin, Elizabeth departed the room and entered her father's study.

Previously, Elizabeth had never had anything more than a brief glimpse through the occasionally open door of her father's study. As she entered it now, she looked around with some distraction, unable to take much in given the apprehension she was feeling. Her father sat in an old chair which appeared to have seen better days, and though his eyes did not betray any more emotion that Elizabeth had come to expect, they were fixed upon her with an almost pitiless sort of implacability.

The man was silent for a few moments, regarding her, weighing her person and her character, Elizabeth thought, and though she could not say for a certainty just how keen his powers of observation were, she felt as if her secrets and feelings were being ripped from her and laid on the desk for his perusal.

But she refused to be intimidated by her father. He was only a man, and whatever purpose he had in calling her into his room, he would find that she would not simply acquiesce to his schemes like a dog begging for a scrap. Her time with her uncle and aunt had given her more backbone than that!

"You should be at no loss to understand why I have called you in here," said Mr. Bennet, finally breaking the silence.

"Indeed, sir, you are mistaken," replied Elizabeth, holding her chin up high. "I am quite unable to account for your actions. If you are concerned for my behavior toward *your* guest, then I assure you that I did not intend to be rude."

"Perhaps you should be more respectful toward your future husband."

All at once, tears welled up in Elizabeth's eyes, and she cried, "No!"

But Mr. Bennet's stare was pitiless and unyielding. "You *will* marry Mr. Collins, Elizabeth. I have already promised you to him."

Chapter XV

Elizabeth's mind worked desperately, trying to determine how she should act. Of one thing, she was certain: her spirit would be crushed as Mr. Collins's wife. She had no doubt that her days would be miserable. And the thought of submitting to marital duties with the man . . .

No, it could not be. Every part of her cried out with abhorrence at the very thought of being so intimately connected with such a man. She would not do it.

"I will not marry him," said Elizabeth in a quiet voice.

Mr. Bennet's eyes pierced right through her, and though his countenance did not change one iota, the depths of his eyes became all that much stormier. He did not say a word, however; he simply sat in his chair, looking at her, as though the very force of his will would compel her to comply.

The silence was unbearable, and Elizabeth filled it. "I know that you have the measure of the man, father. You know that he is in every way ridiculous. He is imbecilic, his opinions make no sense, he flatters that patroness of his as though she were the queen of England, and his personal hygiene is suspect. You would be condemning me to a life of misery and degradation with such a husband."

"And did you not condemn your mother and sisters to such a life with your actions?" queried Mr. Bennet.

Elizabeth huffed impatiently. "I know not how you can still blame me for what happened. No reasonable person could hold me accountable."

"That is a matter of opinion."

"Then you may have your opinion. I shall not be moved. I will not marry Mr. Collins."

Mr. Bennet leaned forward and fixed her with his stare, his countenance shifting into an expression which was truly forbidding. "You will marry Mr. Collins, Elizabeth, and you will marry him soon. You have been the one to ruin this family's prospects. Thus, it falls to you to repair them. Marriage to Mr. Collins would provide a home for your mother and any unmarried sisters should I predecease your mother."

"Should you not have provided for them?" cried Elizabeth. "Perhaps you should live up to your duty as a landowner and stir yourself from your bookroom on occasion. Then perhaps diligence might have helped you set something aside for their eventual care.

"And as for my mother specifically, you are well aware of the extravagance of her expenses in her zeal to dress her daughters to best advantage. Her every thought is to see them all married off as if they were nothing more than sheep being sold to the highest bidder!"

"Do you blame her?" demanded Mr. Bennet, his voice rising in response to her own. "As there is no heir to this estate, her future prospects are grim!"

"They would not be grim if you had done your duty!"

Mr. Bennet shot to his feet, and he moved around the desk to stand in front of her chair. He was much smaller than Mr. Darcy, and years of indolence appeared to have sapped his strength further. But though he was not an overly large man, Elizabeth was herself a small woman, standing taller only than Mary of all her sisters; as a result, Mr. Bennet's face, with its wild eyes boring into her mere inches away from her own, induced a feeling of fear in her breast which she had not ever expected to feel in the presence of this man. She did not know of what he was capable, but at that moment, she very much feared that he would strike her.

"You will listen to me, *Miss Elizabeth*." Her name was uttered with as much scorn as she had ever heard from another person. "Mr. Collins is my heir, and he will one day inherit this property. I care not if he is stupid. I care not if he ever bathes, or if he rolls in the muck and fornicates with pigs. I care not if he takes up a rod and beats you every day with it until you beg him for mercy.

"You *will* marry him. I have decreed it as your father, and as you are still underage, you will obey me. You will go to the church at a time of my choosing, you will repeat your vows before the priest, you will sign the church register in the presence of witnesses, and you will go to Mr. Collins's home and become his wife. Once that happens, I will have no more responsibility for you."

"You have not taken responsibility for me for many years," said Elizabeth.

Mr. Bennet's hand shot out and slapped Elizabeth. He did not strike her hard enough to leave a mark, but it stung nonetheless. His pitiless eyes told her that it was only the beginning if she did not obey his commands.

Deciding that it was best not to challenge him further to his face, Elizabeth looked away calmly. Inside, she was a roiling mass of emotions and fears. But one thought rose above the rest: this was not over. She would not submit meekly to his Machiavellian edicts!

"That is better," rumbled her father after a moment. He stood straight again and leaned back against his desk. "Mr. Collins is not the most intelligent of men. I suspect that should you wish it, you could rule over him without any effort whatsoever. If the thought of being married to him is so distasteful you may think of that at least. You would not only be mistress of Longbourn, but also its master."

Though she was seething, Elizabeth held her tongue. She would not give this man the satisfaction of an answer.

"Now, we will go out and announce the *happy news* to the family. I doubt very much that Mr. Collins is intelligent enough to detect your . . . reluctance to marry him. In fact, I believe the man has much too high of an opinion of himself to even begin to fathom such a thing. It would be best, however, if you were to avoid any overt display of displeasure. We would not wish your marriage to begin on a sour note, now would we?"

Elizabeth glared at him, but Mr. Bennet only watched her with that dark amusement of his. Now Elizabeth could see clearly what his expressions and amusements the previous evening had meant. He was not only fixing his laxity in his own ineffectual way, but he was also offering her up to a man she could not tolerate for revenge! And all at once, Elizabeth recognized her father's pettiness.

Silently, Elizabeth vowed that she would not sit still for this injustice. One way or another, she would triumph and avoid the fate her father had decreed for her.

For now, Elizabeth had no choice but to follow her father back into the parlor, where the rest of the company awaited them. Several curious faces met their arrival, and though Elizabeth could not be certain, the expression of distress on Jane's face told her that their argument had likely been heard. Mr. Collins, however, was all expectation; he surely understood what was about to happen, though he seemed to have no understanding of what a loud argument between father and daughter before the announcement of an engagement could mean. Elizabeth had never before felt more contempt for another person.

"Thank you all for waiting so patiently for our return," said Mr. Bennet, his voiced laced with sardonic amusement and another quality which Elizabeth took to be disdain. "I have an announcement to make."

Elizabeth was watching Mr. Collins, and the expression on his face grew all the more beatific while confusion reigned on the faces of everyone else in the room. Elizabeth seethed, but she kept her silence. There was no point in speaking up now.

"As it happens, Mr. Collins has come to Longbourn with an express purpose. It is therefore my *pleasure* to announce that Mr. Collins and our Elizabeth have come to an agreement. They are engaged and shall be married at the first opportunity."

Bedlam did not ensue as Elizabeth would have expected. Rather, her sisters looked on with confusion and a variety of other emotions—Jane appeared distressed, Mary suspicious, and Catherine and Lydia relieved that they would not need to submit to the attentions of the parson. But it was Mrs. Bennet's reaction which startled Elizabeth the most.

"Elizabeth?" asked she, her voice laced with skepticism. "Surely you cannot mean that." She shook her head to indicate her lack of understanding.

"Mr. Collins," said Mrs. Bennet, addressing the clergyman directly, "would not my Mary suit you better as a wife? She is pious and charitable, and I think she would be a better wife than . . ." Mrs. Bennet swallowed and directed a glance at Mr. Bennet nervously. "Well, let us just say that she would be much easier to handle than . . . my second-born."

Mary gasped and stared at Mr. Collins with horror, and Elizabeth felt all the satisfaction of knowing that she was not the only who could not abide the thought of being married to the man. But she had no need to worry, as the man himself rose to his feet and bowed to the entire company with aplomb.

"I assure you, madam," said he, "that I am fixed on Miss Elizabeth for my wife. I was quite captivated by your good husband's description of her charms, and the reality has been beyond my expectations. She will be delighted, I am sure, to become the mistress of Hunsford, and I do not doubt she will be exceedingly grateful for the attentions of my most esteemed lady patroness, though I am certain that she will wish to display the humblest deference before her ladyship."

He turned to Elizabeth and fixed his eyes upon her, licking his lips in a most loathsome manner. "I take this opportunity now to state without reservation the depths of my regard for you, my lovely fiancée. The violence of my feelings for you is only matched by my eagerness to show you the delights of married life."

Elizabeth's disdain rose to ever greater heights of the ridiculousness of this man. His inelegant comments disgusted her, and if she had been at liberty, she would have broken a vase over his empty head.

"Your behavior this afternoon shall be discussed in greater detail at a later date," continued the detestable parson. "For the moment, let us seal our engagement with a kiss, my dear cousin."

He moved toward her with arms outstretched, but Elizabeth sidestepped him and went to sit beside Jane without saying a word to him. Mr. Collins appeared confused for a moment at her avoidance, but soon the smarmy smile was etched yet again on his face.

"Ah, I understand. I assure you that your actions are only increasing my affection through suspense, and I esteem you all the more because of it. Self-denial is indeed a process by which we might all approach godliness, and I commend you for wishing to wait until we are married."

A snicker actually escaped Mr. Bennet, though no one else seemed to notice it. And though Mrs. Bennet appeared to wish to further try to persuade the parson, she cast a hateful glare at Elizabeth before she subsided. The time before dinner passed in an interminable manner, and though Elizabeth tried to avoid looking at anyone, she could not help but see a measure of pity upon the faces of her sisters. It was a far cry from the ridicule she had often endured at the hands of Lydia and Catherine at the very least.

"Elizabeth," whispered Jane at one point when Mr. Collins appeared to be engaged with Mr. Bennet, "what is happening? How could you have agreed to marry such a man?"

"Because she is doing her duty, Jane," interjected her father. He had been watching the sisters closely, and his voice was filled with censure.

"You should be happy for her. She will one day be mistress of this house."

Jane fairly wilted under the force of her father's glare, and she said no more. Elizabeth, who was not intimidated by her father's show of displeasure, gazed back at him, daring him to censure her, but he did nothing more than stare at her in that cold way of his.

"Do not worry, Jane," whispered Elizabeth to her sister. "Everything will be well."

The evening was interminable, and between Mr. Collins attempts at courting her good opinion, her mother's ever-increasing hysteria over a soon-to-be-married daughter, and the youngest girls' incessant giggling, Elizabeth found it difficult to maintain her even demeanor. But she was determined that she would not willingly go as a lamb to the slaughter. And she had the ghost of an idea of what she might do to avoid the fate her father had planned for her.

The Gardiners were long departed for Ireland, but they had told her that she could return to their house should anything untoward happen. She would go there if she must, content in the knowledge that the servants left at the house would undoubtedly refuse entrance to Mr. Bennet and declaim all knowledge of her whereabouts should he rouse himself enough to make the attempt to recover her. And even though it meant that she would essentially be a prisoner in the house, it was better than the fate her father had planned for her.

But more than that, Elizabeth's thoughts turned to Mr. Darcy. The man had made her an offer of courtship only hours before, and Elizabeth was certain that he would not be happy with her father bartering her off without her consent when his offer—a most advantageous offer!—was still on the table. Elizabeth decided that the first thing she would do was to go to Netherfield and throw herself on Mr. Darcy's mercy. She thought it possible that she could stay with the Darcys until the Gardiners returned, and as he had a young sister, she could merely act as if she were visiting the sister. Their courtship and ultimate engagement could be announced afterward. Surely her father would not persist when confronted by a man of Mr. Darcy's influence and wealth.

The trick was to get to Netherfield. At first, Elizabeth was inclined to wait a few days in order to lull her father into a false sense of security. Then she could simply walk the three miles to the estate, explain everything to Mr. Darcy, and hope that he would be willing to offer her his protection.

But there were several flaws with that plan. The first was that she would have to spend several days pretending to at least tolerate Mr. Collins's advances, a thought which caused her to shudder with revulsion. The bigger problem, however, was the way her father watched her all through that night. The man was not stupid—in fact, she suspected that he might even be considered uncommonly intelligent. She suspected that he was aware of the fact that she was not reconciled to this match in the slightest. And she feared that the longer she waited, the more vigilant and watchful he would become. That would necessitate her making her move as soon as possible, thereby catching him by surprise.

As she looked around the dinner table, Elizabeth avoided looking at the much-despised visage of Mr. Collins. The younger girls were chattering together as was their wont, though Elizabeth could see that Catherine's heart was not it. Several times, she glanced over at Elizabeth, and from what Elizabeth could see, she appeared to be struggling with the thought that something was amiss. Jane was beside herself with worry, though Elizabeth tried to reassure her with smiles whenever she could, and Mary, while inscrutable, often looked between Elizabeth and Collins with a perplexed air, as if trying to puzzle something out.

As for the perpetrators of the night's travesty, Mr. Collins was blathering on about his patroness, his home, and his expected marital felicity in his ponderous tone, and Mrs. Bennet was interjecting comments concerning the wedding arrangements, though she was in no way excited about the prospect. At the head of the table, Mr. Bennet sat watching the proceedings, and if his eyes tightened at some nonsense proceeding forth from the mouth of his wife, he said nothing further.

Elizabeth was done with the lot of them, she decided, except for dear Jane and any other sisters who might want to reconcile in the future. If she had to choose her path all over again, she would have accompanied Mr. and Mrs. Gardiner to Ireland.

Of course, that thought brought on a pang of its own, for if she had done so, she would not have experienced the pleasure of furthering her acquaintance with Mr. Darcy. His request for a courtship could not have been extended, and though she would be free of her father's edicts, she would still be a single girl with an uncertain future.

There was nothing to be done. She would simply have to escape that night and throw herself on Mr. Darcy's mercy. He would assist her—somehow, Elizabeth knew that he would not allow her to be taken from him so easily.

When help finally arrived, it was from an unexpected source.

When dinner was over, Elizabeth excused herself early to retire to her room. As Mr. Bennet had already retreated to his bookroom, her mother simply waved her from the room and continued to speak with Mr. Collins about some nonsense or other. Elizabeth did not care whether her mother was trying to ingratiate herself with her supposed future son-in-law. Elizabeth would never be mistress of Longbourn.

Once up in her room, Elizabeth looked about and set to work. She threw her most important and sentimental belongings into a case along with a few dresses which she did not wish to leave behind. She left most of her personal effects where they were, not wanting someone to question where her possessions were gone should anyone think to look in on her before she had a chance to escape.

While she was thus engaged, a soft knock sounded on her door, startling Elizabeth. Quickly, she pushed the case she had been packing under her bed until it was out of sight, and then sitting on the bed, she called out permission to enter.

The door opened, and Elizabeth peered with astonishment at the person who stood there. It was Mrs. Hill, the housekeeper.

"Miss Elizabeth," said the housekeeper hesitantly, glancing over her shoulder.

Immediately understanding that the woman feared discovery, Elizabeth motioned her forward into the room and closed the door once she had entered. It was obvious that Mrs. Hill was uncomfortable, and Elizabeth smiled, attempting to put her at ease. Then she asked why Mrs. Hill had come.

In a thoroughly diffident manner, the housekeeper looked down, but she roused enough courage to say, "Miss Elizabeth, I beg your pardon, but it is the understanding of those of us below stairs that you are betrothed to Mr. Collins."

Unable to contain her surprise, Elizabeth gasped, which served to draw Mrs. Hill's attention.

"Then it is true?"

Anger flooded through Elizabeth, though she was able to restrain herself from making a caustic remark. This woman was not her enemy, after all.

"I have consented to nothing," said Elizabeth stonily. "Mr. Collins may think that he has gained my hand, but he shall soon find out that I do not mean to surrender lightly."

It was only after Elizabeth's feelings had obtained their release that she realized that she should not have spoken so openly to a servant who might report her words back to the master.

She need not have worried, as an expression of compassion descended over the woman's face.

"It is as I suspected. I cannot understand what the master is thinking, to be forcing you to marry such a man."

"He is thinking of obtaining an easy solution to his problems," said Elizabeth in bitterness. "He cannot bestir himself to actually provide for his family, so he forces me to become their salvation."

The servant apparently did not know what to say to Elizabeth's caustic words, so she ignored them.

"Mr. Gardiner asked me to watch over you, and I have done my best to do so. I am truly sorry that I was not able to divine Mr. Bennet's purpose in recalling you ere now."

"You are not to blame, Mrs. Hill," said Elizabeth, her anger bleeding away. "My father is the author of this travesty, and I shall not put the blame at the feet of anyone else."

"Do you mean to accept your lot?"

Elizabeth snorted. "Never. I shall leave this house tonight and never return."

"Then I shall assist you."

"No, you must not!" cried Elizabeth. "If my father found out, you would lose your position."

The woman's answering grin was positively amused. "I doubt it, Miss Elizabeth. The mistress could not do without me, and the master would never hear the end of it should he relieve me of my position. Besides, I would prefer to lose my position than to allow the master to do this. I could not live with myself if I did so."

Though Elizabeth tried to protest, Mrs. Hill remained firm, and Elizabeth was forced to give way. They spoke for several more moments before the housekeeper departed to return below stairs before she was missed. Heartened by the plan she had devised with the faithful housekeeper, Elizabeth decided to give the appearance of retiring for the night.

Not long after the housekeeper left, another knock sounded on the door, and though Elizabeth debated simply ignoring it, the knock was so soft that Elizabeth knew it could not be her father's.

At her prompt, the door opened, and a head of golden tresses appeared. "Elizabeth?" called Jane.

Relieved to see her dearest sister, Elizabeth motioned for her to enter the room, which Jane did, though she still appeared to be uncertain of her reception.

"Elizabeth . . ." Jane trailed off before summoning her courage and continuing. "Are you well, Elizabeth?"

"As well as can be," replied Elizabeth with an indifferent shrug.

Jane frowned. "I am not certain I believe you."

"Indeed, all shall be well."

"But what of Mr. Collins? And Papa?" Jane appeared to be struggling with her emotions. "I cannot imagine that you have agreed to marry Mr. Collins, of all men. I believe I know your opinion of the man, Elizabeth."

"You are correct, Jane," said Elizabeth. "I did not agree to marry him."

There was a grim set to Jane's countenance when Elizabeth confirmed her suspicions. "How can Papa do this?" asked she, tears appearing in the corners of her eyes. "Surely he can see that you have no feelings for the man."

"Oh, I assure you that I have plenty of feelings for the man!" Elizabeth could not keep the bitterness from her voice. "Contempt, anger, and disgust are foremost among them."

"But Elizabeth," said Jane, stepping forward to take her hand, "what will you do?"

Though she thought for a moment to illuminate Jane concerning the particulars of her plan, Elizabeth reluctantly decided to keep it from her sister. Jane was too good-hearted, and if Mr. Bennet asked, Elizabeth was not certain her sister would be able to keep her confidence. Besides, she did not wish to burden Jane with the knowledge that she planned to throw herself on the mercy of Mr. Darcy.

"Do not concern yourself, Jane," said Elizabeth quietly. "But know that I will not allow my father to do this to me without a fight."

Tears welled in Jane's eyes. "Will I see you again?"

Elizabeth laughed and embraced her sister. "How could I throw off such a wonderful sister? I assure you that we will meet again, Jane. It will likely not be for some time, but it will happen."

Jane smiled through her tears. "I shall miss you. It has been very enjoyable having my little sister with us again."

"And I shall miss you," said Elizabeth, forcing the words out through the emotion coursing through her. She would not trade her years with the Gardiners for anything, but at that moment, Elizabeth cursed her parents for causing her to miss so many years of being loved by a most angelic sister.

The sisters spoke for a few more moments, Jane for the most part admonishing Elizabeth to be well, and then Jane departed, leaving Elizabeth to her empty room and her thoughts. It was not many more moments before Elizabeth decided to retire herself. It would be some time before the house settled down. Until that time, she might as well get a little rest. Then she would make her escape.

Regardless of Elizabeth's intentions, sleep was impossible to come by. In the window of her mind, she kept replaying the events of the evening, running over the state of her relationship with her father and mother, and wondering at the events which had led to the state between them. A part of her wondered what her relationships with her parents would have been had her life not been overturned. Would she be closer to her mother or father? Would she be a favorite of either or both of them?

No, she doubted that would be the case. The thought of being her mother's favorite was quickly rejected. The woman was silly and vapid, and she would automatically choose her youngest and silliest—the one most like her—as her favorite. And as for her father . . . Well, Elizabeth could not imagine being close to Mr. Bennet either. He was a strange man, and she did not believe that he would have emerged from his bookroom for anyone. It was best that she depart and disappear from the Bennets' lives forever.

When the appointed time arrived, Elizabeth roused herself from her bed and prepared to depart. She had not changed into her nightclothes, so it was a simple matter of twisting her hair into a knot and taking her case out from where it was hidden underneath her bed. As she moved to the door, she turned and took one last look at the room she had inhabited for the past two months. There was very little in the way of memories attached to this room, and she certainly had no fondness for it. No, she would not miss Longbourn.

Once outside her door, Elizabeth closed it quietly behind her, making her way down the hall and subsequently the stairs as quietly as she could manage it. There was not a sound to be heard throughout the house. Satisfied she was about to make her escape, Elizabeth turned and made her way deeper into the house, and eventually made her way to the kitchen. There, espying Mrs. Hill near the back door, she approached her with a smile of gratitude.

"Here is your outer wear, Miss Elizabeth," said the housekeeper, helping her into her pelisse. "I have sent the footman to his bed. There should be no impediment to your escape.

"Thank you, Mrs. Hill," said Elizabeth with some emotion.

The woman nodded. "Are you certain you will be well?"

Elizabeth nodded. "It is no more than a three-mile walk to Netherfield. I do not suppose there will be brigands in between here and there."

Though her words were intended to be a jest, Mrs. Hill paled slightly. "I wish there was something more I had been able to do, Miss Elizabeth. But I dare not call upon John, the stable boy, as I believe he would run directly to Mr. Bennet with such news."

Reaching out a hand, Elizabeth touched the woman's arm, partially as a thankful gesture and partially to reassure her.

"It is of no moment, Mrs. Hill. The roads around Meryton are very safe. I do not doubt that I shall arrive at Netherfield completely unscathed. Once again, I thank you for your unstinting devotion and care. I shall miss you dearly."

"And we shall miss you, Miss Elizabeth. But I believe you go to a much better place. May God bless your journey."

Almost overcome with emotion, Elizabeth favored Mrs. Hill with a watery smile before turning toward the door. The housekeeper opened the door and made a shooing motion to Elizabeth, though she was not unaffected by emotion herself. Steeling herself for what was to come, Elizabeth turned to the door and stepped through it.

And was confronted by the thunderous expression of her father.

Elizabeth gasped and shrunk back from the man, but he made no move toward her. He merely watched her, though he was wearing an insufferable smile of satisfaction, clearly enjoying the fact that he had anticipated her flight.

"I see I was right to be suspicious of you. I did not think you would accept your lot without argument."

"No, I will not, father," said Elizabeth, gathering herself. "Mr. Collins is a fool, and I will not marry him."

"You will," was Mr. Bennet's maddening and emotionless reply. "If I have to tie you to the pew and recite your vows for you, I will see you married to him. You owe it to your mother and sisters."

"I owe them nothing!" cried Elizabeth. "Certainly not to a woman who made my first nine years of life miserable."

Mr. Bennet snorted and turned to the housekeeper, regarding her as a lion might eye a fat pig. "I expected my daughter to try to escape. However, I did not expect your involvement in this, Mrs. Hill."

An attempt at defiance from the woman was admirable, but she soon crumpled under his pitiless stare and looked toward the ground.

"The only reason I am not removing you from the premises is because of your long years of service to my family. You will go to your room and return to your duties on the morrow. And you will have no further contact with Elizabeth."

Mrs. Hill looked up at Mr. Bennet at these edicts, and she appeared to be on the verge of some retort. But Elizabeth knew that she would not escape this night and that she did not wish for Mrs. Hill to lose her position.

So Elizabeth put a calming hand on her shoulder. "Please, Mrs. Hill. Do as he asks. There is nothing further to be done tonight."

It was evident that she wished to be of further use, but Mrs. Hill nodded once in Elizabeth's direction. "Very well, Miss Elizabeth. I will return to my room."

"Selfless to the last," jibed Mr. Bennet as the housekeeper retreated. "I know not how you managed to pull her into your schemes, but I shall tell you this—if I catch her acting contrary to my will again, no length of service will save her from dismissal."

Elizabeth locked her father in a disdainful glare. "I would not have her dismissed on my account."

"And yet you have brought the woman to the very brink tonight."

"You may believe what you wish, father. Perhaps I have more faith in the innate goodness of my fellow man. Of course, there are always exceptions."

Her father snorted, but he said nothing in response to her blatant innuendo and instead took her by the arm, leading her back up the stairs. Their progress was not silent, and as the stairs ran past the entrance to Mrs. Bennet's bedchamber, they awoke her, and she cried out with fright, howling some nonsensical lamentation about how highwaymen had entered the house.

"Be silent, Mrs. Bennet!" snapped Mr. Bennet as he led them past her room.

"Now, Elizabeth," said her father as they arrived at the door to her room, "you will retire immediately. There are to be no more adventures this night.

"John!" barked Mr. Bennet.

In the dimness of the corridor, a tall man, lean but with corded muscles under his shirt, stepped forward. Elizabeth realized that he must have been following them from below, though she had not noted his presence at the time.

"You will keep watch outside Elizabeth's door tonight. See that she does not leave the room for any reason."

"Yes, Mr. Bennet," said the man in a soft voice.

Elizabeth shuddered as he looked at her with a merciless stare, and she immediately opened the door and slipped into her room. Behind her in the hall, the mocking voice of her father drifted into the room as though on wings of sound, "Good night, my little Lizzy."

Though Elizabeth attempted to rest, her sleep was fitful. Images of her father staring mercilessly and handing her off to a ridiculous demon named Collins flitted in and out of her dreams. Interspersed with those dreams, she found herself pursued by some nameless calamity which never quite managed to catch her, but which she conversely could not escape. It was a miserable night, made even more so by the fact that Elizabeth spent her waking moments wondering how to affect her escape from her father.

About the best plan she could muster was to wait until Mr. Darcy visited. If she could catch him before he approached her father, she could make him aware of what had occurred. She was certain his regard was real, and she had no doubt he would not take kindly to her father's actions.

Finally, when the morning had arrived, though the landscape outside her window was still laboring under the absence of light, Elizabeth rose from her bed and dressed in a simple but serviceable gown. It was gray and drab, and it suited her mood. She then opened the door to the room and confronted the stony visage of her captor.

"The master said you were not to leave your room."

"Does the master intend for me to starve?" asked Elizabeth imperiously. "I wish to go down to breakfast. You may accompany me to see that I do not run if you must."

The man seemed to consider the matter for the moment before he stepped away from the door and motioned toward the stairs. He said nothing further, but his pointed look seemed to suggest that he would not be gentle if she should be so foolish as to run.

The breakfast room was empty, as her father had not yet appeared this morning, and with the stable hand waiting outside the room, Elizabeth entered. A maid soon arrived with a tray of muffins—it still was quite early, and Elizabeth felt a momentary pang of remorse for imposing upon the staff in such a manner. She forced herself to eat a few bites of the breakfast which had been provided.

The true reason she had insisted on being allowed to come down for breakfast was quite different from what she had told the man. On the far side of the breakfast parlor, down a short hall, sat the tray on which the Bennets normally set their outgoing correspondence. Having written a letter to her uncle that morning in her room, she proceeded to exit the breakfast room and inserted the letter under some others which were already there. She then returned to her breakfast without anyone being the wiser.

After she had returned to her room—under the watchful company of the detested stable hand—she sat at the window, watching the outside world. It was still quite early, so the landscape was as of yet gray, but while Elizabeth sat there, she watched the gradual increase of light, noting the abundance of pale pink and red pastel brush-strokes playing on the undersides of some fluffy clouds floating in the distance. When the sun finally peeked over the horizon, bathing the house in a dazzling array of light, Elizabeth reflected that it was ironic that the sunrise should be so beautiful on such a dark morning.

Her contemplation of the heavens was interrupted when the door to her room opened and Mr. Bennet walked in. Elizabeth rose to her feet and regarded him with no little derision. He took a letter from his pocket, tossing it on her nightstand with a sharp twist of his wrist. It was the letter she had written to her uncle.

"I anticipated this from you as well," said her father. His manner was all insolent smugness, as if he believed himself so very superior for having guessed at her ploy.

"But then, I might as well allow the letter to be sent," continued he in a conversational tone. "By the time it made its way into the hands of my brother, it would be much too late for him to do anything."

"What do you mean?" asked Elizabeth, her eyes narrowing in suspicion.

"Put on your best dress, Elizabeth, for today is your wedding day."

Shocked, Elizabeth gaped at him. "You cannot do this!"

"I assure you that I can."

"The banns have not been read!" sputtered Elizabeth. "The church has not been booked. Nothing has been prepared. You cannot simply decree something and expect that it will be accepted by the church."

"Mr. Jones will marry you because I tell him to. The rest of it does not matter. Now, I suggest you prepare yourself, for you will be married today!"

"You cannot make me marry him!" cried Elizabeth. "Mr. Darcy asked only yesterday if he could court me, and I told him he could!"

That brought her father up short, and he peered at her for a moment before a truly unpleasant smile came over his face. Shaking his head, he said: "I had not thought you desperate enough to lie in order to save yourself."

"I am *not* lying," said Elizabeth with an indignant huff.

"So you say," returned her father, his manner all insolence.

Elizabeth glared at him. "Do you suppose that *no man* will look twice at me, or am I so repulsive that my only recourse is to be shackled to an imbecile like Mr. Collins?"

"I *suppose* that you spin tales of regard so that you may purchase a little time in which to make your escape. I also *suppose* that a man of Mr. Darcy's standing in society would not even look twice at penniless waifs such as my daughters.

"But do not concern yourself, Elizabeth. Should Mr. Darcy come to request your hand, I will ensure he understands how happy you are to be marrying such an amiable and eligible gentleman as my cousin."

And with that, Mr. Bennet turned and departed from the room.

Elizabeth stared after him, wondering if her father had taken leave of his very sanity. Could he not see what a boon it would be to have a connection to such a wealthy man as Mr. Darcy? Would it not raise the chances for *all* of his daughters to make a good marriage?

And the sudden nature of this wedding was beyond her comprehension. While she could not state with any certainty what had been done, she knew at the very least the banns had not been read in Longbourn church as she had attended each of the past three weeks. How could her father think that he could force a marriage without the proper forms being met?

Still, his face and voice had been utterly implacable, and Elizabeth knew that he was serious. He seemed intent upon making her marry his cousin; nothing she said had made the slightest dent in his resolve.

Elizabeth glanced around the room quickly, and espying the window, she went over to it and opened it, peering out to see if there was anything she could use to climb down.

There on the ground, however, stood the stable hand watching her. "You may wish to reconsider, missy," said he. "It would be a shame if your only escape was to fall to your death."

Elizabeth glared imperiously at the man before she shut the window and began to make for the door, only for it to open from the other side.

"I must say that I did not expect that *you* of all my daughters would be the first to be married," said Mrs. Bennet as she bustled into the room. "Still, I suppose I must do what I can to make you presentable."

"You might as well save yourself the trouble, mother. I will not marry the man."

Mrs. Bennet clucked and moved to Elizabeth's closet to look at her dresses. "Your father says that you will. What you say does not truly matter, now does it?"

"Has the entire family gone mad?" cried Elizabeth. "I will not marry the man. I *detest* him!"

"He is not precisely what I would have chosen for a son-in-law, but since it is you, I suppose it is fitting. It is not as if you deserve much more."

Elizabeth's eyes narrowed, and she glared at her mother. As the woman was busy nosing about her closet, she did not see the daggers with which Elizabeth was impaling her through her eyes.

"As for your possessions, I suppose we can pack them up and send them after you. Though I must own that my Lydia would look very well in some of these frocks." Mrs. Bennet sneered at her. "It is not as if you will require them in Kent with such a husband."

"Even if my father forces me to the altar, I assure you that I will not speak," said Elizabeth, keeping her voice calm. "He can force me to the church. He can force Mr. Jones to marry us. He may even be able to force me to sign the register. But I promise you, mother, that regardless of what my father does to affect this travesty, it shall not make it any more valid."

"You will do as you are told!" cried Mrs. Bennet as she whirled on Elizabeth, one finger jabbing at her in accusation. "It is because of you this family must rely on Mr. Collins. It falls on you to ensure that he has no choice but to provide us with a home when your father is gone."

Elizabeth laughed, a harsh grating sound which caused the woman to gape at her in surprise. "Mother, I believe that you must be the most insensible woman of my acquaintance. Do you not see that you are condemning yourself by supporting my father in this?"

Faltering, Mrs. Bennet looked on with incomprehension. She quickly recovered again and turned away. "It is unfortunate that a daughter of mine should be married with such haste. However, I believe it is well that there is no time to plan anything, as I would be loath to plan even the plainest of wedding breakfasts for such an ungrateful daughter such as you."

"I cannot fathom why you would wish for me to be the next mistress of Longbourn, mother," said Elizabeth over her mother's prattling.

"It truly does not signify who marries Mr. Collins as long as we have the man tied to us," replied Mrs. Bennet. "Though I certainly would not wish for my Jane or Lydia to be tied to the man. Both are meant for much greater things."

"You might wish for the devil himself to marry Mr. Collins instead of me, mother. You would not like me as mistress of Longbourn."

That caught Mrs. Bennet's attention, and she turned toward Elizabeth with wide eyes.

"Mr. Collins is stupid and servile, mother," said Elizabeth in a low voice. "Do you think it would take more than a few days for me to gain complete control over him? And if I was to return as mistress of this house after my father is gone, do you think I would be inclined to be merciful to you?"

Fear positively blossomed in Mrs. Bennet's face as the implication of Elizabeth's words began to sink in to her consciousness.

"I promise you, *Mama*, that if I am forced to marry Mr. Collins and it is accepted as legal, then I will make your life a living hell. The leakiest and smallest tenant cottage would look like sheer paradise next to where I will have you housed. And you will never entertain again, not unless you wish to be seen in the drabbest, most threadbare clothes I can find to dress you in."

"But I am your mother," said Mrs. Bennet, her voice weak and her eyes wide with fright. "You must respect me and care for me."

"Like you have cared for me? Remember back to what I was subjected to as a child. Then you will have a glimpse of how much charity I will hold for you in my heart."

For a moment, Mrs. Bennet stood stock still, gaping at Elizabeth. Then all at once, she was fleeing through the open door, screaming for her husband. Elizabeth watched her go, knowing it would not be enough to dissuade Mr. Bennet. But though it might not have been admirable, it had felt good to be able to make her mother fear *her* for a change.

The ensuing argument echoed through the halls of Longbourn, Mrs. Bennet's wails intermixed with Mr. Bennet's angry shouts. Elizabeth thought to follow her mother to her father's bookroom and stir her up into a further frenzy, but she was prevented from doing so by the detestable stable hand, who had entered the house yet again and barred her way from proceeding down the stairs. But though her mother's lamenting cries were heard throughout the house, her father stood firm in his intent.

"You are ruining me, Mr. Bennet!" wailed her mother. "To have such a demon child as mistress of Longbourn! Have you no compassion upon my poor nerves? Let Mr. Collins wed Mary instead."

"Not another word, Mrs. Bennet! The decision has been made.

Elizabeth will wed Mr. Collins!"

"But what shall I do? Mr. Gardiner will not take me in. I shall have to throw myself on the mercy of my sister Phillips!"

"You believe too much in your daughter's angry words. Mr. Collins, if nothing else, is a creature of duty. You shall not be left undefended."

Mrs. Bennet's reply was much quieter, though it was accompanied by a loud sob. But Elizabeth vowed to herself that her mother would receive no such consideration from her if this travesty was allowed to proceed. She might have no way to obtain vengeance upon her father, but her mother would feel her wrath—of this, Elizabeth was determined!

"Elizabeth, what is happening?" asked Jane as she appeared in the door of her room. All of her sisters had similarly been summoned by the commotion in the house. Jane's eyes were wide with fright; she had likely never heard her parents' voices raised in such tones, though when Elizabeth thought on it, the day she had left Longbourn behind had witnessed a similar scene.

"I am being forced to marry Mr. Collins today, Jane."

Jane's eyes widened, and she gaped at Elizabeth, seemingly unable to comprehend, let alone formulate a response.

Perhaps it was something Elizabeth could have predicted, but Lydia huffed and rolled her eyes, saying. "Is *that* all?" She then turned back into her room and slammed the door behind her.

"Surely you are mistaken," said Mary as she, Jane, and Catherine—the latter with frightened eyes—all moved toward her.

"That is far enough," said the ever-present stable hand from where stood in front of Elizabeth's door. "The master has decreed that no one shall enter Miss Elizabeth's room except her mother."

Jane's shocked features instantly transformed into a fierce scowl, the likes of which Elizabeth had never seen before on her face. "Stand aside, John! I will speak with my sister."

The poor man—if he could be termed as such—gaped at Jane with surprise, but though he did not move, Jane was able to slip past him into Elizabeth's room. Though he had been instructed regarding Elizabeth, touching a gentlewoman was no small matter, and he was not willing to chance the repercussions which could result from handling her sisters in such a manner.

"I will not wed Mr. Collins," said Elizabeth once her sisters had gathered in her room. "But my father seems to think that I must be the one to restore the family's fortunes, and he is determined that I shall be the means of repairing our family fortunes."

"But surely Mr. Collins could not be party to this," said Mary slowly, as if trying working through the implications as she spoke. "He is a clergyman, after all . . . ."

"I know not what Mr. Collins's involvement is," replied Elizabeth in an impatient tone. "But I know he is stupid enough to believe anything my father chooses to tell him."

Catherine gasped, tears appearing in the corners of her eyes. "But if Papa makes you marry Mr. Collins, then what about the rest of us? Does he already have our husbands chosen for us?"

Elizabeth shook her head. "I am certain you have nothing to concern yourself over. *I* am the one who has been singled out for this honor."

"I do not understand," said Catherine, looking at Elizabeth with a frown. "What do my father and mother have against you?"

This time, it was Elizabeth's turn to be shocked. "You mean you do not know?"

"It was never spoken of after you left, Elizabeth," Jane was quick to say. "The girls were too young to remember."

"That is not what distresses me, Jane," said Elizabeth through a veil of tears. "Of course they would not wish to speak of the matter. But my mother and father have taught you all to hate me, yet they have never given any reason for it. I have been made the pariah, the faceless, hated sister, despite no reason ever being given for my being shunned. There is no direction for this hatred. It is all so senseless."

Sitting down heavily on her bed, Elizabeth gazed at her hands, unseeing, too heart-sick over what was happening to even feel properly. "I wish I had never returned."

She truly was bereft. She had no family, no connection to anyone in this house, no reason to ever be here again. The Gardiners had offered to take her with them to Ireland and to fight her father's control over her. Never before had she wished so fervently that she had listened to their wisdom. Perhaps she might have been spared this pain.

"I have known what happened for years," said Mary. "And though I have not shown it since you arrived, I have never held it against you, Elizabeth."

"I do not understand," said Catherine in a plaintive voice. "What happened?"

"Not now," snapped Jane.

"Tell her, Jane," pleaded Elizabeth. "At least let her know the truth so that she may judge for herself. And tell Lydia, though I doubt she will listen."

"'Judge not, lest ye be judged,'" murmured Mary.

Down below, a door slammed, and Elizabeth thought it was the sound of the door to her father's sanctuary impacting against the wall behind it as it was flung open. Her father's voice echoed up through the house.

"I will not discuss this any further, Mrs. Bennet! You will return to your room and compose yourself. We shall discuss this in a rational manner when I return."

The sound of her father's heavy footsteps sounded on the stairs, and Elizabeth knew that he was coming for her.

Desperately, she turned to Jane, and drawing her sister close, she said softly, "Tell Mr. Darcy that I did not do this willingly."

Jane looked at her, puzzled by this sudden plea. "What do you mean?"

"Just tell him," entreated Elizabeth, willing her sister to comply.

There was only time for a brief nod, and then Mr. Bennet entered the room. He scowled at his assembled daughters, cowing each of them with the force of his glare. But Elizabeth would not be intimidated by this man!

"Girls, you will return to your rooms, this instant."

Catherine wilted under the force of his stare and fairly scurried from the room in fright, but not without first casting a worried glance at Elizabeth. Mary, though she did not seem intimidated, evidently decided that there was nothing she could do. She gave Elizabeth's arm a squeeze before retreating from the room.

Jane, however, glared at her father and would not budge from Elizabeth's side.

"I will stay with my sister."

To say that Mr. Bennet was unimpressed was akin to saying the French Tyrant was a minor obstacle to peace. "You will return to your room, Jane. Do not disobey me."

"My sister deserves someone to stand up with her through her ordeal. I will not leave her alone."

With sudden violence of movement, Mr. Bennet grasped Jane's arm and dragged her from the room, ignoring her protests.

"Jane!" cried Elizabeth, following closely after her father. "It is well. *I* will be well. Do not worry for me."

"You should listen to your sister, Jane," said Mr. Bennet.

He opened the door to Jane's room and thrust her inside, closing it behind her. He then turned to the stable hand, who was watching the proceedings impassively, and fixed him with a stern glare.

"None of the ladies of the house are to leave their rooms until I return. You have my leave to restrain them if they make the attempt.

"You!" barked he, turning to a maid who had been hiding just out of sight down the hall near the servant's stairway. "Go down and get Mrs. Hill. Instruct her to bring the keys to the house up and lock the doors of all these rooms. John, you will watch Mrs. Hill as she does this. She may bring trays to their rooms later so they may break their fasts, but they are not to be allowed out until I return and command it."

The stable hand nodded, but Mr. Bennet had already turned to Elizabeth. "Will you come with me willingly, or shall I carry you to the church?"

"I will not do this willingly, father. Whatever you have done to ensure this charade goes forward, you can be certain that I will never consider it to be legal or binding upon me."

Mr. Bennet nodded. "I suspected as much."

Taking her arm in a vise-like grip, Mr. Bennet dragged Elizabeth from the room. She thought to struggle with him, but it was clear that she had no real chance of escaping.

"Do you think that Mr. Collins will believe that I am a willing bride, with all the commotion he has been subject to this morning? I am surprised we have not seen him yet, pontificating over the need for family harmony."

Her father let out a bark laughter. "Once again, I have anticipated you. I expected that you would not go to your fate easily, and I sent him on to the church before the festivities began."

Though she would not give the man any credit, it appeared as if he had given thought to any eventuality and planned for them all with meticulous foresight.

"And what makes you think I shall submit to Mr. Collins?"

"I care not what you do." By this time, Mr. Bennet had led her out the front door, and they began to cross the lawn toward the church which stood in the distance. "Once you are married to Mr. Collins, it will be up to him to control you." He fixed her with a sidelong look. "I will tell you that I have advised Mr. Collins that he will need to take you firmly in hand. You should think about that when you resist him."

Elizabeth laughed. "If you think that William Collins can 'take me firmly in hand,' I believe that you are sadly overestimating his capacities."

Her father shrugged and continued to walk at a fast pace. For the first time since she had been led outside, Elizabeth felt the chill in the air. It seemed to pierce her all the way to her very bones, as the thin dress was little protection against the elements. But even that coldness was nothing compared to the chill which was extending tendrils out from her very heart, grasping her in its grip like a never-ending winter.

Soon, Mr. Bennet had bustled her into the church where the two parsons were awaiting her, Mr. Collins looking at them with a saintly smile etched across his features and Mr. Jones watching them through rheumy eyes with a vaguely confused air about him. It was clear that neither understood the true state of affairs.

With an abruptness which momentarily threw Elizabeth off balance, Mr. Bennet stopped and fixed Elizabeth with a fierce expression. It almost seemed as if Elizabeth could see her death in the depths of his eyes.

"Remember that I still have authority over you," hissed he. The look in his eyes almost seemed to pass into madness. "If you say one word which leads either of these men to believe that you are here by anything other than your own will, you will feel my wrath, and it will not be pleasant."

By now, Elizabeth was convinced that her safety—and perhaps her very life!—was in danger should she not obey, and as Mr. Bennet had already raised his hand to her once, she did not doubt his ability to do so again.

But he did not give her time to think on the implications; rather, he began to walk once again toward the pair of parsons waiting for them. "You may proceed, Mr. Jones," said Mr. Bennet as they came to a stop before the parson.

The ancient man looked on him with confusion. "What of your lady wife? Does she not wish to witness her daughter's marriage?"

"Mrs. Bennet is overcome with joy at the thought of a daughter being married," said Mr. Bennet, his lips curled in a sarcastic sneer. "We must not wait for her."

"But the witnesses—"

"You and I will suffice," snapped Mr. Bennet. "Continue!"

Mr. Jones blinked, but he did not protest any further. Elizabeth thought that he was too senile to understand what was truly happening, and she therefore did not hold it against him.

"Miss Elizabeth, please stand next to Mr. Collins," said Mr. Jones, gesturing toward both of the principles.

Loath though she was to even stand next to the man, Elizabeth was forced to move by her father's firm grip on her arm. Mr. Collins watched the proceedings, and he smiled at her, though she was repulsed by the naked lust in the man's eyes.

"Such modesty is becoming of a young maiden, but soon it will not be required. Your display of reluctance is charming, and my love for you is increasing each moment by leaps and bounds. How I am anticipating the joys of marital bliss!"

Elizabeth glared at him, and she heard a soft snort from Mr. Bennet, but she did not deign to respond. Elizabeth decided that all of this did not matter in the slightest. No one would believe such a travesty to be legal.

Mr. Jones soon started with the wedding passages from the Book of Common Prayer, but Elizabeth was not listening, refusing as she was to dignify the proceedings with any sort of seriousness.

As Mr. Jones droned on, Elizabeth glanced at her father out of the corner of her eye, watching as he impatiently waited for the parson to get to the point. Not for the first time, she wondered just what was motivating Mr. Bennet. While the belated desire to protect his family must be a part of it, Elizabeth knew that it could not be all. As she thought about it, she became convinced that it was more about revenge than anything else.

What a petty and selfish waste of a man her father was!

The service went on, and Elizabeth barely heard Mr. Collins make his vows. When it came time for her to do the same, she glared at the parson and refused to open her mouth.

"She does," interjected Mr. Bennet with a glare at the parson. "Move along."

For a brief moment, the parson turned his gaze upon Mr. Bennet, his eyes wide with surprise, and it appeared that he was about to protest. But his words died in his throat, as Mr. Bennet fixed him is a savage glare and enunciated quite slowly and clearly, "Finish the ceremony, Mr. Jones."

The parson jerkily nodded and continued, moments later pronouncing them man and wife. The words hit Elizabeth's soul with the force of a hammer blow, and tears began forming in her eyes. She dashed them away angrily as her new *husband* grasped her hand tugged her over to where the register waited. Mr. Collins signed it, but when he passed the quill to Elizabeth, she merely glared at him.

"Elizabeth," said Mr. Bennet in a low voice, "you will sign that document, or you will face my wrath."

Her eyes flicked to her father, and Elizabeth regarded him with cool fury through the tears which descended—whether they were tears of sorrow or of rage, she could not even determine herself. She noted that Mr. Bennet's hand was twitching, and she knew that he would not allow her to resist him, not when he had gone so far already.

Knowing that she had lost the battle—but vowing the war was still to be fought—Elizabeth snatched the quill and scrawled in the indicated space.

This was not over. She had not even begun to fight.

Chapter XVI

It was with high spirits that Darcy arose that morning and prepared for the day. Though he had at times been somewhat confused at the rapid progression of his feelings and had wondered if he was doing the right thing in offering for a penniless country miss with connections to trade, it simply felt right to be near her and to offer her his heart. And thus, he dressed in his best trousers and coat, as befitted such an auspicious day.

The life of Fitzwilliam Darcy had not been an easy one. There were undoubtedly those who would scoff at the thought that a man who was in possession of vast earthly resources should consider his life to be hard. But they did not know the true man. Possessing a naturally serious and sober disposition, Darcy had never found it easy to do many of the things that others took for granted, and he was further pressed by the fact that he had been left with a great family estate and the care of a much younger sister at the age of two and twenty. Both of these responsibilities were great ones, though in different ways, and both constituted an immense weight on his shoulders.

Even if he had not been made master of Pemberley at so young an age, Darcy would not have been one of the coxcomb dandies caught up in the web of their own selfish desires. Still, at an age when those of his acquaintance would have been engaged in hunts, house parties, balls, and other engagements, Darcy had been learning to manage his estate such that he could live up to the legacy of past Darcy masters. And though he had grown to enjoy the duties therein and to take pride over the stewardship he had inherited, there had still been times when he had wished that he was at liberty to enjoy his life a little more. It was only recently when he had begun to appear more in society, and this was only at the insistence of his uncle and aunt, the earl and countess.

As for his sister, God could not have created a gentler and more loving creature than Georgiana, and Darcy was proud of her and her accomplishments. Unfortunately, she had been cursed with a disposition even more reticent than his own, and he had at times struggled in trying to coax her from her shell. His cousin Fitzwilliam helped in that regard, as he was naturally more gregarious, but due to Colonel Fitzwilliam's duties in the army, Georgiana's care fell to Darcy more often than not.

This was one of the foremost reasons why he had been so drawn to Miss Elizabeth Bennet. She was naturally lively, yet she possessed a sense of calm confidence that he had never before encountered in a woman so young. Darcy foresaw a close and loving relationship between his younger sister and the woman he was courting, and he was confident that if anyone was able to assist Georgiana in gaining more confidence, it was Miss Elizabeth.

But he would not marry a woman simply because he thought that she would befriend his sister. There was something positively magnetic about the young woman, and he had not known her an hour before he had started to feel the pull of her attractions. She was intelligent and learned, could hold her own in any debate, played and sang like an angel, and was beautiful to round it all out. The thought of being unaffected by her charms beggared belief.

So as soon as he was at liberty—a matter of the Netherfield tenants had arisen that morning to delay his departure—he ordered his stallion saddled and made his way toward Longbourn, intent upon soliciting Mr. Bennet's permission for his courtship of Miss Elizabeth. He had no great opinion of the master of that house, but he knew that any father in England would be happy to give his daughter away to a man who possessed a reported ten thousand a year. A man of Mr. Bennet's standing and situation in the world should be falling all over himself to grant his permission.

These thoughts played in Darcy's mind as he rode up to the front of the house, where he was met by a tall stable hand who took the horse's head and steadied him while Darcy dismounted.

"I am uncertain how long I will be here," said Darcy to the man's unspoken query. "For now, please rub him down and give him a few oats to eat. I shall give you further instructions as required."

The man pressed his knuckles to his forehead and led the animal away while Darcy focused upon the house. Having been here several times, he knew that it was a modest yet comfortable house, and though it was certainly nothing to Pemberley, it was not dissimilar to those owned by some of his own neighbors in Derbyshire.

He strode forward to knock on the door, and while he waited, he noted that there was something . . . different about the house, which he could not quite place his finger on. It was nothing physical that he could detect; everything seemed to be in place, and nothing about the structure itself had changed. It was more intangible, almost as if the entire neighborhood was holding its collective breath.

A moment later, the door opened, and the elderly housekeeper stood in front of him. The moment she saw him, her face blanched, and she looked down, causing Darcy no small amount of confusion.

"Good day," said he, handing her his card and trying to ignore the ominous presentiment which was welling up within him. "Will you ask Mr. Bennet if he can spare a moment of time for me?"

The housekeeper acceded in a quiet voice and asked him to wait while she spoke with the master. While he waited in the entrance hall, he noted that no one else in the house was in evidence; the entire house was silent.

And that was when it hit him. He had been to Longbourn on several occasions, and never had he seen the place as quiet as it was that day. There were always servants bustling about, giggles from the younger girls, or the loud voice of the mistress to clutter the air and assault the ears with its tumult. This morning, however, the place was quiet as a grave. The sense of foreboding deepened and tugged at his consciousness, and he wondered what had happened.

"Mr. Darcy," called the housekeeper, interrupting him from his thoughts, "the master will see you."

Nodding in thanks, Darcy allowed himself to be led to the master's study. What he found there was not what he expected.

The last time he had entered the room, he had noted the books on every surface, the furniture, and the person of the man who inhabited the room. This time, however, the man who sat in his chair across from the weathered desk dominated Darcy's attention. He almost seemed a shell of the man Darcy had met before. His face was cast in a somber frown, and near his right hand, which trembled periodically, was a half-empty glass containing something stronger than mere port—brandy, unless Darcy missed his guess. The glass was sitting next to a tray which held several flasks of liquor, and from the bleariness of Bennet's eyes, Darcy suspected that he had been imbibing for some time, though it was still early in the day.

But it was more the hopelessness on the man's face, the absolute expression of *self-loathing* which caught his eye. This was a shell of a man, and he seemed to be shrinking at a pace which Darcy could almost see.

"Have you come with tales of phantasms and other bogeymen, Mr. Darcy?" Mr. Bennet's voice was rough with disuse—or perhaps overuse—and he peered at Darcy, eyes narrowed in sardonic amusement. But underneath Mr. Bennet's bluster, Darcy sensed the man's despair as strongly as if he had shouted it out loud. "Or are you here to report some other unfortunate in the militia who has garnered your disapproval?"

"Neither, Mr. Bennet," replied Darcy evenly. There was no particular reason to become offended by Bennet's current behavior, as Darcy was not even certain if the man was in command of his full faculties.

"Oh? The last time you came to warn me about someone, the man accosted my daughter and was subsequently shipped off to who knows where. As the militia defends us from the French, I would not have you displacing each of them with tales of wrongdoing. We might be vulnerable to invasion."

The man was testing him beyond all endurance, but despite how Bennet chose to act that morning, it would not do for Darcy to lose his temper. This was the father of the woman with whom Darcy wished to enter a courtship, and he would not antagonize the man.

"The rest of the militia is safe from me, Mr. Bennet," said Darcy, keeping his tone measured and even. "Wickham was a special case, and I could not allow him to prey upon the people of the Meryton."

Mr. Bennet snorted. "So you say." The man waved him to a nearby chair. "It appears that you have something else to say, sir, so I suggest you get comfortable. I am certain you will not mind if I have a drink." So saying, he drained the rest of his glass in one swallow.

Frowning as he took his seat, Darcy watched as Mr. Bennet reached for his brandy flask. His extended hand shook, and as he grasped the flask, the shaking became so pronounced that he almost deposited a goodly amount of the amber liquid in his lap rather than in the glass. When he finally managed to pour the sparkling liquid into the glass, he sat back in his chair, taking a healthy swig before peering at Darcy with bleary, blood-shot eyes. Eyes that were haunted, as if the legions of hell had chased him over hill and dale all night.

"Well?" said he, his tone within a hair of being overtly hostile. "Why have you come here?"

"I have come to request a courtship with Miss Elizabeth," said Darcy, deciding it was best to come to the point.

Mr. Bennet's reaction could not have surprised him more. The man's eyes suddenly focused on Darcy and widened for a moment before Bennet burst into laughter. For a moment, Darcy was affronted at the fact that this small man of limited means had the audacity to laugh at his proposal.

"Well, well, who would have thought it?" said Mr. Bennet from between gasped breaths which sounded more like sobs than laughter. "I never would have imagined that you would descend from your high horse and deign to request to court one of my daughters. But you are too late. You would have been too late had you approached me the morning after you arrived in Meryton."

"What do you mean?" asked Darcy, his affront giving away to open alarm.

"Elizabeth was married this very morning. She is on her way to Kent even as we speak, the new wife of my cousin, William Collins."

For the briefest of moments, Darcy stared at Mr. Bennet in incomprehension, but the implications of the man's words soon roared into his skull at the speed of a herd of stampeding horses, and Darcy instantly saw red.

"What?" asked he with deadly cold intent.

His tone seemed to sober Bennet, and the man looked at him, all laughter forgotten. There seemed to well within the man some forgotten measure of spirit as he stared at Darcy in a manner which could only be termed as imperious.

"She was married this very morning, Mr. Darcy. I suggest you look for another woman more suited to your position in life. Elizabeth would never have fit in with your set."

Forcing aside the anger pulsing like a torrent through his veins, Darcy glared at the older man. "Miss Elizabeth could not have consented to this."

Mr. Bennet's eyebrow rose, and rather than being angry, he appeared amused. "I suppose she told you this?"

"Does her acceptance of my request for courtship not prove it?"

With a shrug, Mr. Bennet turned back to his brandy. "It matters little. I am her father, and I decided her marriage to my cousin was in the best interest of my family. Further discussion on this is pointless."

"You would actually wish your daughter to be miserable, married to a buffoon, than happy, married to me? And have you not considered how much more I could do for your family than your heir could?"

"I have yet to see any evidence that she would be happy with you," said Mr. Bennet, ignoring Darcy's second question.

"She accepted me. I cannot imagine that she went to her fate willingly!"

"Again, it is now a moot point since she is now married."

"What did you promise your cousin, Mr. Bennet?" demanded Darcy. The man's tone and clear disregard for the happiness of his daughter incensed Darcy, and it was taking all of his willpower not to physically lash out at the man.

But Mr. Bennet simply glared at Darcy, his face screwed up in a disdainful scowl. "I must ask you to leave now, sir. This matter does not concern you." He paused, and an unpleasant smile came over his face. "She cannot have been attached to you. She never mentioned this courtship in order to save herself from marrying Collins, and in the end, she did what she was told."

For a brief moment, Darcy was taken aback. Why had she not told her father? But then reason reasserted itself. If she had not mentioned it, then it must have been because she knew it would not move her father. Besides, it was of little matter—Darcy was not about to let this go until Miss Elizabeth herself told him that he had no hope.

"This does concern me," said Darcy, rising with deadly intent. "It began to concern me the moment your daughter accepted my offer of courtship."

Directing one final glare at Mr. Bennet, Darcy turned and made his way to the door. But before he opened it, he turned back to Mr. Bennet, noting the man's unfriendly stare, which had been burning holes in his back. To say Darcy was not intimidated by the man was an understatement. If Elizabeth should wish it, he would ruin the man once he had recovered her.

"I hope you are happy with the thirty pieces of silver you received from Mr. Collins for selling your daughter to him. As a learned man, I expect you will understand the reference."

The man blanched at Darcy's words.

"It seems you are already feeling the effects of your betrayal," said Darcy with a grim smile. "May it haunt you all the days of your life."

Before Mr. Bennet could summon any retort, Darcy opened the door and stepped through it, shutting it with more force than required.

Angrier than he had ever been in his life, Darcy stalked down the hallway to the entrance, where he found the housekeeper waiting for him with his outer wear in hand. Though he could not find a smile to thank the woman, he nodded at her, and he was surprised when she spoke to him.

"Will you go after her, sir?"

Realizing that this woman was an ally who had been witness to the happenings of the morning, Darcy nodded before drawing her outside the house, where they could speak more freely.

"Miss Elizabeth accepted my courtship yesterday. I assume she did not marry Collins willingly?"

The housekeeper shook her head and began to wring her hands, her distress a palpable entity. "I am sorry, sir. I failed to protect her."

At Darcy's gentle prodding, she imparted the events of the morning, from her ill-fated attempt to smuggle Miss Elizabeth from the premises the previous night to all that had happened since then; she noted Mrs. Bennet's distress, the girls' support of their sister, and Mr. Bennet's decision to lock them in their rooms while he forced Miss Elizabeth to the church. At the end of it all, Darcy's rage, which had already been impressive, had risen to such heights that he briefly considered returning to Mr. Bennet's room and extracting some measure of payment for all Miss Elizabeth had suffered. But knowing that such actions would not help her, he suppressed the desire and turned back to Mrs. Hill.

"And was that fool Collins a party to this?"

"Only in that he married her," said Mrs. Hill with a derisive huff. "The man is so stupid that I do not doubt that the master simply used him."

Darcy nodded. It matched his own opinion of the matter.

"That dear girl does not deserve all this family has put her through over the years," said the housekeeper in a pleading tone.

Not for the first time, Darcy wondered what this great secret concerning the Bennets could possibly be. But before the thought could even coalesce, Darcy dismissed it as irrelevant. Perhaps Miss Elizabeth would give him an accounting once he found her. Until then, he would concentrate on what needed to be done.

Fixing his gaze on the housekeeper, Darcy said, "Will Mr. Bennet become angry with you for speaking to me?"

The woman scowled, but behind the expression, Darcy could see a slight flicker of fear. "It does not matter. Mr. Bennet can do as he will. I could not leave that poor girl to his mercy."

Taking the woman's words as confirmation that her position might be in jeopardy, Darcy smiled at her. "Mrs. Hill, I thank you for all you did to attempt to help Miss Elizabeth. Should you require it, you will always have a position in one of my homes. I shall speak with Bingley—if it becomes necessary, go to him, and he will see that you are well situated."

"Thank you, Mr. Darcy," said the housekeeper with a curtsey. "I will be well."

With a bow, Darcy stepped out from beneath the portico and called for his horse, already furiously making plans.

The return ride to Netherfield was accomplished quickly, though Darcy did not gallop back as was his first instinct. It was already early afternoon by the time he left Longbourn, and as the preparations for his departure would take some time, it would be next to impossible for him to arrive at Rosings that day.

Part of him wished to race off immediately and remove Miss Elizabeth from the parsonage—for to Darcy, she would *never* be Mrs. Collins. But the more rational part of him was aware that regardless of his anger at Mr. Bennet, Miss Elizabeth was, at least nominally, Mr. Collins's wife, and Darcy had no authority to simply barge into the man's house and remove the young woman. The situation had to be handled carefully.

The one thing which kept returning to Darcy's mind, however, was the thought that he might not be able to do anything about the marriage despite his suspicions that there were several irregularities to be found in how it had been accomplished. Though his mind shied away from the very thought of the idiotic Collins engaging in the marital act with *his* Elizabeth, he knew that if the man was able to consummate the marriage, then the church might very well turn a blind eye to how it had all come about.

But Darcy knew Elizabeth. He knew how strong-willed and how fierce she could be. It was the only thing which kept him from rushing off to Kent that very moment with the intent to impale the stupid man if he should so much as touch her. Darcy did not doubt that she would attempt to avoid Collins that night, and if she had no other recourse, she could simply refuse to allow him into her bed. And Darcy was certain that Collins—a man who looked to others to direct him in all things—was not the sort to force the issue. If Elizabeth refused him, then he would no doubt be angry, but whatever else he was, he was not violent. Lady Catherine would not employ a man with any history of such behavior.

It was with these thoughts that Darcy at length made his way to the front drive of Netherfield. After arriving at the front entrance, he passed the reins off to a hostler and issued instructions that his carriage should be readied for immediate departure. Darcy then entered the house, intent upon finding its master.

What he found instead was the master's sister.

"Mr. Darcy, we had quite despaired of your return!"

Never before had Bingley's sister grated on his nerves as she did at that moment. Her high-pitched simpering beat at his ears like the cries of a score of loud crows, and the cloying scent she used had him irrationally wishing he could bathe and have his clothes thoroughly laundered to remove the stench. He had no time to deal with the woman now.

"I am sorry, Miss Bingley, but a matter has arisen which demands my attention. I must prepare to depart."

An expression of horror fell over Miss Bingley's face. "Leave?" cried she. "But Mr. Darcy, you have only been here for a month. We expected you to stay for two." She walked toward him with a smile in a manner which she obviously considered seductive. "Surely this matter may be concluded through correspondence."

Only years of conducting himself in a proper manner prevented Darcy from snapping at the woman. "I will leave immediately, Miss Bingley. I apologize for any inconvenience this might cause you."

With that, he turned and stalked off toward his rooms without a glance back in her direction, though not without a quick word to the butler to have his valet summoned and to inform Bingley of his imminent departure.

It was a mere thirty minutes later when Darcy arrived in Bingley's study. His emotions were a mass of competing thoughts and feelings, and several times, he had had to restrain himself from rushing off as had been his instinct all along. Though he could not state such with a certainty, Darcy thought that he was in love with Miss Elizabeth, and the idea of her being left to Collins's mercy was almost more than he could bear.

But he fancied himself a good judge of character, and he believed that Miss Elizabeth was as enamored of him as he was of her. Barging in without proper consideration could easily give rise to rumors which would be damaging to both of them, so Darcy had made the decision to trust in her. He would join her in Kent and begin to work on having the marriage annulled; there was little else to be done.

The hall in the vicinity of Bingley's study was quiet, but as Darcy traversed it, he thought he saw a swirl of skirts and caught a whiff of a sickeningly sweet scent drifting upon the air. With a scowl, he ignored it. Miss Bingley was nearby, undoubtedly hoping to gain some intelligence concerning his early departure. She would not receive it; she would learn the particulars in due time, but it would not be from him.

Permission to enter the room was granted, and Darcy let himself in, taking care to ensure the door was closed behind him. As it was made of thick, sturdy oak, he doubted that Miss Bingley would be able to hear anything through it.

The room was not as handsome as Darcy's office in Pemberley, but of course, the entire building was not the equal of his own estate. Still, it contained a sturdy desk situated before a large windowed wall, and it gave an impression of solidity and constancy. The desk itself was littered with papers—not unlike Mr. Bennet's had been, thought Darcy, his mind following incongruous paths—which bespoke the occupant's naturally disorganized nature. Darcy had to suppress a smile; he had despaired of ever inducing Bingley to be more organized, and as the man seemed to be able to find anything he needed with minimal fuss, he supposed that it worked for Bingley, though it would drive Darcy himself to distraction.

Bingley was pacing the room, clearly agitated and worried. Darcy's sudden departure must have caused him to assume that something serious had occurred. He would be correct, though Bingley could not have conjectured the truth of the matter.

"Darcy," exclaimed Bingley as he entered the room. "What is this I hear about you departing early? I hope your family is all well."

"They are indeed well, I thank you."

"Then why the rush to leave?"

This time, it was Darcy's turn to pace, as he was uncertain how to address the matter with his friend. In the end, he decided simply to be blunt.

"I asked Miss Elizabeth for a courtship, Bingley."

A smile of delight broke out on Bingley's amiable face, for which Darcy was grateful; he knew his friend had the highest opinion of Miss Elizabeth.

"I cannot but congratulate you, man," said Bingley. "She is a jewel, to be sure." His smile was soon replaced with a frown. "Then why the sudden need to depart? Have you spoken with her father?"

"After a fashion, Bingley," said Darcy, the scowl he had worn after departing Longbourn returning easily to his countenance. "I must leave because in asking for Mr. Bennet's permission, I learned that he had forced her to marry his cousin."

Bingley's jaw dropped, and he gaped at Darcy. "Forced her to marry him? When he had your offer before him? I must own to being completely at sea, Darcy. How could this have come about?"

Forcing himself to remain calm, Darcy recounted the events of the morning, including what he had witnessed himself and what the housekeeper had told him. Once he had finished his tale, he noted that Bingley had become almost green at the implications of Darcy's communications. Darcy believed that Miss Elizabeth had been singled out for this treatment from her father, but if Mr. Bennet was capable of forcing one daughter to marry against her will, then he would almost certainly be capable of doing the same to any other of his daughters. Such a thought no doubt passed Bingley's mind as well.

"Is the man mad?" cried Bingley. "I know a father has control over his children until they become of age, but this is completely incomprehensible!"

"I know. And I shall see it annulled if it is the last thing I do."

Caught up as he was in his own worries, Bingley clearly had not considered the effect on Darcy, nor had he considered the reason for Darcy's departure.

"I apologize for focusing on my own thoughts, Darcy. But surely you cannot think that an annulment will be granted. Annulments are very rare indeed, as I am certain you well know."

"I am," said Darcy. "But consider what we know about this marriage. Mr. Bennet forced his daughter to be married in front of a priest. The housekeeper testified that the bride was unwilling. I suspect her sisters would confirm it, should they be canvassed. In addition, were the banns read? We have been in church these past weeks, and the curate has never announced such a thing. And has Mr. Bennet obtained a special license? Though I cannot be certain, I very much doubt it.

"When you add it all up, this entire event contains so many irregularities that it might as well be considered a farce. I intend to discover exactly what has happened and petition the church to put the marriage aside."

Bingley nodded slowly. "Have you approached the parson?"

Darcy shook his head. "I was rather preoccupied when I left Longbourn and thought only of returning to Netherfield. I will let the church handle it; I am certain they will send someone to investigate when I bring it to their attention.

A knock sounded at the door, and rather than granting permission, Bingley approached the door and opened it himself, revealing the butler and an agitated Miss Bingley.

"Sir, a note has just arrived for Mr. Darcy."

"I told Mr. Colford that I would see that it was delivered to Mr. Darcy, but he would not give it to me," said a clearly vexed Miss Bingley.

Eyes narrowing, Darcy glared at Miss Bingley, certain that she had intended to pry into his correspondence.

The butler did not appear ruffled. He simply offered the letter to Darcy and said, "The instructions were very clear. The letter was to be delivered to none other than Mr. Darcy himself."

"Thank you, Colford," said Darcy, accepting the letter.

The butler bowed and departed from the room, Bingley closing the door behind him before an obviously upset Miss Bingley could enter. Darcy decided that it was not worth making an issue of her behavior; Bingley would control his sister, or he would not. Darcy would not have anything to do with the woman, so it signified little.

Looking down at the letter, Darcy noted that it was simply addressed to him in a feminine hand. He glanced up at Bingley, noting his friend's interest, and broke the seal, opening the letter and noting that it contained one page written in a delicate script.

Mr. Darcy,

I beg you will forgive the impertinence of my writing to you, but as events this morning spiraled out of control more quickly than any of us could have imagined, I found myself almost literally in shock due to the unfeeling actions and implacable will of my father. I was not informed of your visit until after your departure and was thus unable to pass the message with which my sister charged me. Thus, I determined to write a letter to you, trusting Mrs. Hill to ensure that it is placed in your hands.

My sister has not confided in me, yet given her words this morning, I suspect that something has happened between you which makes my sister's situation that much more desperate. I cannot imagine what you must be feeling at present if my suspicions are at all correct. But before my father dragged my sister off to the church this morning, she charged me most to inform you that she did not go of her own free will. How my father could possibly behave in this manner, I cannot fathom. But Elizabeth was not a party to it, and she fought it until the very end.

Please forgive Elizabeth, as she is blameless in this matter, just as she has been blameless for the misfortunes which have befallen my family. My parents to this day continue to lay the fault at her door, but since she was naught but a small child at the time, I cannot hold her accountable. Perhaps I have said too much, but I wished you to know that I do not doubt that whatever regard you had for my sister was returned in full measure, little though anything can be done concerning it now.

Please think on my sister fondly, Mr. Darcy.

God bless you,
Jane Bennet

"Well, what does it say?" prompted Bingley once Darcy had perused the letter at least twice.

Not trusting himself to speak, Darcy merely offered him the letter, which Bingley took and began to read. It was only a moment before he looked up.

"It appears Caroline was right," said he in a soft tone. "There does appear to be some great mystery concerning Miss Elizabeth."

"I suggest you control your sister, Bingley," said Darcy. "She should not speak so, especially given what Miss Bennet has now told us in confidence. I do not doubt that the rumormongers would be merciless should any hint of this get out."

Bingley nodded. "I will handle Caroline. I assume this does not change your plans?"

"Not in the slightest. In fact, it only spurs me on. I cannot imagine anything more powerful than the testimony of her older sister."

Extending his hand, Bingley returned the letter to Darcy, who folded it and secured it in his coat pocket. It was a boon to have the housekeeper's words confirmed by the testimony of Miss Bennet, but Darcy would still approach the situation with caution. He now trusted, more than ever, that Miss Elizabeth would never submit to Collins. That allowed Darcy to be a little more deliberate in making his way to Kent.

Turning his attention back on Bingley, Darcy noted that his friend was focused inward, a frown of concentration fixed upon his countenance. It was so unlike Bingley. He was gregarious and happy most of the time, though he could be sober and deliberate when required. He was also of a rather impetuous disposition, and Darcy thought that this natural impulsiveness might be of benefit in his own situation with Miss Bennet.

"I must depart, Bingley," said Darcy, drawing his friend's attention. "But before I go, I thought to advise you that if you are decided on Miss Bennet, that you had best move forward with alacrity."

A more typical expression appeared on Bingley's face, and he replied, "I would have thought you would warn me away from so strange a family."

"It would be a little hypocritical of me, do you not think? I have every intention of seeing Miss Elizabeth's sham of a marriage annulled and then making her my own wife." Darcy frowned. "I doubt we will ever have anything to do with her parents, however, and I have no doubt that she would not wish to in any case."

Bingley sobered. "I believe I know enough of your implacable resentment to understand you capable of that, my friend."

"Then I must depart." Darcy directed a pointed look at his friend. "Miss Bennet is a gem, Bingley. Do not let her escape."

Nodding, Bingley stepped forward and clasped his hand in a firm grip. "Then we shall be brothers, Darcy. I wish you well."

With that, Darcy departed. As he was leaving, he caught a glimpse of Miss Bingley as she descended upon Bingley, undoubtedly eager to pry any information she could glean concerning Darcy's departure and the letter he had received. But Darcy turned his mind to other thoughts. He must decide how to approach the situation and, more importantly, how to extricate the woman he intended to marry from her predicament.

The journey to Kent was miserable for Elizabeth. As if it were not terrible enough to be forced to leave Longbourn in the company of Mr. Collins, the carriage they used belonged to her father. Clearly, Mr. Bennet had offered it up in an effort to remove the "newlyweds" from Hertfordshire as quickly as possible. Elizabeth thought it cowardly of him, and it did not assist in softening her hard feelings for the man; of course, it was likely impossible for anything to do that at this point.

Some hours later, they arrived in London, where Mr. Collins arranged for a hired carriage—again, she suspected it was done at her father's expense—for the final leg of the journey into Hunsford. The family carriage was to return to Longbourn, where Elizabeth would have hoped the conveyance rotted and burned if it had not been for her concern for the safety of at least a few of her sisters.

Throughout all that miserable day, Elizabeth could not help but be amazed at Mr. Collins and his inexplicable inability to see what was right in front of his eyes. She was not certain whether to attribute it to abject stupidity or willful blindness but concluded that it was likely a mixture of the two.

"We are finally alone, my love," Mr. Collins had said when the carriage first lurched into motion and began to leave Longbourn behind. "I dare say you have been longing for this moment as much as I."

He had attempted to sidle up to her and draw her close to him, but Elizabeth had been quick in moving to the other side of the carriage, though she refused to make any verbal response.

But her actions had not deterred Mr. Collins; indeed, nothing had seemed to affect his equilibrium or his good spirits.

"Ah, your feminine delicacy is truly something to be admired! I shall respect it, knowing that the day can only end in one manner." The disgusting leer which accompanied his statement, not to mention the lascivious manner in which his eyes raked over her form, had made Elizabeth feel unclean, but she had resisted saying anything, determined to remain silent. If only she could induce him to do likewise!

Unfortunately, Elizabeth was not naïve enough to believe that she could ever induce him to silence. Instead, the man kept up an unending monologue the entire length of their journey, speaking on such disparate topics as the state of the roads and the countryside in which they travelled. The random comments concerning his lady patroness with which he interspersed such subjects did nothing but make the monotony of the road seem even more pronounced.

By the time they arrived at Hunsford, the daylight was waning. There were only a few servants at the parsonage, but they had gathered together at the return of the master and were waiting in the drive to the house as the carriage pulled up.

The parsonage itself was a handsome building, and for once, Elizabeth thought that the man's overweening sense of pride might actually be somewhat warranted. It was a two-story house, seemingly quaint and comfortable, and it was situated in the midst of several strands of woods, with the fields of the great estate it served on the other side of the road. If Elizabeth looked around toward the back of the house, she could see signs of a small park which undoubtedly contained gardens and perhaps even some small area in which to indulge in a morning stroll. The entrance was protected by a small portico, and the door appeared to be made of the same solid English oak which typically decorated the doors of most houses in the country.

In other circumstances, Elizabeth thought that she would have been very comfortable there indeed.

Mr. Collins stepped out of the carriage, and though Elizabeth considered refusing to alight, she decided it would serve no purpose. Therefore, she stepped down and stood in the gravel, though she did reject the parson's hand when it was raised to assist her.

"Mrs. Collins," began Mr. Collins in a grandiose tone, "welcome to your new abode. I trust that you will find our home to be comfortable and convenient, and I would count it a most sensible mark of your foresight if you should call on Lady Catherine de Bourgh regarding anything of which you are unsure, for she has the most particular experience and will direct you in everything in which you stand in need."

"Perhaps you should introduce me to the servants, Mr. Collins," said Elizabeth, not wishing to allow him to become lost in the raptures of lauding his patroness.

"Of course, my dear."

The servants, which consisted of a pair of maids, a manservant, and the cook—the last of whom was a woman of the village employed to come to the parsonage and prepare Mr. Collins's meals—all welcomed their new mistress, and though Elizabeth could not call her mood the best, she attempted to be kind to them. Having the servants' support could only be beneficial, and she did not wish to antagonize them.

When the introductions were out of the way, Mr. Collins dismissed the servants to go about their various tasks, instructing the cook to have the dinner meal delivered to the table within the next hour. He then proceeded to lead Elizabeth into the house, taking the opportunity to display his house with all the silliness she had come to expect of him. Just as he had exclaimed over every item that his eyes fell across at Longbourn, so he described in minute detail every chair, couch, and book which they came upon, clearly trying to impress her with the comfort of his situation. Elizabeth, of course, could only gape at the insensitivity of his actions.

"Mr. Collins, should we not prepare for dinner?" asked Elizabeth once his effusions had sapped her patience to the point where she could not remain silent any longer.

Gaping at her as if astonished by the fact that she would interrupt his monologue, his ruddy face began to take on a scowl, so Elizabeth again spoke up:

"You did request dinner for an hour after our arrival, did you not? By my count, we are rapidly approaching that time."

"Of course, you are correct, my dear," said Mr. Collins. "How clever of you to remember."

"In that case, I shall retire to my room and change," said Elizabeth. With a swirl of her skirts, she turned and left him, catching a glimpse of his surprise that she would summarily dismiss him.

Finding that her belongings had been placed in the master's room, Elizabeth immediately commissioned the manservant to move them to the next bedchamber, which the man did without comment, though his eyes bespoke his surprise. Elizabeth ignored it; she wished for the servants' good will, but she would obtain that by treating them with kindness and respect. If she could induce their loyalty, perhaps she could also induce them to refrain from gossip.

Though Elizabeth thought to simply refuse to go to dinner with the man, she knew that until she was able to extricate herself from his house, she would have to continue to act in a cordial manner. Thus, with the help of one of the maids, she removed her gray dress and changed into a plain evening gown, cursing Mr. Collins for having blathered on so long that she had no time to bathe the dust of the road from her body.

"Would you like your hair done up again?" asked the maid who was assisting her.

Elizabeth regarded herself in the looking glass, and after deciding that she was presentable—and that she had no wish to appear to best advantage in front of the man with whom she would be dining—she declined. "It shall do."

Though the maid appeared perplexed, she made no comment. "Shall you require my services afterward?"

Turning, Elizabeth smiled at the girl, who appeared only a few years older than she was. "I am sorry, but I do not remember your name?"

"Jessica, madam."

"Thank you, Jessica. I appreciate your assistance. Would it be possible for bath water to be drawn so that I may wash after dinner?"

The maid smiled. "I believe so, Mrs. Collins. I will inform Tom, the manservant. It will be ready by the time you have returned."

"Thank you, Jessica," said Elizabeth, grasping the girl's hands in thanks. It was irksome to be addressed with the odious man's name, but Elizabeth decided that she would not ask be addressed otherwise. If she was able to escape, there would be enough gossip as it was. She did not wish to increase it by asking the girl to call her by name.

Mr. Collins was waiting in the dining parlor, and he greeted her in his typical way when she arrived:

"Mrs. Collins, you are indeed a vision of loveliness tonight. I count myself the most fortunate of men, for I believe that Lady Catherine herself would pronounce you more than handsome enough to adorn the arm of her parson. I welcome you to dinner on the first night of our married lives." Mr. Collins bowed low.

"But before we begin, I have a matter I would discuss with you." Mr. Collins paused and looked at her with an expression which was unusually grave. "I noted that your belongings had been moved from our bedchamber into one of the guest chambers. Surely you do not mean to sleep in separate beds."

"Is that not what is normally done, Mr. Collins?" asked Elizabeth. "You *are* aware that most gentlemen sleep in different chambers from their wives. I assumed you would want to be fashionable since you will eventually join the ranks of landed gentlemen."

It was several moments before Mr. Collins's confusion and displeasure changed to pensiveness. "Indeed, I had not considered the matter. Of course, you are correct. And I suppose that, having lived in your own room for many years, you would be eager to retain your own chamber. How intelligent of you to have thought of it!"

"Thank you, Mr. Collins," said Elizabeth, ruthlessly suppressing any show of amusement.

"I suppose it shall not be any great impediment. After all, the doors to our respective chambers are a matter of a few feet apart. The distance is negligible!"

"A happy thought, indeed," murmured Elizabeth.

With a great show of solicitousness, Mr. Collins pulled her chair out and saw her seated before taking his own seat, all the while a vacuous grin of anticipation engraved upon his face.

At his signal, the servant brought in the meal, and the two began to dine.

To be more correct, Mr. Collins began to stuff food in his mouth as was his wont, while Elizabeth, nervous and wondering how she could avoid her married duties, was able to eat only a few bites.

"This is a banquet fit for a king!" enthused Mr. Collins as he savored each morsel. "I must thank Lady Catherine on the morrow for insisting upon just what the menu would consist of this night."

Elizabeth shook her head with a grim frown upon her face which she ensured was unseen by the parson. She might not have bothered, for all the attention the man was paying her.

"And her ladyship also suggested this particular vintage of wine," continued the parson as he grasped the bottle sitting on the table and presented it for her to look at. "She was most insistent that this particular vintage would be helpful in setting the mood for our activities later tonight. 'Mr. Collins,' said she, 'you must be very solicitous of your wife on your first night with her. The proper vintage will allow her to relax and ease her worries of the unknown. As the daughter of a gentleman, she will have been given little instruction of what passes between man and woman once they are joined in holy matrimony.'"

It was true that the parson delivered her ladyship's words in his typical pompous manner, but Elizabeth thought that his patroness's words actually appeared to contain a modicum of sense for once. As a sheltered young woman, Elizabeth had only a basic understanding of the marriage act, and she imagined she would be nervous even if this was a true marriage with a man she trusted and loved.

But these thoughts passed through her mind in moments, as her attention was caught by the bottle of wine which Mr. Collins was brandishing as if it was a spear. The liquid eddied about in the bottle, its deep red color seeming almost the color of blood to Elizabeth in her heightened sense of alarm. But it also seemed to represent her salvation on that night.

For the next hour as they ate, Mr. Collins kept up a steady monologue about anything which came to his mind. As always, his comments centered heavily on his patroness, but he also spoke concerning his situation, the people Elizabeth would meet, and the happy situation of the parsonage, interspersing all this with his expectations of how she would come to appreciate her position and be of use to the people whose welfare he oversaw.

Elizabeth was not as annoyed by the sound of his voice as she normally would be, for as Mr. Collins droned on, he consumed vast amounts of food and, with it, the wine in the bottle. He never noticed that Elizabeth did not drink a drop of the liquid. He also did not notice that whenever the amount in his glass ebbed, Elizabeth would refill it, making certain to ensure that he was never without a steady supply of the red liquid.

Though she would not have thought it possible, either Mr. Collins was less able to hold his drink than she would have thought, or the vintage he had procured was far more potent than Elizabeth would have suspected. For as he ate, his words slowed and slurred, and in the end, his head dropped to the table. Before long, a loud snore rent the air and assaulted her ears.

Rising from her seat, Elizabeth considered the man, wondering if she should have the manservant haul him off to his bed or leave him there to snore beside the remains of his beef and potatoes. And though she would rather do nothing at all, she decided that it would not do for a new wife to show so little consideration for her husband.

But she would not help him herself. He deserved no such consideration from her. So she left him there, returning to her room and the bath which awaited her, grateful that she had been successful in putting the man off. Now she had only to figure out how to do it until she was able to make her escape.

Chapter XVII

The next morning, Elizabeth stirred from her sleep after a fitful night to hear the chatting of birds and the blowing of the breeze outside the window of the bedroom. The house was quiet and still, and though she was well aware of where she was the instant she awoke, she could almost imagine that she was back in her uncle's house and that at any moment her aunt would enter the room and lovingly awake her from her slumber. Would that it was true and not simply fantasy.

With these pleasant thoughts, she opened her eyes, noting that it was still early. Due to the lateness of the season, the sun had not yet arisen, though its rays had begun to lighten the late gray November sky. As the sky lightened, Elizabeth considered her situation. The previous evening, she had been able to manage Collins with almost laughable ease, but she knew it would not always be so. The man was a fool, but though he might be convinced of her eagerness in the confines of his own small mind, Elizabeth knew the longer she demurred, the more suspicious he would become. While she was by no means bereft of thoughts on how to avoid the man, not much time would pass before she would either have to leave or affect an annulment.

Much, she decided, depended on Mr. Darcy, the man who should even now be in the business of courting her. Elizabeth was almost certain Mr. Darcy would follow her to Kent. She based this belief on her certainty that he was not only in love with her, but that he would also not take kindly to being defeated by a man such as Collins. Male bravado could be a powerful ally for her. And though Elizabeth truly felt that Mr. Darcy was the man with whom she would be happy spending the rest of her life, she was not ungrateful for the thought that defeating her father's scheming might be a prime motivating factor in Mr. Darcy's actions.

If Mr. Darcy eschewed any further contact, then she would need to move on her own. She was confident that she could obtain an annulment when the full facts of her father's actions became known, but the trouble would be in gaining an audience before someone who would be able to take the steps that she, as a woman, could not. She had an idea or two about how to do this, and if Mr. Darcy did not come soon, then she would put them into motion without him.

Such actions would not be necessary, she decided as she threw back the counterpane and sat up in her bed. She was certain he would come. The thought of how she had last seen him, his hair blowing in the wind as he stood beside his large stallion and watched her as she returned to Longbourn—that look was not one which a man gave to a woman in whom he had a merely slight inclination. Mr. Darcy would come. Elizabeth would only be required to maintain her patience until he was able to arrive.

Sighing with regret at her predicament, Elizabeth rose and dressed herself, tying her hair back in a simple knot. She decided to go outside to take a quick walk through the park around the house. Though the sun had not risen over the horizon and the air was a little cool from the wind, Elizabeth found herself invigorated by the exercise and determined that she would do this every morning, if only to allow her some time away from the detested parson.

Finally, as the sun broke over the line of trees to the west, Elizabeth stood and faced it, watching its rise. The magnificent sight of the rise of the fiery orb as it cast its rays upon the land below like a lover's kiss inspired her, and for a brief moment it helped her to forget her current situation and enjoy the varied wonders of nature.

It was much later by the time Elizabeth made her way inside, as she had found a bench and sat gazing at her surroundings for some time in wonder. She had to acknowledge Mr. Collins lived in a beautiful locale.

When she finally returned to the house, it was to a sight which was so comical that she had to put a hand in front of her mouth to stifle a snicker from escaping. There, in the entrance, stood the heavyset form of her husband.

Mr. Collins was obviously not well that morning, as his bloodshot eyes, the wet cloth he held to his forehead, and his frequent moans of pain would attest. Elizabeth felt not one iota of sympathy for the man; he had received much less than he deserved, she was certain.

"Mrs. Collins," said he as soon as he espied her entering the house, "I must . . . That is to say, I feel ashamed . . . I cannot apologize enough for my behavior last night, madam."

"In what way, Mr. Collins?" said Elizabeth as she took off her gloves and handed her pelisse to one of the maids who attended her.

"Why, for neglecting you!" cried the parson, though he immediately moaned due to the pain which the outburst had caused in his throbbing head.

"Perhaps we should take this to a more private setting," suggested Elizabeth. Without waiting for a reply, she turned and began to walk toward the dining room, where she was followed by Mr. Collins's muted words: "Indeed, you are correct, my dear."

Privately, Elizabeth could not imagine that such a dullard as William Collins could possibly exist, and she might never have believed it had she not had the proof of the man shuffling behind her.

Upon entering the dining room, Elizabeth took her seat and began to spoon breakfast items on her plate, noting with distaste that Mr. Collins apparently preferred the same type of heavy breakfast foods as her family. Shaking her head, Elizabeth made a note to herself to speak with the cook to order some of the lighter fare that was her preference. She was, at least for now, mistress of the parsonage, and she saw no reason why she should have to suffer through the kind of meals which made William Collins so rotund.

At the head of the table, her husband eased into his chair, wincing at the movement and the sound of her utensils clinking against the dishes. It was only after a moment's consideration that Elizabeth refrained from deliberately making more of a racket, deciding that she had already compromised enough of her principles. She would not be deliberately cruel, regardless of how much the man in question deserved it.

"As I was saying," said Mr. Collins, pressing the wet cloth tightly onto his forehead, "I must apologize for the manner in which I over-imbibed last night. At the time, I had no idea how much wine I was consuming, I assure you."

"You did not?" asked Elizabeth, though inwardly she was laughing at the man's absurdity.

"I assure you, no. I have often found that the pleasure one feels at the moment of imbibing can in no way compensate for the effects one is subjected to afterward. Furthermore, Lady Catherine herself has seen fit to instruct me on the matter. In her usual condescending way, she explained that over-indulgence is for the lower masses, stating that those of us who inhabit a higher plane must of a necessity behave in such a manner as to display our superiority. If we do not, then we are no better than those over whom we have authority. I have never before behaved in such a manner, I must assure you in a most animated fashion."

Those words confirmed all of Elizabeth's suspicions. Lady Catherine was a nosy busybody who considered herself to be above all others. Elizabeth already knew exactly what manner of woman she would be introduced to, and she suspected that she would be meeting the woman before much time had passed.

"But what I most regret, my dear Elizabeth," continued Mr. Collins, "is that I have disappointed you. I certainly never imagined that my wedding night would proceed in such a fashion, and I am certain that you are of like mind. I must give you my most abject apology for offending and upsetting your delicate sensibilities."

Elizabeth stifled a giggle into her hand and turned to Mr. Collins. "I am not at all offended, sir, nor am I disappointed. The wedding night proceeded in a most agreeable fashion, as I am both rested and comfortable."

"You are universally charming!" cried Mr. Collins, reaching out for her hand and, grasping it clumsily, depositing a sloppy kiss on its back.

Elizabeth glared at him and snatched her hand away, rubbing at it with her handkerchief.

"I promise you that I shall not behave thus in the future." A smile of anticipation came over the man's face. "In fact, since I believe that I shall be recovered by this evening, we may start anew as soon as may be."

Watching him coolly, Elizabeth replied, "There is no need to concern yourself with me, Mr. Collins. I assure you that I am quite content.

"In fact, I have heard that wine is very beneficial. Perhaps you should take to drinking it every night with dinner for the purpose of improving your health."

Though Mr. Collins was clearly perplexed by her observation, he shook his head, producing another wince which was calmed by his damp cloth. "I assure you that I have no desire to do so. Not only am I bound to do as my patroness instructs, I am also greatly anticipating our connubial bliss. I am certain we shall be very happy together."

Mr. Collins continued to preach on his expectations for their union, though he did so in between winces whenever he unintentionally became more animated. The drone of his voice began to fade into the background as Elizabeth contemplated some of the measures she could take to discourage his amorous advances. Perhaps she should ensure to have wine at the table every night; he might not be fooled into drinking too much again, but at least she would have a bottle handy which she could break over his thick head should nothing else cool his ardor. She doubted even Mr. Collins could mistake such a blatant act for anything other than her disinclination to allow her *husband* his *connubial bliss*. At least, however, it would gain her another night free from his advances.

The expected visit from Mr. Collins's patroness came that morning, almost too early for normal visiting hours. Given what she had heard of the woman, Elizabeth suspected that Lady Catherine did not believe that the rules of polite society applied to her. Her subsequent behavior proved that fact.

She was a large woman, tall and slender, standing nearly a head taller than Elizabeth herself. Though disposed to be critical of the lady, Elizabeth was forced to acknowledge that Lady Catherine had likely been a handsome woman in her youth, though her weathered features and hair—which was gray peppered with black—indicated that the lady was likely well into her sixth or seventh decade. She was also every bit the imperious noble Elizabeth had expected her to be, observing her surroundings with a haughty and critical eye. Lady Catherine had not been in the house for a minute before she berated a nearby maid for some imagined deficiency. Once she had seen to that task—seeming indifferent to what she had just done—she sat in the high-backed chair situated at the end of the low table in the sitting room. Elizabeth and Collins sat on a sofa immediately to her right, and the lady soon proceeded to study Elizabeth. Lady Catherine's expression almost seemed to indicate that she was a queen being forced to entertain the lowliest milkmaid in her kingdom.

"So this is the new Mrs. Collins," said Lady Catherine after a few moments. "In truth, I had doubted your reports of the handsomeness of your cousin's daughters. I must own, however, that she appears to be a pretty sort of girl."

"Indeed, she is, your ladyship, and I am not indifferent to my good fortune in securing such a handsome bride. In fact, if I may say so—"

"I understand that you are one among five daughters," interrupted Lady Catherine. As she did so, Mr. Collins immediately ceased what he was saying and put a hand to his mouth.

Elizabeth, though she was amused and disgusted at the same time, could only respond in the affirmative. "I am the second of five sisters, Lady Catherine."

"All as handsome as—"

Again, Lady Catherine cut the parson off. "And you have been living with your uncle in London, Mrs. Collins?"

"I have, your ladyship," replied Elizabeth.

"You would do well to remember this piece of advice, Mr. Collins," said Lady Catherine, turning to the parson, who was listening intently. "This estate you are set to inherit is not able to support so many children as the Bennets have produced. I would suggest you have only the minimum of children in order to better support your family. The requisite heir and perhaps another boy should do nicely."

"As always, your advice is timely and wise, your ladyship," said Mr. Collins, his attitude that of one who was caught in the throes of ecstasy. "We shall take care to produce only male children, in accordance with your most excellent direction."

It was all Elizabeth could do not to shake her head at the parson's stupidity. But nothing showed on Lady Catherine's face to suggest a similar frame of mind, and the considering expression she had worn since she had arrived had not changed one iota. Elizabeth felt like a side of pork being examined to determine whether it was worth purchasing.

"And you, Mrs. Collins. Since you have lived with your aunt, can I assume you have been instructed in the proper way to manage a house? I will not stand for the wife of my parson executing her duties in anything less than the proper and most exacting fashion. I assure you that I am very attentive to such a thing."

Taking a deep breath and reminding herself that she would not be required to deal with this harridan for long if all went as she hoped, Elizabeth answered, "My aunt was diligent in ensuring that I was given the proper instruction. She shared the task of managing her home once I became old enough to be involved. I assure you that I am more than capable of managing the parsonage, Lady Catherine."

"More than capable, indeed," said Mr. Collins. "I assure you, your ladyship, that as per your most exacting and explicit instruction, I would never choose for my wife a woman who could not manage my house. My wife shall be diligent in following your most excellent advice to the very letter."

Lady Catherine turned to look on Mr. Collins, and though her expression did not waver in the slightest, Elizabeth had the distinct impression that she was exasperated with his frequent interruptions. It was a suspicion which appeared to be shared by Mr. Collins, as he fairly wilted under the great lady's stare, as evinced by his sudden inability to look at her and his increased mopping of his brow.

"Mr. Collins, I believe it is time for you to begin working on your sermon for this Sunday's service. Perhaps you should retire to your bookroom in order to do so."

His mouth agape, Mr. Collins stared at his patroness before glancing at Elizabeth. Elizabeth had to acknowledge that perhaps the lady was not quite as senseless as she would have thought.

Mr. Collins turned back to Lady Catherine when it was clear that his wordless plea would not be answered and said, "Your ladyship, perhaps I should remain while you instruct my wife, so that I may ensure that your directives are being carried out properly."

"Now, Mr. Collins!" said the lady imperiously.

Mr. Collins stood and fairly scurried from the room, his brief defiance dying an unceremonious death in the face of Lady Catherine's command. Of course, he was not able to depart without bowing and scraping as he sidled along. It took a full minute—and a clearing of Lady Catherine's throat—before the door finally closed behind him.

Though unaware of what the lady specifically wished to discuss with her, Elizabeth was at the very least grateful for the fact that Mr. Collins was no longer nearby.

"Mrs. Collins," said Lady Catherine as soon as the parson had quit the room, "may I speak frankly?"

Intrigued, Elizabeth indicated that she would take no offense.

"You seem like an intelligent young woman. Pray, what is your age?"

Though it was an impertinent question, Elizabeth decided that there was no point in refusing to answer. "I am not yet twenty, your ladyship."

The lady nodded slowly. "I had expected Mr. Collins to choose your eldest sister. She should have been the first to be wed unless she was already promised to another."

Elizabeth had no desire to discuss the details of her father's betrayal. "Jane is not promised, but a young man recently moved into the neighborhood and has fixed his attentions upon her."

"Then this young man had precedence, and as your father had an abundance of daughters to offer, he was not required to redirect his eldest daughter's attentions."

Lady Catherine paused and seemed to consider Elizabeth for a moment before she spoke yet again. "As we agreed, I shall speak frankly. You seem to be an intelligent young woman. I believe you cannot have missed your husband's less than stellar intellect."

Surprised though she was that Lady Catherine would refer to the man in so blunt a manner, Elizabeth could only agree with the woman's opinion.

"He shall require constant supervision, Mrs. Collins. You must be the one to provide it."

Incredulous at the suggestion that she must be her so-called husband's keeper, Elizabeth gaped at the woman. "You wish for *me* to supervise Mr. Collins?"

"Are you not his wife? Yes, I do indeed expect you to take on that responsibility. I have too many people within my purview to continually devote myself to preventing Mr. Collins from making a fool out of himself. It is one of the reasons I encouraged him to find a wife."

Elizabeth could not believe what she was hearing. Lady Catherine knew that she had given the living to a man of mean understanding and little social grace, and she expected his new — and unwilling! — wife to bear the responsibility of making him respectable. Needless to say, Elizabeth was little inclined to blunt William Collins's incompetence when in company.

Of course, it would not be prudent to state such to the lady in question. Elizabeth was very aware of the fact that a living could not be taken away without extraordinary circumstances, and she was certain that foolishness did not fall under that contingency. But while Lady Catherine could not force Mr. Collins from the parsonage, she had the ability to make his life truly uncomfortable and, more importantly, the ability to make Elizabeth even more miserable than she already was. She would not mind William Collins as if he was her child, but she would not purposely alienate Lady Catherine either.

Luckily, the lady did not seem to require a response and seemed to take Elizabeth's concurrence as inevitable. "Furthermore, I expect you to be an active and useful sort of person. As the people within the parish have been without a parson's wife for several years now, they will benefit from your assistance. You will extend it and become known in the neighborhood as soon as may be."

"Yes, your ladyship," replied Elizabeth. In this instance, she had no reason to oppose Lady Catherine's will. Helping the people of the area was something she would do without question. Not only would it take her away from Mr. Collins, it would fill her time, and it was only proper.

If Elizabeth had thought her instruction to be over, she was sadly mistaken, as Lady Catherine had only begun to speak. The lady spent most of the morning in the parsonage's parlor, discussing with Elizabeth exactly how she was expected to behave, how she was expected to manage the parsonage, and when she was expected to approach Lady Catherine for her opinion. The subjects were wide-ranging and covered such topics as how much meat to purchase for consumption, the exact number of chickens Elizabeth would keep, how to manage the servants, and what time she should retire at night. And through it all, Lady Catherine kept up a running monologue and rarely required Elizabeth to give a response. When the lady did request a reply, Elizabeth quickly learned that her noncommittal murmurs would be taken as agreement, for it was clear that the lady believed any directives would be obeyed without question.

For Elizabeth's part, she was far too amused by the woman's audacity and the depth of her meddling to be offended by it. Lady Catherine had no faults, as she owned herself, and Elizabeth found Mr. Darcy's assessment of his female relation to be so close to the mark that she was often forced to put her hand in front of her mouth to avoid laughing out loud.

When Lady Catherine finally took her leave, Elizabeth was relieved to see her go. Furthermore, it was fortunate that Elizabeth had managed to withstand the great lady while not giving offense. It was only a victory of sorts, but she viewed it as a victory nonetheless.

After a full night and day spent in her room, Jane was finally able to leave and move about the house. Her father had returned from the church the previous day and had quickly retired to his library; then, unless Jane was mistaken, he had promptly drank himself into oblivion while Jane and the other ladies of the family waited in their respective chambers, fretting over what had happened and wondering what their future held. Jane's last glimpse of Elizabeth had been through her window when Mr. Bennet had held her firmly by the arm and hustled her down the short path to the church to meet with Mr. Collins.

Only Mrs. Hill bringing them trays at mealtimes had broken the monotony. The stable hand stationed out in the hall had denied their appeals to leave their rooms long after it was necessary, stating that Mr. Bennet had instructed him to keep them confined until he approved their release. Frustrating though it was, they had no choice until something had reminded the master of the house that he had not yet released his family. That morning, the stable hand had disappeared, and Jane had been able to leave her room for the first time since the previous morning. It was nothing more than luck that she had been able to convince the housekeeper to arrange for a letter to be delivered to Mr. Darcy at Netherfield. In truth, Jane was well aware of the fact that the letter would almost certainly do no good whatsoever. But she hoped that with the true knowledge of the events of that morning, Mr. Darcy would find it in his heart to forgive Elizabeth, even if nothing could be done to release the young woman from the bonds of her marriage.

When Jane was finally able to leave her rooms, all was quiet in the house. It was still quite early in the morning, and her mother and younger sisters were therefore still abed. Unfortunately, that state of affairs would change far sooner than Jane would have hoped.

The first interruption to her solitude was her sister Mary. Seeing her was not a trial in and of itself, as Mary tended to be of a more reserved disposition than the other ladies of the house, but Mary was not as quiet as she normally might have been. As soon as she saw Jane in the sitting room gazing out the window, she crossed over and sat close, her agitation quite clear in her taut posture and tightly clenched hands.

"Have you broken your fast?" asked Mary as she sat close to Jane.

Jane managed nothing more than a wan smile. "I am afraid I have not been able to muster much of an appetite."

Nodding, Mary was silent, struggling for a few moments, and then she finally blurted, "How could our father have betrayed Elizabeth in such a manner?"

"He has not simply betrayed Elizabeth," was Jane's response. Mary's eyes widened at Jane's insinuation, though she did not argue the point. There was nothing to argue, for it was nothing more than the literal truth. "I suspect that we are finally seeing exactly what manner of man he is."

Jane was a forgiving sort of girl. She had always believed in the basic goodness of her fellow man, and she thought that everyone deserved a chance to prove themselves sincere. But her parents' behavior since Elizabeth's arrival had shown her the cruelty they could display, and though she had always known that her mother had possessed the capacity for a startling level of vindictiveness, her father's behavior had been something of a surprise. His indolence was established. His taciturnity and tendency to hold his wife in contempt was well understood. But Jane had not ever suspected him capable of forcing a daughter to marry a fool against her will. This was made even more astonishing by the fact that all signs suggested that Elizabeth's relationship with Mr. Darcy was almost certainly more extensive than any of them had realized. Marriage to Mr. Darcy would benefit the family even more than marriage with Mr. Collins would. Surely their father must have seen that!

Mary was obviously shocked, though it was likely more because Jane had voiced such thoughts than because Mary disagreed.

"What do we do now?" asked Mary.

"Is there anything we can do?" asked Jane. She was unable to keep the bitterness from her voice. "Everything has changed, and none of it is for the better."

"I do not think it has changed," said Mary. "I believe that for the first time, our eyes are truly opened. You were right, sister."

There was nothing Jane could do to dispute that sentiment. Silence descended over the two sisters, and they remained in the sitting room together for some time, each lost in their own thoughts.

At length, their peace was interrupted by the intrusion of their youngest sisters. But while Kitty appeared to be subdued, Lydia was as brash as ever, talking to her elder sister in a loud monologue and rarely pausing for Kitty to respond.

As they sat on a sofa in the middle of the room, Lydia looked about and sighed with an exaggerated smile of contentment. "It is so nice to have one's house back to oneself. Luckily, we shall not have to put up with *that* person again any time soon."

"Contrary to what you believe, Elizabeth is every bit as good as anyone in this family, Lydia," said Jane, incensed at her sister's senselessness. "It is typical, I suppose, for an ignorant child such as you to espouse such feelings when you know nothing of the situation."

Lydia appeared shocked that Jane would speak to her in such a manner and retorted, "Mama and Papa both hate her. What further evidence do I need?"

"Perhaps an opinion of your own," snapped Jane. "Unfortunately, we know that shall never happen, as there is no room in your empty head for any thoughts other than redcoats and flirting."

"I cannot imagine why you would attempt to defend that . . . that . . ." She did not continue, which was just as well.

"Be silent, Lydia!" said Mary, causing Lydia to look at her with astonishment. "Before you pass judgment on your sister, you should learn exactly what our parents have held against her. And even then, you should hold your tongue; forgiveness and charity are like unto Christ, after all."

"I shall not listen to this," declared Lydia. "Come, Kitty. We shall return to my room until we can go into Meryton to see the officers."

Lydia stood, but Kitty did not follow. She sat, biting her lip and looking at Mary and Jane in mute appeal.

"Come, Kitty!" snapped Lydia.

"You may stay with us if you like," said Jane, taking pity on her second youngest sister.

"I would prefer that," said Kitty with a sigh of relief.

Though Lydia appeared as if she was about to berate Kitty for her desertion, the cold glares of her elder sisters seemed to induce her to think better of it.

"Then I shall go to Meryton and keep the officers to myself," said Lydia in an airy tone as she turned to leave. "I believe they like me much better anyway."

And with that, Lydia flounced from the room, the sound of her footsteps echoing up the stairs as she returned to her room. All three remaining sisters breathed a sigh of relief; Jane did not think she would have been able to bear her silliest and most vindictive sister that day, so it was just as well that she had left.

"Has Lydia always been . . . ?"

"Spoiled?" finished Mary. Jane might not have been so blunt, but she certainly could not disagree with the sentiment.

"Brash?" continued Mary, ticking a finger every time she made a new point. "Improper? Unfeeling? Insensible? Childish? Petulant?"

"I believe that is enough, Mary," Jane interjected.

Mary turned to Jane and eyed her blandly. "Do you disagree?"

With a sigh, Jane replied, "No, but I do not think we should abuse our sister when she is not here to defend herself."

"On the contrary," replied Mary with a significant look at Kitty, "I believe this is exactly the time to discuss our sister's behavior."

A wide-eyed Kitty listened with growing consternation until she could no longer be silent. "Are you suggesting that I have been the same?"

"You have a tendency to follow in whatever Lydia does, dear," said Jane, giving her sister a sympathetic smile. "Often, your behavior emulates Lydia's. You generally do not instigate this behavior, but you willingly follow it."

For a moment, Kitty could not speak, so surprised was she. When she was finally able to speak, she could only blurt out, "Surely Lydia is not *that* bad!"

Mary huffed with annoyance. "Are we speaking of the same person? Kitty, Lydia has been very close to disgracing herself and her family on several occasions. If she is not checked, then it is only a matter of time before she succeeds in doing so, and it will be to the detriment of us all."

When Kitty appeared as if she did not understand, Jane spoke up again. "We could be tainted by association, Kitty. If the sin is grievous enough, we could be shunned by the entire neighborhood. We would not be invited into any respectable society, and our chances of making any kind of a match would disappear."

"Then why does my father not take Lydia into hand?" asked Kitty, though her voice was quiet and strained.

"I have asked myself that many times," said Jane.

Again, Mary interjected with some less than diplomatic remarks. "He does not take her into hand because it is far easier to simply shut his bookroom door on us and pretend that Lydia's behavior does not exist." Mary paused for a moment, thinking. "Actually, I think he finds it more amusing than anything."

"I do not wish to disgrace the family," whispered Kitty.

Jane and Mary shared a look. If there was at least some good to come of this situation with Elizabeth, then it might draw the Bennet sisters closer together. It might also allow them to pull Kitty back from the precipice. It was unfortunate that Lydia would not be governed by anything other than her own selfish desires.

It was then that Jane noticed a single rider approaching Longbourn, and she moved to the window to discover who it was. When she pulled the drape aside, she could see the rider clearly. It was Mr. Bingley.

"I must go out and meet Mr. Bingley."

Mary nodded. "It is best that you speak with him outside of the house. I will stay and speak with Kitty."

What went unsaid was that Mary would begin to talk to Kitty about proper behavior, and though Jane knew that Mary was overly moralistic, she felt that Kitty was ready to learn. Jane would speak with her herself after Mr. Bingley left. For now, she wished to know if Mr. Darcy had received her letter and, perhaps more urgently to Jane's own peace of mind, if the events of the previous day had damaged Jane in Mr. Bingley's eyes.

Swiftly, Jane made her way from the sitting room and out into Longbourn's entrance hall, where she came across Mrs. Hill, who was moving to answer the door.

"I will see to Mr. Bingley, Mrs. Hill."

The housekeeper nodded. "Will Mr. Bingley be staying for tea?"

Jane considered the matter. She did not wish for Mr. Bingley to meet with her parents—perhaps ever again!—but with her father entrenched in his library and her mother still lamenting the fact that Elizabeth was to be the next mistress of Longbourn, Jane judged it likely that they would not appear at all that day.

"I will speak with Mr. Bingley, but I believe it likely that he will."

"Very good, Miss Bennet," said the housekeeper.

She retrieved Jane's outer wear and helped her into her clothes before retreating from the room. Jane moved to the door and opened it as Mr. Bingley was dismounting from his horse.

"Let us speak over there," she said as she moved toward him and motioned to the side of the house.

Mr. Bingley seemed to understand that she did not wish to speak to him inside, and he extended his arm for her to take, accepting her gentle guidance as they made their way around the house, through the gardens, and back into the interior of the property where they would not be easily observed. When they had arrived, Jane turned to regard her suitor.

It was the compassion in his eyes which undid her carefully constructed façade. Jane had intended to speak of the matter dispassionately, reciting the facts while attempting to discern if Mr. Bingley would turn away from her for having a family so unsuitable to a man in his position. She knew that there were several grounds for him to withdraw gracefully and not incur any censure. But in seeing the way he regarded her, Jane's control over her emotions was negated, and a sob escaped.

Before she even knew what was happening, Mr. Bingley was there before her, coaxing her to rest her head on his shoulder, patting her back in a manner which was completely improper. But it was also a balm to Jane's troubled mind, and she allowed herself the luxury of tears. She cried for her sister, who had been thrust into an unwanted marriage with a senseless man she could not respect; she cried for her sisters, whose prospects seemed to be murky and uncertain; and, perhaps most of all, Jane Bennet cried for herself, lamenting her loss of innocence and the death of her inherent belief in the goodness of her fellow man. All of her assumptions concerning others had been laid bare, and she now realized that wishing that others were good would not *make* them good. There was a lot more evil in the world than she would ever have wanted to acknowledge to herself.

But one cannot cry forever, and though Jane could not determine how long she had sobbed out her heartbreak, her tears eventually subsided, and she rested her head on the broad expanse of Mr. Bingley's strong shoulder. And when she had calmed enough to think rationally again, she had to chuckle at herself; she could not ever remember letting her emotions out in such a manner. It was most unlike her.

Lifting her head, Jane inspected Mr. Bingley, noting that a rather large wet spot had appeared on the shoulder and front of his jacket, and she gave him a watery smile of apology.

"It appears that I have ruined your coat, Mr. Bingley."

"Think nothing of it, Miss Bennet," was his earnest reply. Though he was normally ebullient and happy, little trace of that man was present this morning. Instead, he was somber and serious, much like Jane felt herself.

"I thank you for allowing me to unburden myself, sir. I have never allowed my control to relax as much as I have today. It is far more cathartic than I could have imagined."

"Shall we sit?" asked Mr. Bingley, gesturing at a nearby rough bench. "I believe it would do you good."

Smiling again, Jane agreed, and soon they were perched on the indicated bench, both sitting on the edge and facing slightly toward the other.

"Now," said Mr. Bingley when they were comfortably situated, "what has happened here? Mr. Bennet forced Miss Elizabeth to marry your cousin? I can scarcely credit such a thing."

"It is true. I would never have believed my father could act in such a manner, but I was witness to it myself."

In a halting voice, Jane began to describe the events of the previous morning, detailing what she had seen and what her father's actions had been. She told him everything she knew, leaving nothing out. She did not worry about the propriety of the situation, knowing that Mr. Bingley was not the type to carry tales.

By the time she had finished, Mr. Bingley had risen and was pacing in agitation, a state which continued for some minutes, as he seemed to be struggling within himself. When he turned to her, it was with an expression which almost bespoke fear.

"What kind of man is your father?" asked he with some contempt. "Does he mean to marry off *all* his daughters in a similar fashion?"

Jane's breath caught in her throat. The meaning of Mr. Bingley's words could not be misinterpreted, and after all the heartache of the previous day, the mere thought caused a warmth to well up within her. She then chastised herself for thinking in such a manner, as the surety of her admirer's regard did not lessen Elizabeth's plight in any way.

"I do not think so," said Jane in response to his question, pushing all other concerns aside. "My father is much too indolent to exert himself again."

"Then why was your sister singled out so cruelly?"

Extending her hand, Jane persuaded Mr. Bingley to return to the bench, and she kept hold of his hand as she spoke to him.

"You are aware that Elizabeth lived in London for many years with my uncle, Mr. Gardiner." At Mr. Bingley's curt nod, she continued: "There was a very good reason for her removal, Mr. Bingley. Her life at Longbourn when she was a child was very difficult, and even though I was a child myself, I remember fearing for her. My father was never harsh with her, but he allowed my mother to do with her what she wished. And my mother treated her as if she was a worthless stray, fit for nothing more than scraps and threadbare dresses. Elizabeth's removal to London was her salvation."

Mr. Bingley regarded her intensely. "Your parents hold a grudge against her."

"Yes," replied Jane simply. "It stems from when she was a very young child. I am sorry, but I shall not speak of the reason without Elizabeth's approval."

Mr. Bingley shook his head impatiently. "I understand, and I would not wish to pry. Miss Bennet, we live in a society where . . . well, let us just say that a father has control over a child until they come of age. I am certain you are well aware of this.

"But though I have heard of parents entering their child into an arranged marriage against the child's wishes, I am astonished by your father's lack of decency and his lack of any feeling for your sister. Marrying her off to a man who she has just met without any consideration—well, I am astonished!"

Pausing, Mr. Bingley fidgeted in agitation, and though he seemed to struggle to find the words, he continued in a rush, clearly attempting to say what he meant to say before his words failed him. "I am tempted to remove you from this house immediately and make you my wife before Mr. Bennet can focus upon you to give away to another of his foolish relations."

His concern and his obvious care for her warmed Jane's heart once again. But though her heart cried out for her to urge him to follow through on his notion, she could not. She was not in any danger, and she did not wish to start married life under the scandal of an elopement, which was the only way he would be able to follow through with such a scheme.

"I will be well, Mr. Bingley. I thank you for your concern, but it is unwarranted in this instance."

Though he watched her carefully, the tension seemed to bleed out from him in an almost visible manner. "That is well," was his quiet reply. "Though I would do it in an instant if required, you deserve the best, and I would not have our engagement begin on the heels of such sorrow."

Jane blushed and thanked him for his sincere convictions, more certain than ever that this was an estimable man who would care for her in every way possible.

"Now, let me assuage your concerns slightly," said Mr. Bingley. "Darcy received your letter and was heartened by it. It arrived just before he departed for Kent."

Surprised, Jane peered at Mr. Bingley, wondering what he was about.

But Mr. Bingley anticipated her confusion, as he continued gently, "From your letter, I suspect Miss Elizabeth never had the chance to tell you, but Darcy had asked her for a courtship two days ago. He went to Longbourn yesterday to ask for your father's permission, which was when he learned of the sudden marriage."

"What does he hope to accomplish?" asked Jane.

"He seemed to believe that there is a possibility that the marriage could be annulled," replied Mr. Bingley. "And given the fact that no banns have been read, the bride was not willing, and your father had to practically drag her to the church, I believe that Darcy is right. There is compelling evidence that the marriage cannot be legal."

"Can it be possible?" asked Jane, hope shining within her heart for the first time since the dreadful events of the previous day.

"Put your trust in Darcy and your sister," was Mr. Bingley's gentle reply. "If anyone is able to obtain an annulment, it would be Darcy. And your sister does not appear to be the sort of girl to simply acknowledge defeat. I have never met Mr. Collins, but given what I have heard of the man, I dare say he has more than met his match in your sister."

"I very much hope so, Mr. Bingley," said Jane. The hope his words had engendered had found fertile ground within her mind, and that hope was sprouting, growing at a rapid pace. Perhaps Elizabeth would manage to extricate herself from the quandary with Mr. Darcy's help. She would pray for them.

Chapter XVIII

*I*t was ironic, Darcy decided, as his coach approached Rosings on that fine autumn morning, that he should be back within six months of his final leave-taking from his aunt. The massive estate house loomed in the distance like a massive web with strands to trap and hold, and he knew that the spider who made her home within would bind him without a moment's thought should he not be vigilant. He and his cousin had visited his aunt's domain annually for the past several years, maintaining the estate books, smoothing over any difficulties his aunt's imperious manner might have caused among her tenants, and overseeing the early stages of planting, which generally occurred some weeks earlier than it did at Pemberley.

But what Darcy had not told Miss Elizabeth was that he had informed his uncle—on whose commission he made the journey there every year—that he would not extend the same courtesy in the future. Lady Catherine had been more than usually insufferable that spring in her insistence that he and Anne formalize their engagement, and as neither had ever wished for the other as a marriage partner, they were of no mind to pay heed to her words. Lady Catherine, perhaps sensing that the two in question were less than eager to bow to her demands, had badgered them mercilessly, and it had finally resulted in an unpleasant encounter in which Darcy had stated openly that he would not marry Anne and had made a precipitous departure from the estate with Colonel Fitzwilliam. Darcy regretted that he had not informed his aunt that he would never marry Anne several years ago, but as they were all in the habit of simply ignoring her directives in order to promote family harmony, it had seemed like the best option available at the time.

What his aunt would make of his early return was a matter which any intelligent being would be able to conjecture. In fact, Darcy fully expected that almost the first words out of her mouth would be something to the effect that he had finally come to his senses. But Darcy did not intend to get into an argument with her again, so avoidance would once again be the order of the day. He needed her good will for the moment so that he could meet with Miss Elizabeth and determine what was to be done.

When Darcy alighted from the carriage and strode into the house, no one was present to greet him, and upon making his inquiries, he was told that the lady of the estate was away on some matter of business and that her daughter had retired to her rooms after breakfast. Darcy instructed that Anne be informed of his arrival, and then he went to his rooms to quickly wash off the dust of the road and change his clothes. It was about thirty minutes later that he made his way down to the sitting room in which Lady Catherine normally held court.

Life had not been kind to Anne de Bourgh, which was one of the primary regrets Darcy had in vowing not to return to Rosings. She was petite and cursed with a weak constitution which allowed for little activity, though privately Darcy thought that Lady Catherine's authoritative manner in declaring what she was and was not capable of doing was as much to blame for Anne's lack of robust health as anything else. While Darcy himself favored his father's features, Anne appeared to be in every way a Fitzwilliam, from her blond tresses to her small, slightly upturned nose. She was not unattractive either, he thought, little though her looks affected him. Their primary reason for Darcy's decision not to follow Lady Catherine's wishes was due more to a certain incompatibility of character rather than due to any more physical considerations. They were too alike, they had decided early on, for both possessed a rather quiet disposition. They would each benefit enormously from livelier partners. In fact, Darcy had long thought that his cousin the colonel would better suit Anne than he.

"Darcy," said Anne as he entered the room and bowed to her. "To what do we owe this pleasure? I thought it clear when you last departed that you would not return."

Cursing himself for his lack of foresight—*of course* Anne would look on his sudden and unannounced arrival with suspicion—Darcy stepped forward and took a seat close to her own.

"I have not come to bow to your mother's wishes, Anne," he said, watching for her reaction.

He was not disappointed. She immediately became less guarded, and she looked on him with a hint of amusement. "In that case, I wonder why you have braved my mother's displeasure yet again. You do know how she will view this sudden return, do you not?"

"Of course. And I mean to allow her to continue with her delusions while I am in residence." Darcy paused. "Has it been uncomfortable for you?"

"No more than usual. Mother has always considered you the more troublesome creature, and she has therefore focused on you. I am the dutiful daughter who will do as she directs, after all, so she does not bother me concerning the matter over much, though she does tend to talk about it incessantly."

"Even after I was clear that she should not expect the alliance in the future?"

Anne raised an eyebrow. "Do you really believe that would deter her?"

Shaking his head, with as much amusement as disgust, Darcy returned his focus to the purpose for his arrival. "I am actually here for an entirely different reason, Anne. And it is one which your mother will not like in the slightest."

"Do tell," replied Anne with a twinkle in her eye. "While I can think of many things of which she would not approve, there are only a handful which would result in her immediate and loud displeasure."

"And this is one of them." Darcy was not trying to be grim, but he was well aware of how Lady Catherine would ultimately view his errand once it became known to her, and he fully expected that the confrontation which would ensue would make their argument that spring seem like lovers' murmurings in comparison.

"Tell me, Anne, have you heard anything concerning the new wife of your mother's parson?"

"What can Mr. Collins have to do with your arrival?" asked Anne.

"Please humor me."

Though Anne looked on him with suspicion, she did not demur. "They only arrived at the parsonage yesterday, as I understand." Her expression became positively mischievous as she continued, "Of course, this is all very incomprehensible, as to the best of my knowledge he was not engaged when he left Hunsford four days ago. That seems a little too precipitous even for a marriage based on a compromise, though Mr. Collins is certainly stupid enough to compromise a young lady without even realizing what had occurred."

"This is no compromise," said Darcy though clenched teeth, his indignation rising. "In fact, Miss Elizabeth — for I will not deign to refer to her by that odious man's name — was forced to marry her cousin by her father. And this only the day after I requested to court her."

"I think you had best explain, cousin. This begins to sound like a novel."

Nodding, Darcy did just that, explaining the circumstances of the last several days, watching for a reaction from his cousin. There was none. Anne was just as capable of hiding herself behind an inscrutable wall as he was himself.

"That is quite the tale, Darcy," said Anne once he had finished. "And though I would not cast aspersions on your young lady, I am afraid I must echo her father's sentiments. Why did she not speak of her understanding with you in an effort to save herself? I would think that marriage to you would be an inducement enough to ensure that her father would refrain from forcing her to go forward with his schemes."

"Not from what Mr. Bennet himself told me," replied Darcy. "The man was set on the match."

"I cannot believe that he would have persisted in light of the advantages you would have brought to such a marriage. Beyond the obvious monetary benefits, introducing her sisters to a much higher level of society would have increased their chances of a good match. Surely he could not have ignored that.

"Regardless, you have not answered my question. Why did Mrs. Collins not speak to her father of your proposal?"

Darcy scowled, but Anne seemed unimpressed by his displeasure, merely regarding him with an imperious glare. It was quite similar to her mother's, though he would not voice such an unflattering comparison to her.

"I do not know," said Darcy. "I mean to have an accounting from her as to her reasons for staying silent."

"What do you think?" pressed Anne.

"I believe that it might have been due to a misguided attempt to resolve her own problems," said Darcy. "Or perhaps she simply did not expect it to sway her father."

Anne was silent for a few moments, considering the matter. "What do you mean to accomplish by coming here?" asked Anne. "Since the marriage has already taken place, there is nothing more you can do."

"You do not know Miss Elizabeth Bennet," replied Darcy. Anne looked pointedly at him at the use of the woman's maiden name, but Darcy ignored it. "She is as intelligent as Collins is obtuse. I doubt very much that she has submitted to him."

"But still, annulments are granted so infrequently—"

"Leave that to me. I believe there are enough irregularities concerning this sham of a marriage that a case may be made for its dissolution."

At that moment, the door opened, and Lady Catherine strode into the room. Her appearance was a little wild, no doubt due to the fact that she had just alighted from a carriage, but more because of the almost feral grin with which she regarded him. It brought to mind his fanciful thoughts of her as a spider, weaving her webs to entrap small insects in her domain. She would soon find out that he was more wasp than house fly.

"So, you have finally returned," said Lady Catherine, her tone one of insolent triumph. "It has taken you longer to come to your senses than I would have thought, Darcy, but I always knew you would come around to my way of thinking. Rosings is too great a prize for you to ignore."

Darcy could almost hear Anne's soft snort, and though he was angered by his aunt's reference to the estate being more important and of greater worth than the person of his cousin, Anne was obviously accustomed to such language from her mother.

"Lady Catherine," said Darcy as he rose to his feet and executed the barest hint of a bow. "I apologize for arriving unannounced."

"Never mind that," was his aunt's dismissive reply. "This is a momentous occasion indeed."

"It is nothing more than a friendly visit to my cousin and aunt," replied Darcy with a significant glance at Anne.

Lady Catherine did not miss the glance, and though she obviously did not understand what it signified, she was not about to miss the opportunity to try to induce him into offering for her daughter.

"Well, since you are here now, you must stay for a month complete. In fact, if you are to be here, you may as well send for Georgiana and stay for Christmas. It would behoove her to become accustomed to Anne's presence."

Darcy was not about to be drawn into this discussion yet again. "Georgiana is busy in London at present with her companion. It is our plan to spend Christmas at Pemberley as usual."

A wicked gleam appeared in Lady Catherine's eye. "That is probably for the best."

She did not say anything further, but Darcy knew exactly what her thoughts were. There was nothing to be done but to ignore her words. It did not take long before Darcy became weary of his aunt's commentary, and as he was eager to devise a way to be in the company of Miss Elizabeth Bennet, he soon excused himself in the company of Anne, knowing it was about the only way his aunt would allow him out of her presence.

"Will you visit her at the parsonage?" asked Anne in a quiet voice as they quit the room.

"I believe it might be a little early for that," replied Darcy. "I have only just arrived, and visiting hours are already past."

Anne snorted. "I should think that a little impropriety would be worth saving your lady love from the clutches of her servile husband."

Darcy had to acknowledge that she had a point.

"Besides, I doubt Mr. Collins would ever bar the august nephew of his lady patroness from his house, no matter the time of day or night, should he condescend to call."

Making a face, Darcy nodded tightly. "I believe I shall walk out and try to determine the best method of approaching her."

"Very well. But Darcy, a word of advice, if you will." He turned to his cousin, only to see her watching him with a serious expression. "I would suggest you refrain from calling her Miss Elizabeth. Until you can prove otherwise, she is Mrs. Collins and should be addressed as such. You do not wish for my mother to guess your purpose here."

Little though he liked it, Anne was right. It *was* distasteful to think of such a bright light connected in such a manner to that man, but he could not take the chance of Lady Catherine's early displeasure.

"Agreed. If you will excuse me."

"Go, Darcy," called Anne as he walked away. "I will distract my mother in your absence."

And so Darcy left to meet the woman of his dreams, grateful that Anne and he were of one mind in this instance. He hated to think how much more difficult this would be if Anne had truly desired a proposal from him.

With Lady Catherine's departure, nothing further was holding Elizabeth to the parsonage for the day. As the sun was shining and the day was fine, she determined to walk out so that she might avoid him for a little while. Mr. Collins's work room was situated in a corner of the house which overlooked the road to Rosings, a circumstance which was undoubtedly beneficial to the parson, as he would have the first intelligence whenever Lady Catherine drove by. As the lady departed, Elizabeth, knowing that Lady Catherine would drive past that very room, immediately made herself scarce. It was child's play to leave through the front door and depart in a direction where she would not be seen, the strands of trees surrounding the house hiding her escape. The air was brisk and Elizabeth immediately found herself at home on the grounds of Rosings.

Elizabeth had to acknowledge that Lady Catherine was mistress of a beautiful estate, not that the accident of birth which led to her being so situated credited her in the slightest. Still, the woods through which she walked were a delightful mix of beech, oak, and pine, and Elizabeth could not help but imagine the bounteous glory of the trees should they be crowned in their summer mantle.

She walked for some distance, reveling in the warm autumn air which was a blessing on such a day and thinking of her situation at present. The anger she had felt had largely subsided, and she was able to think more rationally than she had been able to the previous day.

In truth, she had no proof aside from her estimation of Mr. Darcy's character that he would follow her to Kent. She still believed that he would, but she began to see that it might very difficult to extricate herself from this marriage if she had no outside assistance. Various thoughts and feelings flowed through her, from her the anger still present beneath the surface of her emotions to vague plans of what she would do should Mr. Darcy not come, the most outlandish of which was the thought of boarding a ship and fleeing to the Americas.

But it all turned out to be unnecessary, for as she moved around a bend in the path she was walking, there stood the man himself.

Mr. Darcy had obviously slept quite ill, and as she took in his less than immaculate condition, a feeling of utter longing and belonging welled up within her. Being with this man felt so *right*, so *natural* that any doubts she had had of his constancy were immediately banished from her mind. Elizabeth still could not state whether she loved him, but she was now well aware of the power he held over her, and she knew that she could easily come to love him, given the time and the opportunity.

It did not hurt that he gazed at her with such intensity. Elizabeth was certain that Mr. Darcy was just as affected by their meeting as she was.

"I had not thought to see you walking the grounds," said he, his voice gravelly with emotion. Then his lips curved into a slight smile. "I suppose that I should have foreseen it, knowing what a great walker you are."

"I think you may attribute my presence due more to a desire to avoid Mr. Collins than the desire for exercise," replied Elizabeth.

Though Mr. Darcy's countenance darkened at the mention of her supposed husband, he seemed to throw it off with effort. "Whatever the reason, I am grateful. I was pondering how I might gain an audience with you."

Motioning to the path from whence he had come, Mr. Darcy waited until she began to walk, and then he fell into place next to her. Neither spoke for some time, but as they walked, they each took comfort in the presence of the other. Though Elizabeth longed for him to take her into his arms, to feel the comfort of his strength, she was mindful of the situation. In the eyes of society, she was still Mrs. William Collins, and as such, she could not be observed by others in the embrace of another man without utterly ruining both her reputation and Mr. Darcy's. Discretion was called for.

"It was a most unwelcome surprise when your father told me you were already wed," said Mr. Darcy after a few moments of walking.

"It was a most unpleasant surprise when *I* discovered my father's intentions," countered Elizabeth. "I tried to flee the night before, but my father anticipated me."

Mr. Darcy turned his startled gaze on her. "You tried to flee?"

Blushing, Elizabeth nodded. "I had thought to go to Netherfield and throw myself on your mercy. If nothing else, my uncle's staff would have let me in at his home in London, and they would have concealed my presence from my father, had it come to that."

"Would it not simply have been better to tell your father that I had already requested a courtship?"

Elizabeth turned an unaffectedly astonished gaze at him. "He indicated that I had not told him?" At Mr. Darcy's nod, Elizabeth shook her head and attempted to master her emotions. "I *did* tell him. He chose not to believe that such a thing was possible."

"And then he lied to me," said Mr. Darcy.

"It appears to be so."

They walked on in silence for several more minutes before Mr. Darcy sighed and turned to her. "Miss Bennet, I find myself confused over this situation. Though parents often arrange marriages for their children, your father's actions are astounding. Unless he has purchased a special license—something I judge unlikely—your marriage has not the sanction of the church. What can he be thinking?"

"Revenge," was Elizabeth's simple reply.

"I beg your pardon, Miss Bennet," said he haltingly, "but may I ask—what do your parents have against you?"

Elizabeth would rather not have to tell him of her history, but she knew that it was imperative that she do so. Still, the thought of having his good opinion for one more night was appealing, and as the day grew long, she had much rather not chance tarnishing his image of her at the present.

"Mr. Darcy, can we wait until tomorrow for my confession? I believe it will be necessary for me to return to the parsonage very soon."

The very mention of her return to Mr. Collins's domain brought a scowl to his face. "I believe I would prefer to remove you from *that man's* influence immediately."

Elizabeth put a hand on his forearm for a brief moment in reassurance. "I am well able to manage the likes of William Collins, Mr. Darcy. This situation has the potential to be very difficult for us both. If you were to take me from what society sees as my lawfully wedded husband, the backlash would be immense."

"Of course you speak the truth," said Mr. Darcy, even as it was clear to see that he little liked the necessity. His expression then became apprehensive, and he turned to regard her with trepidation. "Have you . . . What I mean to say is . . ."

Elizabeth was confused, never having seen Mr. Darcy act in such a reticent manner.

"Miss Bennet," said Mr. Darcy after a monumental internal struggle, "were you able to . . . *manage* Mr. Collins last night?"

At first, Elizabeth was confused, and then flashes of the previous evening illuminated her consciousness, and she blushed as Mr. Darcy's meaning suddenly became clear to her.

"I was able to manage him quite well indeed," said Elizabeth after taking a few moments to compose herself. "In fact, Mr. Collins awoke this morning with a rather severe indisposition. It seems he indulged in a little too much celebration over my father's success in forcing me to the altar with a particularly fine vintage which Lady Catherine herself had recommended for our wedding night. Of course, I cannot confirm the quality of the wine myself, as I did not consume a drop."

At that, Mr. Darcy burst out laughing in such a manner as Elizabeth had never seen from him before. She found that she quite liked it when he laughed—his face was transformed from its normally serious lines, and it rendered him uncommonly handsome when so changed.

"I should never have doubted you, Miss Bennet," said Mr. Darcy, still chuckling to himself. "It appears as if you are able to handle the man masterfully. Do you have another bottle of the vintage on hand for tonight?"

"No," said Elizabeth, "but I am already planning how to avoid him yet again. I dare say that Mr. Collins will find it quite difficult to consummate his marriage, though he has taken great pains to assure me that he is greatly anticipating connubial bliss."

This time, Mr. Darcy's response was pure disgust. "The man truly has no concept of proper behavior. To speak of such things openly with a maiden is the height of crassness."

"Insensible, indeed," murmured Elizabeth.

They walked on for several more moments, each lost in their own thoughts, until Elizabeth, taking stock of her surroundings, turned to Mr. Darcy.

"Loath though I am to return, I am certain I shall already incur Mr. Collins's disapprobation for having left the parsonage at all. I believe that I had best return."

"Then let me escort you to the nearest edge of the woods," said Mr. Darcy, gesturing to a path which Elizabeth judged led back in the direction of Hunsford.

"What are your thoughts on ensuring this marriage is examined and rejected?" asked he once they were well on their way toward Hunsford.

"I hope that your presence indicates your willingness to assist?"

"You agreed to a courtship with *me*, Miss Bennet," said Mr. Darcy with a pointed glance which seemed to pierce her to her very soul. "I am not a man who relinquishes that which I desire to anyone, least of all to one such as Mr. Collins. I believe that I see several instances in which ecclesiastical law has not been followed that would render this marriage invalid. I will do everything in my power to ensure that it is."

Warmed by his words, Elizabeth nodded, but there was one more problem which weighed on her mind. "And will I not be a social pariah if we do obtain an annulment? I would not wish to stain your family's honor, sir."

"You need not worry about that," replied Mr. Darcy. His tone was dismissive, but Elizabeth could see that he was considering the matter with all the gravity she had come to expect of him. "I doubt that word of this will get back to London, and even if my aunt deplores the fact that I will marry you—as I am certain she will, given her aspirations for Anne and me—she will do nothing to damage the Fitzwilliam name in public, and she will subside without making a scene in any of our social circles, though I do not doubt her private diatribes will be lengthy and spectacular.

"And given what I know of how the marriage came about, I suspect that if the details are ultimately made known to society, your father and Mr. Collins will receive the lion's share of the derision, given how they have behaved in the affair.

"Besides, I despise society and its pretensions." This last, he said with nearly a growl. "If society should shun us, then it would not cause me a moment's concern. We may retire to Pemberley and live out our lives in peace."

Though it sounded heavenly, Elizabeth was still concerned. "But what of our children, should we be blessed with them? They will need our good name in society for when they are grown themselves."

"That is true," acknowledged Mr. Darcy, "but by then, the matter will be long forgotten, for some other delicious scandal will have reached the attention of London's wagging tongues. Besides, I tend to choose friends that view London society in the same manner as I do. I am certain most of those friends will stand by me, so we have little to fear."

Elizabeth hoped, rather than believed, it would be thus, but she made no further mention of the subject. "Then I will leave the annulment to you. I will deal with Mr. Collins and ensure the man does not lay so much as a finger on me, and you shall work on having the marriage annulled."

"We shall conquer this, Miss Bennet," said Mr. Darcy, stopping and turning to gaze at her. "We must simply be patient."

"Thank you, Mr. Darcy." Elizabeth paused, looking at him through eyes which were quickly misting with emotion. After all she had been through these past months, it was comforting to have a man nearby who wished for nothing more than her happiness.

"I wanted to say that . . . that I am grateful for your constancy, Mr. Darcy." She smiled and blushed a little before forging on. "I cannot say how our courtship will turn out, but I find myself anticipating the opportunity to know you better. I say this not because of my thankfulness, but because I believe you are the best man of my acquaintance." She flashed him an impish grin. "I am certain you will acquit yourself as a suitor most admirably."

"And I long for the opportunity to show my devotion," was Mr.

Darcy's quiet reply. "It is ironic that some of our courting period shall pass while you are at least nominally married to another man."

"Ironic indeed!" said Elizabeth.

Elizabeth reached into her pocket and produced a letter to the Gardiners. "I wrote to my uncle the morning before my father dragged me off to church, but my father prevented me from sending it. I wrote a new letter based on my changed circumstances this morning, hoping I would be able to post it. Will you see to its posting, Mr. Darcy?"

"I will send it express, Miss Bennet," replied Mr. Darcy, taking the letter from her hand. "When he learns of these events, I do not doubt that Mr. Gardiner will return from Ireland post haste. He may even arrive before Christmas if he hastens enough."

"I hope that is the case. But I truly must be going."

"Of course," said Mr. Darcy, bowing to her. "Please let me know if there is anything you require. Should you dispatch a note to me, I will come immediately, regardless of the circumstance."

It took no greatness of thought to note that Mr. Darcy was concerned that Mr. Collins would demand his rights. Elizabeth was warmed by his desire to keep her safe, but she knew that Mr. Collins, ineffectual and stupid as he was, was no match for her.

"Thank you." Though her reply was quiet, she was certain that Mr. Darcy heard it and could feel the emotion behind it.

There was nothing further to be done than to return to the parsonage, and after curtseying to Mr. Darcy, Elizabeth departed. But it was as if some invisible bond stretched between them, calling to her and inducing her to look back at him several times as she made her way back toward Hunsford. And every time she looked back, he still stood there, a tall statue of a Greek god, watching as she walked away. In that moment, Elizabeth thought that her feelings for Mr. Darcy were becoming very strong indeed. It would not be long, she sensed, before she was able to say that she loved him.

Which made the current situation even more pitiable. She could not fathom what she would do if the church would not hear her pleas, but the thought of being chained to William Collins for the rest of her life was unbearable. Not when she was rapidly coming to know what it was to care deeply about Fitzwilliam Darcy.

Chapter XIX

As expected, Elizabeth was subjected to Mr. Collins's displeasure on her return to the parsonage. He expressed his feelings in a way which was long and rambling and centered about the idea that he did not think it proper for her to be wandering country lanes alone. Elizabeth was certain the man did not consider it to be proper because he believed it infringed upon his authority as head of his house.

"In summary, Mrs. Collins," said he as his long-winded discourse lurched and stumbled to a halt, "you must understand that a man in my position cannot tolerate a wife who is constantly plodding through the countryside, her hair wild and her clothing tossed to and fro in the wind. If you feel you must take a constitutional, then I suggest you walk in the garden behind the house. In that way, you will always be in close proximity should I have need of you, and you will in no way be behaving in a manner which is unseemly. It is to your credit that you wish to keep yourself young and attractive for your husband by partaking in the benefits of constant exercise," here, he paused and turned a lascivious smirk on her which she barely managed to refrain from removing from his face by means of a hard slap, "but it is not necessary. My love for you has already grown by leaps and bounds, I assure you. It is now more important for you to behave as the young married woman you have become rather than as a carefree young girl. You recently resigned that estate, after all."

His arguments completed, Mr. Collins ceased speaking and looked at her expectantly, but Elizabeth did not respond. In fact, she decided that his silly soliloquy was not worth a reply, and she steadfastly held to her purpose of not responding to his idiocies.

"Have I made myself clear?" asked Mr. Collins after a few moments of uncomfortable silence.

Elizabeth sat looking at him placidly for several more moments before she rose to her feet. "I believe I shall speak to the cook about dinner. I will inform you when it is ready."

For the briefest of moments, Mr. Collins appeared confused by her sudden non sequitur, but he quickly recovered and favored her with an unctuous smile. "Of course, my dear. I shall await your summons to the dining room."

Then, with a leer, which he no doubt intended to be flirtatious, he left the room, taking the time to bow every few steps. Once he was out of her sight, Elizabeth heaved a sigh of relief. The man had obviously deduced—incorrectly—that she would obey his directives, no doubt due to her delicacy and reluctance to discuss the issue. As she was already highly anticipating meeting Mr. Darcy on her daily rambles, Elizabeth had no intention whatsoever of agreeing to so unreasonable a demand.

They were soon situated in the dining room, and while Elizabeth's appetite was greater than it had been the day before, she still ate relatively little. Mr. Collins, on the other hand, seemed to relish every morsel which passed his lips. For once, the conversation was muted and understated, and Elizabeth, though she did not know the reason for his uncharacteristic reticence, did not question it either. Silence was said to be golden, after all, but that was most especially true when it came to William Collins.

After dinner, they retired to the drawing room, where Mr. Collins once again became voluble, but whereas his words normally consisted of whatever was passing through his mind at any given time, he seemed on this night to center upon his happiness toward their situation. Furthermore, he seemed to expect that tonight was the night when all his expectations for their felicity would come to pass.

As was her habit, Elizabeth allowed the man to drone on for some time without making any response while she concentrated on thinking of Mr. Darcy and how he had looked so very handsome that day when they had met. But this time, Mr. Collins did not continue on interminably. Instead, he paused after speaking for some time and then turned to her and said:

"Perhaps it is time that we retired, Mrs. Collins. I find that I am eager to start our married life in earnest. Shall I come to you in thirty minutes?"

Though she knew exactly to what he referred, Elizabeth decided a little ingenuous behavior was in order.

"For what purpose, Mr. Collins?" said she, her brow wrinkled up in a frown of confusion. "Do you wish to read together tonight?"

"No, my dear," was the reply. "I mean to come to you so that we may consummate our marriage. I am certain you are as eager as I, so I should not wish to keep you waiting!"

"Consummate?" echoed Elizabeth. Perhaps she was overdoing it slightly, but the man was not clever enough to detect her pretense, and she was enjoying confounding him. "I am certain you are the consummate rector in Hunsford. You do not need my approbation."

"I was referring to the marriage act," replied Mr. Collins. It seemed as if her manner was beginning to wear on him, as his reply was more than a little testy.

Widening her eyes in mock understanding, Elizabeth shook her head. "I am afraid that will be quite impossible, Mr. Collins."

A frown of confusion settled over his face like night falling. "I assure you it is not, Mrs. Collins. In fact, it is not only expected of married couples, but it is also necessary to beget children. As a sheltered young lady of gentle birth, you would not have any knowledge as to what it actually entails, but it is a wondrous gift given to us by our Lord which allows us to participate in the act of creating life. There is nothing more natural and just than for two such as you and me to cleave together once we have been married."

In fact, though Elizabeth was a sheltered young lady, she was not as bereft of knowledge as the parson thought. Though her uncle would certainly not allow her to read the type of book which would explain the matter to her in full, she was a curious and intelligent woman and was thus able to read between the lines. Besides, her aunt was a woman of decided opinions who did not hold with the idea of sending a young woman into the marriage state only to be scared half to death by learning what occurred between man and woman. She had not been explicit, but she had given Elizabeth enough information concerning what lay in store to bring her comfort should she marry, though she had left enough unsaid to leave Elizabeth an innocent.

And unfortunately for Mr. Collins, the thought of engaging in such intimate acts with *him* was beyond repugnant to Elizabeth.

"You are correct, Mr. Collins," said Elizabeth slowly. "I do not know much of the matter. But I am aware of the fact that it cannot be done when a woman is suffering from her womanly indisposition."

"In-indisposition?" echoed the parson, confusion written upon his brow.

"Surely you are aware of this?" asked Elizabeth innocently, secretly rejoicing that the parson did not know nearly as much as he thought he did. "A woman suffers from an indisposition frequently which makes what you suggest quite impossible."

"Of what are you talking, Mrs. Collins?" demanded Mr. Collins. It was clear that he was becoming somewhat cross. Elizabeth was certain she knew just how to deflect him.

"It is somewhat . . . embarrassing," replied she. "But there is blood involved, and it can be quite messy, you understand. I thought you knew of this."

The parson clearly had little understanding of the matter, but it was equally obvious that the thought of blood upset him, and he pursued the matter no further. "A thousand apologies, my dear, but I had not realized what you meant. It is truly unfortunate that you have been visited by such a calamity at such an inauspicious time." He regarded her, his air faintly radiating suspicion, before he said, "Excuse me, but how often does this indisposition intrude, and how long do you expect it to last?"

"It is difficult to say," said Elizabeth, though she had to fight to keep the laughter at bay. "It comes without any warning, and sometimes it can stay for some time. I will be certain to inform you when it has safely passed."

Mr. Collins nodded sagely. "It is unfortunate indeed, but I believe that I will be quite content waiting for you to be ready to receive me. Far be it for me to rail and murmur when the Lord sees fit to try my patience in such a fashion. Rather, I believe that the suspense caused by the additional wait will increase my love tenfold, and the fact that I can imagine the act will keep me quite well while we wait."

Elizabeth looked at the man with distaste. Surely a parson should not be given over to such "imagination" as Mr. Collins suggested, and she rather thought the only suspense involved with the situation was whether she would be able to avoid laughing in the man's face when he began spouting his inanities. She therefore simply smiled at him, though she was surprised that he was not able to detect the frostiness of her mood, which should almost have frozen him solid.

"Then it is fortunate that you have acquired such patience, Mr. Collins. I believe that I shall take my leave to retire."

And without waiting for an answer, Elizabeth departed the room, ignoring the parson as he bowed and scraped and wished her a pleasant night, all the while expressing his happiness and his willingness to wait until she was ready. Inside, however, she was wondering how she would be able to manage to remain calm throughout the ordeal. She was ready to strangle Mr. Collins, and it was only the second day in his company!

For the next several days, Elizabeth felt that the only thing that kept her going was the knowledge that Mr. Darcy was nearby. Dealing with Mr. Collins in any fashion was exhausting, and though the man did not directly bring up the subject of their marital duties, his constant innuendo about how much he was anticipating them and the delicate compliments he seemed to believe necessary exposed to her a degree of civility entirely beyond what was endurable.

Thus, she took every opportunity to visit the woods of Rosings, and there Mr. Darcy would meet her away from prying eyes, his presence like a balm to her bruised soul. That was not to say that Mr. Collins was happy with the fact that she continued to walk great distances in defiance of his orders. On the contrary, he was as voluble concerning the matter as he had been that first day. By this time, however, Elizabeth was becoming adept at ignoring the man while appearing as if she was actually attending him. Yet every day after he had once again demanded that she avoid the activity, he appeared to be satisfied in his own mind that she would begin to obey his wishes upon the morrow.

Those times with Mr. Darcy were enough to induce Elizabeth to forget her cares for a brief moment and to immerse herself in no more weighty matters than simply coming to know the man better. They spoke of many subjects—politics, literature, and their respective childhoods, among other things—and it was not long before Elizabeth began to take the measure of the man who was so assiduously paying court to her. As for the annulment, Mr. Darcy had sent some letters which he hoped would lead him to the proper authorities, and when it was time, he would leave to see to the matter personally. Elizabeth was dreading the time when he would not be in residence, but she knew it was necessary.

Elizabeth had always known that Mr. Darcy was an intelligent man, but it was not long before she began to understand that he was even more estimable than she had suspected. They had canvassed literature previously, so Elizabeth was well aware of his capabilities there. He was also a responsible landlord, and his account of his actions with regard to his estate in the north revealed him to be a liberal master who was involved intimately with the business of his estate. Furthermore, though he was by his own admission not at his best in company, he was an ardent suitor, concerned with everything about her, including her comfort and her feelings. Underlying his words appeared to be a depth of feeling which would prove him to be an ardent lover once they were allowed to progress to the point of being able to announce their relationship openly.

It was truly unfortunate that this season of courtship should be so marred by this sham of a marriage which Elizabeth's father had forced on her. As the days progressed, she found herself becoming ever angrier with her father for robbing her of the magical wonder of Mr. Darcy's full attentions.

While they did speak of the situation at times, they restricted the subject to Elizabeth's account of how she was dealing with Mr. Collins and Mr. Darcy's efforts to determine how to release her from the marriage. It was an unspoken agreement that they should avoid speaking of the matter in favor of taking the opportunity to further become acquainted with one another.

Only once was this embargo broken. And while it was concerning a subject which Elizabeth would prefer not to have spoken of, she knew she owed Mr. Darcy an explanation.

"So you believe Mr. Bingley will make my sister an offer?" said Elizabeth as they were walking through Rosings' woods the day after he had arrived in the neighborhood.

"We had that conversation just before I left," confirmed Mr. Darcy. "Bingley is in the habit of having his head turned by a pretty face, but it does not take long for him to lose interest. As your sister has held his attention for so long, I suspect that it shall not wane."

"Then I imagine my mother shall be in a frenzy of preparations, and they will both wish they had eloped before they finally arrive at the altar."

A shadow passed over Mr. Darcy's face, and Elizabeth, realizing what she had inferred, could only wish that she had held her tongue.

"Was your mother in such a state before your departure for the church, Miss Elizabeth?"

The pointed question could only cause Elizabeth to blush, and she knew that the conversation she had dreaded for so long was at hand. "I assure you not, Mr. Darcy. My mother, though she was undoubtedly happy to be rid of me, is not of the opinion that my nuptials were worth celebrating. And when I made clear to her what her life would be like should I become mistress of Longbourn, she was quickly seized by a desire to see that the marriage never came to pass."

Mr. Darcy appeared intrigued by her words, but he did not respond to them. "Miss Bennet, perhaps it is not precisely proper to speak of it, but I find myself exceedingly curious as to the reasons behind your unusual relationship with your parents. I know you would have told me ere now had I allowed it, but I deferred that conversation. Will you not now share your burden?"

"I am well aware that you are owed this explanation, Mr. Darcy," replied Elizabeth with a sigh. "Though I might wish to leave it unspoken forever, I cannot in good conscience keep it from you, as I know that it might materially change your opinion of me."

Though Elizabeth was stoically looking to the side, she felt a hand on her arm which arrested her progress, and she looked up at the man near her, almost melting at the expression of utter compassion with which he regarded her.

"Miss Bennet," said he, "though I obviously have no knowledge of the matter at hand, I cannot imagine that I would *ever* turn away from you. Please share this great secret with me."

"It is not precisely a secret," said Elizabeth. The man's manner was utterly disarming her, and though she still regretted the necessity and wished she could avoid it, her apprehension had receded as the mist flees before the sun. "Anyone in Meryton who is of age knows at least the basics of the subject, though it is not much talked of any longer." Elizabeth paused for a moment, trying to determine how best to tell her story. "Have you heard talk at all of a Bennet heir?"

Mr. Darcy frowned. "I understood that Mr. Collins was your father's heir."

"That is true. But there was another—my father's son, who died in infancy."

The look with which Mr. Darcy favored her suggested that he already had a suspicion of what Elizabeth was about to say, but he remained silent, his eyes urging her to continue.

Elizabeth sighed. "My brother Thomas was actually my sister Mary's twin and was the first born between them. His birth fulfilled all my mother's wishes, though perhaps she still wished to have a second son to inherit should anything happen to the first. Thomas was by all accounts a healthy babe, though as twins, both he and Mary were a little smaller than most.

"You must understand, Mr. Darcy, that the events I am about to relate to you took place when I was a small child, and I have no memory of them. What I know I have pieced together through conversations with my uncle, and even though he was not privy to exactly what happened, I feel that it is essentially accurate. My parents have never deigned to tell me exactly what they hold against me.

"I was an inquisitive child and a trial to my mother's nerves. In that, I was different from Jane, who was always quiet and well-behaved and able to amuse herself for hours with the simplest of activities. After my mother gave birth to twins, only months after I turned two years of age, I was apparently fascinated with my younger siblings, much as a girl will obsess over a new doll, or perhaps more akin to the feelings of a child for a puppy. I would continually watch my mother and the nursemaid when the infants were awake, and I would watch the twins as they slept, fascinated by the new life which had arrived in our home."

Elizabeth took a deep breath, and the memory of the old pain clawed at her with icy fingertips. "On a hot day in the summer, when my brother was less than two months of age, I lay down beside him as he was napping and fell asleep. In my sleep, I somehow rolled over onto him and smothered him.

"You can imagine what happened when we were discovered. My mother's fears of being removed from her home when my father's cousin inherited the estate were born that day. And as I became older and began to understand what I had done, a feeling of guilt settled over me which I can recall from my earliest memories.

"From that day forward, I became a pariah in my own home. My father, while he did not join in the abuse, allowed my mother to treat me as she would. I was shunned, and my sisters were told I was worthless and disobedient. While my mother only struck me on rare occasions, I was often sent to bed without dinner for some imagined naughtiness. At the age of nine, I contemplated taking my own life, Mr. Darcy."

By this time, Elizabeth had tears streaming down her cheeks, though she made no effort to dry them. Mr. Darcy had kept a grave silence as she had related her past, and more than once, his compassion had almost proved to be her undoing. But Elizabeth stoically kept her composure, determined to relate the entire story before her courage failed her. She was spent by the time she fell silent.

"That is an extraordinary tale, Miss Bennet," said Mr. Darcy. "Here, let us sit so that you may regain your composure."

He led her to a nearby bench which had been hewn from a log, and after seeing to her comfort, he sat by her side. Though it was not proper by any stretch, he reached out and grasped one of her hands between his own, caressing it in soothing, mesmerizing circles.

"Now, there are one or two points I would like to clarify. First, in my experience, infants are put into cribs to sleep for their own protection, not only from falling, but also from other dangers such as curious toddlers. As a child of two, how could you have climbed into the crib to sleep with your brother?"

"I know not, Mr. Darcy," replied Elizabeth, taking the handkerchief he pressed into her hand and drying her tears. "It is something which has come up in conversation with my uncle. He suspects that my entreaties to see my brother annoyed my mother—who has always been flighty—and that I was put down to sleep with my brother either by mistake or by design in order to silence me."

"And your father has never spoken of it."

Elizabeth laughed, though the sound was devoid of mirth. "Does my father ever speak of anything? A more taciturn man would be difficult to find. My father ignored and avoided me before I left his house, and other than the day he forced me to the altar, he has confined his interactions with me to an expressionless stare."

"Then your uncle stepped in?"

"When I was nine, my uncle and aunt visited for Christmas a few months after they were married, and they removed me back to London with my father's permission."

Mr. Darcy fell silent, and they sat on the bench listening to the wind as it played through the bare branches of the trees. Here and there, the sounds of bird calls echoed through the woods, and Elizabeth thought she could hear the chattering of squirrels, though the season was rather late. The sensations evoked by Mr. Darcy's continual stroking of her hand were almost soporific in nature, and Elizabeth soon found herself drifting. She had slept badly since her arrival in Kent, and she almost felt as if she could succumb to the lure of sleep out here in the woods, with Mr. Darcy watching over her like a guardian angel.

At length, however, he spoke. "Miss Elizabeth, would you like to hear my interpretation of the events you have just related?"

Though by now she was certain he would not be severe with her, Elizabeth smothered a sense of apprehension and nodded.

"It is unfortunate that your brother did not live, but a child of two has not the capacity to understand the consequences of their actions. Even a fairly simple desire, such as the desire to see a beloved brother, can have consequences far beyond what a child can understand." Mr. Darcy looked intently into her eyes, and she could fancy that he was trying by force of his will to induce her to agree with his assessment.

"Miss Bennet, in the end, I believe that the exact sequence of events is irrelevant. What your parents have subjected you to is unconscionable. Only the basest of parents would hold the actions of a child against them, no matter what the tragic consequences were. I urge you to release whatever guilt you still carry."

"I have tried, Mr. Darcy," said Elizabeth. "It is still difficult for me to talk about it, but my years with my uncle and aunt taught me that lesson, though it was not easy to learn. I mourn my brother's passing, but I know that I did not bring about his death with malicious intent."

Mr. Darcy nodded. "Even in the short time in which I spoke with Mr. Gardiner, he impressed me as a sensible man. And now I find that I am indebted to him."

Curious as to his meaning, Elizabeth cocked an eyebrow at him, a little of her spirit returning in the wake of her confession.

"If he had not taken you into his home and molded you into the exceptional young lady you are today, than we may have met under very different circumstances, and you might have been a very different person." Mr. Darcy paused, and a shadow fell over his eyes. "We might not have met at all."

"But we have, Mr. Darcy," replied Elizabeth. His words caused her heart to soar, and she now felt happier than she had since before she came to London. If her penance for what had happened—her time with her family, the trumped-up marriage to Collins, the pain of all that had occurred—was to be the price for the love of this wonderful man, then Elizabeth would pay it gladly a hundred times over.

"I know that there is still much to do," continued Mr. Darcy, "but once you are free of Collins, I wish to bring you under *my* protection quickly."

Elizabeth's joy dimmed slightly. "But I am still not twenty. Even if I am free of Collins, I doubt my father will agree to allow your suit."

A fierce scowl met her concern. "Leave that to me. Given how the man has behaved, I will feel not an iota of remorse should his refusal force me to act against him. You will be my wife, Elizabeth. That I promise you."

What was there to say to such a declaration? There was nothing she could say. And though Elizabeth knew that the greatest care must be taken in her behavior, she could not but wait with breathless anticipation as Mr. Darcy lowered his head. Then his lips were suddenly on hers.

It was nothing more than the briefest of contact—a mere grazing of his lips upon hers—but the feeling behind it and the tenderness of Mr. Darcy's expression was enough to leave Elizabeth breathless, as though he had kissed her with abandon. But more than that, it was the promise, the unshakeable testament that he would abide by his words and that they would ultimately be together. And in that moment, Elizabeth felt the first stirrings of love flutter within her breast. What a thing it was to be inspired to such feelings and to inspire them in her turn!

The moment was over quickly, and though Elizabeth felt her face flaming as if warmed by the heat of a blacksmith's furnace, she could not look away from Mr. Darcy. This was where she belonged. She was home.

"Come," said Mr. Darcy, rising to his feet and pulling her along with him. "We should return you to the parsonage before you are missed."

They began walking through the wooded paths, and Elizabeth reflected back on this most wonderful of days. She knew that she would always cherish it, above even their ultimate wedding day or anything which was to come afterward. For on that day, she had truly learned that she was worthy of the love of a good man.

A few nights later, Elizabeth found herself in the sitting room of Rosings Park, where Lady Catherine was holding court. When she arrived back at the parsonage, Mr. Collins had met her with the invitation—though Elizabeth felt it was more like a summons—from his illustrious patroness for dinner that night. It was the first time since her arrival in Kent that they had been so honored with an invitation, and Elizabeth was almost certain that it would have been forthcoming earlier if Mr. Darcy had not arrived the next day. And there were two others present that evening—Mr. Darcy's cousins, Anne de Bourgh and Colonel Fitzwilliam.

It was not long before Elizabeth felt she had taken the measure of the two new acquaintances. Anne de Bourgh was a quiet woman, likely a few years younger than Mr. Darcy, and though she was not what one would commonly term as "pretty," she was at least pleasant-featured and seemed to be a kindly sort of person. Of course, it was difficult to tell, as Miss de Bourgh was rarely allowed to say anything without

Lady Catherine restating or outright contradicting everything she said or even simply speaking for Miss de Bourgh so that she might avoid the bother of speaking for herself. Elizabeth could also see evidence of the woman's weak constitution in her coloring, which was much paler than Elizabeth's own, and in the thinness of her figure. Miss de Bourgh's method of dealing with her mother was often a roll of her eyes or a small shake of her head. Elizabeth thought she would be well worth knowing if one could only get past her mother.

By contrast, Colonel Fitzwilliam was bluff and good-humored, his pleasure at meeting Elizabeth evident in the wideness of his smile. Colonel Fitzwilliam was at least as tall as Mr. Darcy, but though he was not nearly so handsome—and she was willing to acknowledge that she might be prejudiced—he was by no means ill-favored or bereft of charm. Elizabeth quickly felt disarmed in his presence and was soon chatting with him happily.

"I am very happy to make your acquaintance, Mrs. Collins," said Colonel Fitzwilliam after sitting on one of the sofas near to her. "Darcy has told me much of you, and I dare say he did you justice, even with his typical reticence."

"I am happy to have Mr. Darcy's good opinion." Elizabeth forced herself to avoid looking at the man, who sat at Lady Catherine's side. "Very happy indeed."

Colonel Fitzwilliam smiled and nodded at her while shooting a glance at his aunt, who was in the midst of graciously accepting Mr. Collins's fawning. "I understand you are recently arrived at Hunsford. How do you like the parsonage?"

Something in his manner told Elizabeth that he was aware of the truth of the situation, and she relaxed ever so slightly at the thought of having another ally so close at hand. "It is a comfortable home and by no means lacking in shelves in the closets. I believe that Lady Catherine has graciously bestowed her . . . kindness upon the one man who will willingly accept whatever she deigns to share with him."

The colonel laughed. "I have no doubt of it. I dare say that I understood Mr. Collins's character within a few moments of meeting him this previous spring."

"What are you talking of, Fitzwilliam?" interrupted Lady Catherine in a strident tone. "I shall not have guests in my house speaking in low tones and keeping confidences. I will share in the conversation."

"We were speaking of your generosity in bestowing your advice upon Mr. Collins, aunt," said the colonel. He winked at Elizabeth in a manner which Lady Catherine could not see, nearly prompting

Elizabeth to giggle.

"Indeed, your ladyship is most kind and condescending to offer such pearls of wisdom," was Mr. Collins's grandiose interjection. "We are exceedingly grateful, I assure you, and whatever you impart to us, I promise shall be executed with alacrity. And might I add—"

"It is very discerning of you to recognize good advice when you receive it," said Lady Catherine, speaking over whatever William Collins was saying at the moment. The parson almost appeared to have swallowed his tongue in his haste to be silent, a circumstance which did not go unnoticed by any of Lady Catherine's relations. Perhaps it was not exactly kind to laugh at the stupid man's mannerisms, but he was so ridiculous that Elizabeth could not blame the cousins' hastily hidden smiles.

"I could not do otherwise, Lady Catherine," replied Elizabeth, watching as the grand dame inclined her head as if it was nothing more than her due.

The conversation continued for some time until they were called into dinner. Lady Catherine insisted that Anne and Mr. Darcy sit on either side of her, leaving Elizabeth in the company of her supposed husband and Colonel Fitzwilliam. But though Mr. Collins spent much of the meal pontificating in his ponderous tone, Elizabeth and the colonel were able to garner much amusement from baiting and observing the man, so it was not a total loss.

"I really must say that I find your wife quite enchanting, Mr. Collins," said the colonel near the end of the meal. "I am sure you must feel yourself to be fortunate indeed to have persuaded such a woman to become your wife."

The parson preened and smiled beatifically, no doubt thinking that it was a compliment to him that the colonel liked his wife so much. "Indeed, I am. My wife has many charms in her favor, and though her portion is small and her future was bleak, I flatter myself that I saw past the material disadvantages and recognized that she was perfectly suited to a man in my position. I dare say that you will not find two such partners possessed of such a commonality of purpose, such a unity of thought."

"Indeed, you are correct." With a glance at Elizabeth betraying his amusement, Colonel Fitzwilliam continued, "I have yet to meet a couple such as you."

Elizabeth was forced to cough into her handkerchief, which she had raised to her mouth when Mr. Collins had begun speaking. It truly was beneficial to her state of mind to have such an intelligent and amusing man as Colonel Fitzwilliam nearby to make her life more bearable!

After dinner, they adjourned to the music room, where Lady Catherine expressed a fervent desire for some music. Of course, as she was the only one present who possessed any skill whatsoever on the pianoforte, Elizabeth was elected to exhibit before the company. Far from being annoyed at the lady's imperiousness, Elizabeth was grateful for the opportunity to avoid more "instruction" at the lady's hands. She was pleased when Colonel Fitzwilliam offered to sit with her and turn the pages.

When she had played the first piece, Lady Catherine spoke up. "Your playing is quite proficient, Mrs. Collins. I understand that you had access to masters during your sojourn in London."

"Yes, Lady Catherine," replied Elizabeth, quietly beginning to play another song which she had memorized. "My aunt was diligent in seeing to that part of my education."

"As she should have been," replied the lady. "I am glad to see that the necessities of polite society are recognized even by one as far down the social scale as your aunt."

Elizabeth caught Mr. Darcy's eye as his aunt spoke, and he appeared as if he thought she might be offended by his aunt's rather crass and rude statement. But Elizabeth only favored him with the slightest of smiles. She was not about to be offended by the ill-judged opinions of a woman who was so very self-absorbed.

"Indeed, she was, your ladyship. I have never wanted for any instruction in those subjects in which all accomplished women must have knowledge."

"Ah, but who decides the requirements to be deemed accomplished?" asked Colonel Fitzwilliam with a twinkle in his eye. "I have seen many a woman who is called accomplished merely because she nets a fine purse."

"Indeed, you are correct," said Mr. Darcy. "It is a term which is much too liberally applied."

Elizabeth arched an eyebrow in the manner she knew he found charming. "And how would you define the term, Mr. Darcy?"

"Oh, an accomplished woman must possess the usual skills, among them an aptitude for music, an understanding of modern languages, and so on." His expression became downright playful at that moment. "But I must own that should a woman not improve her mind by extensive reading, then the rest of it is all wasted."

By Elizabeth's side, the colonel was forced to hold back a guffaw, as he clearly understood Mr. Darcy's reference to her penchant for the written word, which they had discussed during dinner. Unfortunately, it was near impossible for Mr. Collins to remain silent for any length of time.

"And it is my assertion that there is no young woman so accomplished or so elegant as your dear daughter, Miss Anne de Bourgh, for there is in her carriage a nobility and intelligence such that it may render any other pretenders for the title as nothing. You must be very proud of her indeed."

"You are mistaken," replied Anne with a bit of a blush. "I am not accomplished."

"Of course you are," snapped Lady Catherine. "Mr. Collins has the right of it. Though you do not currently play, net purses, paint screens, or any of that other nonsense that the world thinks so highly of, I am confident that should your health have allowed it, you would have been the most accomplished of your sex."

Lady Catherine turned to Mr. Darcy. "Anne is uniquely suited to whatever endeavor she should bend her will toward, do you not agree?"

Anne looked skyward, her cheeks flaming with mortification, but Mr. Darcy merely said, "I am certain my cousin is most capable."

The murmur of conversation in that part of the room rose, and Elizabeth was left to her playing, which she attended to before she could be singled out by Lady Catherine. Beside her, the colonel was smiling at the inanities to which he had just been a witness, and after some few moments, he turned to her and with a grin said:

"My aunt is right about one thing—your playing is very fine indeed."

"Thank you, Colonel Fitzwilliam. It has often been my companion these years. I do enjoy the activity very much."

Elizabeth stayed at the pianoforte for the rest of the short time they were there, and she thought that Lady Catherine might command her to cease playing, but the lady seemed content with her audience and made no further comment toward her. When it was nearing time for Elizabeth and Mr. Collins to depart, Mr. Darcy stood and made his way to Elizabeth's side, stopping when he was in full view of the pianoforte to stand there with the ghost of a smile on his face.

"I am relieved to know of Mr. Darcy's opinion of me," said Elizabeth, a playful mood rising up within her. "His countenance is often so forbidding that if I was at all unsure, then I might think that he disapproved of me."

"I am not so very stern," said Mr. Darcy as the colonel chuckled.

"And you are well aware of my opinion of you, so you may drop any pretense."

"There is no pretense, sir," said Elizabeth. She wished to smile at him and show him the full brilliancy of her feelings for him, but under the hawk eye of Lady Catherine, it seemed wiser to moderate her expressions.

"I am glad to hear it. But we must speak quickly before my aunt summons me back."

Elizabeth nodded her head as she continued to play.

"Tomorrow, I will be leaving the estate, and though I do not expect to be gone long, I wished you to know of it before I leave."

"Is it concerning my . . . particular problem?"

"It is," confirmed Mr. Darcy. He leaned forward and in a low tone said, "I will be speaking with Mr. Collins's superior. I hope that I am able to prompt an investigation into certain matters which have occurred in the past week. Your situation should be addressed at the same time."

"Thank you, Mr. Darcy," said Elizabeth very quietly. "I am beyond grateful for your help."

Mr. Darcy only smiled. "I am helping myself as much as I am helping you."

"And Anne and I will be here to support you," said the colonel as he cleared his throat pointedly.

Mr. Darcy nodded and stood up straight again, no doubt knowing that he must be careful in front of Lady Catherine.

"I do not doubt that it shall be entertaining in the extreme," continued the colonel in a jolly tone. "I have not had this much fun in ages."

At that moment, Mr. Collins announced that they must depart, though it was clear that his announcement was made with the greatest reluctance. Elizabeth could not imagine that the man would ever willingly suggest that he leave the lady's presence, which indicated that Lady Catherine had spoken to him at some point in the past about the appropriate length for one to stay after dinner.

The carriage was offered to convey them back to Hunsford, and Elizabeth departed in the company of her husband. And though she did not have an opportunity for a personal farewell with Mr. Darcy, she knew that he could see the depths of her heart in her eyes. And she left, content in the knowledge that the necessary steps to release her from the yoke of Mr. Collins were about to be put into motion.

Chapter XX

𝒯he night of the ball at Netherfield, Jane Bennet prepared herself as she usually would for such an event, but her heart was not in it. For ten years, she had done without Elizabeth's presence, but now that she had been tantalized with her dear sister's sparkling company for those few weeks, Jane felt that there was something important missing from her everyday life. For the first time, she found herself feeling resentful of her father.

The Bennet ladies gathered in the entrance hall of Longbourn, and as Jane looked at her sisters, she could see how subdued they were. She was not the only one who had been affected by Elizabeth's forced departure. Of course, the exception was Lydia, ignorant as she was, for she had loudly proclaimed that she was happy to be rid of her elder sister. But Kitty, Lydia's close follower no more, had been more thoughtful of late and was disinclined to follow her younger sister's example. And if Mary moralized less, then Jane could only be happy for the change. How strange that such a material difference could have been caused by their father's betrayal of their sister.

"Let us depart, girls," said Mrs. Bennet as she bustled into the room. Mrs. Bennet was no longer inclined to complain and moan about whatever upsetting thing Elizabeth had told her.

"Where is my father?" asked Jane, though she had much rather avoid him.

Mrs. Bennet huffed and waved her hand in exasperation. "Your father will not be moved. He claims he will not attend the ball with us."

In truth, Jane was not surprised. Mr. Bennet had rarely removed himself from his bookroom since he had forced Elizabeth from the house. Regardless, to avoid a private ball given by a newcomer to the area at the largest estate in the area was beyond rude.

The rest of her sisters did not comment, nor did they appear to care about their father's incivility. Soon, the Bennet ladies were filing out to the carriage, and they got under way, and if the carriage was less cramped than it might otherwise have been, it was cold comfort indeed.

The drive in front of Netherfield was decorated with a string of lanterns which illuminated the night, and the manor house glowed and hummed with activity. Servants, their uniforms crisply pressed, stepped forward to assist the Bennets from their carriage, bowing and welcoming them to Netherfield. They entered the house to the sight of the master of the house approaching, his face split with a smile wider than any Jane had yet seen adorning his face.

"Mrs. Bennet, Miss Bennet, welcome!" exclaimed he as he grasped Jane's hand and kissed it.

"Thank you for your welcome, Mr. Bingley," enthused Mrs. Bennet. "It is very kind of you to have invited us."

"It is no trouble at all, Mrs. Bennet," replied he. But while Mrs. Bennet preened and tittered and acted as if Mr. Bingley had paid her the highest of compliments, Jane, who had spent more time in Mr. Bingley's company than anyone else in Hertfordshire, could tell that he was much less enthusiastic and much more reserved than was his wont. Given their previous discussion, Jane could not help but conjecture that he now disapproved of her parents.

With a mischievous smile, he excused them—Mrs. Bennet had already turned her attention to Lady Lucas, who was nearby—and led Jane to the side, saying, "I hope you have saved the first dance for me, Miss Bennet."

Jane flushed. "Of course, Mr. Bingley."

"Excellent! And I believe that I will require the supper set, too, if you please."

Her blush deepened, and Jane thought she was almost glowing scarlet. "It is yours if you wish, Mr. Bingley," replied she, though her voice was little more than a whisper. "Are you certain you wish to make so . . ."

"I have never been so certain of anything in my life, Miss Bennet." The pure emotion in Mr. Bingley's voice pulled Jane's eyes up to his, and for a moment, she thought she was floating on a cloud, weightless and free. The intensity in his gaze almost reminded her of when his friend watched Elizabeth.

"Then it is settled," she managed after a moment of trying to find her voice.

"Good." Mr. Bingley paused and looked about. "If you will wait for me, Miss Bennet, I will complete my duties in the receiving line and then come and collect you. I would very much like to escort you into the ballroom."

As he returned to finish receiving his guests, Jane watched him, taking the time to calm her racing heart and compose herself. Whatever deficiencies Mr. Bingley now saw in her family, his behavior proved his enduring good opinion of *her*. There was something . . . eager in his attentions this evening. Jane did not dare contemplate what exactly this might portend, but there was an excitement in her which could not be repressed. It seemed like a momentous evening.

At length, when the receiving line had all passed through, Mr. Bingley excused himself and approached Jane, his irrepressible smile once again fixed upon her. "Shall we, Miss Bennet?"

Nodding, Jane put her hand on his arm and allowed herself to be guided into the ballroom. The large room was filled with the residents of the surrounding countryside, milling about, speaking with one another. The band at the far end was already engaged in prelude music, and the soft strains of the strings wafted over the room like the most delicious scent. The room itself had been decorated in the soft shades of gold and red, and though Jane doubted that it had been Miss Bingley's intent, the subdued lighting almost suggested a hint of romance in the air. It was altogether the most breathtaking scene Jane had ever witnessed.

Soon, the time for the first dance had come, and the dancers formed up on the floor, the honor of leading the dance falling to Jane and Mr. Bingley. The music began, and they commenced the steps of the dance. The first pass was executed with all the gracefulness of a swan, and when they closed once again and he took her hand, Jane, unable to keep her concern for her sister at bay, even on this most magical of nights, said:

"Have you heard from Mr. Darcy?"

"Only once, when he informed me that he had arrived safely."

The dance took them apart for several moments, and when they once again approached each other, Jane continued:

"I am very grateful that Mr. Darcy should take it on himself to assist my poor sister."

"I believe that his own interest is engaged in this matter, Miss Bennet."

"So I understand. But many men would not continue to pursue a woman in the face of such . . ." Jane paused, glancing around to ensure that no one was attending to their conversation. "What I mean to say is I think very highly of Mr. Darcy for not wavering from his purpose despite all that has happened."

"He will not," was Mr. Bingley's firm reply. "A steadier character than Darcy's I have yet to meet."

They separated, and it was a few moments before they once again met on the floor. Mr. Bingley's gaze upon her rivalled his friend's in intensity when he said:

"I will not waver either, Miss Bennet. Of that, I assure you."

Blushing, Jane nodded her head, feeling blessed that she and her younger sister had protectors of such constancy.

The night was magical. Jane rarely had occasion to sit, as her hand was solicited for every set, and since Mr. Bingley was the host, he did not sit out a dance either. He performed his duties with the aplomb of a truly amiable man. And if neither of their eyes left the other even when they were dancing with other partners, no one in the room could fault them, and all Meryton was afire with speculation as to when their engagement would be finalized.

Jane herself never realized how much she gazed at Mr. Bingley, but she did know that for perhaps the first time in her life, she was truly happy. She was being courted by a man of principle and honor, and she had hope that her dearest sister would be released from her predicament by her own admirer.

Unfortunately, with a family such as hers, it was impossible for the entire evening to pass without some sort of vexation rearing its ugly head. And though Kitty did not embarrass her as she might have previously, there was no change in the behaviors of Mrs. Bennet and Lydia. Her mother spent the entire night speaking loudly of her expectations for her eldest daughter and the handsome and very rich man from the north, and nothing Jane said could quiet her rhapsodies. It took all her fortitude to ignore the words which continually spilled from her mother's mouth, but Jane was able to take heart in Mr. Bingley, who looked at her with commiseration and mouthed, "Courage!" to her on more than one occasion.

Lydia was a different matter altogether. She flirted and laughed, flitting from one officer to another, and given the way some of them looked at her with naked lust engraved on their faces, Jane knew it would not be long before her sister disgraced herself and all her family. But it took Mary's plea before she finally decided to act.

"Jane, can you not do something about Lydia?" pleaded Mary. The night had progressed, and it was almost time for supper, and given the wine flowing freely, Jane knew that Lydia's behavior would not get any better as the night grew longer.

Nodding, Jane slipped away from her sister, and marching up to Lydia, she took her hand and directed an apologetic smile at the young man with whom she was currently flirting.

"Jane, what are you doing?" squawked Lydia as Jane led her away. "I was speaking with Denny!"

"I care not!" cried Jane as they reached the entrance hall.

Jane spied a door to the side of the hall and, opening it, discovered a small room that was empty. She quickly guided her still protesting sister inside.

Ever impetuous, Lydia made to get past her, saying, "Let me return to the ball. I was having ever so much fun!"

"You shall not until you have heard what I have to say!" snapped Jane.

Lydia blinked, seeing Jane angry for perhaps the first time, but her whining and protestations did not stop.

"Lydia, stop it! You are on the verge of disgracing us all with your behavior. I demand you behave with more decorum!"

"Mama is not displeased with me!"

"When is Mama *ever* displeased with you?"

Jane looked at her youngest sister, and as she noted the pout on Lydia's face and the firm set to her jaw, contempt for the girl rose within her. Lydia was not unintelligent, but her strong will and exuberant demeanor had never been checked with instructions on proper behavior, and it made her unwise.

"Now, you listen to me, Lydia," said Jane, speaking slowly and clearly to ensure her sister understood she was serious, "if you do not cease this unseemly behavior, then I will ask Mr. Bingley to remove you to an upstairs bedroom where you will stay and miss the rest of the ball."

Lydia's chin jutted out in defiance. "You have no authority over me. I shall act as I see fit."

"Perhaps she has no authority, but I would hope you would obey your elder sister."

Startled by the voice, the sisters turned as one to see Mr. Bingley enter the room. And though Jane had always thought of him as a congenial man, the events of the past few days had proven that he was able to summon a stern bearing as well. He walked toward them, and after nodding at Jane with an affectionate smile, he turned a hard and unforgiving glare back upon Lydia.

"I must own that though I have seen your improper behavior in the past, Miss Lydia, I have never seen you throw caution to the wind with such abandon. Perhaps it is the absence of your father which has prompted this departure from decent behavior?"

The flush of Lydia's cheeks told Jane all she had to know. Mr. Bennet had never been much of a deterrent before, but his mere presence—even in spite of his propensity to ignore her excesses—must have kept the girl in check to a certain extent.

"In this matter, I support your sister," said Mr. Bingley. "If you do not cease this unseemly flirting, loud laughter, and your other attempts to make a spectacle of yourself, then you shall be confined to a bedroom with a footman guarding you to ensure you do not leave."

"You cannot do that!" cried Lydia.

"I assure you that I can," was Mr. Bingley's merciless response. "Given how your mother likes to exclaim about how I am courting her eldest daughter, do you think she will gainsay me in this matter? Furthermore, your father is not present—not that I believe he would care in the slightest should I remove you from the ball.

"In truth, Miss Lydia, you are not old enough, you do not have the appropriate experience as to the consequences of your actions, and you have never, I dare say, been taught how to moderate your behavior. I now wish that my invitation to this ball had excluded you. I do not wish the evening to be ruined by the actions of an ill-mannered child."

Lydia gasped, and tears appeared in the corners of her eyes. But Mr. Bingley was merciless, and Jane dared to think that he was masterful. This was a man who, being fully cognizant of the mores of society, took action to correct a situation which was getting out of hand. If only her father had the same kind of character!

"Be that as it may, you are here, and you may stay as long as you conduct yourself properly. We will now return to the ballroom, where you will speak quietly and not run about with every officer in attendance. And I assure you that I will be speaking with Colonel Forster about his officers' behavior, if he has not already noticed himself.

"Am I very clear about what we expect of you?"

A sullen nod met Mr. Bingley's demand, and though Jane thought that Lydia might be cowed for the time being, she highly doubted that her ways were to be so easily changed.

"Very good," said Mr. Bingley. "Now, let us return before we are missed. Miss Bennet, if you will?"

Jane took Mr. Bingley's extended arm, noting that Lydia reluctantly grasped his other arm, and allowed herself to be led back to the ballroom. Their entrance, though it did not go unnoticed, did not create as much of a stir as Jane had feared. She did notice Miss Bingley's glare, and she could not fault the woman for it; after all, Lydia's behavior must be of concern for her as well, given the attention that her brother had been paying to Jane since his arrival.

"Miss Lydia, are you engaged for the supper set?" queried Mr. Bingley as they entered the room.

"With Captain Carter," said Lydia, her sullenness giving way slightly to anticipation.

"Carter is a good man," replied Mr. Bingley with a nod of approval. "You may wait until he approaches you for the set. But remember: behave yourself, or you shall be removed from the ballroom in disgrace."

A resentful glare met his directive, but it soon withered in the face of Mr. Bingley's fixed and pointed look. She subsided with a nod.

Having noticed them entering the room, Mary approached, her posture screaming her uncertainty. "Will you please stand with Lydia until her partner for the supper set comes to claim her?" asked Jane.

Apparently, Mary's question was answered, and she sighed with relief and agreed to their request. Jane was led away by Mr. Bingley as the first strains of music for the supper set were floating out over the ballroom. Taking the opportunity of their close proximity, Jane leaned toward her companions and said:

"Thank you, Mr. Bingley. She would never have listened to my demands alone."

"It is quite all right, Miss Bennet," replied Mr. Bingley. He directed a soft smile at her which melted her heart. "I would not have you discomfited when it is within my power to prevent it. I dare say that your sister is not beyond redemption. All she needs is a little guidance."

Jane grimaced. "Unfortunately, she is not likely to receive it from my parents."

Mr. Bingley grimaced in sympathy, but there was not much he

could say.

The other event to mar the beauty of the ball happened later that evening, near the end of supper. Jane had, as per convention, partnered with Mr. Bingley for supper, and much of her equilibrium had returned. As Mrs. Bennet was sitting in a completely different part of the room, her words had no power to bring shame to Jane, who made the decision to focus on her dinner partner and not whatever mortifying words were issuing forth from her mother's mouth.

It was as the supper hour was coming to a close when Mr. Bingley excused himself to see to some matter of the musicians, leaving Jane by herself for a moment. She stood and went to the table on which the punch sat, taking a cup for herself and reflecting on the evening. It was then that Miss Bingley approached her and greeted her as if she were a close friend.

"Miss Bennet, I hope that you are enjoying yourself this evening?"

"I am indeed, Miss Bingley," replied Jane, who had already complimented the woman on her arrangements. "You have created a wonderful evening for your guests and should take pride in that fact."

Miss Bingley fairly preened, though her words were a deflection of praise. "It is nothing, I assure you. In a country town such as this, the demands which would prevail in London society may be relaxed for a more informal evening. I have not done anything extraordinary."

Jane inclined her head, determined to take the woman's words at face value, though they could just as easily have been construed as being critical of country society.

"I understand that your sister was lately married to your cousin," said Miss Bingley. "How is she adjusting to life as a married woman?"

Feeling somewhat uneasy, Jane demurred. "I have not yet had a chance to hear from my sister." Jane did not think the events surrounding her sister's marriage had been much talked about in the area as of yet. Mrs. Bennet did not speak of it, and though Elizabeth's absence that evening had been noted, not much had been made of it. Miss Bingley must have heard it from her brother.

Miss Bingley nodded in a commiserating fashion. "Married women do not necessarily possess the time required to write to their single siblings. I know when Mrs. Hurst was married, I hardly heard from her for a sixmonth!"

"I have every expectation of hearing from Elizabeth before long."

"Then that is well indeed," said Miss Bingley. "I suppose she was not in residence for the past ten years, so you must be very well able to do without her."

"On the contrary, Miss Bingley, I miss her exceedingly so."

Miss Bingley took no notice of her comment. "It must be of great comfort to your mother for your sister to marry her husband's heir. You will all continue to have a home once your father departs to meet his maker."

Jane looked at the woman askance. Surely Miss Bingley must be in her brother's confidence, knowing that he was on the point of making her an offer. Though uncomfortable with this conversation, Jane could only respond:

"I would hope to have my own home long ere that happens."

"And so you shall," said Miss Bingley. "But it is truly a shame that Mr. Darcy has departed from Netherfield. His presence is such a comfort for Charles." Miss Bingley turned an excited, almost sly gaze on Jane and said, "I dare say that he . . . Well, perhaps it is best not to excite speculation. But I am certain that I shall not remain in my single state for much longer."

Jane turned a disbelieving eye upon Miss Bingley, wondering if the woman had witnessed the same events that she had herself these past weeks. The insinuation that Mr. Darcy would soon be offering for her, after Jane already had confirmation that Mr. Darcy had asked Elizabeth for a courtship, showed a blindness to the facts of the situation which was shocking.

"It is particularly gratifying to be singled out by such a man," continued Miss Bingley, blithely unaware of Jane's consternation. "I believe that everything has passed as it was meant to. It is of paramount importance that people marry within their sphere, after all, and I am happy that everything has worked out so well.

"Now that events are proceeding in such a proper manner, I might soon be able to call another dear friend my sister." Miss Bingley leaned toward Jane, and as if imparting a great secret, she whispered: "Charles and Miss Darcy are such *dear* friends. And though Charles often takes a fancy to a new acquaintance, his affections always return to his friend's sister. I dare say we will be hearing wedding bells before long."

An immense feeling of disdain welled up within Jane, and for the first time, she saw Miss Bingley for exactly what she was—a petty, insincere, social climber who did not care about who she stepped over to get what she wanted. Her insinuations about staying in the proper sphere were almost laughable considering the fact that she was nothing more than the daughter of a tradesman giving herself airs. In that moment, Jane wanted to put the woman in her place more than almost anything she had ever wanted in her whole life.

"I believe you should not put too much hope in your brother marrying Miss Darcy," said Jane in a frosty tone. Miss Bingley started when she spoke, undoubtedly considering Jane far too modest and self-effacing to speak in such a manner. "Considering the fact that he has all but declared himself to *me*, your ambition will never be realized.

"And given how much Mr. Darcy avoids you, I seriously doubt he will ever offer for you, regardless of whether my sister is available or has, as you say, 'married within her sphere.' I am a gentleman's daughter, as is my sister, and I am certain we must both be acceptable as a bride to any young man. And my sister is every bit Mr. Darcy's equal, no matter what her social status or married state. Perhaps you should remember that."

With that, Jane turned and walked away, leaving the woman to stare at her in stupefaction.

It was just as the dancing was beginning again that Caroline stalked up to Bingley with a fierce scowl and demanded his attention.

"Charles, I would speak with you immediately!"

Bingley turned to regard her with some amusement. He had not missed the fact that Caroline had just been speaking with the woman he loved, and he had also witnessed her smug self-satisfaction turn to befuddlement in the wake of that conversation. It seemed that Miss Bennet had finally shed her diffident manner and seen Caroline for what she was and had then put her in her place accordingly.

"You would speak with me about what?" replied Bingley mildly. "I am engaged with Miss Lucas for the next set."

"She can wait," said Caroline. Her shortness only served to amuse Bingley rather than to annoy him as it would have in the past.

Bingley was not unaware of Caroline's shortcomings. But as one who did not in general like disputes, he had attempted to carefully inform his sister that Darcy was not interested. When she had angrily denied his words, he had left her to her own delusions. Darcy could take care of himself, after all.

He knew that Caroline would not take his intention to propose to Miss Bennet well, aspiring, as she did, for him to make a match with Miss Darcy, through the most convoluted bit of reasoning Bingley had ever come across. But Bingley was firm in his purpose. He would propose to Miss Bennet, and if he had his way, he would do so before the night was complete. He fancied he owed Darcy for his firmness of purpose, not only because Darcy had advised him to secure Miss Bennet as soon as may be, but also on account of his friend's guidance over the years of their acquaintance.

A sidelong glance at his sister revealed that she would not give way. He would have to speak with her, lest she make a scene. It was just as well—now was as good a time as any to have this conversation.

"Very well, Caroline, but I will not leave Miss Lucas without informing her that I will not be able to dance with her. I shall meet you in the hall as soon as I have a word with her."

Caroline's demeanor told him what she thought of his intention, but she wisely bit her tongue and nodded in a distinctly impatient fashion. She then stalked away from him in high dudgeon.

After seeking Miss Lucas out, Bingley bowed to her and said with a smile: "I apologize, Miss Lucas, but my sister has brought a matter to me which demands my attention. Could I trouble you to reserve another dance for me this evening?"

Miss Lucas smiled and said, "It is no trouble at all, Mr. Bingley. I am free two dances hence."

"Then it is settled," replied Bingley, bowing and turning to leave the room. It was truly fortunate that Miss Lucas was such an agreeable young lady. Many with whom he was acquainted would have taken such an application as an insult.

Upon exiting the ballroom, Bingley made the short journey to the hall swiftly, eager that this tête-à-tête should not draw the attention of those in attendance. When he arrived, his first sight was of his sister pacing like a caged lion. She rounded on him as soon as he appeared.

"What are you thinking of, Charles?" spat she.

"Perhaps if you would be more explicit, then I might be able to answer you," replied Bingley, unimpressed by her show of pique.

"You know very well of what I speak. This infatuation with Jane Bennet has gone too far. I cannot believe that you would disgrace our father's memory with this . . . this . . . ill-advised dalliance with a young lady who is by no means suitable to be your wife."

"And in what way is Miss Bennet unsuitable?" asked Bingley. He held control of his temper, displaying in his mind a Darcy-like iron control over his emotions, but it was a near thing.

Caroline threw up her arms in disgust. "She has no fortune, no connections, and the most insupportable, improper family I have ever had the misfortune to meet. In short, she has nothing to recommend her, and her mother will end up being a millstone around your neck should you continue in this fashion." Caroline stopped pacing and her eyes narrowed. "Tomorrow, we shall return to town and leave this inconsequential speck behind us. You shall overcome this infatuation in due time, I have no doubt."

"I will not," said Bingley, standing up straight and refusing to bend to his sister's machinations.

"Yes, you will!" snapped Caroline. "I insist. I will not put up with that insignificant little country miss as a sister."

"Then you had best leave my house and go live with our relations in York, for I shall not be moved."

"What is it about these Bennet sisters which causes men to lose themselves like rutting dogs?" cried Caroline. "I shall not accept this, I tell you. She shall be the ruin of our entire family!"

"What is the meaning of this?"

The third Bingley sibling stepped into the hallway and approached them. "I can almost hear you in the ballroom *above* even the sound of the music, Caroline. If you do not wish our guests to overhear you quarrelling like a pair of hyenas, then I suggest you desist immediately."

Caroline appeared flustered at her sister's words, so Bingley took advantage of her momentary speechlessness and turned to Louisa.

"I suppose that you are in agreement with Caroline?"

His hard, accusing tone was not lost on Louisa, and she paled slightly. "I have not the pleasure of understanding you."

"Caroline is trying to convince me of the unsuitability of Jane Bennet to be my wife. I suppose that you are here to support our sister and try to dissuade me from my course?"

Louisa paled and glanced at Caroline—who was watching, her face almost chiseled from stone—before she turned back to Bingley with a conciliatory expression. "I will not lie to you, Charles. I am concerned, primarily with the . . . lack of decorum betrayed by some of her family members."

"And her lack of dowry and connections?" said Bingley in an accusatory tone. "What of those?"

"Those facts are to be considered, of course," said Louisa. "But if you feel strongly enough for Miss Bennet that they are not material, then I understand. It is not what I would wish for you, but you are your own man, able to make your own decisions."

Though Caroline shot Louisa a poisonous look of the betrayed, Bingley focused on his elder sister, and he nodded, though it was with an uncharacteristic abruptness. "I appreciate you voicing your concerns in such a fashion, Louisa. They are noted. But you, of all people, must understand the very great benefit of marrying due to the desire to be with someone for whom you possess an affection rather than due to merely prudent concerns."

His sister's flush told Bingley that his barb had met his mark.

"I do indeed, Charles," said Louisa. "You have my support if Miss Bennet is truly what you want."

"Oh this is very touching indeed," scoffed Caroline, "but it is immaterial to the matter at hand. Our father gave us the task of improving our family's name in society, and I will ensure that his wishes are carried out.

"Your marriage to Hurst was regrettable," continued she, "but ultimately necessary, as it allowed us to enter into higher society. With our marriages, Charles and I will ascend even higher. There is no more discussion to be had. Be prepared to depart on the morrow."

"You have stated your directives; now hear mine," hissed Bingley, stepping up to his sister and glaring down at her. Caroline was no small woman, but Bingley towered over her, and for a brief moment, he enjoyed that feeling of authority.

"I will not depart on the morrow or any other time in the near future. If you wish, you may depart yourself. But if you do stay, then you had best heed my words. I will brook no more interference in my relationship with Miss Bennet, and I will hear no more attacks against her. I intend to declare myself to her at the first opportunity and will not be dissuaded."

"You will receive no support from me if you persist in this madness," declared Caroline hatefully. Then she stalked off without a backward glance.

Bingley watched her go sadly. "What happened to the sweet, affectionate child she used to be?"

"That child was consumed by her ambition to ascend to the heights of society," replied Louisa. "I will handle Caroline, Charles. You return to your lady and make your plea."

Heartened by his sister's encouragement, Bingley did something he had not done in many years—he leaned forward and embraced her, pouring his gratitude out in his actions. "Thank you, Louisa. I will."

And with that, he turned and strode back to the ballroom, noting as he did so that the first dance after dinner was in its final stages before drawing to a close. Spying Jane Bennet where she stood by the side speaking with Miss Lucas, Bingley was gratified that she was not engaged in this set, and he was seized by the desire to stake his claim to her hand. With such thoughts in mind, he strode toward the two women and bowed before them.

"Miss Lucas, would you mind very much if I was to steal your conversation partner away for a few moments? I promise we shall return before our dance together."

Though she appeared surprised, Miss Lucas was not bereft of sense, and she immediately seemed to understand his purpose. She was also discreet enough to keep her composure and not voice any such thoughts. Her response was an amiable:

"Of course, Mr. Bingley. I need to speak with my mother anyway."

With a nod, Bingley led Miss Bennet away, confident that Miss Lucas would keep the particulars of his request from common gossip. As there was a balcony nearby, Bingley led his love there, and they slipped out into the chill of the night.

Having achieved his objective, Bingley turned to regard Miss Bennet, noting how her countenance shone in the light of the moon and how her hair appeared to almost give off a soft glow of its own. She was luminous and beautiful, her outer beauty only matched by the beauties of her soul. And she was calling out to him in that moment in a manner which he fancied only he could interpret. She truly was his destiny.

"Miss Bennet, I find that I cannot go any longer without baring the contents of my heart. But though I have never been more certain of anything than I am of my feelings for you, I wish to be sensitive of your desires. May I continue?"

Though the light was scarce, Bingley was certain he could see tears glistening in her eyes as she nodded shyly and waited. Bingley had never had any doubt that she would welcome his addresses, but in that moment, a feeling of peace such as he had never felt before welled up within him, and he stepped forward and grasped her hand, bringing it up to his lips.

"You are a jewel among women, Miss Bennet, and I am exceedingly fortunate to have found you. Your light, your goodness, your kindness; all of these thing shine and echo within my heart, bearing witness to me that your equal simply does not exist. I will never be more grateful for anything, than I am for the decision to lease Netherfield, as it led me to you."

Bingley smiled at her, lifting her chin so that she faced him, noting the tears of joy which streamed down her cheeks. "I would be most happy if you would consent to be my wife, Miss Bennet, and join me in happiness for the rest of our days. Will you marry me?"

"Nothing would make me happier," said Jane in a tremulous whisper. "For I love you so very dearly."

Taking advantage of their newly acknowledged state, Bingley drew her to him and settled her against his breast next to his heart. This was where she belonged, and he would never allow her to leave.

Jane could hardly believe her good fortune. The man she was not so secretly in love with had proposed, and she was to be married!

But thoughts of joy were tempered by the knowledge of what her mother's reaction would be should the engagement be announced at the ball. Of course, it could not be announced yet, as Mr. Bingley would have to approach her father to make it official, but that would not deter her mother. Though it was distasteful to hide it, Jane knew that for her own peace of mind, they would need to keep it between themselves.

"We should return to the ballroom before we are missed," said Mr. Bingley into the quiet.

Jane smiled and drew away from him, gazing upon him happily.

"I shall approach your father for his permission." He turned a stern gaze on her which she knew instinctively was not actually directed at her. "Your father will not oppose our match, will he?"

"I doubt it very much, Mr. Bingley," said Jane. "What happened with Elizabeth was obviously an aberration. It shall not be repeated."

"That is good," replied he, "though it would not make a jot of difference to me. I shall take you to Gretna Green if necessary."

A thrill ran through her at his pronouncement, but Jane assured him that it would not be necessary in this instance. She then paused and addressed her concerns.

"If you are willing, I would like to keep our engagement between ourselves for now."

Mr. Bingley looked at her intently before nodding. "You fear your parents' reactions?"

"Primarily my mother's," said Jane with a grimace. "We shall not have any peace once she knows, as she will crow before the neighborhood unceasingly."

"Your wish is of course my command. I can wait a few days, though I must own that I am anticipating a little proclaiming of my own!"

Jane blushed, and she agreed with a shy smile. Mr. Bingley raised her hands to his lips again and then escorted her back into the ballroom. It appeared that their short absence had gone all but unnoticed, as their return did not garner the attention she had feared it would. But while they did not receive the notice she had feared, her mother, speaking loudly with some of the local matrons on the far side of the room, caught her eye before they had taken two steps into the room.

And it was settled in Jane's mind. Their future did not include Netherfield, as it was far too close to Longbourn for Jane's peace of mind. She was certain Mr. Bingley would be amenable to looking for an estate in some district far from Meryton. Truly, it was possible for a woman to be settled too near to her family, and for Jane, anything closer than several days' travel by carriage was too near indeed.

Chapter XXI

Three days after his departure from Rosings, Mr. Darcy returned. For Elizabeth, those three days had been an exercise in patience, and she now fancied that she possessed that particular virtue to a great degree. Mr. Collins was his typical verbose self, and he seemed particularly attentive in those days, even to the point where it became difficult for Elizabeth to escape to the peace and solitude of her walks. She finally managed it on the third day, but her escape had been a close one—she could not have abided his presence any longer without lashing out at him.

As they had promised, Mr. Darcy's cousins visited frequently, and their visits helped to form a sort of barrier between Elizabeth and her so-called husband. Colonel Fitzwilliam was particularly masterful, engaging Mr. Collins in conversation, with tales of his exploits being prominent in their discourse. And if Mr. Collins was not interested in stories about the engagements in which the colonel had fought or in his accounts of his duties and the foibles of his general, he was not about to offend the nephew of his patroness by professing a disinclination for his company.

But the true revelation was Anne de Bourgh. Elizabeth had not been certain what to make of the young woman. On the one hand, Elizabeth had Mr. Collins's description of her, though she knew not to give full weight to the man's praise. Her own observations, however, had told her that the woman would likely be aloof. To find her to be a pleasant, though somewhat shy, woman in desperate need of a friend was a welcome surprise. Given enough time and opportunity, Elizabeth thought they could be quite close friends indeed.

The second day after Mr. Darcy's departure, when Miss de Bourgh and the colonel were visiting, the subject of Elizabeth's enforced marriage and her life in London had arisen, and Elizabeth had surprised herself by relating to Miss de Bourgh the pertinent events which had led to her living with her aunt and uncle. While she could not have imagined sharing the events with someone who was, after all, a virtual stranger, sharing it with another woman turned out to be an incredibly cathartic experience.

"Your parents are contemptible," was Anne's blunt reply once Elizabeth had finished speaking. "To blame everything on a child of two is completely beyond the pale, and you should give no credence whatsoever to anything they say."

Caught as she was between the emotion of the moment and Anne's rather blunt statement, Elizabeth did not know whether to laugh or cry. "It took me some time to come to that conclusion," replied Elizabeth after a moment of regaining her composure. "It *was* difficult as a child."

"That is to be expected," said Anne. "But you are intelligent enough to see it now, so I would advise you to give it no thought in the future. Allow your parents to wallow in bitterness."

The talk turned to Anne's situation with her mother, and though Anne was not nearly as explicit as Elizabeth had been, still she shared some of her past and her feelings about a mother who attempted to dominate every facet of her life.

"I would not have you believe that I dislike my mother," said Anne at one point. "She has cared for me for more years than I can count, and there were many periods where I was very ill indeed. She has not the ability to show her love in an affectionate manner, but I have always been aware of her love for me. In fact, her love is part of why she has always been so insistent about this ridiculous engagement which she speaks of so frequently. In her mind, she believes that marriage to Mr. Darcy is the best thing for me, and she will not be moved from that opinion."

Elizabeth cocked her head sideways in amusement, her curiosity overcoming her amusement. "Were you never tempted by your cousin?"

"There were times as a young girl I might have indulged in a fantasy or two," said Anne. "But as I became older, I came to realize that we are poorly suited. Darcy and I would not make a good couple."

Elizabeth rather suspected that Anne was actually far more interested in her *other* cousin, the colonel, even if the woman did not realize it herself. Their camaraderie was clear for all to see, and they teased each other and spoke with great animation when together. The colonel's affections were less visible, as he was agreeable to all, but Elizabeth felt that he could be nudged along to a greater affection for Anne given the right circumstances.

Of course, she made no mention of this to either of the two principals. Not only did she not know them well enough to state such a thing, but Elizabeth was no matchmaker. It would be better for them to come together due to their own efforts rather than have another meddle in their affairs. They experienced enough meddling from Lady Catherine!

Before Mr. Darcy's actual appearance, the parsonage was graced with another visitor—and one who Mr. Collins apparently knew well.

"Mr. Forbes!" cried he when the visitor was announced. "I had no notice of your coming, or I should have ensure that you were greeted with all the pomp which is your due as my superior."

It was with a congenial smile and an unaffected manner that Mr. Forbes responded: "That is quite unnecessary, I assure you, Mr. Collins. We are all God's servants, are we not?"

While Mr. Collins hastened to assure the man that he agreed without reservation, Elizabeth watched the scene and was able to take her first impression of the man. Mr. Forbes was a slight and rather diminutive man, possessed of a kindly face with piercing blue eyes set within. He also carried himself with an air of confidence, his demeanor defying his rather small size. He was not much older than Mr. Collins, Elizabeth deduced, as his hair was rather thick and brown and lacking in any gray, from what she could see.

"Perhaps you should introduce me to your lovely wife?" prompted Mr. Forbes when Mr. Collins's effusions went on for several minutes.

"Yes, of course!" cried Mr. Collins. "How thoughtless of me! Come here, my dear," continued he, extending a hand out to Elizabeth.

Though she would by no means have allowed Mr. Collins any supposed authority over her, Elizabeth decided that it was best to observe convention and avoid offending Mr. Forbes, who at this moment held her fate in his hands. Thus, she moved and rested her hand as lightly as she dared on Mr. Collins's arm.

"Mr. Forbes, please allow me to introduce my lovely wife, Elizabeth

Collins. Elizabeth, this is Reverend Forbes, an acquaintance from my days at the seminary and now my direct superior in the church."

Elizabeth curtseyed in response to the bow offered by the gentlemen, and she looked up at him with hope shining in her eyes. She fancied that he did not miss it, given the quelling look he gave her.

"Enchanted, madam," was all he said.

They sat in the parlor for some time, and Elizabeth ordered a tea service, content that the man was finally here and that she might finally be nearing an end of her time in purgatory. Mr. Forbes was all that was gentlemanly—he was kind and attentive and possessed a well of patience which was required any time one was in close company with Mr. Collins. They spoke of little of substance, confining their conversation mostly to Mr. Forbes's journey to Hunsford and the fineness of the weather this late in the season.

"Should I have had word of your coming, I would have planned my day accordingly," said Mr. Collins. His slight fretting did not go unnoticed. "As it is, I must depart soon to the village."

"But God's work is more important than visiting and drinking tea, is it not, Mr. Collins?"

Mr. Collins made a face that Elizabeth fancied was a wish that he was at leisure to indulge in further fawning on the man, but his answer was all agreement. "It certainly is, Mr. Forbes. It is merely that we meet infrequently and that I believe I would benefit further from the wisdom you bring."

"I shall be here when you return, Mr. Collins." He turned and smiled at Elizabeth. "In fact, if it is not too much trouble, I believe that I will stay the night and depart on the morrow."

The rapturous agreement of Mr. Collins was almost comical, as he praised his superior and insisted that it was no trouble whatsoever. For her part, Elizabeth simply agreed quietly, certain that Mr. Forbes would use the time to speak with her while Mr. Collins was away. As it coincided with her own desires quite well indeed, she could have no objection.

"Then perhaps you should go about your business, Mr. Collins. I am certain your wife will be able to entertain me during your absence."

"Indeed, she will, for she is ever so obliging and well-versed in all the social graces. I will leave you in her capable hands so that I may return as soon as may be."

Once Mr. Collins had departed, Mr. Forbes turned his gaze upon her, and though he was not harsh, his expression contained a little more severity than she would have wished. He appraised her in silence for a few moments before he spoke, and if he was sharper than she expected, he was also kind and considerate of her feelings.

"I must say that I was shocked to hear Mr. Darcy's account of how you came to be in Kent, Mrs. Collins. Perhaps you should explain to me why you wish to effect an annulment."

Elizabeth thought it prudent to be cautious. "What did Mr. Darcy tell you?"

"Please indulge me by telling me in your own words what has happened," replied he. Then, in a conciliatory tone, he continued: "I ask you answer me not as a means of discovering any discrepancies between your account and what Mr. Darcy has already told me, but because I wish to understand your feelings."

Chewing her lip, Elizabeth thought over the man's words and decided she had no choice. After taking a deep breath, she began to speak, telling him of the circumstances which had led her to Kent. She did not go into her past with her family and the reasons for it—*that* she would not tell another soul if she could help it—but she touched on the years she spent with her aunt and uncle, the events which had led to her return to Meryton, the arrival of Mr. Collins, and the forceful insistence of her father that she be married. When she had finished, Mr. Forbes looked at her with some compassion.

"You have told me a great deal more than Mr. Darcy did. I will assume that this is because he did not live these events as you did.

"However, I am also certain that you have not told me everything, though I suppose most of it is not relevant to the subject at hand. Regardless of how you became estranged with your family, the fact of the matter is that you were and that your relationships with your parents were such that your wishes in the matter were not taken into account.

"Now," he said after a brief pause, "I am certain you are aware that a father has authority over a child until that child reaches the age of majority?"

"I am aware of that."

"The authority vested in a father includes that of making an alliance the father deems fit. I am certain that as a member of the gentry, you have heard of marriages which were arranged between parents. However, dragging a daughter to the altar and forcing her against her will is not something the church will tolerate in a general sense. And even more so, the marriage of two persons without the banns having been properly read is a breach of our ecclesiastical law. These are two serious concerns. Is there anything else you can think of which would potentially make this marriage invalid?"

Elizabeth nodded. "I did not properly sign the register."

His interest piqued, Mr. Forbes looked at her askance. "That is quite unusual. Normally, a rector would not allow the newly married to depart without signing the register. Furthermore, I would have thought your father would have seen to it, given how much trouble he went to in order to bring this about."

"I did sign it," said Elizabeth. "My father threatened me with retribution if I did not. But what he did not realize is that I did not sign it with my name."

"You deliberately signed the wrong name?" asked Mr. Forbes.

"I did," said Elizabeth, holding herself straight and proud.

The chuckle which met her statement was not at all expected, but it was welcome nonetheless.

"It appears that you did whatever you could to avoid this fate your father chose for you. Though I am not happy to see God's laws flouted in such a manner, I applaud you for your determination, Mrs. Collins. You are clearly a lady of much character and intelligence."

The moment was broken, however, when Mr. Forbes once again regarded her with a seriousness which could not be feigned.

"I must ask, Mrs. Collins—are you certain you wish to have your marriage annulled? It is not an easy thing to grant, and if you obtain your desire, it may have adverse effects on your future. Many who receive annulments become social outcasts, as I am certain you know."

"I do wish for it," replied Elizabeth. Though she had intended to keep her composure, the carefully constructed wall she had erected since leaving London began to break apart, and she felt herself falling prey to her emotions. "I know it is not generous to speak of a person in less complimentary terms, but I can hardly think of anyone less suited to be my husband than William Collins.

"I have nothing left to lose, Mr. Forbes." Elizabeth could hardly see the man through the tears in her eyes. "I will refuse to allow him into my bedchamber as I have done until now. He will get no heirs to my father's estate from me."

Though he appeared surprised at her words, Mr. Forbes nodded. "It is easier to undo a marriage which has not been consummated." He gazed at her a trifle severely. "It would be best if you would remember that, though I cannot condone such behavior in a general sense."

Elizabeth nodded.

"One more question for you, Mrs. Collins," said Mr. Forbes.

At that moment, the door chime rang, and Elizabeth rose, though she had not recovered from her bout of emotions. Mr. Forbes rose with her and, smiling kindly at her, put his hand on her arm to forestall her departure.

"Let the maid answer the door, Mrs. Collins. I was expecting another to join us.

"While we wait, I would like an answer to my question. Was Mr. Collins a party to what happened in Hertfordshire?"

A bark of laughter escaped Elizabeth's mouth. "He was there, was he not?" At Mr. Forbes's stern look, Elizabeth relented. "I do not think that Mr. Collins was aware of my reluctance, as I did not have the opportunity to tell him openly. You have perhaps noted that Mr. Collins is not precisely . . . intellectually gifted?"

A tight nod met her statement.

"I believe that Mr. Collins could not imagine that I would be anything less than eager and grateful for his attentions. My reluctance since then has been put down to certain . . . feminine indispositions and my 'desire to increase his love by suspense.' So from that perspective, he was not a party to it, I suppose."

The door opened, and Mr. Darcy was shown into the room. Elizabeth regarded him as if she was a drowning woman and he the only one who could save her. But though he regarded her with his typical intensity, he was equally circumspect in his greeting to her.

"Mrs. Collins," said Mr. Forbes, "even if your husband was not a party to what happened, the church still expects its clergymen to behave in a certain manner. And it is expected that a man who marries a woman takes the opportunity to confirm that she is at least resigned to the match, regardless of what he has been promised."

Having said that, Mr. Forbes turned and greeted Mr. Darcy, and Elizabeth asked him to sit with them. She was unsure as to why Mr. Forbes had asked him to join them, but she was certain it would be made clear in due time.

Indeed, the churchman was not inclined to exchange pleasantries. Instead, he turned his stern gaze upon them both and said:

"What has not yet been explained concerning this matter is the reason why Mr. Darcy—a man wholly unconnected with you—has taken up your standard. Would either of you care to enlighten me?"

Anyone witnessing their faces would have likened them to a pair of children caught in an act of disobedience. Elizabeth felt herself flush, and though she could not look at Mr. Darcy, she thought that he was as red and embarrassed as she felt.

"Mr. Darcy asked me for a courtship the day before my father forced me to the church," said Elizabeth in a halting tone.

Mr. Forbes nodded. "Though it was not outside the realm of possibility for Mr. Darcy to have offered his assistance due to nothing more than pity, I expected that there would be something else at play here."

Once again, the man turned a stern eye upon them both. "Can I trust you both to rein in your passions and conduct yourselves with decorum?"

"Of course," said Mr. Darcy, though he appeared very much the errant schoolboy. "I would never dishonor Miss . . . Mrs. Collins in such a manner."

"Good," replied the clergyman with a nod, though he did raise an eyebrow at Mr. Darcy's near faux pas. "I am well aware of what you are both feeling right now." He paused and took them both in with an amused smile. "I have been married for some years to my dear wife, but I recall the days of waiting very well indeed. Attraction and desire between you is understandable, but we must leave everything to its proper season.

"I will do what I can to right the wrong which has been done to you, Mrs. Collins, but your plight is not an excuse for you to indulge in inappropriate behavior. I will expect you to remain at a respectful distance from Mr. Darcy until this has been resolved."

When Elizabeth and Mr. Darcy both murmured agreement, Mr. Forbes became much more pleasant again, so much so that Elizabeth dared to ask him another question.

"How long do you anticipate it will be?"

The man's compassion was unmistakable in the way he regarded Elizabeth. "Mrs. Collins, I ask for your patience. An annulment is not a minor undertaking, and the investigation alone will take some days. I will send an agent for the particulars concerning what has happened in Hertfordshire, including the application to your father's rector, the marriage registry, and the matter of the banns not being read. I will inquire with the curate here in Hunsford myself before I leave tomorrow."

At Elizabeth's look of consternation, Mr. Forbes merely smiled at her. "There is no need to worry, Mrs. Collins. I have no intention of making your situation any more difficult than it already is. I will canvass the curate and give him strict instructions not to mention anything to Mr. Collins. Though perhaps it is unusual conduct an investigation in secret from one of those involved, in this instance, given the behavior of your father and Mr. Collins, I believe it is warranted."

The conversation turned to general matters, and it was not long before Mr. Darcy excused himself, citing a need to return to Rosings to attend his aunt. Elizabeth was sorry to see him go, but as she needed to see to supper, she had some duties with which she could occupy her time. Mr. Forbes was shown to a room where he could refresh himself ahead of the supper hour, leaving Elizabeth by herself. The hope which had smoldered within her had now burst into flame, and she was hopeful that she might someday soon be free of the odious Mr. Collins.

That evening was filled with inanities aplenty, and though Elizabeth knew Mr. Collins was a sycophant of the first order, that evening in the company of Mr. Forbes taught her much about the man who was, at least at the moment, her husband.

For she learned that Mr. Collins was not only Lady Catherine's devoted servant and toady, but he was also not above licking the boots of anyone he deemed as being higher in the social order than he was himself. If Elizabeth had not already had such low expectations for his behavior, she might have been mortified by the way he fawned over Mr. Forbes, showering him with praise about anything which entered his mind. As it was, Elizabeth was able to endure the evening quite well indeed, for though Mr. Collins was his typical voluble self, Mr. Forbes was everything which was agreeable. For once, there was intelligent conversation to be had.

Still, as the minutes and then hours passed by, Mr. Collins wore on her patience, and by the time she retired, it was all she could do not to snap at her husband for embarrassing her at every turn. She went to her bed gladly that evening, believing that a night's rest would restore her spirits.

The next morning, Mr. Forbes did not stay long. He departed to go to the church and was there for some time in the company of Mr. Collins and Mr. Dawson, Hunsford's curate. Elizabeth was not certain how he had managed it, but because Mr. Collins made no mention of the matter, she could only assume that Mr. Forbes had been successful in diverting his attention while he spoke with Mr. Dawson. It was Mr. Forbes who returned to the parsonage alone to retrieve his belongings and take his leave. It was then that he gave Elizabeth a final few words of encouragement.

"Your suspicions were correct, Mrs. Collins. The banns were never read in the parish, which leads me to believe that they were not read in Hertfordshire either."

Elizabeth only nodded; she had been certain that was the case.

"There still is the possibility that Mr. Collins or your father purchased a special license, and I will investigate that as well. However, given the expense, I rather doubt that was the case unless Lady Catherine was somehow persuaded to supply the funds to her clergyman.

"If there is no special license, then the neglecting of the banns will make your case that much stronger."

"Thank you," said Elizabeth with fervency.

"It does not mean the annulment will be granted," warned Mr. Forbes. "The church will sometimes sanction a marriage even if the proper forms have not been met for the simple reason that it is deemed better that a marriage which has already taken place should not be split asunder."

"I understand," replied Elizabeth, the reality of the situation clear to her. "In that case, there would be nothing left for me here."

"This is not something from which you can simply run, Mrs. Collins," said Mr. Forbes, his tone awash with compassion. "You would be little more than a pariah, forever alone."

"That would be preferable to putting up with such a demeaning marriage for the rest of my life," replied Elizabeth. In reality, she was so very exhausted with thoughts of her situation that she did not wish to consider the matter any longer. Whatever happened would happen. It would do no good to think on it without respite and make herself even unhappier in the process.

"Have hope, Mrs. Collins. I believe that the chances of your marriage being dissolved are as good as any other I have seen."

And with that, Mr. Forbes departed, leaving Elizabeth alone to her thoughts and to what she suspected would be a terrible period of waiting, not knowing what her fate would be.

It truly was terrible, and at times, Elizabeth did not know how she managed to withstand the suspense. Mr. Darcy was, as always, a boon to her troubled soul, but mindful of Mr. Forbes's admonishments, Mr. Darcy and Elizabeth did not meet in the woods again; it would not do to have gossip concerning clandestine assignations and unfaithful wives work their way through the neighborhood.

Rather, in that time Elizabeth began to make herself useful in the neighborhood, visiting the sick and elderly, assisting by disbursing baskets of food and supplies to the less fortunate and taking on all the duties of a parson's wife. At first, she was able to own to herself, she had done it simply to keep herself busy and, perhaps more importantly, away from Mr. Collins, but as she continued to involve herself in the doings of the parishioners, she began to enjoy herself. She did not know what was in store for her should she eventually be free to marry Mr. Darcy, but she knew that managing the house, caring for tenants, and being a useful, active sort of person would all be expected of her. She looked upon the days spent in such endeavors as a training period of sorts for her ultimate destiny of becoming Mr. Darcy's wife.

And she found that what she was doing was making a difference in the community. Her husband was not a popular minister. Not only were the people well aware that anything they told him might be carried back to Lady Catherine, but most of the advice he gave to those in need was deemed to be so nonsensical as to be utterly worthless.

But while Elizabeth avoided him as much as possible, she found that his insinuations that he was becoming impatient to finally consummate their marriage were becoming more blatant. As it was nearing two weeks since her marriage, she knew that soon his patience would be exhausted and that he might become aware of the fact that she was avoiding his attentions. What he would do then was a matter of some conjecture. Elizabeth was certain that he would not become violent, but she was also certain that he would try to force the issue in some manner.

In the meantime, there was nothing to do but wait, pray, and attend to whatever duties she could. And hope. Hope was a large part of her life.

"Is there a letter from Elizabeth today?"

Shaking his head in resignation, Edward Gardiner turned to his wife. "Nothing. I have a few letters from my partner in London, but nothing from Longbourn."

Sarah frowned. "It has been more than a week, Edward. I am worried."

Gardiner could only commiserate with his wife. He had always been of the opinion that his brother by marriage had called for the return of his daughter for some particular reason, but he had never quite been able to determine what exactly that reason was. The subject had never really been put to rest between them—they both wished that Elizabeth had allowed herself to be persuaded not to return to Longbourn, but Gardiner had vowed that he would not dictate her life to her, and he had thus given way and allowed her to return. They had relied on her frequent communication to calm their worries and assure themselves that she was, at the very least, content with her family.

"She has never gone this long without writing," fretted Sarah. "Something is wrong."

"We do not know that for certain. Her letter may simply have been lost in the mail."

A withering glare met his assertion, and Gardiner had to acknowledge that he did not truly believe it either.

"Elizabeth's letters have changed since we left her there, Edward. You know they have."

"I know, my dear. There is a distinct want of cheer in her communications of late. She tells us that all is well, but I am aware of her propensity to put a cheerful facade to the world."

"It is more than that. It is specifically because she does not wish to worry us."

Gardiner sighed and went to his wife, taking her hands within his own. The children were ensconced with their governess, and though there was a frigid wind blowing in from the sea, the house he had rented for their use while they were in Ireland was cozy. It merely wanted Elizabeth's cheery presence to make it into a lively home for the duration of their stay. Such cheer had been lacking since their arrival due to the inhabitants' habit of worrying over the state of their beloved niece.

"My business is almost complete, Sarah. Shall we depart instead of staying for the Christmas season as we originally intended?"

"Yes!" was Sarah's instant cry.

Gardiner was forced to grin at her eagerness. They had anticipated this family holiday greatly, but her attachment to Elizabeth was so strong that she did not even hesitate.

"Then I shall go and complete my business as soon as may be so that we may depart."

Sarah nodded, though a smile was playing about her mouth, and Gardiner knew that his own attachment matched hers. They truly had been blessed to have Elizabeth in their home for all those years. Hopefully, she would reside with them again before she inevitably left to establish her own home with her eventual husband.

They busied themselves with their respective tasks, but they had not been engaged in such for long before the door chime rang. A few moments later, a maid entered and handed Gardiner a thin package.

"This express has just arrived, Mr. Gardiner," said she in her lilting Irish accent.

After exchanging a glance with his wife—and noting that Sarah appeared apprehensive at the arrival of an express—Gardiner stepped forward to take the letter. He thanked the maid, who immediately departed, and looked down at the missive.

"It is from Kent," said he with some surprise.

"Kent?" echoed his wife. "Do you do business with anyone in Kent?"

"Not with anyone who would be sending me an express," replied Gardiner before he broke the seal. There was another sealed piece of paper inside the first. Gardiner looked at the writing on the outside of the second sheet and gasped. It was Elizabeth's.

"What is it?"

But Gardiner could not respond. His attention caught by the words on the paper, he read the short note before turning to Elizabeth's missive and opening it, his fury growing as the import of the words leapt off the page and assaulted his senses like darts piercing him with all their fiery rage.

Sarah could clearly see that something was amiss, as she rose and walked toward him as soon as she saw his change in demeanor. "Edward, what is it?"

His outrage overcoming his ability to speak, Gardiner chose the simple expedient of thrusting the letters at Sarah, allowing her to take them while he began to pace, muttering imprecations at Bennet under his breath. It was not long before his wife was as angry as he was himself, but Sarah, fortunately, was able to keep her wits about her.

"I was afraid your brother had some specific reason for demanding Elizabeth's return," said she. "But I had not imagined him capable of *this*!"

"At this moment, I am trying to decide whether to ruin the man or simply run him through," said Gardiner.

"I would appreciate it if my husband would not go off and get himself thrown in prison for killing his brother-in-law," said Sarah wryly.

Gardiner stopped his pacing and stared at her. "You are taking this rather calmly, are you not?"

"Only because you have not stopped to think, husband." Sarah stepped forward and put a calming hand on his shoulder, and then she led him to the couch. "Look here: Elizabeth writes that she has some hope of being free of this cousin of Bennet's."

"You and I both know it is very difficult to undo a marriage."

"Perhaps. Now, what do you know of Mr. Darcy actually going to Kent to be of assistance to her?"

"I am sure I know nothing of the man other than what I told you of meeting him on the way to Meryton and what Elizabeth has told us in her letters," said Gardiner.

"Does it not strike you as strange that a man who is only barely acquainted with her would travel to Kent in order to help her extricate herself from this marriage?"

Comprehension dawned, and Gardiner stared back at his wife in surprise. "Are you suggesting that Mr. Darcy admires Elizabeth?"

"Why else would he involve himself in such a manner? You did tell me that you thought he was interested in Elizabeth."

"I thought the man was friendly and that he appeared to look on her with favor, but their acquaintance was only minutes old when I observed them."

"Well, it appears as if it has deepened significantly since then, though our reticent niece has not seen fit to state it explicitly in her letters."

"And if Mr. Darcy is involved . . ."

"Then she might have a chance of actually having the marriage annulled," finished Sarah. "He certainly has the standing and social clout to enable him to bring it to the church's attention."

It did make a certain amount of sense, though Gardiner was still struggling to understand Sarah's comments about Mr. Darcy's supposed interest in Elizabeth. Though Elizabeth was a gentleman's daughter, an alliance with her would be less than what society expected of a man of Mr. Darcy's stature.

"In that case, we had best continue our preparations to depart," said Gardiner. "I feel a sudden desire to have an urgent discussion with my *brother*." The contempt with which he referred to Bennet seemed to be matched by his wife. Or exceeded, if anything. But Sarah stayed focused on the important part.

"And find Elizabeth. I wish we had not left her there."

"We will not make that mistake again," replied Gardiner, taking her hands in his. "Until then, let us make certain to depart as soon as we can. It is time we returned."

Chapter XXII

"No, Caroline, I shall not give way!" cried Bingley, standing and staring down at his sister with considerable pique. The breakfast table between them lay forgotten like so much dross. "I have proposed and given my word. I shall not back out now!"

"But Charles—" exclaimed Caroline, her anger rising to meet his own.

"No!" said Bingley. Lowering his voice and glaring at her, he told her, "Listen to me, Caroline. I will not have this discussion again. If you cannot stay silent, then I shall send you to Aunt Esther. Now, leave off!"

Throwing down his napkin, Bingley stalked from the table. He headed for the entrance and called for his horse once he had exited the house.

Outside, a blustery wind whipped about, its dreariness a match for Bingley's mood sour mood. The ten days since Jane Bennet had accepted his hand had been difficult ones for a number of reasons. The fact that it was still not official had given Caroline ammunition to use against him, and her never-ceasing haranguing on the subject had worn on his nerves until he had finally snapped that morning. Of course Caroline would be the catalyst for such an unusual outburst.

Within moments, his horse was saddled, and he began riding over the parched and windswept fields to Longbourn—and hopefully to the final sanction of his engagement.

If Bingley was to be honest with himself, he was annoyed with the world *and* Jane Bennet as well, though such an emotion could not stand in the face of her intrinsic goodness. And Miss Bennet was indeed everything which was good. But her request on the night of the ball—though understandable due to what she endured in her home on a daily basis—had turned Bingley's life into a nightmare of sorts. Not only had Caroline used the opportunity to badger him concerning the engagement—her latest inanity that morning had been to try to convince him that Jane was reluctant because she did not know how to tell him that she actually did not want to marry him—but he had also put off some business in London due to the fact that he did not wish to leave Miss Bennet behind. He feared Mr. Bennet would promise her to some other sycophant relation during his absence.

He knew that Miss Bennet herself was not to blame. She had wished to keep their engagement a secret between them, as she was afraid of her mother's reaction; given what Bingley knew of Mrs. Bennet, Miss Bennet had every reason to dread the histrionics which were certain to ensue. But the time had now come.

Longbourn was the same as Bingley had left it the previous day. The estate was silent other than the sounds of animals in the distance, and Bingley thought it likely that Mr. Bennet was still keeping to himself in his bookroom, a hermit steadfastly refusing the company of those around him. Given the quietness, Bingley suspected that Mrs. Bennet was away from home; otherwise, he would likely have heard the woman during his approach to the manor.

A few minutes later, Bingley was walking the grounds in the company of his angel, her sisters Miss Catherine and Miss Mary following them at a respectful distance, acting as chaperones. As they walked, Bingley listened to Miss Bennet's conversation, which usually enthralled him, with only half an ear while he tried to determine exactly how to convince her that it was time to formalize the engagement.

"Miss Bennet," said Bingley, stopping to gaze into her beloved face. "Jane. I would like to formalize our engagement as soon as possible."

She looked at him and nodded. "Though I would almost wish to keep it from my mother indefinitely, I believe it is time."

Bingley returned her smile with a grin of his own; apparently, he had not needed to concern himself with her ultimate agreement. But he was curious all the same. They began to walk again, and Bingley said:

"I know I have not much to offer, but surely you do not think your mother will disapprove of our engagement."

Miss Bennet glanced up with wild eyes before she noted his grin and returned it with one of her own. "You shall simply have to be persuasive since you are so poor a suitor." She sighed and then chuckled. "Of course, it is much more likely that she will *frighten you away* than disapprove of you."

A chuckle escaped Bingley's lips, but though Miss Bennet's words were stated in a lighthearted fashion, there was an underlying tension in her manner which told Bingley that her words were not made entirely in jest.

"I assure you that nothing can drive me away," said he, looking at Miss Bennet with an earnestness of manner, trying to reassure her of his constancy. "Your mother may shout her acclaim from the rooftops for all to hear between here and London, and I shall not go away."

"Perhaps you should reserve your judgment until she has shown us off to every family in the neighborhood," said Miss Bennet with a playfulness of manner he would have attributed to her younger sister.

"Perhaps I should!" said Bingley in like fashion. But then the thought of what lay before him sobered him, and he turned to Miss Bennet. "I will approach your father this instant. Have you any suggestions on how I might make my application?"

"I do not." She sighed, and the grimace of lingering pain appeared before his eyes. "I do not understand my father. I never have. But given how he has behaved since Elizabeth went away, I doubt he will oppose you."

Bingley could only nod. A few moments later, they had returned to the house, and Bingley stood before her father's door, contemplating what he would say to the man. He would brook no refusal on the matter, but he also knew that there was every possibility that the coming discussion would not be pleasant. Still, it had to be done.

After rapping on the door sharply, Bingley was forced to wait, as there was no immediate response. It was only after he knocked a second time that he heard a voice from within demanding to know what he wanted. He decided that it was permission enough, and he opened the door and walked in.

The sight that met him shocked Bingley to silence. Mr. Bennet stared at him through eyes sunken in a face which appeared weathered and worn. The man appeared to have aged substantially in just the few days since Bingley had seen him last, and as he gazed at the man he would have as a father-in-law, Bingley was struck with a certain dark satisfaction. Given the scarlet-lined eyes, the unfocused stare, and the lined, careworn face, he fancied that Mr. Bennet was paying for his sins in a most painful manner. A haunted conscience was no small burden.

"What do you want?" was the man's demand as Bingley stepped into the room.

There was not much point in belaboring the matter. "I am here to ask for the hand of your eldest daughter in marriage," said Bingley in a tone which demanded attention.

Mr. Bennet peered up at him as if confused. He then shook his head slightly and turned away, rubbing his eyes as if he had not slept in a fortnight. "And I suppose you have already applied to Jane for her consent?"

"I have," confirmed Bingley. "Miss Bennet has done me the singular honor of accepting and making me the happiest of men."

A snort escaped the elder gentleman, and Bingley stared at him in anger.

"My cousin said that phrase to me over and over," said Mr. Bennet, though Bingley wondered if the man even remembered that someone else was in the room. "I wonder how he feels about the matter now. She cannot be making it easy on him, I think." He laughed then, though it was a sound which Bingley could only liken to the fraying of a rope to the point of snapping.

It was best not to allow Mr. Bennet to continue to think of *that* situation, much though Bingley wished to give the man a piece of his mind.

"Have I your blessing, Mr. Bennet?" prompted he.

"I do not know what you think you might have done to punish yourself in such a fashion," said Mr. Bennet, "but if you truly want to enter the married state, then you have my permission. I have two conditions."

Frowning, Bingley motioned for Mr. Bennet to continue, though the man was not even watching him. It did not matter.

"First, you will leave this room and never return to it. Second, you will make the announcement to Mrs. Bennet without my presence. I do not wish to be subjected to the raptures of *my wife*," his voice liberally oozed with contempt, "on the subject."

Bingley was affronted for Mrs. Bennet's sake. He had no great opinion of her, and he was well aware that her ways could indeed be trying. But Mr. Bennet had *married* the woman, presumably with the full knowledge of her character. He was not an unintelligent man, after all. For a man to treat his wife with such contempt was so completely unpardonable that he almost wished to take Mr. Bennet to task.

But there was nothing to be done about it. Speaking out in her defense would not bring the man to any repentance; he was much too far gone for that.

"I will announce it to your wife when I return to the sitting room. Is that sufficient?"

Mr. Bennet merely took up his brandy decanter and waved Bingley from the room. Bingley was only too glad to escape.

He took a moment outside in the hall to compose himself. It was well that he would be removing Miss Bennet from the house, as it was obvious that Mr. Bennet had no desire to protect his daughters, if indeed he ever had. Some thought would need to be taken for the welfare of the other girls, and Bingley resolved to Darcy when the opportunity arose.

Squaring his shoulders, Bingley marched toward the sitting room where his beloved waited. Miss Bennet caught his eyes as soon as he entered the room, and though Mrs. Bennet—who had returned in the interim with her youngest and silliest daughter in tow—immediately cried out at the sight of him, he smiled and nodded slightly at Miss Bennet, seeing her sag in relief.

"Mrs. Bennet," said Bingley, interrupting her before she could speak more than a syllable or two, "I have an announcement to make."

Mrs. Bennet did not even allow Mr. Bingley to say anything further. She screeched and launched herself at Miss Bennet, showering her with affection and exclamations of rapture and satisfaction about how important her daughter would be and claiming foreknowledge of the event. It was a most boisterous and happy celebration, and Bingley himself was the focus of much of it, excited as Mrs. Bennet was that her ambition had now been realized. It amused him and almost made him want to like the woman, for all her improper exclamations.

When they finally were able to calm Mrs. Bennet, she immediately tendered an invitation to dinner which Bingley was forced to decline. Louisa and Caroline would need to be told of this development, and due to the snit Caroline had been in lately, Bingley decided it would do no good to delay.

"But Mr. Bingley!" Mrs. Bennet fairly shrieked. "Surely you can spare us an evening for such a momentous occasion. If you would but tell me your favorite dishes, I shall have cook prepare them in your honor!"

"Another time, Mrs. Bennet," replied Bingley. It was clear that he would need to be firm with this woman. Miss Bennet, though she was certainly not weak, was so self-effacing and good that he could well imagine her deferring to her mother in fear of offending her.

"But Mr. Bingley—"

"Mama, Mr. Bingley has said he must go," interrupted Miss Bennet. "He must announce our engagement to his sisters as soon as may be."

Perhaps there was more steel than Bingley had expected in his future wife. He caught her eye with an admiring look, relishing the fact that she blushed slightly before returning one of her own.

"Then you must come tomorrow," said Mrs. Bennet, stubbornly refusing to desist.

In this, Bingley decided that he could afford to be generous with the woman. Regardless of what he thought of these people, they would be family, and he needed to establish the fact of their intimacy at the earliest opportunity. He could take stock of the situation at a later date and determine then whether to maintain any kind of relationship with them.

"I will speak with my sisters when I return, Mrs. Bennet. I do not believe we have any fixed engagement scheduled for tomorrow, but I will confirm our attendance with a note."

His acquiescence spurred Mrs. Bennet on to ever greater frenzied fluttering, such that it was several more minutes before he was able to extract himself. When he finally insisted that he must depart, he was walked to the door by his angel amid her mother's assertion that Miss Bennet *must* see her newly minted fiancé to the door. Though Bingley might have been offended on her behalf had the circumstances been different, he took it in stride, as it corresponded nicely with his own wishes in the matter.

"I wish I was coming with you," said Miss Bennet as she walked by his side to the door.

"Just remember that your day of release approaches, Miss Bennet," replied he. "But enough of this formality. As we are now engaged, I should like to call you 'Jane,' if you are in agreement."

She blushed a pretty rose color, but she nodded her head in shy agreement. Bingley was delighted. "And I expect you to call me Charles."

"I will, Charles."

"There is one more thing I wish to discuss with you," said Bingley, his earlier thoughts returning to him. They reached the outer entrance and stepped out onto the portico, where a groom was waiting with Bingley's horse. Bingley stopped Jane with a motion and paused to look into her eyes. "I am afraid for your sisters. They are left in the care of a woman with little sense and a man who seems intent upon killing himself with drink."

Jane sighed. "I am worried, too, particularly for Lydia and Kitty, though Lydia is headstrong and determined to walk her own path. With my mother encouraging her every step of the way, she will eventually do something to embarrass the family."

"Then we shall invite them to London to stay with us as soon as is practicable. Perhaps Lydia can be instructed on the proper way for a young lady to behave while there."

Turning to him, her eyes shining with emotion, Jane said: "You would do that for my sisters?"

"Jane, they are soon to be *my sisters*. And I am certain that Darcy could be persuaded to assist as well. If we promise Lydia balls and parties, then I am certain she will be eager to accept and will feel equally loath to return to Hertfordshire."

"But that will leave my mother by herself," fretted Jane.

"With all due respect," began Mr. Bingley carefully, wishing to state his opinion but not offend his fiancée, "Mrs. Bennet has, by her treatment of your sister, brought this upon herself. She and your father both have."

"I understand, Mr. Bingley. But the dutiful daughter in me tells me to honor my mother, regardless of the pain she has dealt in this life to my dearest sister."

"And it does you credit. But the person being so honored must conduct themselves in such a manner as to deserve that honor first."

"You are right, of course." Jane paused and turned to look out across the drive, a pensive frown on her lovely face. "But if my mother should make amends . . . then we must forgive her and take her back into our society."

"*If* her amendments are undertaken in a sincere fashion." Putting his hand to her chin, Bingley gently turned her head until she was once again facing him. "Jane, I have no desire to slight your mother. But I have a very high opinion of your sister, and though I do not know her well, the fact that Darcy thinks so highly of her speaks volumes.

"Fitzwilliam Darcy is not in the habit of brooking disappointment." Bingley paused and laughed at his own words; they sounded dreadfully pompous. "I have never known Darcy to give up merely because an endeavor was difficult. I fully expect to learn that he has managed to free your sister from her predicament, and when he does, I expect they will marry. I would always wish for your sister to be comfortable in our home, and I would give her precedence over your mother. I do not know the details, but I suspect that it is not your sister who is to blame for this distance between her and your parents. Am I correct?"

Jane nodded, though she was clearly unhappy about having to agree to such a critical assessment of her mother.

"Miss Bennet," began Bingley with compassion, "I understand your reluctance to speak of any censure of your mother, and it does you credit. Again, I do not know the details of this matter which your parents hold against your sister, but their behavior is not proper, regardless of who is culpable for whatever misfortune has befallen your family."

Straightening, Jane looked up at him with resolve. "You are correct, of course."

"In that case, we are decided. Once we are married, we shall attempt to be of use to your sisters."

"Thank you." Her words were quiet, but they were also infused with feeling, and Bingley was pleased to bask in the approbation of his beloved.

In a few moments, Bingley took his leave, happy with the way the day had gone. He was now engaged to his angel, and they were in agreement about their future efforts for her sisters. Now, he was only left to inform his own.

As Bingley was riding away from Longbourn, he passed by the church and happened to notice that someone was entering. The man's clothes indicated he was a cleric, and he almost appeared to be on official business.

Grinning, Bingley urged his horse on. There was no way he could know exactly what was occurring, but since Darcy was interested in a woman who had married under suspicious circumstances, it was highly likely that the man was there to investigate. Bingley had no doubt that Darcy had the ability to effect such an investigation. He was highly adept at getting what he wanted.

Her mind full of her fiancé, Jane Bennet went to bed that night, reflecting that Charles Bingley had turned out to be more than she had ever expected him to be. It was a heady feeling to have inspired the love of such a man. Jane could hardly wait to start her new life.

In truth, Jane had thought that Mr. Bingley, for all his amiable qualities, had been perhaps been a little too deferential to his sisters' opinions, particularly toward his younger sister, as she was by far the more forceful of the two. Considering what Jane had discovered about that lady's character, it would be worrisome to enter into a marriage with a man who was ruled by his sister.

But in the past days, Mr. Bingley had shown himself to be his own man, and though she had heard something of what had passed between him and his sister—though Mr. Bingley was too much of a gentleman to be explicit—she was now satisfied with his resilience.

A knock on her door startled Jane from her thoughts, and she called out to the person on the other side to enter, drawing her robe about her. The door opened, and Jane was surprised to see Mary in the doorway.

"May I come in?" was her sister's quiet query.

"Of course, Mary," said Jane, curious about her sister's presence. Mary had always eschewed such rituals as this, though Jane had on occasion shared her bedchamber with her youngest sisters. Of course, Kitty and Lydia's general silliness made it very difficult for Jane to enjoy those times, even if having her sisters in her room did bring comfort and reduce the loneliness she often felt in her home.

"I just wanted to say," began Mary after they had settled on Jane's bed, "that I am very happy for you, Jane. Mr. Bingley is an excellent man. You will be very happy."

"Thank you, Mary," said Jane. Mary was so diffident that Jane was certain that she was finding it difficult to say the words, even though they were almost expected. "I believe that I shall be very happy indeed."

Her congratulations spoken, Mary settled into an uneasy silence. Jane had always thought of herself as the most reticent Bennet girl, but with Mary struggling to converse even this much, she wondered if that were true. But it was also clear that Mary had something to say, so it seemed best to allow her to do so.

After a few minutes of struggle, Mary looked at her and smiled a little helplessly. "I was wondering . . . That is, I mean to say . . ." Mary stopped and huffed with frustration. "It is difficult to speak when I have kept to myself for so long. I dare say I share less than ten words a day with anyone in my family."

"We all do seem to be immersed in our own concerns," said Jane gently, hoping that her sister would unburden herself.

"A selfish family indeed," murmured Mary

Though she was perhaps inclined by habit to defend them all, Jane was forced to agree with Mary's assessment.

"I wonder how much would have been changed had our sister not been chased from our home," said Mary with an abruptness which spoke to a rush to get the words out before her courage failed her.

So this was the crux of what Mary wished to speak of. Jane did not know why it was her engagement which had brought out a wish to discuss the matter further, but she was grateful for it nonetheless. She herself had seen something estimable in Elizabeth, and she wished for her sisters to acknowledge it, too. Elizabeth's forced marriage to Mr. Collins had opened their eyes. Now it was time for them to acknowledge that the excuses they had built up in their minds for the state of their family were nothing more than an unwillingness to own the truth. It was their parents' failings which had led to the state of their family.

"Elizabeth would have made us all better," said Jane. "We are truly made less without her. You, Papa, and I are reticent in company—"

"To say the least," interjected Mary with a ghost of a smile.

Jane acknowledged her words with a nod and continued: "Exactly. So do you not think that we would have benefited from Elizabeth's livelier presence, especially when, unlike with our mother and younger sisters, that liveliness is accompanied by proper behavior?" Mary could only nod. "And perhaps Papa might have done well with an intellectual equal. Elizabeth is very intelligent and has many interests which could have benefited him if he had only taken the trouble to discover them."

A dubious frown met her declaration, though Mary did not say anything. Jane herself struggled to imagine her father as anything other than the distant and somewhat frightening man in whose home she had been reared. Of course, the death of his son and heir might have changed him into the man he was now. It was impossible to know.

"And what about Kitty and Lydia?" continued Jane. "Might they not have been made a little less wild had they had someone as an example of proper behavior before them, one who would have had the courage to reprimand them with the sharpness they require?"

"Well, they cannot be many degrees worse," muttered Mary. "And I grant you that Elizabeth might have been able to keep them better in line than you or I. That outcome seems likelier than our father being anything other than what he is."

"Perhaps," agreed Jane. "But I am certain that this family has suffered inordinately from what happened, and though you might not remember it, Elizabeth suffered the most."

"I do remember," was Mary's quiet reply. "I have tried not to think of it, but I do remember. I wish I had behaved better."

"I do not recall any overt unkindness on your part," said Jane, placing her hand on Mary's shoulder in a gesture of comfort.

"No, but neither did I welcome Elizabeth back when she returned. Indeed, you were the only one to treat her with any kindness or even any respect at all. Regardless of what happened when she was a child, she did not deserve such treatment."

Happy to hear her sister's words of repentance, Jane leaned over and engulfed Mary in an embrace, and Mary returned it with as much emotion as Jane imparted herself. Mary had always been distant, even as a young child. But now, for the first time in her life, Jane actually felt close to her sister and believed that a strong relationship between them was possible.

"I think that Elizabeth is also very forgiving," said Jane, still holding her sister tightly. "I know from my experience that she wants nothing more than to have a relationship with her family. If you make the overtures, then I am certain she will be happy to accept your friendship."

Mary sighed and pulled away. "But I do not think that I shall have an opportunity to extend my apology for some time. Not with her marriage to Mr. Collins and her removal to Kent." Mary paused and huffed in indignation. "I cannot believe that a man of the cloth would behave in such a reprehensible manner as Mr. Collins did. It is only for Elizabeth's sake that I would refrain from wishing the man to lose his position!"

Smiling—this was the sister Jane had come to know, after all—Jane leaned forward again and in a mischievous voice said, "If you can keep a secret, then I have something to tell you."

At Mary's eager nod, Jane launched into the story of all that had occurred outside Mary's notice these past days. The sisters talked until the wee hours of the morning, and Jane could not be happier. Perhaps there was a chance for a relationship with some members of her family. It was all Jane had ever wanted.

Chapter XXIII

Time has a strange way about it. It can be the most elusive concept in the world, passing almost like a thief in the night, gone without warning and without notice, leaving one wondering how it had disappeared. On other occasions, its passage is akin to the torturous journey of a tortoise across a sandy beach. Unfortunately for Elizabeth, the time after Mr. Forbes's departure was very much the latter.

Had she been left to the sole attentions of the pernicious parson, she might have been a fit candidate for bedlam. Mr. Collins had never learned the very great benefit of silence and had especially never learned that speaking would prove to all the world that he was as foolish as he was stupid. Life in his company was a never-ending stream of conversation, and none of it was in any way interesting or intelligent. The fact that he had no original thought in his head was confirmed by the fact that his pronouncements echoed what she had often heard from Mary during her short time at Longbourn; Elizabeth suspected that most of his material concerning the deportment of young ladies was memorized verbatim from Fordyce. The other words which spewed forth from his mouth were so recognizable in their pomposity that Elizabeth was certain that they came directly from the mouth of his patroness. And the thoughts he spoke of their situation merely caused her to struggle to refrain from rolling her eyes.

What actually worried Elizabeth, however, was that his patience with her continued refusal to consummate their marriage appeared to be all but exhausted. If he should succeed in this design, it would certainly make it more difficult to annul the marriage, but more importantly, her feelings for Mr. Darcy were such that capitulation was akin to a betrayal of that gentleman.

Thus, Elizabeth was forced to use every weapon in her arsenal to avoid the rector's attentions. Once it became obvious that her "female issues" could no longer be the reason for her reticence, she began inventing excuses to keep him away. One evening, she pleaded a headache—prompting the man's insistence upon caring for her, which she, of course, firmly rebuffed—while the next she retired early, claiming fatigue due to the day's activities. On another occasion, she insisted that he show her the length and breadth of Rosings' park, an activity to which he agreed with alacrity but soon came to repent; much as had happened at Longbourn, Mr. Collins found himself breathless before they had walked more than a quarter of a mile. On that evening, he had almost fallen asleep in his mashed potatoes, which had been a source of great amusement to Elizabeth. One night, she took the simple expedient of locking her door and ignoring him when he attempted to delicately gain her attention.

She was convinced that the man would not attempt to break the door down, not only because he was simply not a violent man, but also because of his fear of what his patroness would say should she discover he had ruined one of the doors in the parsonage. The events of the first evening, where Elizabeth had tricked him into overindulgence in spirits, were only repeated once, and on that occasion, she was certain she was only successful since the man was brooding over the fact that even though his marriage was nearly three weeks old, his conjugal bliss was still a matter of his imagination rather than fond remembrance.

But the rope was straining and fraying, and Elizabeth was certain it would snap before long. And when it did, Elizabeth could well imagine what form his displeasure would take. No doubt there would be more of his long-winded soliloquies about female comportment, obeying one's husband, and the proper behavior for married couples.

Had she not had Mr. Darcy and his cousins to turn to, Elizabeth was certain that she would have succumbed to madness long before. Mr. Darcy and Colonel Fitzwilliam visited every day, and though Miss de Bourgh could not, constrained as she was by her dictatorial mother, she had appeared on her own several times and in the company of her cousins on occasion.

One night after Elizabeth had again claimed a headache, she and Mr. Collins were invited to Rosings Park for supper and cards. Though Elizabeth's nerves were frayed by the necessity of maintaining constant vigilance, she had dressed herself and made her way alongside her insensible husband, ignoring his prattling about windows and chimney pieces throughout their walk up to the front entrance of the grand estate.

They were shown into the sitting room where Lady Catherine held court. And after they entered the room, the expected inanities began.

"Mr. Collins," said Lady Catherine when she saw him, "I distinctly remember impressing upon you multiple times the importance of punctuality, yet you walk in at this hour. I expect that you will correct this oversight the next time you are invited to Rosings."

It was all Elizabeth could do not to laugh in the lady's face. Not only were they almost five minutes earlier than the appointed time, but Lady Catherine said this every time they arrived, regardless of what time they walked through the door. Elizabeth had even contrived for them to be ten minutes late one day, thinking that the lady would do more than simply berate them, but her speech had not altered in the slightest. Elizabeth suspected that it was one of the ways in which she exercised her control and supposed superiority over her parson.

Mr. Collins, of course, was incapable of contradicting her ladyship. "Indeed, you are correct," said he in a groveling tone, his knuckles almost dragging on the floor due to the depth of his bow. "I shall instruct my wife thus and take care that we arrive on time in the future."

Of course, Lady Catherine hardly heard his humble reply, as she had turned back and directed her pronouncements at her nephews, who were seated nearby. Mr. Collins, eager to bask in his patroness's august presence, immediately hastened to her side, resembling nothing more than a crab scuttling across the beach. Noting a smile from Miss de Bourgh, Elizabeth returned it and moved to take a seat next to the heiress.

"Mrs. Collins," said Miss de Bourgh quietly in greeting when Elizabeth sat. "I trust you are well?"

Eyes darting to where the parson was now seated as close to Lady Catherine as he could contrive, Elizabeth sighed. "I am coping, Miss de Bourgh. Being forced to live in close quarters with such a fool has been difficult, to say the least."

"Your feelings of exasperation are understandable," murmured Miss de Bourgh, glancing herself at the man in question. "He truly is the perfect man to be my mother's parson, you must own."

This time, Elizabeth did roll her eyes, an act which prompted a giggle from her companion. "That does not speak highly of either of them. No offense to your mother, of course."

"None taken, though it would certainly not be an untruth. I am well aware of my mother's faults, I assure you." Miss de Bourgh paused and looked at Elizabeth closely. "Has Mr. Collins been . . . difficult to keep in check?"

Elizabeth's cheeks flamed at even so oblique a mention of her avoidance, but she nodded once. "He is becoming impatient. I am certain of it."

"I wish I could help more. I would invite you to stay at Rosings with me for a day or two, but I know that my mother would suffer apoplexy."

Giggling, Elizabeth allowed that it was so. "No doubt the pollution of the venerable halls of Rosings could never be cleaned should such a low-born woman such as myself stay here for a night."

"Your impression of my mother is rather droll," replied Miss de Bourgh with a straight face. "One would almost think you have heard her speak."

The two ladies laughed, and at that moment, Mr. Darcy approached and, with a bow, greeted Elizabeth before beginning his own quiet inquiries into her state. Unfortunately, Elizabeth was not able to spend much time conversing with him, as they were called in to supper, and Elizabeth was escorted by Mr. Darcy, who also escorted Miss de Bourgh. The rest of the evening passed in a fashion typical of an evening at Rosings.

The true excitement of the evening began after they left Rosings to return to the parsonage.

"A most agreeable evening indeed, my dear," said Mr. Collins as the carriage departed from the grand house. Lady Catherine, eager to impress her guests and maintain the distinction of rank at every turn, had insisted upon their return to the parsonage through the auspices of one of her carriages. "I flatter myself that anyone in our position would consider Lady Catherine's favor as a most blessed circumstance. Is it not so?"

Privately, Elizabeth could not imagine anything worse than such a meddling crone overseeing their every action. Still, she allowed it to be so, eager to maintain whatever good humor her husband possessed.

The quickest way to lose his good opinion was to criticize the woman, after all.

"Indeed, I believe that this is a providential occasion, my dear," continued Mr. Collins, a gleam entering his eye. "We have dined yet again with the most condescending Lady Catherine de Bourgh and her relations, and I am certain that such attention from her ladyship can be construed as nothing less than her wholehearted approval of my new wife. And as such, I believe that the night where we finally become one has arrived, and I flatter myself that you, my dearest wife, are as eager as I to partake in the delights assigned to married couples."

His statements both annoyed and alarmed Elizabeth. It was a trial not to stare at him in disbelief, as he had been making hints such as this from almost the exact moment they had first arrived in Kent. However, he had never spoken in quite as blatant a manner as this, and the look in his eyes suggested that his patience was all but exhausted.

Elizabeth replied with a noncommittal monosyllable which seemed to satisfy Mr. Collins. He bowed — a curious affectation, as they were still sitting in the carriage — and he regarded her with anticipation.

"In that case, my dearest Elizabeth, I believe that we should retire as soon as we reach the parsonage. I shall give you twenty minutes to prepare before I come to you."

The rest of the journey back to the parsonage was filled with Mr. Collins's conversation, and while that was not unusual, he continued to speak of their future felicity in a manner which Elizabeth found quite unseemly. Thus, when the carriage stopped in front of the parsonage, she opened the door and stepped down, hurrying into the house with alacrity, amusing herself with the thought that he almost certainly considered her haste to be because of her eagerness for his visit. In truth, Elizabeth hurried into the kitchen, where the keys for the various rooms of the house were kept, to make certain that all keys to her bedchamber were in her possession before she retired to her room and entered, making certain that the door was locked behind her. Now, more than ever, she was thankful for the foresight which had resulted in her insisting upon her own room.

Quickly preparing herself for bed, Elizabeth braided her hair and donned her longest and heaviest nightgown before settling down in bed and waiting for the inevitable. If she was to be honest with herself, Elizabeth knew that she was not truly fearful for what the parson might do; she was more curious as to what form his displeasure would take.

In the end, it was a little more than ten minutes after she had entered her room—Mr. Collins, it appeared, was not any more adept at telling time than he was at any of the other tasks at which Elizabeth had witnessed him failing so abysmally—when his knock sounded on her door.

"Mrs. Collins," said he as the reverberation of his raps echoed through the room. "I have come to you." His tone was a particularly wheedling sort of voice which he no doubt thought to be affectionate.

When there was no reply, he attempted the door experimentally, his efforts to turn the handle intensifying when it became obvious that it would not turn.

"Shall you not open the door, my love?" asked he after a few moments of ineffectually turning the knob. "It is time for there to be no more secrets between us."

Elizabeth stayed resolutely silent, refusing to give the man any reason for hope that his advances might meet with any success. His attempts to enter the room became more insistent, and the noise of him turning the handle and eventually pushing on the door in an attempt to enter into the room sounded loud in the stillness of her room.

"Mrs. Collins, this is unseemly," said he, his voice raised in displeasure. "I have been patient in deference to your delicate sensibilities, but there comes a point where further delay cannot be tolerated. Open this door!"

The sound of his shoulder hitting the door resounded throughout the room, along with his now insistent and furious turning of the handle. But it was all for naught, as the door refused to yield. Elizabeth was grateful for the sturdy construction of the parsonage.

"Very well. I shall return," said the man, his voice overflowing with anger.

Elizabeth listened to the sounds of his retreat down the hall and to the stairs. Knowing that she guessed correctly at his actions, Elizabeth waited for his return, thinking about how the stupid man still did not understand her disinclination for his company and her disgust for his person.

Soon, his footsteps once again sounded, this time swift and clipped, up the stairs and to the outside of her door. "Where is the key to this room, Mrs. Collins?" demanded he. "Let me in!"

When Elizabeth refused to speak, the man once again pushed on the door and turned the handle with a furious vigor.

All at once, the noise stopped, and silence reigned in the hall. After a moment, he spoke again, his voice conciliatory this time. "Mrs. Collins, please open the door. It is time for us to become a couple in every sense of the word. Further delay is not proper."

He said nothing further of the matter, and moments later, the sound of his footsteps echoed down the hall. The noise of his own door closing arose with a crash, indicating his rage as he entered his own room and shut the door behind him with undue force.

Elizabeth heaved a sigh of relief, confident that he was defeated for the night. But though she fell into a fitful doze, it did not last long, as the parson was back to try her door before long, and though he said nothing, the sound of his stalking footsteps, followed by his abuse of the handle and his subsequent heavy pounding on the door, served as a testament to his anger.

And so it continued through the night. Mr. Collins would attempt to enter the room for a few moments, and then upon being frustrated with his failure, he would retreat back to his own, returning to make the attempt again and again. There was little sleep to be had for Elizabeth that night, as she was afraid to settle into a deep sleep. It would not do to be woken by the man in the event that he actually managed to bypass the door. It was a long night, and by the morning, Elizabeth was almost contemplating simply leaving the parsonage for good.

Mr. Collins accosted her the moment she entered the breakfast room the following morning, his displeasure as well as the obvious effects of a sleepless night written on his face.

"Mrs. Collins," said he, "what did you mean by locking me from your room last night?"

"I am sorry, Mr. Collins, but I have not the pleasure of understanding you," said Elizabeth, deciding that it was best to utilize simple avoidance as long as possible. "I found myself fatigued upon our return last night and retired as soon as we arrived at the parsonage."

His mouth working in astonished soundlessness, Mr. Collins gaped at her. "Do you not remember my comments from last evening? It has been nearly three weeks since our marriage. The time is here for us to become one, as I am certain an intelligent young lady such as you must understand."

"Become one?" asked Elizabeth, feigning ignorance. "Did we not become one when my father forced me to the altar and insisted I sign the register?"

Perhaps it was not wise to refer to her reluctance in so blatant a manner, but Elizabeth was angry, and her good judgment had been impaired by disdain for this man. But in this, she appeared to be fortunate, as once again the sight of a befuddled Collins met Elizabeth's sight, and if she had not been so disgusted by the man, she might have found it amusing. However, proving that he was a man prone to hear what he wished to hear and nothing more, Mr. Collins ignored the second part of her statement and focused on her seeming lack of understanding.

"Now I see, my beautiful wife," said he with an expression of utmost condescension. "I had thought that your excellent mother would explain the matter to you in full before our marriage, but perhaps the ceremony was completed in such haste that a communication of this sort was not possible. You have been ignorant of what happens between man and woman once their marriage has been sanctioned, and I suppose that I should not be surprised that an elegant and innocent female such as yourself would not possess such knowledge.

"Regardless, I shall enlighten you, and by the time I have finished explaining the matter to you, I am confident you shall be as willing—or dare I say eager!—as I am to finalize our marriage in the solemn act of communion between two souls. You see, Mrs. Collins—"

"Thank you very much for your words," said Elizabeth, speaking over the man's blathering. Resisting his advances, tolerating his never-ending prattling, and even living in the same house as the man were all very well, but Elizabeth would not subject herself to an explanation of the marriage act from the man. She had much rather die than allow him to continue in such a manner!

"As the weather is fine, I believe that I shall take my constitutional before I attend to Widow Morris. I bid you a good morning, sir."

And with that, Elizabeth swept from the room. Her last glimpse of Mr. Collins was the man staring at her as she exited the parsonage, his jaw slack with the shock of her exit.

Elizabeth stayed out pacing the grounds of Rosings as long as she was able, not wanting to return to the parsonage to once again bear the complaints of her husband, despite the fact that it meant that she was away from the parsonage until quite late in the afternoon. Mrs. Morris was a wonderful old soul who appreciated Elizabeth's attempts to care for her, and she told the most interesting stories of her late husband, who had been the blacksmith in the small community for many years.

Finally, however, Elizabeth was forced to turn her steps toward the parsonage and brave the displeasure of her husband. She did not know exactly what form his anger would take, but she could not imagine that his frame of mind was at all good given the manner in which she had left him earlier without even taking leave.

Her suspicions were proven to be correct, but as she walked up to the front door of the house, she noted the presence of one of Lady Catherine's carriages with a groan. Anne always visited in her phaeton, which meant that the lady herself was undoubtedly within. A visit from the woman was never a circumstance to be looked upon with equanimity; this interview promised to be much worse.

Knowing there was nothing for it, Elizabeth entered the house, passing her outer wear to Jessica, who was waiting for her within the entrance.

"Lady Catherine has come?"

"Yes, madam," replied the maid, her eyes lowered in deference. Elizabeth had cultivated a friendship of sorts with the young woman, and Jessica would only behave in such a manner if something uncomfortable was occurring. Whatever Lady Catherine's purpose was, it could not be an innocuous visit.

"Very well," said she to Jessica, giving her an encouraging smile. "I shall go in directly."

The parlor's interior held three disparate people: her husband, Mr. Darcy, and Lady Catherine. But while Mr. Collins turned to regard her with a petulant scowl and an injured air and Mr. Darcy with one of excessive worry, Lady Catherine's countenance was nigh unreadable other than a slight tightening of her eyes and a somewhat calculating stare. An awful premonition began to form within Elizabeth's breast.

"Mrs. Collins, how good of you to return to the parsonage," said Lady Catherine as soon as Elizabeth had entered the room. "How can you account for such a long absence?"

"After my morning walk, I visited Hunsford village, and I have been with Mrs. Morris, offering her comfort." Elizabeth was not about to concede any wrongdoing, and if what she suspected was true, Lady Catherine would undoubtedly interrogate her, trying to uncover something lacking, as a fisherman might inspect his nets for holes.

"Surely that cannot account for the length of your absence. Mr. Collins informs me that you left before even breaking your fast."

Turning a less than amused eye on the parson, Elizabeth regarded him, noting the way in which he projected himself to be the injured party. "How . . . good of him to relate such details to your ladyship in minute detail. One wonders if he is always this loquacious about matters which should be left private."

"Mr. Collins tells me everything!" said Lady Catherine. It was impossible to miss the pride in the lady's voice at such a proclamation. "There is no detail about the parish and those lives within the realm of my influence which I would not wish to know. I am most decidedly attentive about all such things, I assure you."

Knowing that Mr. Collins related *everything* to the woman was one thing, but having it proudly proclaimed by her was another. Not only did it appear that the parson was betraying the parishioners' confidence by relating to his patroness what was said in the confessional—a grievous breach of church law, if true—but it seemed almost certain that Mr. Collins had told her ladyship everything which had occurred since their arrival in Kent, though the man had almost certainly not explained anything which had happened in Hertfordshire. He would certainly wish to keep any hint of impropriety from her ears, if he even now comprehended that what had passed between them had been in any way improper.

"How . . . fortunate a circumstance for you, Lady Catherine," said Elizabeth. The fact that the lady's countenance tightened into a disapproving scowl bespoke the fact that Elizabeth had been unable to keep the scorn from her voice.

"Mrs. Collins, I warn you not to trifle with me. However you may choose to attempt to deflect the matter with impudent comments, you will find me steady to my purpose. My character has been celebrated far and wide with an uncommon frankness, and I assure you that I will not depart from a lifetime of such conduct.

"Now, Mrs. Collins, among the communications your husband has imparted to me, one statement he has made is that though your marriage is already weeks old, it remains unconsummated. Is this so?"

Elizabeth glared at the small-minded man, incensed that he would speak of such an intimate matter with another, but Mr. Collins merely glowered back at her. She should have guessed that he would not keep quiet about this. The man was incapable of gainsaying Lady Catherine concerning the slightest detail, and he would not doubt wish to have her firmly take his part in any dispute.

"Lady Catherine," interjected Mr. Darcy, looking highly uncomfortable, "perhaps we should not interfere in so delicate a matter as this."

"Be silent, Darcy. This is a most grave matter, and I must have Mrs. Collins's response."

Mr. Darcy bristled at being spoken to in such a matter, but Lady Catherine had already turned her attention back to Elizabeth. "I am waiting, Mrs. Collins."

"That is an impertinent question, and I shall not dignify it with a response," said Elizabeth with some disdain.

"Mrs. Collins, I insist upon being satisfied. Have you submitted to your husband as is your duty as a wife?"

"You may insist all you like, but it will have no effect on me. I will not respond to such an impertinent question from someone so wholly unconnected to me."

Mr. Collins's eyes fairly bulged out of his head at Elizabeth's words and tone, and Lady Catherine gave her an infuriated look. "Unconnected with you?" cried she. "I provide this living to *your husband* which so handsomely feeds you and provides a roof over your head. You would dismiss that connection?"

"You are no relation, Lady Catherine, regardless of how closely my husband works with you. I would not answer your questions if they came from my mother, who I must own is a much closer connection. This line of questioning is improper and unseemly, and I will not respond."

Eyes narrowed to mere slits, Lady Catherine looked on Elizabeth with derision. "I believe your refusal to speak of the matter is tantamount to an admission of guilt, Mrs. Collins, and I can only wonder at the effrontery, the lack of common sense, and the sheer impropriety of your behavior. I have never heard of a woman denying her husband his rights as a married man as you have. I demand that you immediately cease this behavior and submit to it as is proper."

Elizabeth said nothing, content to sit there and glare at Lady Catherine. The other woman appeared to take her silence as an opportunity to instruct her on exactly what she must do. But Elizabeth had decided not to listen. Instead, she looked over at Mr. Darcy, noting his discomfort over his aunt's continued diatribe. When their eyes met, an understanding passed between them, and they both smiled slightly, sending encouragement to the other. In this fashion, Elizabeth was able to tolerate Lady's Catherine's copious words on the subject.

But when the afternoon started to wane, Elizabeth decided that enough was enough. She stood in an abrupt fashion, startling Lady Catherine to silence for a moment, and curtseyed, though with the minimum deference required.

"If you will excuse me, I must see to supper."

And with that, Elizabeth departed the room, expecting for the great lady to call her back before she was able to make her escape. But no word of opposition was voiced, and soon Elizabeth had vanished from their sight. But she paused at the closed door to see if she could hear any reaction to her departure. The sounds of conversation welled up from within the room, and though Elizabeth could not hear exactly what was being said, the lady's voice rose above the murmur:

"Go to her tonight, Mr. Collins. I am certain you shall have no trouble with her."

Stifling a laugh, Elizabeth fled to the kitchen. If Lady Catherine thought her cowed, then the lady was less discerning than Elizabeth had ever thought. William Collins would be named King of England before she would ever submit to him.

Elizabeth soon learned that Mr. Collins was not quite the simpleton she had thought, a realization which at once amused her and concerned her at the same time. Lady Catherine had departed before Elizabeth had returned to the parlor, but though the lady had seemed certain that Elizabeth would do her duty as the lady saw it, Mr. Collins had no apparent conviction of the same.

Rather, throughout the evening, Mr. Collins watched her with suspicion, though he tried to hide the fact that he was doing so. To say that his attempts at obfuscation were ineffectual was a massive understatement. He was as obvious in his watching eyes and narrow stares as Lydia was in her flirting at the local assembly.

When Elizabeth went to bed, she was uncertain as to whether Mr. Collins would make the attempt to once again enter her room. His behavior seemed to suggest that he was not in agreement with his patroness's conclusions on the matter. But his reverence for her and his seeming belief of her infallibility were such that Elizabeth felt certain that he would at least make the attempt. Thus, when she heard the rattle of the doorknob only a quarter hour after she had retired, Elizabeth was not surprised that he had trusted his patroness's judgment.

What did surprise her was when he left directly and did not bother her for the rest of the night. Of course, she did not truly believe that he had given up; on the contrary, Elizabeth had every confidence in his inability to see what was right in front of his eyes.

And she was proven right.

The next morning, Elizabeth emerged from her room to the sound of wind howling through the trees beside the house, the lash of rain against the windows, and the dreary, reluctant light filtering through the windows like a disobedient child afraid of imminent punishment. There would be no escape for her today amongst the groves of Rosings

Park.

Elizabeth entered the dining room to the sight of her husband with food already piled high on his plate and the newspaper set out in front of him. Upon seeing her, he put down his paper and stood, peering at her with an unctuous smile.

"My dear, it is so good of you to join me this fine morning," said he with a low bow which would have been appropriate if she had been the queen herself. "I must say that you are looking lovelier than the reddest roses in my garden. But when have you ever looked anything but enchanting and radiant?"

The sight of his lascivious leer almost prompted Elizabeth to quit the room forthwith, but against her better judgment, she sat in a chair which he pulled out for her and filled her plate with a dainty selection of breakfast foods, determined to stay only long enough to eat a little food and depart from his odious presence.

"Might I inquire of how you intend to spend your morning, my dear?" asked Mr. Collins.

Elizabeth regarded him with some mixture of exasperation and disbelief. Did he truly think that fawning over her and courting her good opinion would change her mind about his attentions? If he did, then he had a far higher opinion of his own charm than was warranted. Elizabeth fancied that a charging boar held more charm than William Collins.

"I believe that I shall attend to some sewing," replied Elizabeth after a moment. "There are a few articles which I would like to complete for the Smith children as soon as may be." What Elizabeth did not tell the parson was that she wished to complete them before her annulment was ready to be heard, as she knew there would be no peace for her to pursue such things after Mr. Collins was made aware of what she was planning.

"Marvelous!" enthused the parson. "It is as I suggested to Lady Catherine herself. She advised me, before I left for Longbourn, to choose a useful gentlewoman who would be active in the community and work towards its betterment, and I dare say that I have chosen one who will do me credit in that respect. You are to be commended for your eager interest in the children of Hunsford and for your diligence in doing that which our Lord commands. I am heartily glad of having you in my life."

The parson paused, and though he did not say anything more, Elizabeth was certain that he had forced himself to refrain from referencing her refusal to allow their marriage to become any more intimate than it was.

"I believe that I shall join you in the parlor, my dear," was all he said.

"Do you not need to work on your sermon, Mr. Collins?" suggested Elizabeth.

"Indeed, I believe that my sermon is already complete," said Mr. Collins, though the look in his eye—smug and knowing—suggested that he knew something that she did not. "I find myself wishing to know my good wife better, and I am assured that our marriage will proceed in a much more . . . felicitous manner if we will only take the time to know one another better."

And nothing Elizabeth said on the matter would deter the man; he was determined to press his suit. Privately, Elizabeth was beginning to wonder if she should simply stay in her bedchamber and refuse to emerge.

"Really, Darcy, you are pacing about, growling and snapping like a menagerie lion. Shall you not sit for a time?"

Darcy turned and scowled at his cousin, but he did not cease his stalking about the floor. The wind and rain made a visit to the parsonage difficult, and should he go out in the inclement weather, he would arrive looking like a vagabond.

Still, he would have braved all that and more for Elizabeth, who was worth everything he owned. But Fitzwilliam and Anne had persuaded him against the scheme, arguing that there was nothing which could be done and that he would only make matters worse should he barge into the parsonage like a vengeful spirit.

The thought of his cousins' arguments deepened Darcy's scowl, and he turned and directed it at Fitzwilliam. The colonel was unimpressed by his display of displeasure.

"You know very well that it is not proper for you to spend every waking moment with Mrs. Collins." Surprisingly, it was Anne who had spoken up. Though she had been amused at his discontent, she had not said anything until now. "Mrs. Collins will be very well, I assure you."

Stopping and leaning against one of the large windows, Darcy gazed out at the sodden landscape, though he saw none of it. His mind was at the parsonage, and he could not help but imagine that fool Collins attempting to make Elizabeth his once and for all. Darcy swore to himself that marriage or no marriage, he would run the man through if he so much as pulled a hair from Elizabeth's head.

"You did not see the pair of them, Anne," rasped he. "That idiotic parson whining to your mother that his wife would not give him his due was akin to the sight of a child being denied some amusement. And Lady Catherine continually berated the woman I love for not doing her duty, as if her wishes in the matter were of no consequence."

"In my mother's defense, she is unaware of the circumstances of the Collins's marriage."

"Even if she knew of them, do you imagine she would empathize with Miss Bennet?" demanded Darcy, as he turned to stare at his cousin.

Anne sighed, gesturing with an open palm. "No, I am certain she would not. You do not need to explain my mother's faults to me, Darcy. I am intimately familiar with her character."

"I do not mean to disparage your mother, Anne," said Darcy with a regretful sigh.

"Come now, Darcy!" cried Fitzwilliam. "Of course you do. There is so much, after all, to work with. She and Collins are made for each other — each more ridiculous than the other."

"Have a care, Fitzwilliam," admonished Darcy, though he could not disagree with his cousin's sentiment.

"It *is* my mother to whom you refer, cousin," said Anne with a frown.

"Of course it is," replied Fitzwilliam with a smug grin. "No one is more familiar with her foibles than you, dear cousin."

"I hardly think this is cheering Darcy."

By this time, Darcy was not even paying attention to them, as his mind had returned to the parsonage. "The worst part of the whole disgusting display," continued he with an absentminded frown, "was after Miss Bennet left the room. Lady Catherine stood there, holding court with that sniveling toad, telling him that *his wife* would now accept his attentions gratefully, as if *the great Lady Catherine de Bourgh* had changed Elizabeth's mind with nothing more than her displeasure. I am certain that had I not been in the room, she would have instructed him to force the matter."

"You are so much more critical of my mother on this visit, Darcy," said Anne. "You have almost always refrained from voicing such thoughts in the past, though I am certain you have harbored them. How can you account for it?"

Exasperated, Darcy rose and began to pace the floor again, even as Fitzwilliam snorted and said: "Can you not account for it yourself, Anne? The enchanting Mrs. Collins is in danger, and as Darcy harbors such feelings for her, his outrage is roused in her defense, which in turn has dulled his inhibitions."

"That is not all, Fitzwilliam," said Darcy, passing a weary hand over his face. "Meeting Miss Bennet indeed changed me substantially, but I have begun to realize just what my aunt's pretentions of breeding are. They are nothing more than a vain attempt to aggrandize herself and rationalize her need to feel superior.

"And the worst part of it is that I have realized these very traits within myself," said Darcy, so quietly that he was not even certain his cousins could hear him.

"Come now, Darcy," cried Fitzwilliam, "you can in no way compare with our aunt in that respect. No offense to you, Anne."

But Anne just waved him off. "Are you speaking of anything in particular?"

"I have not told you of how I met her," said Darcy, a quiet introspection settling over him. "It was at a coaching inn north of London on the way to my friend Bingley's rented estate. She had just emerged from the inn and had stopped there, closing her eyes and basking in the light of the golden sun overhead. Had I not known better, I might have thought the light radiating around her like a halo indicated the presence of some heavenly personage. I have never been so affected in all my life.

"And yet subsequent events led me to believe that had she lived all her life in Hertfordshire with her improper family, then I might not have given her a second glance. She was dressed in fine fabrics, and her mode of dress has always been more fashionable than her sisters. And her uncle, who I first mistook for a wealthy man of status—what might I have thought of him had I met him and known in advance of his situation in life?"

"But Darcy, unless I am very much mistaken, you have only met the man once," protested Fitzwilliam. "Are you suggesting you know his character after so short an exposure?"

"Of course not. But I could tell that he is a good man, and he would have to be, to have raised such an estimable woman as Miss Elizabeth."

Fitzwilliam conceded the point with a nod, and Darcy continued. "But the thought of how I might have behaved and what I might have thrown away with that behavior has caused me to examine my feelings and interactions these past weeks, and I cannot say that my self-examination has pleased me. I am a prideful being. I am only glad I was given a chance to amend my character before I betrayed my flaws to her. I doubt I would ever have claimed her good opinion had I not changed first."

"Surely you are too harsh on yourself, Darcy," said Anne.

Looking up, Darcy caught the eyes of both of his cousins, noting that they were regarding him as if seeing him for the first time. "Are my words so surprising?"

The cousins exchanged a look, and Fitzwilliam spoke up, though hesitantly. "We have always known of your fastidious nature, Darcy. You are a credit to your family, your heritage, and all with whom you come into contact. If you were a little prideful in yourself or your heritage, well, it is a less serious flaw than it could have been."

Darcy sighed. "Which answers my question."

"Do not take it to heart," said Anne. "You could have been blessed with my mother's brand of pride, so it could be much worse."

A slight smile fell over Darcy's face. "It speaks well to the fact that you are able to maintain a sense of humor."

But inside, Darcy was already brooding again. If that idiot Collins laid one finger on his Elizabeth, Darcy would not be responsible for his actions. But at the same time, his cousins were correct. Elizabeth could handle the man. He merely needed to have faith in her.

By the time evening fell, Elizabeth was at her wit's end. A full day stuck with the company of Mr. Collins was intolerable, and through it all, Elizabeth had not known whether she should laugh, cry, or simply break a bottle over the bore's head. If she had thought the parson's pathetic attempts at wooing her that morning were laughable, the sheer heights of ridiculousness to which the man was capable of ascending had not even been reached. His attentions continued throughout the day, and nothing was beneath his notice. He complimented her on her hair and dress, flattered her skill with a needles as she sewed the clothes for the children, waxed long and—in his mind, at least— eloquent about her beauty and accomplishments, and tried to convince her of his undying love and devotion.

But underneath it all, Elizabeth thought she saw something else in his manner. He was not a sensible man, nor was he clever. While another man might be content to woo with subtlety and persistence, Elizabeth could sense in his manner an ill-disguised impatience which he was only barely able to suppress. It was unsurprising, considering the man had convinced himself of his love for her on the strength of naught more than a day's acquaintance.

Convinced as she was that Mr. Collins thought himself ill-used and denied his right as a married man, she was certain that this phase of wooing could not last, and she soon learned she was right. She simply had not imagined how little patience he actually possessed.

It happened as dinner was ending. Mr. Collins had continued his monologue almost without consideration for his need to breathe when he said something so ridiculous that Elizabeth's finely tuned sense of the absurd overcame her good judgment.

"Felicity in marriage shall be ours, my dear," said he in his pompous manner. "I am convinced that your liveliness and vivacity shall do me a world of good, as I tend more toward gravity and silence."

Unable to help herself, Elizabeth let out an unladylike snort, and Mr. Collins's eyes narrowed.

"I am sorry, my dear, but I was not aware that I had said anything humorous. Perhaps you would like to share whatever thought happened to cross your mind."

His glare was pointed and his displeasure certain, and Elizabeth, frustrated to the point of incivility, could no longer hold it back.

"Silence?" demanded she with a tone fairly immersed in scorn. "When did you mean to display this silence, Mr. Collins? By my count, you have not allowed more than thirty seconds to pass in silence this entire day."

His glare deepening, Mr. Collins said, "If I was not already convinced of the violence of your affections, then I might think that you were mocking me."

"You have only just detected it?" asked Elizabeth with a raised eyebrow. "On the contrary, I thought that I had been quite open in my disinclination for your company and my disdain for your ridiculous pomposity and idiotic statements—and from the very first moment of our acquaintance, I might add."

"I shall not put up with such . . . such . . . such insubordination!" The parson shot to his feet and glared down at her. "I am your husband, and you shall show me respect!"

"Respect?" jeered Elizabeth, rising to her feet herself, sensing that he was on the verge of some more physical response than he might normally contemplate. "You are a being who is worth nothing more than contempt, Mr. Collins, and that is a feeling which I hold for you in abundance."

His mouth working silently, Mr. Collins gazed at her in wonder, and Elizabeth almost laughed at the man again. It appeared that he truly was blind and had not been able to see her disdain for him, though it was almost incomprehensible that he could have missed it.

Then his face fell into an ugly scowl, and he stood up as tall as his slightly hunched form would allow. "This is unseemly, Mrs. Collins," said he, apparently attempting to inject a measure of authority into his voice. "The time has come for you to submit to me, your rightful husband. You will do so tonight, and I will never again hear such disrespect from you!"

"I shall never submit!" cried Elizabeth. "Not if I should be tied to you for a thousand years!"

"Do you wish for me to seek an annulment, woman?" demanded he. His rising voice made it obvious that he was no gentleman. "Are you insensible as to what that will mean to you in your future?"

"If it means freedom from you, then I accept," said Elizabeth. "There is nothing I wish more than to be free of you."

Purpling in anger, Mr. Collins seethed for a few moments before he stepped toward her, saying, "You *will* submit to me!"

He reached for her with both hands extended, but Elizabeth was ready for him. She dodged to the side, avoiding one of his hands while the other became entangled in the skirt of her dress. Elizabeth turned and, in a smooth motion, kicked him in the shin. Mr. Collins howled and released her, shouting imprecations which should never have been heard by a woman of gentle breeding while hopping up and down on one foot.

Taking the opportunity to escape, Elizabeth darted from the room, making for the stairs and the comfort and security of her own room. But as she climbed, Mr. Collins's voice followed her, crying:

"Run away, demon woman! I shall see this marriage annulled! Then you shall receive your just desserts."

But Elizabeth kept moving until she had reached the safety of her locked room, all the while chuckling at the ineffectual dolt. He had done more than she had expected in trying to assert his authority, but she was confident that the worst was now over. With any luck, Mr. Forbes would return soon, and she could throw off the bonds of this travesty of a marriage.

Chapter XXIV

*I*t was in fact the next morning when Mr. Forbes made his appearance. The night had actually been comfortable for Elizabeth, for though she had heard Mr. Collins's petulant stomping to his room and the jolting thud of his door closing behind him, she had heard nothing more from the man the entire evening. The following morning at breakfast, Mr. Collins made a concerted effort to ignore her, the effects of which were made somewhat ineffectual by the petulant glare he would often focus on her when he thought it least likely that he would be observed.

After breaking his fast, the parson retired to his study, where Elizabeth did not see him until an unexpected visitor—unexpected in Mr. Collins's eyes, at least—arrived late that morning,

"Mr. Forbes," greeted Elizabeth as the man followed the maid into the room. Though she had known he would return at some point, his sudden appearance sent Elizabeth's heart racing at the thought that her deliverance might finally be nigh.

"Mrs. Collins. I trust you are well?"

"Tolerably well, sir."

He looked at her closely, as if attempting to confirm for himself the truth of his words, and then nodded. "That is good to hear, madam. Now, if you will have Mr. Collins summoned, I believe it is best to get this business completed as soon as possible."

Though Elizabeth was eager to know the results of Mr. Forbes's investigation, she understood that Mr. Collins could not be excluded from these proceedings. And due to their argument the previous night, Mr. Collins was already aware of her disinclination for the marriage. While the news that she wished the marriage to be annulled would almost certainly cause consternation, he had stated his intention to seek an annulment himself, so it should coincide nicely with his own desires.

Elizabeth was soon proven correct, for after Mr. Collins had entered the room and given his somewhat perfunctory greetings to his superior—perfunctory for a man as verbose as William Collins—he announced his intentions in a most direct and abrupt manner.

"It is truly a sign from God that you have arrived this morning, Mr. Forbes," began he with a hateful glare at Elizabeth. "I have come to learn the most grievous and indelicately sinful nature of this woman with whom I have had the most unfortunate happenstance to be joined in holy matrimony. I must inform you that I will directly seek a most expeditious annulment and will further recommend that this . . . this Jezebel be excommunicated and cast from the church with alacrity. She has greatly wronged me, and her sinful and lascivious state is such that she has no business worshipping in any holy place of God."

Elizabeth stared at the parson, wondering that he was so angry as to make such statements to his superior. For his part, Mr. Forbes frowned, and Elizabeth could tell from his set jaw and the fire in his eyes that he was not impressed by Mr. Collins's rather improper statements.

"On what do you base these claims, Mr. Collins? And before you answer," continued he before the parson could reply, "I would remind you that the Church of England has strict definitions of what behavior warrants excommunication and that it is always preferable to redeem the sinner rather than to simply cut them off from communion with the church. We also expect our ministers to act with the highest of standards and do not look kindly on those who bring baseless accusations upon others for the purpose of revenge."

With these words hanging in the air, Mr. Forbes glared at Mr. Collins, and the latter looked upon him with horror, not to mention some confusion; he had obviously expected to be believed implicitly. "I ask again, Mr. Collins, on what do you base these claims?"

Mr. Collins stared at his superior, and Elizabeth could tell that he was seeking for some way to retract his statement.

"Do you still wish to accuse your wife, sir?" prompted Mr. Forbes with exaggerated patience.

At Mr. Collins's quickly shaken head, Mr. Forbes nodded. "As I thought. In the future, Mr. Collins, I would suggest that you think your statements through with great care, lest you say something which will put events in motion which you did not foresee. Do not attempt to defame another unjustly, as the consequences may be severe."

Surprisingly, Mr. Collins did appear to be suitably chastened, and upon assuring himself of that fact, Mr. Forbes nodded once, his expression becoming somewhat more congenial.

"And as for your stated desire for an annulment, my purpose in journeying here today is to inform you of something involving that very issue. I have investigated certain irregularities with respect to your wedding to Mrs. Collins, and I have made my report. The matter is ready to be heard by the ecclesiastical court."

"Ready to be heard . . ." stammered Mr. Collins. "But I have not yet made any request for such a thing."

"No, you have not," said Mr. Forbes with a pleasant nod. "But I have been investigating such allegations at the behest of your lady wife, and I have found more than enough evidence of improper doings with respect to your marriage that my recommendation to my superiors was that we allow the case to proceed. I have come today to inform you of the time and date of the hearing."

Throughout Mr. Forbes's speech, Mr. Collins's expression went from confused to amazed and then finally to an ever-increasing anger which left the man furious by the time the explanation was complete. And though Elizabeth knew Mr. Collins to be an ineffectual sort of man, she actually believed, by the time Mr. Forbes stopped speaking, that had she been alone with Mr. Collins, he might have tried to strike her.

In rage, Mr. Collins turned on her and began to berate her, saying:

"How dare you, Mrs. Collins! I agreed to marry you and gave you a home and the excellent patronage of my Lady de Bourgh, knowing your unworthy nature and miniscule portion would result in your never receiving another offer of marriage. I am appalled by your betrayal, madam. I should strike you where you sit!"

"'Another offer?'" jeered Elizabeth. "By my account, you never even directly made me an offer! Had you actually deigned to make any such offer to me, it would have been most soundly rejected!"

If she had thought Mr. Collins was furious before, the redness of the rage on his ugly countenance told her that she had not known the levels to which his anger could ascend. He jumped to his feet and began screaming at her, saying, "You miserable, ignorant child—"

"That is quite enough, Mr. Collins!" commanded Mr. Forbes, rising to his own feet and staring down the furious parson. "We are civilized people, and a gentleman does not stand and shout at a lady."

"She is no lady!" spat Mr. Collins. "She is nothing more than a common whore—"

"Silence!" roared Mr. Forbes, stepping forward and placing himself in front of Mr. Collins, his eyes blazing in affront.

The relative sizes of the two men alone should have presented a far different picture than the reality. Mr. Collins was heavyset, and added to that bulk was the fact that he was a rather tall man, though the certain stoop of his shoulders gave the impression of a lesser stature. Mr. Forbes, by contrast was rather diminutive and slender, giving the impression of a man who was in no way capable of enforcing his will physically. But in this instance, the smaller man clearly intimidated the larger, as Mr. Collins blanched at so being called to order by his superior and then dropped down onto the couch with haste, though his hateful glare at Elizabeth never waned. But to this, the overtone of petulance was now added, leading him to appear more the sulky child than the grown man who felt himself able to care for a wife.

"I will not tolerate another outburst, sir," said Mr. Forbes.

As Mr. Collins's attention was torn from Elizabeth, he must have seen something in the other man's air which convinced him that matters would proceed very ill for him if he did not desist, as he nodded his head in a most aggrieved fashion.

"Good," said Mr. Forbes. "Now, I have some questions for you, Mr. Collins. I believe I have the facts, but I would like to hear your own perspective on the events which led up to your marriage." He paused for a moment, looking intently at Mr. Collins. "The first question I have is: did you obtain a special license for the purpose of marrying your wife?"

Elizabeth looked at him curiously, wondering what he could be about. Mr. Collins, however, merely waved his hand.

"I have not the means to purchase a special license, sir."

Mr. Forbes's expression became even more severe. "And your patroness did not purchase one for you?"

"Of course not. Lady Catherine prefers to have the distinction of rank preserved in all things, and she would never outlay funds in such a frivolous manner for someone who is inferior to her exalted position in society."

Nodding, Mr. Forbes said, "I had suspected as much. And the

matter of Lady Catherine's actions in this parish must also be dealt with, but that is a matter for another time. Though I was not able to discover any hint of a special license, your ability to produce proof of the existence of one was about the only thing which *may* have salvaged this situation for your part."

Mr. Collins was clearly confused. "I cannot understand of what you speak, Mr. Forbes."

"You do not?" asked Mr. Forbes with an upraised eyebrow. "Surely you, having graduated from the seminary, understand the requirements of marriage. For the church to sanction a marriage between two participants, it must be solemnized in the parish where one of them is resident. The banns must be read in the home parish of each of the principals for three consecutive weeks, and only then may the marriage license be rendered valid and the marriage take place. The other option is for a special license to be purchased in lieu of the banns being read. If it is purchased, a marriage may take place at any time.

"Tell me, Mr. Collins, were the banns read in Hunsford church before your wedding?"

No answer was forthcoming, as Mr. Collins simply gazed at Mr. Forbes in equal parts fear and astonishment.

"I can see from your reaction that they were not," replied Mr. Forbes with a nod. "The testimony of your curate reflects that truth.

"Now, what of the marriage? Did it seem to you that your bride came to the altar willingly?"

"Her father promised her to me," was Mr. Collins's response.

"I am very aware of Mr. Bennet's actions in this matter. You did not answer my question. Did it seem to you that Mrs. Collins was there of her own free will, or did she appear reluctant?"

Mr. Collins shot Elizabeth a poisonous glare. "She never told me that she did not wish to marry me. In fact, the first I knew of the matter was when she told me herself recently—amid improper words and actions not befitting a lady, I might add."

"Of course I did not tell you," said Elizabeth with some scorn, feeling that she could be silent no longer. "My father did not permit me a choice in the matter."

"Surely you could have said something to me to enable us both to avoid this situation," said Collins, his voice stiff with indignation.

"Would you have listened?" snapped Elizabeth. "I would have thought that a few moments of observation would have told you all you needed to know about my feelings, Mr. Collins. You certainly made no mention of marriage when you arrived, and you even spoke of being betrothed. How should I have known to say anything to dissuade you?"

"You should have done so."

Elizabeth snorted. "I seriously doubt that would have changed anything, Mr. Collins."

His refusal to meet her eyes told Elizabeth all she needed to know about the truth of her statement. Mr. Forbes also seemed convinced of the matter.

"Besides," said Elizabeth, continuing when she knew she had best keep silent, "there are only two reasons why my father forced me to marry you. The first is because he wished to make some effort—however late and ineffectual—to provide for his wife after he passes on. I was the sacrificial lamb in that respect. The second reason is because he holds a grudge against me and thought it would be a punishment to tie me to a fool such as you for the rest of my life."

Mr. Collins bristled at her words, but Mr. Forbes inserted himself into the conversation again to calm tempers. "I believe that we should leave such speculation out of this discussion; it truly serves no purpose."

Though she could not repent of her words, Elizabeth inclined her head and apologized. Truly, all she wanted was for this farce to be over. Whatever came afterward could be dealt with at that time.

"Mrs. Collins makes a valid point," said Mr. Forbes. "Did you not think it strange how she acted that morning? I have discovered that she did not even speak the words to allow her consent to the marriage; rather, her father spoke in her place. Did this reluctance not tell you that something was amiss?"

Again, no response was forthcoming, as Mr. Collins merely stared at his superior with an expression akin to that of hare when it realizes that the fox intends it to be its next meal. And Elizabeth knew the answer to the question. Mr. Collins had not noticed it because he thought entirely too well of himself to imagine for a moment that she would object. She, a young lady of little fortune and few prospects as the daughter of a country gentleman, would undoubtedly be grateful for his condescension. No other consideration would have mattered.

"It appears to me that you never took the trouble to find out the lady's feelings," said Mr. Forbes. "And I shall tell you this: regardless of how our society works and how fathers are responsible for their daughters and may, at their discretion, enter them into betrothals for the advantage of their family, there are still certain forms which must be observed. The banns must be read or a special license sought, and it is generally accepted that the man, whether he is entering an engagement of his own free will or due to a contract, will actually propose to the lady in question, even if her refusal is not in doubt. You may wish to remember this if you have occasion to marry again, Mr. Collins.

"In this instance, it is clear that you behaved badly, though the bulk of the blame must be placed at the feet of her father. The church does not consider women to be chattel, to be married off without their consent. Mrs. Collins has been treated quite badly throughout this entire fiasco."

His words hung in the air like the blade of a guillotine waiting to fall, and for the first time since the interview had begun, Elizabeth saw signs of true fear on Mr. Collins's face. It was just as well, she thought; after all, if he was censured and his life made difficult by Lady Catherine, then perhaps he would face sanction from the church. Though she would not wish for vengeance, she could only applaud such an eventuality, given how poorly the senseless man had conducted himself in this matter.

"The annulment hearing will be held on Tuesday at ten in the morning at the chapel in Westerham. I suggest you both arrive well before the appointed time."

"My . . . my father will not be present, will he?" asked Elizabeth, a trace of unease passing through her.

"He will not, Miss Bennet," said Mr. Forbes in a kindly tone. "Though his behavior has not been beyond reproach, this is a matter of whether this marriage is to be sanctioned or struck down. It was deemed pointless to involve Mr. Bennet now.

"There is one final matter," said Mr. Forbes, looking at both of them in turn. "I apologize for speaking so freely of so delicate a matter, but can I assume that this marriage remains unconsummated?"

At the question, Elizabeth noticed a positively cunning expression come over Mr. Collins's face, and it did not take any great insight to know where his thoughts tended at that moment.

"It has not been consummated," said Elizabeth quickly, not wishing for the man to begin to plot. "Nor will it be."

"That is well," said Mr. Forbes in a deliberate fashion. He turned to look at Mr. Collins. "It would be best if it remained that way. The matter is in the hands of the ecclesiastical court, and it would not do for there to be any more untoward behavior to complicate matters further."

Though the man was a dullard, Mr. Collins obviously understood the reference, for he nodded sullenly to his superior. Elizabeth could only breathe a sigh of relief. Perhaps she would not have to worry about what he would attempt.

It was only a few more minutes before Mr. Forbes took his leave, and Elizabeth walked him to the door and thanked him; he demurred, stating that it was only his duty. As Mr. Collins stomped to his library and closed the door with a thunderous crash, Elizabeth was left to her own devices for the rest of the day. Since the air in the parsonage was now a mixture of stifled rage, petulant ill use, and injured feelings, she determined at once to leave for a long walk and revel in the fact that she would soon be free from the captivity of her marriage.

She entered the woods of Rosings soon afterward, clothed in all the winter accoutrements necessary to ward off the mid-December chill, feeling more at liberty than she had in months. And then, reveling in her newfound freedom, she did something that she had not done since she was a small child—she hiked up her skirts and ran through the woods, joyously feeling nothing but the wind through her hair and against her feet and listening to the harmonious sounds of the forest through which she ran.

It was a full five minutes later by the time she slowed to a walk, the stitch in her side and her great panting breaths forcing her to stop before she would have wished it. For a moment, she leaned against a tree, her breast heaving with the exertion and the emotions of the moment. She would soon be free—free to follow the dictates of her heart and to remove herself from the oppressive presence of the parson and his patroness. The air had never tasted so sweet nor the sunlight felt so bright as it did at that moment.

After her breathing had calmed, Elizabeth opened her eyes, only to see the form of her beloved, standing and watching her, looking like a prince come to rescue a damsel in distress. Elizabeth would never understand what made her act the way she did, as she was not accustomed to being so forward, but before any conscious thought intruded, she swiftly closed the distance between them and reached up to kiss Mr. Darcy full on the lips.

His surprise was evident in the way he stiffened, but he soon responded, enclosing her in the circle of his arms and responding to her kisses with a passion of his own, his tongue dueling with hers in a needful and breathless sharing of himself. Reason reestablished itself quickly—much more quickly than Elizabeth would have wished!—but it was a poignant harbinger of delights to come.

"I am sorry, Mr. Darcy," said Elizabeth as she pulled away from him. "I forgot myself."

"Am I to repine such a passionate reaction to my presence?" asked Mr. Darcy with a raised eyebrow.

Elizabeth laughed delightedly and, taking his arm, pulled him down the path further into the woods of the park. As they walked, Elizabeth was unable to keep a girlish giggle from her lips.

For his part, Mr. Darcy looked at her fondly, asking, "Am I to infer that there is some reason for your current, dare I say, giddiness?"

"You may, indeed, Mr. Darcy. Mr. Collins and I have been the happy recipient of a visit from Mr. Forbes this morning."

"And I suppose the results of his investigation have confirmed that you shall enjoy a happy and prosperous marriage with your Mr. Collins?"

Delighted that Mr. Darcy could tease her, Elizabeth said, "Oh, indeed. There could not be a happier creature than I to be shackled for the rest of my life to such a man."

They both laughed together, and Elizabeth squeezed his arm with affection. "In fact, the ecclesiastical court is ready to hear the annulment case. We are required to go to Westerham on Tuesday."

His responding smile was all Elizabeth could have wanted. "And Mr. Forbes seems to think that the chances of obtaining an annulment are good?"

"He questioned Mr. Collins quite closely concerning the details, and though he had already discovered them through his investigations, he was not pleased to hear what Mr. Collins had to say for himself. Though I am attempting to maintain an even temper and know that something might still prevent the dissolution of this marriage, I find that I cannot help myself. The thought that I shall soon be free of him fills me with a delighted feeling of freedom which I have not felt before."

"And you shall be free, Miss Bennet." Mr. Darcy stopped and stood in front of her, looking down on her with an expression of utmost tenderness. "I believe that I had asked you a question before this business reared its ugly head. You answered in the affirmative, as I recall, and I cannot wait for the opportunity to meet with you as a suitor, as should have been your right for the past month."

"I am anticipating it most keenly, Mr. Darcy," said Elizabeth, a lump in her throat.

They continued to walk, and though Elizabeth tried, she could not suppress a feeling of excitement at her impending release from bondage.

"Miss Bennet," said Mr. Darcy, once again capturing her attention, "have you given thought concerning what you will do should the marriage be annulled? Surely you cannot return to your father's house."

Elizabeth made a face at the mere thought. "Certainly not. And I imagine he would not allow me to be there either, not after my most recent bout of infamous behavior."

Though he turned to her with concern written upon his brow, Mr. Darcy caught her mischievous grin and subsided, no doubt spared of his thoughts of chastising her for her family's failings.

"My uncle and aunt told me to go to their townhouse should I need to. I could simply stay there until their return from Ireland."

Mr. Darcy frowned. "Surely it would not be proper for you to stay at your uncle's house without a guardian present."

"I do not think I have another choice," replied Elizabeth gently. "I have no other relations with whom I may stay other than my aunt and Uncle Philips in Meryton, and I am certain that staying there would not be at all comfortable. It is far too near to Longbourn, and as my mother is close to her sister, the situation would be difficult for my aunt."

Though he only nodded his head, albeit reluctantly, Mr. Darcy was clearly in thought, and Elizabeth was certain that he had some idea of what might be done, though he was not any more forthcoming at that moment. Elizabeth was content to allow him to ruminate on the subject, happy as she was to simply be in his company.

"Perhaps we can discuss this at a later time," said Mr. Darcy after a pause. Elizabeth had been content to simply walk in his company, the silence between them being a very comfortable sort. "I may have an idea, but the matter is not urgent at present."

It was some time later when Mr. Darcy and Elizabeth finally parted. The time they spent together on the back lanes out of sight of prying eyes allowed Elizabeth to regain her equilibrium, and because of that, she felt that she was once more able to face Mr. Collins, content in the knowledge that he might soon be removed from the position of being her husband.

Chapter XXV

*H*appiness was a state that Fitzwilliam Darcy was not able to attribute to his life in a typical sense. Though he was not *unhappy*, he had often found himself in the past to be more characterized by such words as dutiful, diligent, or content. Blessed with a large estate and many holdings besides, Darcy was well aware that his position was one to be envied. But all of these things did not necessarily equate to happiness, which was a fact that Darcy had only recently understood.

Thus, it was with a great level of anticipation that Darcy awaited the opportunity to pay his addresses to Miss Elizabeth. She was, in short, a breath of fresh air—and one he desperately needed in his rather staid and serious life. She had her own demons to conquer, as did anyone. But she would emerge stronger once she had conquered her trials. And Darcy did not doubt that she would be a good influence on Georgiana as well. His sister would certainly benefit from the presence of a sister in her life.

Elizabeth—for he could not now think of her in any other terms than by her Christian name—was already a captivating young woman, but he was certain that she wanted only the right influence and situation in life to blossom into a truly exceptional woman. Darcy meant to provide her with everything he had in order for her to grow into what she was meant to be. The only thing which was required was for the church to declare her current married status null and void.

After leaving Elizabeth close to the edge of the woods and watching her as she made her way back to the parsonage, Darcy returned to Rosings, his feelings awash with a mixture of contentment and impatience. His return to the estate, however, soon erased all such happy thoughts.

He could hear her long before he was actually in her presence, an occurrence which was not at all uncommon on account of the loudness of the woman's voice. It was something he should have anticipated, he thought, knowing of Collins's inability to keep anything from his patroness. But the fact that the man would so quickly scurry to Lady Catherine with his tales of woe and the word of his "betrayal" at the hands of his wife showed a weakness of character which was truly contemptible.

"She is in quite the state, Darcy," warned Fitzwilliam when Darcy had entered the house. "She is insistent that she will go to the parsonage directly and instruct Mrs. Collins to cease her 'unseemly display,' as she terms it."

"That is amusing, coming from Aunt Catherine," said Darcy with no little measure of scorn.

"As true as that statement is, you may wish to moderate your words," said Fitzwilliam, "if you wish to stay close to Mrs. Collins until she is free from that little parson."

Darcy only grunted as he removed his outer garments. It was time to go into the sitting room and try to prevent his aunt from making a spectacle of herself, slim though the likelihood of success seemed.

"Thus far, I have only been able to get a garbled message of what exactly had occurred," continued Fitzwilliam as he waited. "Do you care to share?"

"Mr. Forbes returned this morning." He had shared everything with Fitzwilliam and knew that his cousin would understand the significance of that piece of intelligence.

Fitzwilliam nodded. "I take it, then, that the news is good for Mrs. Collins?"

"The hearing is set for Tuesday in Westerham," replied Darcy shortly. "Given what I know myself, I suspect the chances are very good that the marriage will be struck down."

"Very good," said Fitzwilliam. "But I would caution you to keep your head about you. The dragon lady will make Mrs. Collins's life miserable if she detects any hint of your admiration."

With a glare at his cousin—Fitzwilliam should have been aware that Darcy would never forget himself in such a manner—Darcy turned and entered the room in which his aunt was still loudly pontificating. To her side sat Anne, who appeared to be the unfortunate recipient of her mother's diatribe, though she bore it with a patience that Darcy envied. Still, he supposed that Anne was largely inured to Lady Catherine due to years of constant proximity. Not for the first time, Darcy considered what might be done to ease Anne's situation. It could not be comfortable to continually live with such a woman.

"Darcy!" boomed Lady Catherine when she spied him entering the room. "It is well that you have come. We must take thought concerning what is to be done about that . . . scheming little piece of baggage."

Directing a bland yet even expression at his aunt, Darcy replied, "I am afraid I have not the pleasure of understanding you, aunt."

A wave met his words. "That is because you were once again gallivanting all over the estate rather than attending us as you should. Had you been here, you would have understood the wrong which Mrs. Collins is even now perpetuating upon her poor husband and indeed upon the entire community."

"A great wrong?" asked Darcy with a raised eyebrow.

"The stupid girl has sued for an annulment—and after all Mr. Collins did to give her insignificant family notice and heal the breach. I, in my Christian generosity, advised him to do such a thing, and *this* is how she repays us both!"

"An annulment?" queried Darcy with a lazy lack of interest.

"You are dull today, Darcy!" snapped Lady Catherine. "Pay attention!"

"If you would explain the situation, then perhaps I would understand," said Darcy. Secretly, he was amused by his aunt's displeasure. She was not in the habit of tolerating disappointment or being gainsaid in any fashion, and this business with the wife of her parson must be severely taxing on one who was intent upon having her own way. Yes, Darcy was enjoying this very much.

In response, Lady Catherine glared at him, but evidently recalling her view on the paramount importance of keeping his good will, she swallowed her pique. It was another thing to which she was unaccustomed.

"Mr. Collins has just been here to visit me," said Lady Catherine. "It seems that his wife has been bearing stories of her mistreatment at the hands of her husband and father and has requested an annulment from the church, though I doubt it shall be granted. Somehow—and I know not how — she has managed to prevail on them to hear her case."

"And Mr. Collins was here to pour out his sorrows on your benevolence?"

Lady Catherine completely missed the sarcasm in Darcy's tone. "To whom should he turn if not me? I advise him most particularly on everything, I assure you, and I have found him to be a good pupil, if a little ponderous."

By Darcy's side, Fitzwilliam covered a laugh with a cough, but Lady Catherine, though she did glare at him, made no comment, preferring to stay on the topic of her parson.

"This infamous behavior is not to be borne! The girl should be grateful for the attention he paid her. Of course, part of the blame must belong to Mr. Collins for choosing her. Mrs. Collins is a pretty sort of girl, I suppose, and she seems to be quite intelligent, but her impertinence is of an uncommon sort, and she appears to think too well of herself.

"Regardless, I shall depart to the parsonage posthaste to make my sentiments known to her. She must be prevailed upon to cease this unseemly business immediately and to retract her ungenerous attempt to annul her marriage."

Though he knew it was fruitless, Darcy would not allow his aunt to impose herself upon Elizabeth without his making an attempt at opposition.

"Lady Catherine, have you considered the fact that if the church is investigating the matter, then perhaps something is amiss?"

An imperious glare met his question. "It does not signify. The marriage has been solemnized, and she should accept her fate with dignity."

"If Mr. Collins is found to have behaved badly, should he not be held accountable for his actions? And as for Mr. Bennet, I have met the man, and I was by no means impressed with him. I suggest you allow the church to handle the matter without involving yourself, as it is not, after all, truly your concern."

"I would not consider myself attentive to all things within my domain if I did that."

"Then perhaps you should consider the fact that it will reflect badly upon you if it is found that Mr. Collins's behavior was not beyond reproach. You installed him in Hunsford and sent him to his cousin to look for a bride, after all."

Unfortunately, Darcy's words had the opposite effect from the one that he was intending. Upon hearing his words, Lady Catherine became even more displeased, and she immediately stood, directing her servants to bring the carriage around.

"I will repair immediately to the parsonage and deal with this directly. Mrs. Collins must be brought to see reason!"

Nothing Darcy said from that moment on made any impression upon Lady Catherine's determination to insert herself into the affairs of her parson, so Darcy insisted upon accompanying her when she left. And after speaking briefly with Fitzwilliam and obtaining his agreement that he would stay with Anne, Darcy entered the coach with Lady Catherine and settled in for the short journey to the parsonage. His aunt eyed him with a trace of a frown as he regarded her blandly.

"Darcy, you take a rather unseemly interest in the affairs of my parson."

On the contrary, thought Darcy, *I care nothing for the affairs of your parson. On the other hand, I have a great interest in the affairs of the young lady with whom he claims to be joined in matrimony.*

But Darcy was determined not to be cowed by his cantankerous relation. "And you do not?"

"Mr. Collins is *my* parson, installed in the living that is in *my* power to give," said Lady Catherine, a trace of heat entering her voice. "Thus, his concerns *are* my concerns."

"And some would say that you are taking an excessive level of interest in this matter."

Lady Catherine threw up her hands. "This is not your concern, Darcy. You had best stay at Rosings and get on with the business of deciding on a wedding date with Anne."

"I will not even grace that statement with a response, given the words which passed between us when I last left Rosings."

Through narrowed eyes, Lady Catherine glared at him, but her disapproval was interrupted by their arrival at the parsonage. With one last huff, the lady disembarked from the carriage without even waiting for him to step down and assist her. Darcy was grateful, as he felt inclined to throttle the woman already!

Lady Catherine marched into the parsonage, where she sent the maid scurrying with a glare and entered the parlor without being introduced. Darcy, who followed behind her, noted immediately that Elizabeth sat in a chair and that Mr. Collins, who had not, for once, been watching the road for his patroness, appeared to be sitting close to her and speaking intently to her. That she was uncomfortable was evident, but knowing her ability to withstand her husband, Darcy schooled his features to neutrality and resolved to be patient.

"Lady Catherine!" exclaimed Mr. Collins as he rose and executed a hasty bow. "I welcome you to my humble abode, and I must express my great regret on not greeting you at the door as is your right as my noble patroness. I was just—"

"Yes, yes, Mr. Collins," snapped Lady Catherine as she sat in the high-backed chair which she usually used when at the parsonage. She gave the appearance of holding court, and Darcy was certain that such was her design, not only for the purpose of cowing her voluble parson, but also for the purpose of intimidating Elizabeth. "I have come directly to speak with your wife, and I will not be persuaded from my purpose. For the nonce, you will be silent while I have words with her."

The parson sank to his chair in an instant, but a smug sort of smirk played about his mouth as he glanced in a superior manner at his wife. Elizabeth, for her part, appeared to be less than impressed by the show of displeasure directed at her.

"Well, what do you have to say for yourself, Mrs. Collins?" demanded Lady Catherine after a moment.

"As you have not stated the purpose for your visit, I cannot comment about something of which I have no knowledge."

Silently, Darcy commended her for her fortitude, but his aunt's countenance merely became more severe.

"Mrs. Collins, do you not know who I am?"

"I am very well aware of who you are, your ladyship."

"Then you must know that I am not to be trifled with. You are perfectly well aware of the reason for my visit, yet you attempt to obfuscate in a manner which offends me and injures the respectability of your husband."

"There is no obfuscation, your ladyship," replied Elizabeth. Though she kept her calm temper, Darcy was certain that she was privately annoyed by the lady's impertinence. "Yes, I may have an inkling of what has brought you here today, but I would not dare to assume. I would much prefer to wait until you have stated your purpose before speaking."

"It seems you would indeed dare to assume much!" cried Lady Catherine. "But I shall deal with you later." She turned her demanding gaze toward Mr. Collins, who, though a moment earlier was caught up in the smugness and certainty of his common opinion with that of his patroness, now fairly cowered under the weight of her glare.

"Mr. Collins, I am most displeased, both with you, and with your improper wife. I sent you to Hertfordshire to acquire a wife—a simple and straightforward task. I instructed you on exactly the type of woman you should choose for the position, and yet you have returned with a woman who is not only unsuitable, but is almost the exact opposite of every trait I instructed you to search for. How could you allow yourself to be imposed upon by this Mr. Bennet to marry his most unworthy daughter?"

The poor man—if he could be termed such—did not appear to know what to do or how to act, and no words came forth from his normally garrulous mouth. But as usual, Lady Catherine did not require a response, for after she had reprimanded the parson, she turned her attention back to Elizabeth.

"Now, Mrs. Collins, I have come to the parsonage this morning with the resolve of having my wishes carried out, and I am determined that it shall be so. Regardless of my conviction that you are completely unsuited to be the parson's wife in this parish, your marriage has been sanctioned, and I must insist that you cease this unseemly display."

"I have conducted myself exactly as I should, Lady Catherine," replied Elizabeth. Darcy could only applaud her bravery once again. "As for the matter of this *marriage*, I am not certain what Mr. Collins has told you. But if you would listen to what exactly happened in Hertfordshire, I am certain you would agree that I was used quite ill by my father and by Mr. Collins."

"I have no need to hear of it!" cried Lady Catherine. "The marriage has been solemnized, and though I have no desire for you to be wife of my parson, I have decided, in my Christian generosity, to extend this olive branch to you and allow you to remain. But I must insist upon the assurance of your good behavior."

"The marriage *has not* been solemnized," said Elizabeth. "The fact that there is a hearing scheduled should be an indication of that."

Lady Catherine glared at Elizabeth, and though Darcy thought to intervene, he was silenced by a glance from the young woman in question. It seemed to say that he had best hold his tongue, as she was more than capable of dealing with his aunt, and though the protective streak in Darcy had been aroused, he decided it would be best if he abided by her wishes.

"I will not be gainsaid! You will oblige me!"

"I will not. The church will decide whether Mr. Collins has acted correctly in this matter."

"Mrs. Collins, I am shocked indeed at this behavior. I had come here, thinking to find a reasonable young woman, and yet I find a child. I am not in the habit of brooking disappointment, I assure you. I shall be resolute to my purpose until you give me the agreement I desire."

"Then I must pity you, madam, for I shall *never* give it! You had best cease to importune me on the subject."

Jumping to her feet, Lady Catherine loomed over Elizabeth as a summer storm cloud hovers over the ground below. "I insist!"

This time, however, Elizabeth did not deign to respond. Instead, she simply sat there looking up at the lady, and though it was obvious that Lady Catherine was trying her patience, it was equally evident that she was not moved in the slightest by this display of anger.

"I cannot believe this!" cried Lady Catherine. "I will not be defeated by the machinations of an improper Jezebel. I will be obliged!"

"I can hardly be a Jezebel," said Elizabeth with a wry look. "As I understand the term, a Jezebel is a woman who seduces unsuspecting men. Since I have never even allowed the worm you employ into my bed, I believe that such assertions mean little."

By this time, Lady Catherine had reached a dangerous shade of red in her rage, and Darcy thought for a moment that she might strike Elizabeth with her walking stick. But before he could move to protect her, Lady Catherine turned an icy glare upon the still cringing form of her parson.

"Control your wife, Mr. Collins. If this *woman's* behavior causes a scandal, then you may as well find another parish."

She turned and stalked from the room, her walking stick striking a loud beat as she went, a counterpoint to the sound of her boots hitting the floor. All was silent in the room after her departure.

Though it seemed as if his aunt had forgotten about his presence, Darcy had no desire whatsoever to leave, intent as he was on watching Mr. Collins. The man's face went white at the inference behind Lady Catherine's last words, and for a moment, he appeared too shocked to speak. But then the color rushed back into his face, and his countenance quickly assumed the hue of a ripe tomato, and he turned to deliver what Darcy assumed would be a harsh rebuke to his wife.

But then he stopped and looked at Elizabeth for a moment, and a resolve seemed to settle over him. For her part, Elizabeth ignored him, seeming to simply revel in the fact that Lady Catherine had departed. But Darcy could see something more in the man's calculating look, and he knew exactly what Mr. Collins was contemplating.

"Mr. Collins, a word," snapped Darcy, startling the man, as if he too had forgotten Darcy's presence. Instantly, however, the man's familiar subservient expression appeared, though this time it was colored with a hint of cunning, an expression which was rather incongruous on his stupid face.

"I would be happy to, Mr. Darcy, but I believe that I must have a long overdue conversation with my wife." He shot a stern glare at Elizabeth, who rose to her feet and announced that she had some matters to see to.

"It appears that we have a few moments, Mr. Collins," said Darcy, forestalling the man's obvious intention to prevent Elizabeth's departure.

Mr. Collins was a mass of conflicting emotions, and though he judged better than to force his wife to stay, his struggles were clear for Darcy to read. First and foremost, Darcy thought, was his abject fear of Lady Catherine and the threat of dismissal, but Darcy could also see the man's frustration at Elizabeth's recalcitrance and his inability to force her to behave as he wished. And of course, there were the more unsavory emotions—bewilderment, sullen anger, and, unless he missed his guess, lust for the young woman Darcy loved. But Darcy was not about to allow the man to harm her in any way.

After Elizabeth left the room, Mr. Collins turned his attention to Darcy, and immediately his countenance changed to a look of utmost servility, much as Darcy had seen the man display many times before. It was something that Darcy could use, he decided with a grimness of purpose.

"Yes, Mr. Darcy?" asked he. "How can I be of assistance to an exalted personage such as yourself?"

"First, we may dispense with this fawning. I am not my aunt, Mr. Collins, and I do not require your submissiveness or your flattery."

"But it would not do for me to treat you with anything other than the respect you deserve."

The slightly whining quality to the man's words grated on Darcy's nerves, and he frowned at Mr. Collins, noting his sudden pallor in response.

"As I have stated, Mr. Collins, I do not require your groveling. However, what I do require is for you to treat your wife with the utmost dignity and decorum."

A look of utmost condescension came over the man's face, so incongruous with his earlier deference, and Darcy wondered at this man. He certainly was like none other Darcy had ever met before. Darcy fervently wished that the pleasure had been indefinitely postponed.

"As an unmarried man, you cannot, I fear, have any understanding of what passes between man and wife," said Mr. Collins, his tone a strange mixture of deference and self-assurance. "It is for the man to control and direct his wife in all things, and your aunt has made me painfully aware of my own failure in regard to this necessity. I fully intend to correct my oversight and exert the direction which my wife is sorely lacking.

"You had best focus on your own future wife, Mr. Darcy," continued he in a tone which was even further steeped in condescension. "I am highly anticipating the opportunity to wish you joy with your fair cousin, Miss de Bourgh."

"Mr. Collins, are you completely bereft of sense?" hissed Darcy. "I am well aware of the direction in which your thoughts lie. And I will tell you now that if you harm one hair on the head of your wife, the full force of my fury shall fall upon you without mercy."

"What right do you have to instruct me on how I may deal with my wife, sir?" demanded Mr. Collins, forgetting his deference.

Darcy stood and towered over the small man, and Mr. Collins seemed suddenly reminded of exactly with whom he was speaking. "I have the right of a gentleman concerned for the welfare of a lady. Your conduct in this entire matter has been reprehensible, Mr. Collins. I suggest you take great care lest you find yourself in circumstances even worse than the ones you currently face."

Mr. Collins wrung his hands, his agitation warring with his perceived need to enforce his control over his wife. "But I face dismissal if my wife succeeds in this mad design to throw off our marriage. Whatever shall I do?"

"I care not," said Darcy, his tone pitiless. "I seriously doubt you will escape punishment regardless. Perhaps you should have thought of this before you defied all sense and propriety and allowed Mr. Bennet to wed his daughter to you with only the barest appearance of the proper forms of marriage. I am certain the church does not look kindly upon parsons who willfully disregard ecclesiastical law."

By this time, Collins was looking at him, mouth agape in horror, and Darcy could not help but gaze at him with satisfaction.

"But all shall *most assuredly* be lost if you assault your wife, Mr. Collins. I will ensure it. By the time I am finished with you, you will wish you had never been born. Do we understand one another?"

Mr. Collins nodded his head in a most animated—and absurd—fashion, and the words spilling from his mouth were almost coherent, but the gist of it was that he would not dream of treating his wife with anything but respect.

Grimly, Darcy smiled and thanked him and let himself out of the house.

The next few days were almost pleasant for Elizabeth. Though any interaction whatsoever with Mr. Collins was exasperating and a trial on her patience, there was in actuality relatively little to be had. Simply put, the man seemed intent upon avoiding her in the most assiduous manner possible, and Elizabeth could only be grateful for that. She had waited at the door listening to Mr. Darcy reprimand him and warn him from engaging in any untoward behavior, but she had almost expected Mr. Collins to ignore his directive, given how fearful he was toward Lady Catherine. But other than at mealtimes and a few instances when they came across each other in the house, there was little communication between them. Elizabeth could not be happier for that fact. Apparently, Mr. Darcy's threats had found fertile ground in the imagination of the parson.

A place where this courtesy—if it could be called that—was not extended was in church that Sunday. The topic of the sermon for the week was decided upon by Lady Catherine, which Elizabeth had discovered soon after her arrival in Kent. Knowing that Lady Catherine was in charge meant that she expected some sort of denunciation from the parson, and though he was not willing to cross Mr. Darcy in the matter of his physical conduct, he could hardly fail to use the Sunday services as a way to reprimand his wife according to the wishes of his patroness.

Thus, when the first words out of his mouth that Sunday morning confirmed the subject to be the need for women to submit to their husbands in all things, Elizabeth was not surprised. She also did not refrain from glancing skyward in exasperation, and if the man's suddenly tight glare was any indication, he did not miss the movement.

Nor, it appeared, did Mr. Darcy's relations. Lady Catherine shot Elizabeth several smug smiles throughout Mr. Collins's long-winded and droning speech, but the colonel's features openly betrayed a grin, and Miss de Bourgh could be seen to suppress a giggle at some of his more dramatically pompous pronouncements. Even Mr. Darcy, though clearly not amused when the parson began to speak, seemed to echo a little of his relations' amusement. As for Elizabeth, her amusement at the sheer ridiculousness of the parson made it impossible for her to feel affront at his blatant and ineffectual attempt to embarrass her.

After church, however, was when tempers truly began to flare.

Once Mr. Collins concluded his remarks, he went to the door, as was his wont, to say farewell to those worshippers who had attended the service and to ensure that his patroness and her party had a clear path to the door, as if the lady was royalty.

Thankfully, Lady Catherine waited until most of the congregation had dispersed before doing anything, though Elizabeth was uncertain whether to attribute her wait to discretion. It hardly seemed likely, given how outspoken the woman was, but Elizabeth was grateful nonetheless.

"Mr. Collins," said the lady once the Rosings and Hunsford parties were for the most part alone, "I trust that the situation at the parsonage has improved?"

Clearly, the man was at war with himself. If the surreptitious glances he cast at Mr. Darcy were any indication, it was obvious that the parson feared to anger the man. He could hardly be blamed, as the gentleman was regarding him with a stony severity which promised pain should he speak wrongly. Ultimately, Mr. Collins's old loyalty and, perhaps more importantly, his fear of inciting Lady Catherine's displeasure was a powerful motivator. Thus, he stood for several moments, clearly wondering how he should proceed.

Lady Catherine, however, took his silence as an inability to own that he was unable to control his wife, and the woman turned on Elizabeth with anger etched upon her face.

"Mrs. Collins, have you submitted to your husband and performed your duties as I have instructed?"

"Since I do not consider Mr. Collins to be my husband, I cannot imagine to what duties you refer."

Immediately overcome by anger, Lady Catherine strode up to Elizabeth and began to shout at her. "How dare you, Mrs. Collins! I gave you explicit instructions with the expectation they would be carried out, and still you continue to defy me? This is not to be borne."

"I am afraid you have no choice," replied Elizabeth in a frosty tone. "The church will decide my fate, as it will that of Mr. Collins. I am merely waiting for that eventuality."

"This is not a matter to involve the church in!" screeched the lady.

"The church is already involved," replied Elizabeth, her own tones climbing as she fought to maintain her temper in the face of such attacks.

"Mrs. Collins, do you not understand that you are tainting the very stones of Rosings and Hunsford with your actions?"

"Then you must wish for me to be gone. Believe me, I wish for nothing less!"

"I must insist that you submit to your husband as you have been instructed! I will accept no other answer from you!"

Finally, Elizabeth's temper snapped, and she glared at the meddling old crone with fire in her eyes. "Lady Catherine, if you are so adamant about the need to *submit*, then perhaps *you* should submit to him! I never shall!"

Her eyes fairly bulging out of her head, Lady Catherine stammered for a moment before screaming, "I have never been so insulted in my entire life!"

"Then perhaps it is time for you to receive a taste of your own medicine, as I had not been in your company for two minutes before you had insulted *me*!"

And with that, Elizabeth glared at Lady Catherine and stalked away. She did not leave so quickly that she did not witness the colonel's struggle to hold in his mirth or Miss de Bourgh's hidden smile. Of Mr. Darcy, she could see very little, as his emotions were concealed behind his typical mask of reserve. But he watched her go, and she thought she could detect a hint of approval in his manner, which was rather curious. She had just grievously insulted his aunt, after all!

Elizabeth did not return to the parsonage. She stayed outside and walked the paths of Rosings, intent upon avoiding Mr. Collins as much as possible. She knew that she would not meet Mr. Darcy, as it was better for them to avoid being seen in one another's company as much as possible. Thus, she spent a long and lonely afternoon in solitary reflection, which was certainly much superior to spending time with her husband.

Tuesday could not come soon enough!

Chapter XXVI

When Tuesday morning finally did arrive, it was as if Elizabeth was hearing the siren call of freedom. The preceding days had been difficult in some ways, though easier in others, but the general atmosphere of tension and anticipation was almost stifling, and she was eager to have done with it. No matter what happened today, she was determined to leave Collins behind as soon as may be. She would rather take ship and live in the wilds of Canada than live with an imbecile for the rest of her life!

Mr. Collins said nothing to her that morning. He had not said anything since she had insulted his patroness. His looks, though, spoke volumes as to the level of affront he was feeling, and Elizabeth knew that he was beginning to wish that he had never laid eyes on her despite whatever physical attraction or lust the man felt for her.

The small gig he kept for his journeys to the further flung areas of the neighborhood was hitched, and they soon found themselves on their way to Westerham for the hearing. Elizabeth was amused that the man had not offered to help her up to the seat, but she did not comment. Her thoughts were mostly on Mr. Darcy, who had contrived a moment to speak with her the day before when she had taken her constitutional. Though he had been careful not to speak to her for more than an instant, he had assured her that he would be at the hearing to lend his support. Elizabeth was grateful, and because of his expected presence, she knew that she could suffer through a short ride with her soon-to-be-erstwhile husband.

The church in Westerham was only slightly larger than the one in Hunsford, as the village was not much larger than the parish over which Mr. Collins presided. But it was actually rather new, the previous building having burnt to the ground several years earlier and been subsequently replaced. The sight of the two-wheeled gig caused little notice as they made their way through the town to stop in front of the shining white façade of the house of worship.

Elizabeth quickly alighted, not wishing for one moment to give Mr. Collins any reason to touch her, not that she should have bothered. The man ignored her as he tied the horse's reins to a post and followed her into the church.

The inside of the building was primarily lit by the light of the morning sun flowing in through the large windows along the side of the chapel, though a few sconces had been lit as well. The pews had been moved back slightly to allow for the proceedings at the front where the pulpit was located. On the floor in front of the pulpit, three high-backed chairs had been situated to look back toward the pews, and several other chairs had been set up to accommodate the principals of the matter. There were a number of people in attendance, and most appeared to be official looking, though of the few laymen present, Mr. Darcy standing tall and giving her an encouraging smile, was the one who captured her interest. She dared not look at him nearly as long as she would have liked, and she distracted herself by noting that though the lady had expressed her opinion on more than one occasion, Lady Catherine had not chosen to attend that morning.

"Mrs. Collins, Mr. Collins," a voice spoke up. Elizabeth refocused her gaze and was relieved to see Mr. Forbes approaching with his typical kindness. "Please, if you will step this way, we may begin momentarily."

Grateful to the man for acting to put her at ease, Elizabeth followed him and was soon seated in a chair facing the tribunal, a little to the right of the center. Mr. Collins, by contrast was placed in one a little to the left in the same general position, and it appeared he disliked the thought that he was facing those who would be stern and strict in their interrogations. If Elizabeth was to be honest with herself, she was nervous herself.

Elizabeth glanced around at the chamber, noting the sparsely populated room and the small groups of men discussing what she presumed to be the matter at hand. Most were dressed as Mr. Collins and Mr. Forbes were, all in black with the traditional collar of the clergy tight about their necks. But there was one group of three who were dressed slightly differently; these men wore long, flowing black velvet Chimere over their ivory Rochet and puffy lawn sleeves, with Geneva bands at their throats. Two of the men were likely somewhat younger than her father; one had blond hair and an open countenance, and the other had black hair which had mostly turned white. The final man in that group was tall and imposing, with piercing dark eyes and coal black hair that had only a hint of gray at the temples, for all that he appeared to be older than the other two.

A moment later, the signal had been given, and Mr. Forbes stepped forward to speak. "I now call this hearing to order. The tribunal has been gathered today to hear the petition for annulment from Mrs. Elizabeth Anne Collins, née Bennet. Presiding at this hearing and forming the tribunal will be Their Graces, the Bishop of Chichester, the Bishop of Rochester, and His Grace, the Archbishop of Canterbury."

That was a surprise, and Elizabeth stared at the elder man situated in between the other two bishops with some trepidation. Because annulments were so rarely petitioned and even more infrequently granted, they were matters for the highest echelons of the church. But Elizabeth did not think that His Grace Charles Manners-Sutton, the Archbishop of Canterbury and senior bishop of the Church of England, would concern himself with proceedings such as these. A glance at Mr. Collins revealed that he was in a state approaching terror. The involvement of the leader of the church would almost certainly not bode well for him.

"Thank you, Mr. Forbes," said the Archbishop, his voice a deep rumble. "Please begin."

With a bow, Mr. Forbes launched into his explanation. He detailed how he had learned of Elizabeth's wish to have the case heard and had subsequently journeyed to Hunsford to speak with her, taking the time while there to talk to the curate at Hunsford parish to inquire about the reading of the banns. He then detailed how he had sent an agent to Longbourn church, where the wedding had taken place, and had confirmed that the banns had not been read in that parish either. Finally, he spoke of his efforts to locate any record of a special license and his subsequent discovery from Mr. Collins that one had not been purchased.

The archbishop stared at Mr. Collins, and though it was not precisely an unfriendly glare, it was also not one which allowed the parson any indication that his actions were under anything less than the severest scrutiny. "And the particulars, Mr. Forbes?" asked he, not removing his gaze from Mr. Collins.

"The parson of Longbourn church stated that Mrs. Collins was hesitant from the moment she entered the church to the time it came for her to sign the register."

"And did she eventually sign the register?"

"After a manner of speaking," replied Mr. Forbes. He held up the heavy black book that Elizabeth remembered from the church the morning of her marriage. "I took the liberty of requesting that the register be brought here for examination during this hearing. I will refer back to it when we arrive at that point."

The archbishop nodded.

"It is evident that the bride did not consent to the marriage."

"Pardon me, sirs," said Mr. Collins, evidently finding his courage, "but her father consented to the marriage. As she is underage, that should be all that is required."

Mr. Forbes turned and eyed the parson with some displeasure. "I shall remind you of our previous conversation where I informed you that the church does not consider women to be chattel."

"And the fact that she did not speak to me of her unwillingness to consent?" persisted Mr. Collins.

"I believe we should allow the lady in question to speak for herself." Mr. Forbes turned to Elizabeth and with a smile said, "If you please, Mrs. Collins. I think that we should hear your comments on what happened that day."

"Of course, Mr. Forbes," replied Elizabeth. "What precisely would you like to know?"

"Did you consent to the marriage?"

"I did not."

"And why did you not protest more?"

"Partially from shock." Elizabeth paused. "I was told the night before that my father wished me to marry Mr. Collins, and as I had only met the man and did not feel an inclination toward him, my father and I argued. He ended my argument by slapping me."

Elizabeth tried not to notice Mr. Darcy's anger at her last admission, but her words seemed to generate more understanding.

"And then what happened?"

"I tried to escape that night," continued Elizabeth. "I dressed myself and attempted to slip out of the house after dark."

Mr. Collins gave a glance of disapproval due to what he must have considered to be a display of her lack of propriety, but Elizabeth ignored him. "My father stopped me before I could leave, locking me in my room for the rest of the night.

"The next morning, he entered my room, telling me to dress for my wedding, which was to be held that morning."

"And why did you not protest?" demanded Mr. Collins.

"Would it have made the slightest bit of difference?" scoffed Elizabeth. "You had ignored my attempts to convey to you that I felt no inclination toward you, and my father had made it very clear that my refusal was not an option."

"Did you fear that he would strike you again?" asked Mr. Forbes.

"He never stated it outright," replied Elizabeth slowly, "but it was clear he would do so from the way he acted and the way he held my arm. His grip left bruises on my skin."

"And did you not consider your father the authority in your family for making such decisions?" This question was from the archbishop, and though Elizabeth could not quite read his expression, she did not think that his question was intended to provoke her.

"I barely know my father," said Elizabeth. "From the time I was nine, I have been brought up by my uncle, and not once in those years did my father visit, write, or attempt to contact me. At least, he never did so until he wrote to my uncle to insist on my return. I did not know his reason initially, but I now know it was the purpose of forcing me to marry Mr. Collins."

"But he is still your father. Do you not owe him your respect?"

"Pardon me, Your Grace, but he has never acted like my father." Elizabeth dashed a few angry tears from her eyes as she tried to put on a brave face despite her tribulations. "As a child, I had been neglected and made to feel inferior, dressed in cast-offs and held to blame for all my family's misfortunes. I do not know what might have happened to me had my uncle not intervened. And then I was called back to my father, told I was to marry a man I had only just met, forced to the church, made to listen as my father agreed to my wedding vows in my stead, and forced under the threat of violence to sign the marriage register, all for my father's petty revenge for the grudge he holds against me. Is this the kind of man I should respect?"

The archbishop regarded her, the compassion in his eyes clear in his softened gaze and sad smile. "No, Miss Bennet. I must agree with you." Turning to Mr. Forbes, the archbishop said, "Have you any other evidence, Mr. Forbes?"

"The register, Your Grace," said Mr. Forbes. He approached and placed the book on the table situated in front of the three bishops, opening it for them to see. "If you will look at the second entry from the bottom, you will see Mr. Collins's signature. However, the signature beside his is somewhat . . . surprising."

The bishops examined the book for several moments until the archbishop looked up and pierced Mr. Collins with a look, though he was sporting a bit of a wry smile.

"Mr. Collins, are you aware of your wife's name?"

"Y-yes, of course!" blurted a flustered Mr. Collins.

"What is it?"

"Elizabeth Collins."

"Her maiden name, Mr. Collins."

"Elizabeth Bennet," snapped Mr. Collins, shooting a glare at Elizabeth.

"Then would you care to explain why the name next to yours in the register, though somewhat hastily scrawled, clearly reads 'Marie Antoinette?'"

The shock was evident in Mr. Collins's ruddy face, and he stared at the archbishop for several moments, his mouth working, though no sound was emerging. But all at once, this happy state of affairs changed, and his face mottled with rage. He turned to Elizabeth with a poisonous glare of uncharacteristic intensity and said, in a low and dangerous voice, "You did not sign your name to the register?"

"Of course not."

"Do your name and reputation mean so little to you, madam?"

"It was the only form of protest my father allowed, and had he thought to check, I doubt he would have allowed it either."

Mr. Collins fell silent, and it seemed as if he had finally been defeated by her testimony. But while he might now accept that she did not wish to be joined with him, Elizabeth was certain that the man had far too high an opinion of himself to allow his spirits to be depressed for long. On the contrary, once the immediacy of the situation was passed—and perhaps more importantly, once he was out of his superiors' presence—Elizabeth had no doubt that his anger would make an impressive return.

"Do you need to see the register to be convinced of the fact that your wife's name is not written here, Mr. Collins?"

The parson looked back at the archbishop, and though he did not speak, he shook his head with a grimace.

"Then the last question pertains to the consummation of the marriage. Can we assume that it has not been consummated?"

"Would it change your decision if it was?" asked Mr. Collins.

A harsh glare from all three bishops met his question. "Were you thinking of telling an untruth, sir?"

"No, Your Grace," replied Mr. Collins hurriedly. "I merely wish to ascertain if there was anything I could have done to keep my wife."

"It seems to me that you did not even bother to go through the correct means to *obtain* a wife," said the Bishop of Chichester. "As far as I can see, there is nothing in this farce which is legitimate, and the only choice is to dissolve the marriage, though there is not much to dissolve."

"I am in agreement," said the archbishop. "The only reason that the question of consummation is pertinent at all is the matter of Mrs. Collins keeping herself intact so that she may marry again."

"The marriage has not been consummated," said Elizabeth hurriedly. She did not state that there was nothing in the world which could possibly have tempted her into allowing Mr. Collins to touch her. The bishops would likely have understood—and possibly even agreed!—but she doubted they would have been amused by such a statement.

"Good," replied the archbishop. "My fellow bishops and I will confer, and then we will render our decision."

The three men stood, and they repaired to a corner away from the rest of those in the room, and Elizabeth sat back in her chair, content that the decision seemed as if it were about to be made in her favor. She dared not look at Mr. Darcy, for fear that her feelings would be plain for anyone to see.

It was not long, however, before the three men returned and took their seats, and their attention was quickly focused upon Elizabeth.

"Mrs. Collins—" began Manners-Sutton. Then he checked himself and said, "I suppose we should call you 'Miss Bennet' again. On behalf of the Church of England, I wish to apologize for the grievous wrong which was done to you, not only by your father, but also by one of our own."

Almost weeping with relief, Elizabeth nevertheless squared her shoulders, and in a voice slightly quivering with emotion, she said, "I thank you for your words, Your Grace. Please know that my faith has not been shaken and that I do not blame the church. I merely want justice done. I have no desire beyond that."

The archbishop smiled. "You seem like a very good young woman, Miss Bennet. Please use this opportunity to select your future partner in life wisely. You have been given an opportunity to choose for yourself, and it would be a shame if you were to marry someone who did not appreciate you."

Every instinct screamed at her to look at Mr. Darcy, but Elizabeth managed to resist, and she instead answered, "Thank you, Your Grace. I certainly shall."

Elizabeth had the distinct impression that the archbishop was smiling at her indulgently and that he knew something of her and Mr. Darcy. He said nothing further on the subject, however, instead content to incline his head and move on to his next remarks.

"For various irregularities, including the bride's lack of consent, the neglect of the required reading of the banns, the fact that there was no special license procured, and the improper signing of the marriage register, we declare this marriage annulled and void, struck from the records of the church as if it had never taken place. As much as it is in our power to influence, we hereby state our support for Miss Bennet. She is the wronged party in this matter and therefore cannot be held accountable. We hope that all will accept her innocence and accept her into full society. No dishonor will stain her reputation.

"Mr. Collins."

The archbishop calling his name seemed to snap Mr. Collins from his dark thoughts and glares at Elizabeth, for he looked up. For a moment, Elizabeth thought that he might snap at the archbishop.

"It has come to our attention that there are certain irregularities concerning your stewardship over the parish of Hunsford."

His eyes bulging from his head, Mr. Collins immediately leapt to his own defense. "I know not what Mrs. Collins has told you—"

"Mrs. Collins has said nothing," interrupted the archbishop. "The matter of the annulment has been brought to a close; this is a different matter entirely. It is presumed that you must return her to her father's home—is that not correct?"

At Mr. Collins's sullen nod, the archbishop continued. "Then that is all that will be said concerning the matter. When you return, however, we will take up the matter of these issues within the parish. At that time, we can determine what improvements need to be made."

With that, the bishops rose and filed from the room, leaving Elizabeth with tears in her eyes. She was finally free!

"Miss Bennet," said Mr. Collins, striding up to her in a clipped manner. "You will return to the gig immediately. I wish to prepare to return you to your father without delay."

Elizabeth gave him a measured look and decided it was best to simply appease him. "Of course, Mr. Collins."

So saying, she preceded him down the aisle of the church and toward the door. There, in front of her, stood Mr. Darcy, and though his expression was unreadable, Elizabeth could tell that he was pleased with the result of the hearing. "I will go to the parsonage and see you as soon as may be," said Mr. Darcy in a quiet tone as she walked toward him.

Mr. Collins clearly did not hear him, but he did notice the man speak, for he hurried up to him and, in a tone as deferential as any he had ever used with Lady Catherine, said, "I implore you, Mr. Darcy, do not speak with my cousin. She is now a fallen woman, and any association of her with your exalted self can only damage your pristine reputation and that of your fair betrothed. I shall return this . . . *woman* to her father as soon as may be so she does not stain the fair estate of Rosings with her presence."

The unamused visage of Mr. Darcy turned, and he glared at Mr. Collins, causing the man to step back with alarm. "If I just heard correctly, the archbishop declared that Miss Bennet could in no way be held accountable for what happened and that there was no stain on her honor. I suggest you remember exactly who was to blame for her tribulations."

Once again, Elizabeth was treated to the sight of Mr. Collins's jaw working with no sound issuing forth.

"Until next time, Miss Bennet," said Mr. Darcy as he smiled and bowed over her hand.

Then he turned and left swiftly, leaving Elizabeth to follow behind more sedately. Elizabeth did not know what the future would hold, but she was certain she would enjoy finding out. Mr. Darcy, it appeared, would be an ardent suitor.

The journey back to the parsonage was completed in silence, though the very air about them was charged with tension. Mr. Collins, by the set of his jaw and the redness of his countenance, was quite clearly furious with what had happened. That he blamed her, both for the dissolution of their marriage and for the implied investigation into his activities as parson, was undeniable. Just what he planned to do about it was still a matter of conjecture. Elizabeth expected that his promise to return her immediately to Longbourn was genuine. He would not wish to keep the reason for his disgrace in his company any longer than was absolutely necessary.

Her conjecture was proven when they arrived at the parsonage. The moment Elizabeth alighted from the gig, Mr. Collins jumped down and crossed quickly to her side before she had time to alight. He did not deign to assist her, but when she had stepped down onto the gravel, he grasped her arm in a harsh manner and began to march her toward the house, growling, "You shall return to your room and pack your personal effects as soon as may be."

Elizabeth was not about to accept this treatment from the man, and she stopped and wrenched his hand from her arm, causing him to stumble. The parson straightened and glared at her, but Elizabeth forestalled him, saying, "I will return to my room and pack, Mr. Collins. But you will not drag me like a recalcitrant child."

"You *are* a recalcitrant child!" thundered Mr. Collins, the spittle flying from his mouth.

Elizabeth was not impressed. "No, just a woman determined not to be used by the likes of you."

"You will return to your room. You will pack your belongings. You will be ready to go at first light. If you do not do these things with alacrity, I shall strike you where you stand."

"I am not surprised you would do such a thing, Mr. Collins," said Elizabeth as she walked past him and entered the house. "You are certainly no gentleman."

Perhaps Elizabeth was not wise in her anger, and she half-expected him to follow her and take her arm yet again, but he did not. But as she hurried up the stairs to her room, she heard his heavy footsteps behind her. "I will arrange for our departure in the morning. In the meantime, you must pack. You are not to leave your room. I will have cook bring some dinner to your chambers."

Elizabeth heard nothing more, as she entered her room and pulled out her trunk. Since her family had not seen fit to send more than a few of her dresses, she did not have many to pack, which meant that bringing her belongings in order did not take much time. She had just finished the major part of the task and was about to exit the room when her door opened and the maid entered.

"Do you require assistance, madam?" asked the woman, though she did not look up at Elizabeth.

"I believe I have it well in hand, Jessica," said Elizabeth with a smile. "Besides, I cannot imagine that Mr. Collins would be happy to find you in here."

Jessica sniffed with disdain. "I care not what the master likes, madam. You have been kind to all the staff, and we shall miss you. The master . . . well, he is not thought of with any esteem."

"Thank you, Jessica. While I cannot say that I will miss the parsonage or Mr. Collins, I am grateful that you have taken such care of me and that you all have refrained from gossip concerning the state of affairs between Mr. Collins and me."

"We would never do anything to hurt you. Our loyalty is given to you, not Mr. Collins."

"And I thank you for it." Elizabeth walked forward and grasped the surprised maid in a light embrace, thankful for her foresight to cultivate good feelings among the staff. They were good people, and she would miss them. They were certainly nothing like their odious master. "Jessica, I may soon have another situation in which I will be at liberty to offer you employment. Would you like to work for me when I do?"

"Oh, yes, madam," said Jessica, appearing happy to be singled out in such a fashion. "I should like that very much indeed."

"Then I will make the arrangements as soon as may be. It will not be for at least some months, you understand."

The maid assured her that she did understand, and with a tearful goodbye, Elizabeth shooed her from the room, not wishing her to incur Mr. Collins's wrath. When the woman had gone, Elizabeth glanced about, noting the lack of anything left denoting that this had been her room for the past month. As it was still only a little after noon, Elizabeth determined that she would be absent from the parsonage for as long as she could possibly contrive. Thus, she gathered up her pelisse and determined to walk in the park of Rosings for as long as she could stand the cold weather. Though she had come to enjoy walking very much, she was grateful that her forced walks in the December cold would soon come to an end.

When Elizabeth stepped from her room, however, Mr. Collins was there, blocking her path to the stairs. He appeared to be ready for a confrontation.

"What do you think you are doing, madam?" demanded he.

"I have finished packing my belongings, Mr. Collins. As there is still much daylight left, I thought I would leave for a constitutional in the park."

"You shall not. I will not allow it. You will stay in your room until it is time for us to depart. I have already informed you of this."

Though Elizabeth would have gainsaid the man, she decided that it was better in this instance to simply avoid confrontation. She would be departing on the morrow, and after that, she would never have to lay eyes on him again. Discretion was called for.

"Very well," said she. She turned and entered her room without giving him the courtesy of any kind of acknowledgement.

It was a long afternoon. The time passed slowly, and though Mr. Collins did not try to enter, she could hear his heavy tread throughout the house that day. She amused herself with one of the books she had brought—and had subsequently hidden from Mr. Collins, knowing he did not approve of her reading material—but by the late afternoon, she was beginning to feel restless. Her window overlooked the road, and she had kept a vigil that entire day, looking for Mr. Darcy, who had promised to come.

The supper hour came and went without sign of him, and Elizabeth was beginning to become concerned. She had never known Mr. Darcy to break his word, but still he did not arrive. In due course, Elizabeth ate her dinner in the silence of her room and then retired for the night, all without sign of Mr. Darcy.

The next morning, she rose before it was light and dressed in her best traveling dress, bundling up against the cold for her journey away from Kent. And through all of her final preparations, she wondered what had become of Mr. Darcy. When they departed, there was still no sign of him. But she was certain she would see him again. He had promised.

Chapter XXXVII

A pleased and relieved Darcy returned to Rosings after the hearing, content in the knowledge that his love was now free to follow her own heart. The words of the archbishop were appreciated, but he was happy that this incident had happened in the far corners of the kingdom where it would be unlikely to come to the attention of society. He would have braved whatever censure was required for the pleasure of her hand, but she did not deserve to be made the object of derision of those with nothing to do but gossip.

Upon arriving back at the stables, Darcy swung down from his horse and handed the reins down to the groom. He would visit the parsonage as soon as he could manage and discuss with Miss Bennet how exactly to remove her from the parsonage and where she should go, for he was certain that Collins would not consider her comfort.

As he entered his aunt's house, however, he could hear the strident tones of Lady Catherine demanding his presence. Grimacing, Darcy thought of ignoring her, but he knew that he would have to face her eventually. He did not doubt that he would once again need to disabuse her of the notion that he would marry Anne, and a part of him was annoyed. It seemed as if he had spent his entire adult life fending the woman off. But it was not a discussion he would have again. Today would put an end to all her schemes.

When he entered the room, his aunt watched him, her eyes narrowing. "Where have you been, Darcy?"

Darcy returned her gaze with a cool one of his own. "I attended the hearing in Westerham, aunt."

If anything, her gaze became flintier. "And why would you bother? What can the doings of my parson be to you?"

"Did you not wish to know what was decided?" asked Darcy with a pointed look. "I would have thought you would be demanding to know."

"Of course I do. I am quite attentive to all the doings in my parish, I assure you." Lady Catherine paused for a moment, and then she grudgingly nodded. "I suppose since you were there, you may inform me what has happened."

"The marriage was annulled, Lady Catherine. That is not an unexpected outcome, as I am sure you will agree." Darcy did not miss the wide smiles on the faces of his cousins at that announcement, but he focused his attention on his aunt.

But Lady Catherine did not react with anger as he would have thought. Rather, she nodded as if the matter was of supreme indifference to her. "Very well. I shall deal with Mr. Collins after that . . . woman has been returned to her family.

"But I am surprised at you, Darcy. You have taken an unseemly interest in her fate. She is nothing more than the insignificant daughter of an equally insignificant country gentleman. What can you mean by showing such an interest in her?"

"Perhaps I am merely concerned for the relation of a friend. Her elder sister is engaged to be married to my friend Bingley, and what happens to Miss Elizabeth is therefore of interest to him."

"Do not think me ignorant of your interest in her, Darcy," snapped Lady Catherine. "You would not journey all the way to Kent for such a trifling matter. And I have not missed the way you look at her when you are in company together. I am not blind."

Darcy inclined his head, but he was not disposed to confirm or deny her allegations. When he did not answer, Lady Catherine looked at him closely, a harsh glare on her face, before she turned to Anne.

"Anne, sit up straight!" She turned back to Darcy, not even noting the fact that Anne had ignored her and had not moved in the slightest. "It is now time, Darcy. I have allowed this unseemly delay to go on for long enough. You will formalize your engagement with Anne before you leave this room. I will not be gainsaid."

"As I have stated many times in the past, I will not marry Anne," said Darcy, keeping his tone cool and calm. "Neither Anne nor I wish it."

"It is your duty. There is nothing else to be said, no other decision to make. You have been destined for one another from your cradles, and it was your mother's favorite wish as well as my own. There will be no argument."

"Madam, you still do not seem to understand me, so allow me to make myself clear." Darcy stared into the woman's eyes, allowing his immovable will to show to her that he was not about to be bullied. "There has never been an engagement between Anne and myself. No formal betrothal has ever been drawn up, and there is no legally binding document which makes it necessary for us to marry. Anne and I have discussed the subject many times over the years, and it has long been our decision that we do not suit and do not wish to wed. Thus, all your schemes are for naught. We will not oblige you."

"*Schemes!*" shrieked Lady Catherine, her eyes fairly bulging out of her head. "You insolent boy! I will have you know that this was the fondest wish of your dearly departed mother!"

"If it was so, then why did she never mention it to me?"

"You were but a child when she passed."

"Regardless, it signifies little," said Darcy, moving to a nearby chair and seating himself, "for I have no intention of ever yielding in this matter, and even if you were to persuade me, Anne would not agree."

"Anne will do as she is told!"

"Again, it signifies little."

Lady Catherine shot to her feet, her glare boring into him with all the fury of an affronted woman. "Listen to me well, both of you. This is not a matter which is open for discussion. I *will* see you married if I have to place the article in the newspaper and drag you both to the altar by the ears."

"Oh, do be silent, mother."

So surprised was Darcy that he swallowed the retort which had been on the tip of his tongue in favor of gazing at his cousin with unconcealed astonishment. Never before had he heard Anne stand up to her mother. Anne was stubborn and obstinate at times, but these traits had always manifested themselves in a more silent form of defiance.

"You will not use such language with me, Anne," snapped Lady Catherine. "As I was saying—"

"None of us give three straws about what you are saying," rejoined Anne. "Darcy has told you time and again that he will not marry me.

We will not bow to your whims, so you had best forget that such a notion ever existed."

"You will not gainsay me!" shouted Lady Catherine. She stalked up to Anne, and grasping her arm in a painful manner, she wrenched the young woman up so that she was facing her. "You are *my child*, and you will do as you are told."

"Let go of me, mother."

The next events happened so quickly that Darcy felt as if he were entrapped by molasses. The sound of a slap reverberated throughout the room, and the forceful blow snapped Anne's head to the side. All of this happened before Darcy could move a muscle.

A fury overcame Darcy. He and the equally enraged Fitzwilliam stepped forward to forcibly remove Lady Catherine's hand from her daughter.

"Have you lost your mind?" demanded Darcy. His hands closed around Lady Catherine's arms, and he tore her away from her daughter.

Anne's eyes returned to her mother. She stared in shock for a moment before her eyes rolled back in her head, and she sagged to the floor. Fitzwilliam, who had moved to her side, caught her as she fell, easing her slight form into his arms. For a handful of breaths, complete silence reigned in the sitting room.

"Fitzwilliam, take Anne to her rooms while I deal with Lady Catherine," said Darcy at last, taking control of the situation.

For an instant, it seemed as if Colonel Fitzwilliam might not obey. As he looked down at the still form of his female cousin, the tension seemed to mount within him. The military man within Fitzwilliam was likely demanding that he take action.

"Fitzwilliam, let Anne be your first priority. I will handle matters here."

A clipped nod was his answer, and Fitzwilliam left the room with Anne in his arms, but not before directing a hateful glare at their aunt.

As Darcy watched them go, a notion dawned on him which he had never before considered, though it was so obvious that he felt a fool for not having noticed it before. He suddenly felt certain that Fitzwilliam would not protest the solution he was considering, though Darcy was unsure of Anne's reaction.

"Unhand me, Darcy!" said his aunt, causing him to become aware of the fact that he was still grasping her wrists. "You will unhand me this instant! This is your fault. If you had simply done your duty, then none of this unpleasantness would ever have happened. Now you have filled Anne's head with dangerous notions which she has no business contemplating."

A thunderous glare returned to Darcy's face, and he turned his attention on his aunt. Lady Catherine must have seen something in his gaze, as she blanched and looked away, her struggling all but ceasing.

"This is certainly not *my* fault," snarled Darcy. He moved to the nearby sofa, still grasping his aunt's hands, and forced her to sit there. Then he stood to his greatest height and looked down on her with an unrelenting glare.

"How dare you, madam!" said he in a low and infuriated voice. "To be striking your daughter when she is in such delicate condition is an abominable act of the sort that I should never have expected from you. What were you thinking?"

Darcy was about to berate her more when he noted that her cheeks had bloomed and that she had looked away from him. Her blush was not from embarrassment, he thought; rather, it appeared to be more than that. As if she was the child caught with her hand in the proverbial cookie jar.

And in that instant, Darcy knew. "How long has this gone on, Lady Catherine?" rasped he, desperately attempting to maintain control over his emotions. "How long?"

"I know not of what you speak!" cried Lady Catherine.

Darcy bent over and glowered at her, causing her to shrink back into the sofa.

"How long?"

"Anne is my child! It is my right to enforce her to behave properly and to take her to task whenever necessary. As one without children, you can in no way understand this."

"Have I not a sister many years my junior?" growled Darcy, though he scarcely felt capable of speaking due to his astonishment. He was wondering at the fact that he was truly seeing his aunt for the first time in his life. How could he have been so blind? "But though I have often been more father than brother to Georgiana, I have never slapped her in such a fashion. How long have you been abusing your daughter?"

By now, Lady Catherine was too frightened of his harsh demeanor to do much more than protest violently, though not coherently. It was obvious that he would not gain any information from her.

In a few swift strides, Darcy had crossed to the door of the sitting room. Wrenching it open, he bellowed for the footman, and when the man appeared, Darcy addressed him: "Find Lady Catherine's maid, and bring her here."

The man nodded and departed, and Darcy turned back to his aunt, noting the pallor of her skin and the apprehension with which she regarded him.

"What do you mean to do?"

"I will confine you to your rooms, madam, until we have departed. You will not be given another opportunity to mistreat your daughter."

Lady Catherine made no response, but the tightening of her eyebrows bespoke the fact that her typical imperiousness was making a return. Darcy paid her no heed. Once he had completed his business here and seen Anne to London, all congress between himself and his aunt would come to an end. He would have nothing further to do with the woman.

When the maid returned in the company of the footman, he gave instructions to both of them, noting that he would allow no disobedience to his orders. When he had finished speaking, he turned to his aunt, motioning for her to rise and go to her rooms, promising with his look that he would force her there if necessary. For a moment, he thought she might attempt to defy him. But she quickly seemed to realize that he was in earnest, and with a huff, she rose to her feet and stalked from the room, her head held high like she was departing of her own volition.

Passing a hand over his face and rubbing his temples, Darcy looked out the window, where the parsonage could just be made out in the distance. How he longed to go to Elizabeth! But Elizabeth had proven how she was capable of handling the parson. He would go as soon as he could tear himself away, but for now, he was needed here.

The first thing to be done was to write an express to his uncle, the earl. Henry Fitzwilliam, the Earl of Matlock, was a kindly man and not in any way similar to his sister. Between them, Darcy and the earl had watched over Rosings these past years, managing the estate and preventing its ruin from Lady Catherine's excesses. It had been at his uncle's request that Darcy had visited Rosings every year in the spring, in part to take a little responsibility from his uncle's shoulders and in part because being in company with Lady Catherine once a year was more than enough! His uncle still visited in the autumn of every year and would understand the situation of the estate. More importantly, he would know the state of affairs regarding Anne's inheritance. It was that, more than anything, which Darcy was interested in, given the thought which had occurred to him in the sitting room.

After writing to the earl and leaving some instructions with the staff, Darcy climbed the stairs to the family apartments and went to Anne's room, where he found Fitzwilliam pacing in the sitting room, his face a thunderous cloud of grief and anger.

"What have you done with the old goat, Darcy?" demanded Fitzwilliam the moment he saw Darcy. "Whatever it is, it cannot be enough. I have half a mind to return biblical justice upon the vile woman."

"Calm yourself, Fitzwilliam. I have taken care of the matter for now, but I fear that the situation is much worse than we had thought."

A sharp glance met Darcy's words, but Darcy interrupted Fitzwilliam before he could get started. Knowing the colonel's temper, Darcy wished him to calm a little before he revealed his suspicions.

"Has the doctor been called?"

Fitzwilliam snorted. "Yes, I had him summoned, but the man I sent returned, saying that the doctor was not in any condition to see to Anne. The man is soused, Darcy, and it is not even the middle of the day! Is this the kind of man my aunt has employed to care for Anne's health?"

Aggravated, though hardly surprised due to his aunt's desire to surround herself with toadies like Mr. Collins, Darcy shook his head. "Is there a local apothecary?"

"There is, though I am not certain as to his level of competence. I sent the man out to summon him."

Nodding, Darcy moved to the door to Anne's room and cautiously eased it open. There, lying on the bed, he saw his cousin, her form pale and ghostly with the exception of the vivid pink of a hand-mark staining her cheek. His outrage at his aunt's behavior once again rising, Darcy glared at the sight. Lady Catherine would not have the opportunity to do such a thing again. He swore that to himself.

A commotion sounded behind him, and Darcy closed the door to Anne's room and turned. He immediately noted the arrival of a man of middle years, tall and slender, with gray at his temples and streaking his hair.

"Good day, sir," said the man, greeting Fitzwilliam. "My name is Mayweather. I am the local apothecary."

The two cousins greeted the man and swiftly made him aware of the situation, including the argument, Lady Catherine's assault on her daughter, and the state of the physician who they had attempted to summon. Mr. Mayweather grimaced at that last bit of information.

"It is well that Mr. Douglas was not available. I have little respect for the man, and most of those in the village will not consent to be seen by him."

Darcy frowned. "Then what does he do here?"

"He is your aunt's personal physician," said Mayweather with a significant look. "He tends to your cousin, and your aunt keeps him on."

The cousins exchanged looks, but in the interest of seeing to Anne as quickly as possible, the apothecary was shown into her bedchamber with alacrity.

"What has happened here, Darcy?" asked Fitzwilliam when the man had gone. "I must own to being completely at sea."

"I do not know, cousin, but we shall get to the bottom of this."

It was a tense wait, for though they might not have been concerned in normal circumstances, Anne was of such delicate constitution that neither could state with a surety exactly what their aunt's assault had wrought. The minutes seemed to drag on like hours, but it was actually only a very short time before the man emerged yet again.

"Your cousin will be well," stated he, forestalling any questions. "I have seen to her, and though I do not doubt that her cheek will give her pain, there should be nothing standing in the way of her making a full recovery. I have left a small amount of laudanum to be used should she be in pain, but I do not doubt she will be well. Or at least as well as she can be in this environment."

The apothecary paused, clearly troubled about something.

Darcy motioned for him to continue. "You have something else to say?"

"I found . . . certain unexplained bruises and the like on her person, though they were old, and most were only slight discolorations which were almost completely healed."

"Where?" demanded Darcy, certain that he had the proof he was looking for.

"Her ribs, legs, arms. Virtually everywhere. The locations and number of them were not consistent of bumping into furniture or anything of the like. I hesitate to suggest such a thing, but it seems as if she has been mistreated."

"I will kill her!" snarled Fitzwilliam. Darcy was forced to grasp his cousin by his shoulders to keep him from leaving the room.

"While I would like nothing better than to allow you to have a go at Lady Catherine, you need to keep a clear head, Fitzwilliam. There is nothing to be gained from further confronting the woman. We had best focus on removing Anne from this situation."

"Please do, sirs," said Mr. Mayweather. "I believe I now understand why I was never allowed to examine Miss de Bourgh, though I rather suspect that part of it is because your aunt wished to have someone who would agree with her opinions without delay. I am sorry to speak of your relation in such a manner."

"Believe me, Mr. Mayweather, your thoughts are much more innocuous than mine," said Fitzwilliam.

"Very well," said the apothecary. It was clear that though he was happy to have been of service, he did not wish to stay and witness the aftermath. "I shall take my leave. Please have me called if something else should develop. And please, for your cousin's sake, remove her from this place. A proper physician could likely do wonders for her."

Thanking him, Darcy saw him to the door, promising that they would indeed change Anne's circumstances. In another moment, they were alone, and Fitzwilliam looked at Darcy with anger.

"You knew."

"Not until I spoke with our aunt after her actions," said Darcy. "She would not confirm anything, and as such it was more of a strong suspicion than anything else, though I will own that I had little doubt."

Fitzwilliam raked his hands though his hair and slumped down on the sofa. "We've failed her, Darcy. How could we have come here every year without noticing this?"

"I rather suspect that our aunt has been a little more circumspect than this," said Darcy. "Regardless, let us wait until Anne awakes for more information concerning the matter, shall we?"

As it was, they had several hours to wait before Anne was to wake. During that time, the two men tried to pass the time with conversation and discussions about the future, but inevitably their thoughts would return to the events of the day, and they would lapse into silence. Fitzwilliam asked him about Elizabeth, and tried to convince him to go to the parsonage, but Darcy refused, stating that he was needed here. He loved Elizabeth Bennet, but he was also aware of her abilities. He was not concerned for her, though he did take Fitzwilliam's suggestion and wrote a short note to be delivered to the parsonage. He wrote little more than that he had been delayed at Rosings, but he did not doubt that she would understand. He would visit her as early as possible the following morning, and see to her disposition and removal from the area.

At length, however, Anne did wake, and he and Fitzwilliam were summoned into her room by the maid. Anne was propped up against the head of the bed by a copious number of cushions, and though she moved her head and grimaced a little at the pain she was obviously experiencing, she appeared alert and not a little angry.

Dismissing the maid—not wishing for any part of their conversation to be overheard—Darcy turned to where Fitzwilliam had already taken a seat beside her bed, eagerly leaning toward his cousin. "Are you well, Anne?"

As Anne replied to the colonel that she was as well as could be expected, Darcy once again watched the two of them, alert for anything in their interactions which would betray a closer tie than mere cousins. And though Fitzwilliam was eager, Anne appeared shy and reserved, which was certainly not unusual for her. Still, Darcy felt that there was enough to be seen that his hastily conceived plan might have more than a little possibility of success.

"Anne, I have two questions for you," said Darcy as he approached the bed. "First, how long your mother has mistreated you? Second, why did you never tell any of us?"

Anne's slightly shameful look told Darcy all he needed to know. Fitzwilliam's reaction was, by contrast, an instant reddening of his countenance and a set to his jaw which told Darcy that he was contemplating murder.

"Peace, Fitzwilliam," said Darcy as he crossed the room and sat on the edge of Anne's bed. "I have already sent an express to your father. Unless there is something occurring in London which prevents it, I expect he will be here tomorrow. At that time, *he* can confront Lady Catherine as the head of the family. For now, I wish to understand more of what has happened here."

"Well, Anne?" asked Fitzwilliam, focusing his attention upon her. "We are waiting."

"It is not as bad as all that," said Anne, though in a hesitant voice. "My mother has always insisted upon her will being followed to the letter, and she has been willing to enforce her commands. When I was a child, it was a rap on the mouth with her knuckles. As I became older, such punishment became more sporadic, though occasionally crueler. She has never slapped me as she did today, which is why I was so astonished."

As she said this, Anne's hand rose to her face, and she touched her bruised cheek, only to pull her hand away with a wince.

"As long as I obey and speak in what my mother considers to be a pleasing manner, I have little to fear from her."

"Then what of the signs of bruising that the apothecary found on you?"

Anne appeared surprised at that. "My mother consented to allow

Mr. Mayweather to see me?"

"She had little choice," growled Darcy. "I confined her to her rooms after Fitzwilliam took you away. Fitzwilliam sent for the doctor, but when he was found to be in his cups, we had to look elsewhere for medical assistance."

Nodding, Anne said, "Mr. Douglas's services are generally not required when you are in residence, as my mother does not wish you to see me in anything other than the best light. But when you are not here, he knows only to imbibe at night, as he is not likely to be called in to attend me." Anne barked a laugh that was devoid of amusement. "Mother does so like to have things ordered according to her schedule. Heaven forbid that I should actually fall ill at night when she is sleeping."

"The signs of mistreatment?" prompted Darcy.

"After your last visit here and your refusal to bow to her whims, my mother was incensed," said Anne after some hesitation. Darcy stared at her with chagrin, knowing she meant to protect him from his own self-recrimination. "I generally agree with her in order to keep her claws retracted, but that did not always work. She would berate me, blame me for not being pretty enough to entice you, claim that I made no effort to secure you. She would pinch me, slap my hands, grasp my arm and drag me about, showing me what I must do to catch you."

"Oh, Anne, I *am* sorry," said Darcy.

Anne only waved him off. "I never told anyone, partly because I was ashamed."

"Never be ashamed of another's mistreatment of you," said Fitzwilliam, "especially when it is one who should have your best interests at heart."

Nodding her head, Anne looked on them both gratefully, though Darcy thought they had done little to deserve it. "As the months passed, her treatment gradually slowed, and we had settled down into our typical indifference by November. But then that little parson arrived with his wife in tow, and you followed soon after." Anne paused for a moment, considering her words, before she looked up at Darcy. "My mother was instantly suspicious, Darcy, though I do not think she ever knew the extent of your regard for Miss Bennet.

"I then made the mistake of telling her that I did not wish to marry you," said Anne in a quiet voice. "The faded bruises that the apothecary saw were a result of that bit of defiance."

"Annie, you know that we would have protected you, had we known," said Fitzwilliam.

"I know," replied Anne with a sigh.

"Then why the blazes did you not say something?"

"I believe that we should concentrate on what is to be done now," said Darcy. "There will be time enough for self-recrimination after Anne is removed from this house."

"I was planning to ask you to take me with you when you left," said Anne, looking down at her hands. "I wish to see a physician in London, that I might learn whether there is anything that can be done for me."

"I believe that can be arranged," said Darcy with a smile. He then paused and looked at his cousins, trying to decide how much to say. Given the situation, it seemed as if there was not much point in staying silent. "I have another question. How long have you both had feelings for each other?"

Their reactions were a revelation, for though Fitzwilliam looked at Darcy as if he was daft, Anne actually blushed and looked away.

"Of what are you speaking, Darcy?" demanded Fitzwilliam.

"Anne?" asked Darcy, ignoring his other cousin for the moment.

Anne glanced at Fitzwilliam for a moment, her manner shy and unsure. "I have always known that you and I you do not suit each other, Darcy. But Fitzwilliam is garrulous and happy, his manner far different from our reserved natures."

"Of that, I am aware, Anne," said Darcy with some amusement.

"Come now," exclaimed Fitzwilliam, "I shall thank you not to speak of me as if I was not here."

"Then let us speak *with* you, by all means," said Darcy, turning to Fitzwilliam. "What are your feelings for Anne?"

Fitzwilliam gaped at him. "Who are you, and where is my cousin? Can it truly be that Fitzwilliam Darcy is playing matchmaker?"

Darcy glared pointedly at his cousin. "Is Anne not eligible?"

"Highly eligible," growled Fitzwilliam. "But I should not like put her in the same position as that which we are trying to remove her from."

"And if she *is* willing?"

"Now I shall thank you both not to speak of *me* as if *I* was not here," said Anne, though the starkness of her words was belied by the hint of a smile appearing at her lips.

"The fact of the matter is—"

"Of the facts, as you say," said Darcy, interrupting his cousin, "only a few are important. First, Anne requires protection from her mother. You may amply provide that. Second, you require a woman of fortune, and unless you are hiding her somewhere," Fitzwilliam glared at him, but Darcy ignored the look, "you have not managed to find one in your thirty years of life. Finally, unless I am very much mistaken, you would not be opposed to it on the grounds that it is *Anne*, much as she does not oppose the thought of being married to *you*."

"And what of Lady Catherine?"

"What of her? We are already set on defying her. Is this matter any different?"

"Will Anne lose her inheritance?"

"While I cannot state such with any surety, I do not believe that Anne is anything other than her father's heir." When both Anne and Fitzwilliam were silent, Darcy pressed forward. "It would behoove you both to consider it. Not only would it resolve several problems, but if what I am seeing before me is any indication, I do not doubt that you would do well together. I will leave you to speak of it, if you require a little time."

"Perhaps a little time would be desirable," said Fitzwilliam. "But regardless, Anne goes to London tomorrow."

"I would not have it any other way," said Darcy.

"Thank you, Darcy," said Anne in a quiet tone.

"You are welcome, cousin," replied Darcy. "But in the future, I expect to be consulted should you require assistance."

Anne nodded, seeming happy for the first time in Darcy's memory. "I should like to see your Elizabeth again. She is confident and determined, two traits that I lack. I believe I have much to learn from her."

"I am certain she would be happy to deepen your acquaintance. I know I would be happy to be in a position to make her a part of your life in perpetuity."

"In that case, you had best go and secure her," said Fitzwilliam.

With a slight nod, Darcy excused himself in order to allow his cousins to have their long overdue talk. His thoughts immediately went to Elizabeth. A quick check of his pocket watch revealed that it was already approaching the time to retire, and though Darcy wanted nothing more than to ensure for himself that she was well, he knew that it would be difficult to show up at such an hour. Instead, he resolved on going to the parsonage early the next morning.

Thus, he arose early the next morning and after a quick consultation with Fitzwilliam, he made his way to the stables and then rode to the parsonage. According to Fitzwilliam, the discussion between him and Anne had been a success, though they both decided that they would take proceed slowly in order to become accustomed to their new situation. Darcy wished them well.

When Darcy arrived at the parsonage, he dismounted, tied his horse to a nearby fence, and approached the door, conscious of the fact that it was still much too early for a courtesy call. But he had stayed away long enough. He did not doubt that Collins would wish to remove Miss Bennet from Hunsford as soon as possible, and if Darcy was to make the arrangements himself, he would need to ensure that his voice was heard immediately. There was no telling what an idiot such as William Collins would do should he be left to his own devices.

Darcy's knock on the door went unanswered for several moments, and he was beginning to become worried when the door finally opened and the timid face of one of the maids appeared in the open space.

"Mr. Darcy here to see Mr. Collins and Miss Bennet," said he.

The maid looked about nervously before she replied, "They are not here, Mr. Darcy."

Surprised, Darcy stared back at her. "Not here?"

"They left very early this morning for Miss Bennet's home in Hertfordshire. Mr. Collins declared that he would not have her in his home for one minute longer than necessary."

"When did they depart?"

"More than an hour ago, sir."

"Thank you," said Darcy. He turned and swiftly made his way back to Rosings. A quick change of clothes and a word with Fitzwilliam—who said that he gladly would take care of Anne until the earl arrived—and then Darcy was on his way to Hertfordshire.

Chapter XXVIII

*I*f Elizabeth had thought the previous journey to Kent was uncomfortable, it was nothing compared to the insufferable return to Hertfordshire. Mr. Collins sat in the seat next to her in all his injured silence, intent upon ignoring her. Yet at the same time, his silence seemed to accuse her, for he continually flayed her with his injured glances and displayed his ill-used countenance for her to see.

It was made worse by the fact that Mr. Collins insisted upon taking her the entire way to Longbourn in his two-wheeled and uncovered gig, which was not truly meant for such a journey. Had the season been warmer and the day fine, she might have been able to ignore the man completely and enjoy the scenery as it sped by, but the day had dawned gray, with low clouds threatening snow, and the air held a distinct chill, like winter was finally upon them. Mr. Collins, of course, did not seem to feel the chill of the air; Elizabeth suspected that he was warmed by the force of his self-righteous anger.

Elizabeth attempted to prevail upon him to stop in London and leave her at the Gardiners' residence, but she was no more successful in this appeal than in anything else she requested that morning.

"It would shorten your journey by half, sir," said Elizabeth, attempting to induce him to see reason.

"Surely you can see that such a suggestion is not proper," replied he in a pompous tone. "Of course, I should not be surprised that one such as you would make such a suggestion. But it would be most improper for me to entertain such a thought, even for a moment."

"It is not improper, and the Gardiners encouraged me to make use of the house should it be required. Surely you can see that I will not be welcome at my father's house."

"I care not, madam. I must deliver you to your father's home to be finished with you, and that is what I shall do."

He allowed only one short stop at a small and nondescript inn which appeared on the side of the road soon after they left London behind. Other than that brief interlude, he drove them forward, almost as if the very hounds of hell were pursuing them, driving them back to Mr. Bennet's estate. Considering that it was Lady Catherine who was behind them in Kent, Elizabeth supposed that her fanciful imaginings might not be far from the truth.

Thus, though it was well before noon when he guided the gig up to the front door of Longbourn, Elizabeth was already feeling exhausted and heartsick at the reception she was likely to receive. In the back of her mind, she still worried about Mr. Darcy, wondering what had happened to prevent his appearance at Hunsford.

When she and Mr. Collins pulled up in front of Longbourn, Elizabeth was close to panic. Her father had essentially dragged her to the altar and forced her to marry, her mother never treated her with anything but contempt and ridicule, and her sisters, save for dear Jane, had never given her any reason to suspect they would be anything but hateful. Elizabeth was not looking forward to this reunion in the slightest.

Once the gig had come to a halt, Mr. Collins tossed the reins aside and sprang down with a spryness that was surprising for such a heavyset man. And before Elizabeth could step down from the conveyance herself, Mr. Collins was there. None too gently, he dragged her from the gig and onto the ground and hurried her toward the door.

"Unhand me, Mr. Collins!" gasped Elizabeth, shocked by the violence with which the man was treating her.

"I mean to return you to your father as soon as may be," snarled Mr. Collins. "Remember you have brought this on yourself."

But Elizabeth was not about to allow this man to treat her in this fashion. Twisting her arm, she wrenched it out of his grasp, glaring at him with contempt. "It appears you did not listen to the archbishop, Mr. Collins."

"The archbishop does not understand what manner of woman you are," ground out Mr. Collins. He reached out to grasp her arm again propel her toward the door again.

The door opened before they could reach it, and the countenance of Mrs. Hill appeared. She seemed shocked as she beheld Elizabeth in the company of Mr. Collins.

"Miss Elizabeth—" began she, only to be interrupted by the parson.

"Summon your master, immediately."

Mrs. Hill started and looked to Elizabeth for direction, but at Elizabeth's motion, she backed into the house. Mr. Collins followed closely behind, still clutching Elizabeth's arm. Mrs. Hill turned to approach the door to Mr. Bennet's study, but the door to the parlor abruptly opened, and Mrs. Bennet stepped out into the entrance hall, only to stop short at the sight which met her eyes. Behind her, all of Elizabeth's sisters followed, each showing confusion at the sight of their sister. While Jane appeared happy at seeing her and Lydia openly disdainful, it was the sight of her middle sisters which confused Elizabeth, as Catherine appeared hopeful and Mary seemed relieved.

"Elizabeth?" cried Mrs. Bennet with a frown. "What is the meaning of this?"

Sensing that something significant was about to happen, Mrs. Hill turned and rapped sharply on the door to Mr. Bennet's study, and the door opened immediately, suggesting that Mr. Bennet was on the verge of investigating the sudden commotion in his house. He stepped forward when he saw Elizabeth and Mr. Collins, and he could not have missed the way Mr. Collins was scowling and holding her arm tightly.

"Mr. Collins," said Mr. Bennet, though his attention was settled firmly on Elizabeth, "I thought we had agreed that you and Elizabeth would not return to Longbourn as long as I was alive."

"I am done with your demon daughter!" screamed Mr. Collins. He shoved Elizabeth forward so that she stumbled and fell at her father's feet. "You can have her back, Mr. Bennet, for she is nothing to me now. I hope you have a pleasant life with her."

Mr. Bennet glared down at Elizabeth, but she refused to be cowed. Wincing at the pain of a knee which she had bumped when she fell, Elizabeth gained her feet and dusted off her dress.

"I believe that the marriage has been solemnized, Mr. Collins," said Mr. Bennet. "Perhaps whatever she has done may be ameliorated if you would take her more firmly in hand."

"Your daughter has offended, embarrassed, and humiliated me!" shouted Mr. Collins. "She has claimed ill-use and has sued for annulment, Mr. Bennet."

Shocked, Mr. Bennet stared at Mr. Collins briefly before turning and glancing at Elizabeth. "Annulments are but rarely granted, and one such as my daughter cannot have the resources to affect such an outcome."

"Then perhaps you should ask your daughter how she managed to bring such an eventuality about, for the annulment was granted yesterday morning."

The surprise inherent in her parents' faces was perhaps not unexpected—regardless of how Mr. Bennet had brought the marriage about, he must have thought there was little chance of Elizabeth even managing to induce someone to listen to her grievance, never mind actually obtaining the annulment. But the surprise lasted only a moment before Elizabeth once again witnessed the rage of her father, so difficult to arouse, once again directed at her.

"You have ruined us again!" shrieked her mother, breaking the pregnant silence.

As if that was the impetus needed for them all to break free from their amazement, everyone began talking, and though Elizabeth could not make out much of what was said, the overlying emotion was anger, and her father's appeared to be the most prevalent.

"How could you, a girl with no family and no connections, possibly bring about an annulment?" demanded Mr. Bennet over the din.

"I merely told the truth, father," said Elizabeth, her chin rising in defiance. "That sham you attempted to force on me could not stand up to any scrutiny."

"It was not meant to be scrutinized!" roared her father. "It was meant to finally allow you to repay the debt you owe this family!"

"Oh, Mr. Bennet, whatever shall we do?" wailed Mrs. Bennet. "She has stained the family name yet again, and should you die, Mr. Collins will throw us all out as soon as may be."

"On that, you can be assured," spoke up one William Collins. "I have been most grievously used in this whole affair. The character of your daughter was misrepresented, the situation of the family obfuscated, and the unwillingness of Miss Elizabeth to marry me hidden. Once I have quit this place, you shall hear no more from me until my solicitor brings word of your immediate removal once Longbourn is mine."

Mrs. Bennet began to wail anew, and Mr. Bennet stalked toward Elizabeth, his hands clenching and unclenching as he stalked her as the falcon stalks the hare. But Elizabeth would not be cowed—she would never allow this man to intimidate her again!

"What have you done, you stupid girl?"

"Perhaps you should ask yourself what *you* have done, father," said Elizabeth. "All my life, you have blamed me for something which could not be my fault. Should I feel any allegiance to a man who does not lift even a finger to make things better for his family?"

"You shall not talk to me in such a fashion!"

"And you, mother," said Elizabeth, ignoring the man. "You, who treated me worse than the dirt beneath your feet, taught your daughters to fear and hate me without any explanation other than your own petty narrow-mindedness. Should I feel even the tiniest measure of empathy for your situation?"

Though she knew she was provoking both of her parents beyond what was wise, Elizabeth could not help the words which spilled forth from her mouth any more than she could still the beating of her own heart. It was as if all the hurts she had been subjected to during the entire course of her life had now come to the fore and were being released. And the release felt cathartic. She did not even wish to stop it now that it had begun.

"You—both of you—have behaved in the most reprehensible manner possible," continued Elizabeth with a relentless will to be heard. "You blamed a young child who could not have possessed the knowledge of any possible consequences of her actions, and you made her a pariah, mistreating and shunning her, making her wish she was dead. *I* was that child, father. You have no notion whatsoever of how close I came to ending my own life during those miserable years when I was forced to bear your contempt and ridicule."

"Were you not responsible for what happened?" asked Mr. Bennet in a dangerous tone.

"Is the bird who flaps his wings and causes an avalanche which results in someone's death at fault? Of course not! I cannot even begin to tell you both how much you disgust me!"

Mr. Bennet reached out and struck Elizabeth with the back of his hand, and she went down in a heap. All at once, she heard several voices screaming, and as Elizabeth attempted to rise, Jane moved in front of her, standing there like an avenging angel.

"You shall not touch her again!" exclaimed Jane.

"Stand aside, Jane. It is time your sister finally receives what is coming to her."

"Yes, father, give me what is coming to me," said Elizabeth with a contemptuous sneer. "Show us all exactly what kind of a man you are."

As Mr. Bennet strode forward, pushing Jane roughly aside, a deep voice sounded out, arresting his progress.

"That is enough!"

It was into this scene that Darcy arrived at Longbourn, and he was appalled to see what was happening in that house. He had ridden like a man possessed, certain that his love was in danger. It appeared as if he had been correct to be so concerned—Mr. Bennet was on the verge of causing his daughter great physical harm, and Darcy was not about to allow that to happen.

"You will not touch her, Mr. Bennet," said Darcy as he stalked toward the other man. Something in his countenance must have told Mr. Bennet that Darcy was serious, for he shrunk back. "You will never touch her again if you value your life."

Mr. Bennet appeared to recapture some of his belligerence, as he stuck out his jaw in obstinacy and said, "And what do you have to do with this matter, sir?"

"You know precisely what I have to do with this matter. Had you been more reasonable, more of a *gentleman*, Miss Elizabeth and I might already have been married."

Several gasps were heard about the room, and Mrs. Bennet in particular appeared to be close to fainting. It was, of course, the Bennet matron who spoke first.

"What do you mean? Have you an interest in my daughter?"

Darcy glared at the woman. "I asked Miss Elizabeth for a courtship the day before your husband forced her to the altar with *him*." Darcy waved his hand at Collins, who was standing in mute astonishment. "The fact that your husband did not even take care to observe the barest of requirements is my gain, as it allowed Miss Elizabeth to sue successfully for release from him."

"Oh, Mr. Darcy!" wailed the Bennet matron. "Surely you cannot think to marry such . . . such a . . . disobliging, disobedient, *murderess* such as my second daughter! My Lydia would be certain to make you a much better companion."

"Madam, I had not known your youngest a week before I knew that she is the last woman in the world whom I could ever be prevailed upon to marry." Mr. Bennet gasped, and Miss Lydia turned red, but Darcy continued to speak with pitiless honesty. "She is fit to be no one's bride, considering the way she acts. You had best lock her into her room until she has learned something—anything!—of propriety, for she assuredly knows nothing of it now."

Mrs. Bennet stared at him and then rounded on her husband. "Will you allow him to talk of your daughter in such a fashion?"

Mr. Bennet looked at Darcy through narrowed eyes. "Elizabeth is still only nineteen, and she cannot marry without my consent. You shall not succeed in your purpose."

"If you think even for an instant that you shall deter me, you are sorely mistaken." Darcy glared at Mr. Bennet. "There are ways around such things, Mr. Bennet, and you should remember that I have the power to make life very difficult for you. Do not try my patience!"

Apparently defeated, Mr. Bennet lifted a hand which was slightly shaking to his head and rubbed his temples. "Take her, but leave. She has ruined this family twice already, and she shall not be given an opportunity to do so again."

"I shall," said Darcy, taking Elizabeth's arm and drawing her toward the door. "Do not ever expect to see her again."

"We shall be happy never to lay eyes on her!" shrieked Mrs. Bennet. "Good riddance! I wish you have never been born, Elizabeth Bennet!"

Guiding her outside, Darcy shielded Elizabeth from the accusing eyes of her parents, intent on protecting her to the best of his ability. Outside, Darcy saw the gig in which Mr. Collins had brought Elizabeth to Longbourn, the horse still standing winded in the driveway. Darcy shook his head in disgust at the man's stupidity. To have subjected Elizabeth to a journey in such accommodations was ludicrous on many fronts. Whatever the man intended to do, that horse would not be taking him back to Hunsford tomorrow or, indeed, any time soon.

The difficulty was determining a way to transport Elizabeth away from this place without any real means of doing so. Darcy had left his carriage behind in Kent so that Fitzwilliam might use it to convey Anne to London, so it was obviously not available. And given what she had endured the past day, Darcy did not think it wise to allow her to try to walk to Netherfield. The only way to accomplish her removal was, therefore, to put her on his horse and walk the animal to Netherfield. He would send a servant to retrieve her bag, though the fact that she had nothing else to bring with her incensed Darcy all that much more.

"Mr. Darcy! Mr. Darcy."

Against his better judgment, Darcy turned to see the fawning form of the parson hurrying toward him. The man was wearing an anxious frown, and he made a comical figure as he approached Darcy, bowing low every few steps. If the man so much as put one toe out of line, Darcy would crush him like the insect he was.

"Mr. Darcy!" gasped Mr. Collins as he strode up, even that little amount of exertion causing the man to double over in breathlessness.

"I really must protest, sir. This is not seemly at all."

"What must you protest, Mr. Collins?" Darcy glared at the parson.

The man mopped his brow, clearly recognizing the dangerous note in Darcy's voice. "I must protest this fascination with my cousin, a woman who is now disgraced by virtue of an annulment. I cannot fathom why you have even followed us here, as I know for a fact that Lady Catherine de Bourgh had expected you to formalize your engagement with your fair cousin, Miss de Bourgh. I can only suppose that this . . . this *slattern* has made you forget the allegiance to your family. I adjure you, sir, by all that is holy, do not . . ."

"Be silent, Mr. Collins!" interrupted Darcy.

The parson's mouth snapped shut, and he gazed at Darcy with unconcealed astonishment.

"I know not what hearing *you* were present at, Mr. Collins, but I clearly heard His Grace, the Archbishop of Canterbury, state that the wrong was perpetrated upon Elizabeth and that she herself *had done nothing wrong!* I suggest you remember that, sir, as the moment you return to Kent, you will likely find your own actions under the heaviest of scrutiny.

"And as for your comments concerning me and my cousin, you have no connection to either of us, so it can be of no concern to you. However," continued Darcy when the parson seemed intent upon interrupting, "if you must know, I informed Lady Catherine myself, in the company of my cousin, that we would not marry. In fact, I did this in April the last time I visited, and I was forced to reiterate it only yesterday."

Mr. Collins stood there in the cold, gaping at Darcy in astonishment, but Darcy grimly noted the fact that the man appeared to have some semblance of a self-preservation instinct, as he did not venture to say anything further. "There, Mr. Collins," said Darcy after a moment of watching the man, "though you have clearly overstepped your place, you may take solace in the fact that you have protected the interests of your patroness to the best of your ability. Now, I suggest you return to the house and determine how you will return to Kent."

When the parson opened his mouth to speak—proving that his reverence for Lady Catherine was indeed stronger than his sense of self-preservation—Darcy stepped close and lowered his voice to a hiss. "I suggest you do not speak any further, Mr. Collins. Anything you say might contribute to your future misfortunes."

Thankfully, Mr. Collins turned on his heel and returned to the house, leaving Darcy alone with Elizabeth in Longbourn's driveway.

Chapter XXIX

The next period of time was a mystery for Elizabeth, so consumed was she with what had happened. After the event, all she would remember was brief flashes of memory—Mr. Darcy lifting her up on his horse; the concerned expression on his face as he watched her with all the worry of a lover; brief flashes of the landscape through which they traveled; and the smooth and steady gait of the horse beneath her.

Knowing intellectually and through the memories of a child that her family hated her was quite different from knowing it through personal experience. Even the memories of her father's pitiless glare, her mother's words, and Lydia's indifference on the day of her forced marriage were nothing compared to what she had been subjected to that day. Her father had struck her, and comparing it with the slap she had endured the day before her marriage would be like comparing a puddle to a lake. Her cheek still smarted from where he had hit her, and she would likely have a spectacular bruise to go along with her wounded pride.

She was now bereft of any family or name, as she was certain her parents would no longer countenance any congress between her and any of them. The thought of being forever estranged from Jane brought particular pangs, and Elizabeth, though she tried valiantly, could not suppress a sob.

She barely noticed when their progress stopped, but she could hardly miss when Mr. Darcy pulled himself up on the horse behind her, settling into the saddle and pulling her to him. He shook the reins, and the horse started forward, and Elizabeth, shocked as she was by his actions, could not speak for a few moments.

"Surely this is not proper, Mr. Darcy," said she, attempting—and failing miserably—to inject a hint of levity in her voice.

"I find that I care little for propriety at this moment, Miss Bennet." He regarded her with that heart-stopping smile of his before his gaze became somewhat mischievous. "There is no one about to observe us, Miss Bennet."

"We might still meet someone."

"In that case, what is the worst that could happen? I might be forced to marry you to save both our reputations. I am well able to bear the thought of such an eventuality."

Blushing, Elizabeth could only laugh, it sounded mirthless even to her own ears. She settled up against him, content for the moment to be encircled in his strong arms.

They rode on for several moments, and Elizabeth could tell that they were making better time than previously, which was likely a good thing. The day was waning, and the cool air was becoming biting, and Elizabeth knew that should it get much colder, her pelisse would not be much protection against the chill. It had been a long and exhausting day, and she would not be unhappy to have it end in a warm bath and a cozy bed.

"Although I cannot understand your feelings at this time," said Darcy, the gentle buzz of his voice sounding close beside her ear, "I urge you not to give any credence to your parents' words. You are an exceptional young woman, Elizabeth Bennet, and your parents do not deserve to have you in their lives."

As if his words were the final assault on her already overwrought emotions, Elizabeth felt the hold on her emotions shatter and break. She let loose a hoarse sob that was followed by a torrent of tears. She clung to Mr. Darcy's coat in desperation, crying for the harsh life she had had in her parents' home, for the pain of the severing of her family ties, for the loss of her dearest sister, and for the life lost, that of her brother, who had perished under the most tragic of circumstances. For Elizabeth, it was the first time she had sobbed thus since her aunt's kindness had broken down her barriers when Elizabeth had left Longbourn for the first time all those years ago.

When her tears finally subsided and her sobs stilled, she was content merely to bask in the warmth of a lovers' embrace. And for the moment, Mr. Darcy said nothing either, as he appeared to take as much comfort in her presence as she did in his.

"I would apologize for provoking such a storm of tears, but I had a feeling that you required them."

Elizabeth nodded. "The release of emotion can be cathartic indeed. I have not indulged in them in such a way for many a year."

Though he did not answer her, Elizabeth felt the tightening of his hold, and they continued in silence. It was not a few moments later when Elizabeth began to take notice and interest in their surroundings.

"Where are we going, Mr. Darcy?"

"Netherfield," replied he shortly. "In fact, we shall be there momentarily."

Pulling away, Elizabeth looked up to him askance. "Is that wise?"

"It is not wise to continue out in this cold when you have been subjected to it the entire day."

"Still, for me to show up at Mr. Bingley's home unannounced..."

"Not precisely unannounced," said Mr. Darcy. "I sent an express off this morning when I left, notifying Bingley that I was leaving Kent and warning him of the possibility that we might arrive at his doorstep today. My man is following with my clothes and should arrive today. We will send a footman to Longbourn for your trunk when we arrive there."

"It seems that you think of everything, sir."

A smile met her declaration. "I must warn you, Miss Bennet, that I am of a very serious frame of mind. I am also an organized and dutiful creature, so if you feel you cannot live with such a man, then I suggest you tell me so at once."

Elizabeth feigned astonishment. "What shall I do, sir? It is a daunting prospect to be married to a man without fault."

"I am not without fault. But if you wish for a partner who will devote himself to your happiness and comfort, then I am at your complete disposal."

"I am happy to hear it," said Elizabeth, struggling not to tear up at his response.

Luckily, she was prevented from responding, as Mr. Darcy announced that Netherfield had become visible through the trees. More pressing issues once again plagued Elizabeth's mind, and she turned to look a little fearfully at the rising prominence of the manor.

"I must own that I am not anticipating being subjected to Miss

Bingley's supercilious sneers and affected superiority."

"Leave Miss Bingley to me," said Mr. Darcy.

They soon stopped in front of the manor, and Mr. Darcy let himself down from the horse. He was just reaching up to assist with her own descent when the master of Netherfield, trailed by Miss Bingley, emerged from the front door. Mr. Bingley had a look of concern on his face, but his sister only displayed a fierce scowl, though the expression was erased when she saw Mr. Darcy glance at her.

"It seems you were correct, Darcy," said Mr. Bingley as he approached and shook Mr. Darcy's hand.

"Believe me, Bingley, it brings me no pleasure to be proven correct in this instance."

Bingley nodded and turned to Elizabeth. "I am happy to see you, Miss Bennet, looking unscathed by your ordeal. I assure you that you are welcome to stay at Netherfield."

Elizabeth only had time to thank him and to assure him that she was well when the shrill tones of Miss Bingley interrupted them.

"What can you mean by calling her 'Miss Bennet,' Charles? Do you not know that she has been married to Mr. Collins this past month?"

"My sham of a marriage was struck down yesterday morning, Miss Bingley," spoke up Elizabeth, unwilling to allow the two men to speak for her. "I *am* Miss Bennet, and I would appreciate it greatly if you would not refer to me with the name of the man who conspired with my father to force me to the altar."

If anything, Miss Bingley's sneer of derision became even more pronounced. "So you obtained an annulment." Miss Bingley turned her back on Elizabeth, as if giving her the cut direct, and addressed her next comments to her brother. "Surely you cannot mean for . . . *this woman* to stay here, Charles. Not with the stigma of an annulment attached to her."

"I assure you that I do mean to extend our hospitality to Miss Bennet," said Mr. Bingley, his voice allowing for no argument.

"If it is any consolation," said Darcy, interrupting Miss Bingley when she appeared about to deliver a retort, "I was at the annulment hearing when the Archbishop of Canterbury himself declared that Miss Bennet was in no way responsible for what happened to her and that no stigma should be attached to her."

"You were at her annulment?" sputtered Miss Bingley. "That is singular, Mr. Darcy. I was not even aware that you had seen her lately. I am all astonishment that you would take such an interest in her."

"I take quite a lot of interest in her," replied Mr. Darcy, his manner as serious as Elizabeth had ever seen. "I received her approval of a courtship the day before her father separated us."

This last was said with such a tender look that Elizabeth almost melted in response. Miss Bingley, however, watched them with a slack jaw and bulging eyes; soon, however, her expression became a thin glare of displeasure. The woman would bear watching; now that Mr. Darcy had stated his intentions outright, she would be looking for any opportunity to end Elizabeth's relationship with him.

"Now, Miss Bennet," said Mr. Bingley, a grin affixed to his face in response to their obvious affection, "I shall call a maid to show you to your room directly. I have no doubt that you will wish to refresh yourself after your journey."

Elizabeth curtseyed and thanked him, and she gratefully allowed herself to be led away to her room. Mr. Darcy bid her a quiet farewell and promised that he would see her for supper that evening; then he turned to Mr. Bingley and thanked him. The last thing Elizabeth witnessed before she climbed the stairs to the second level was the sight of Miss Bingley raising her voice in anger and Mr. Bingley giving a firm response. At least, Elizabeth *hoped* it was firm. The woman already promised to be insufferable.

The bathwater was hot and plentiful, and Elizabeth felt her weary body relax in response. So relaxed did she become that she almost fell asleep in the bath, and only the arrival of the maid who had been sent to attend her prevented her from following her body's intentions. But Elizabeth would not allow herself to slight her host—Mr. Bingley had welcomed her into his house against his sister's wishes, and she would not be so rude as to fall asleep before she had attended him for the evening.

When Elizabeth had finished her bath, she dressed in a simple evening dress—what remained of her clothes had arrived in the interim—and prepared to remove herself to the sitting room before supper. She had almost finished her preparations when a knock sounded on her door. After she gave the signal, the door opened, and a young maid stepped in.

"I beg your pardon, Miss Bennet, but your presence is requested in the sitting room."

Frowning, Elizabeth wondered at the purpose for her summons. She had thought Mr. Bingley would be content to allow her to spend the evening in her room if she should desire it. Something must have occurred to prompt the summons.

"Tell Mr. Bingley that I shall come directly," said Elizabeth to the maid, who curtseyed and left the room.

It was only a moment later when Elizabeth left her room, her curiosity afire with the reason for her summons. But it immediately became clear to her. The moment she entered the room, she found herself enveloped in a fierce embrace.

"Jane?" was the only thing Elizabeth was able to manage before she too was crying and hugging her elder sister, afraid that this would reveal itself to be nothing more than a dream if she pulled away.

When the tears stopped and the sisters were able to pull apart slightly, Elizabeth was able to see her sister through watery eyes, and in a voice choked with emotion, she said, "How came you to be here?"

"I could not stay there any longer," sobbed Jane. "I do not know my parents, and to be frank, I do not wish to know them. I never saw such cruelty before as when father struck you. I do not wish to stay in his house."

The last was said in a whispered voice, and Elizabeth, unable to bear her sister's distress, once again drew her close.

"Miss Bennet, Miss Elizabeth," said the voice of Mr. Bingley. For the first time since she had entered the room, Elizabeth became aware of the presence of the gentlemen. "Shall I call for tea? I believe that we have much to discuss."

The sisters released one another, and Elizabeth turned to see the indulgent yet concerned gazes of both Mr. Bingley and Mr. Darcy. Though Mr. Darcy was dressed in the same clothes as he had been previously, he had bathed himself, and his clothes had been brushed, and if he was not his typical immaculate self, at least he appeared to be clean and comfortable.

"What is there to discuss?" asked Jane in a dispirited tone. "I am not yet one and twenty, and though Papa has given consent for my marriage, the thought of living at Longbourn until we marry is insupportable."

"Miss Bennet," said Mr. Darcy, "there may be something we can do. Shall you not take tea with us?"

"Indeed, Jane," said Elizabeth, "we should do as Mr. Darcy has suggested."

Taking a visible breath to calm herself, Jane nodded and allowed herself to be led to a nearby couch. As Mr. Bingley ordered their tea, Elizabeth sat close by her sister, determined that nothing should come between them. Jane, Elizabeth was pleased to see, appeared just as eager to stay as close as possible. Mr. Darcy watched over them as a dog watches over his bone, and though he said nothing, it was clear that his concern for them was more than just friendly. The only one of the house who was not present was Miss Bingley, and Mr. Darcy informed them at a question from Elizabeth that the woman had chosen to remain in her rooms.

When the tea was delivered, Elizabeth assumed the task of pouring, for Jane was clearly still too overwrought to concentrate on such a mundane task. As soon as they all held a teacup in their hand, the discussion began in earnest.

"How did you get here, Jane?" asked Elizabeth with no small measure of curiosity. Though her sister was certainly capable, Elizabeth did not think her the type to walk three miles in the cold.

"I rode," she replied simply. "The stable hand was not present, so I saddled the horse myself and left Longbourn as soon as I was able. I could not stay in that house one moment longer."

"What happened, Jane?"

Jane huffed, which was a sound which Elizabeth had never heard from her before. "More of what usually happens. My father returned to his bookroom as you departed, and my mother was in hysterics, moaning about what would happen when he dies. I think I understand his aversion to her company in a way I never have before."

"That does not make it right for him to ignore her and belittle her," said Elizabeth with indignation.

"No, it does not," said Jane with a sigh. "But I do understand it. For all of his failings, my father is an intelligent man, and my mother would try the patience of a saint."

"It is obvious he married her in a moment of infatuation," said Mr. Darcy. "Unless a person is fortunate enough to make such an alliance with a person with whom one is well-suited, sudden passion and infatuation cannot be a reason for lasting happiness and harmony."

"Indeed, it cannot," said Mr. Bingley. "But that cannot be an excuse."

Mr. Darcy gestured in agreement, and the group fell silent. A stray thought caused Elizabeth to break it.

"And what happened with Mr. Collins?"

"Mrs. Hill saw him to a room immediately, and he showed no inclination to leave it. I am certain he was as fatigued with Mama's hysterics as was I."

"I am glad you have come, Jane. I had thought that my entire family was lost to me. I am happy to be proven wrong about you at least."

"You may have more family available to you than you thought."

Elizabeth looked at Jane askance, and Jane smiled and laid a hand on her arm.

"Kitty and Mary have both changed substantially since you left," said Jane. "Kitty and Lydia had a falling out, so Kitty tends to stay with me and Mary. And Mary told me that she wishes she had treated you better when you were at Longbourn."

It was all Elizabeth could do not to choke up and shed tears at the thought that her sisters might be thawing toward her. She did not know either girl well, as neither had given her the opportunity to know them, but after having been so long denied any relationship with her birth family, Elizabeth could only grasp at the idea of having sisters with eager anticipation.

That thought brought on another, and she turned to Mr. Darcy, noting that he appeared to have the same thought she had.

"Yes, Miss Elizabeth, I am serious in my interest in helping your sisters," said he.

"It seems to me that we have a ready solution for our immediate problem," said Mr. Bingley. "Your father has already given his consent to my marriage with Jane, and the settlement papers are signed. The only thing holding us back is the date we already decided on, which is a month away. If I were to purchase a special license, we could marry at any time, and my dearest Jane would not need to return to Longbourn."

"And it would save you from enduring a month more of engagement," said Darcy with amusement.

Mr. Bingley looked at Jane, his heart in his very gaze, and she blushed in response. "I find that I can bear the deprivation of being denied a long engagement very well indeed," said he. He then tore his eyes away from Jane and said, "Darcy, can I assume you are still set on Miss Elizabeth?"

"I am," replied Darcy without any delay.

"With Jane and I married, Elizabeth could stay with us until your own marriage takes place. That would solve the problem of her accommodations while you are still courting."

"I believe the courtship phase is over," said Darcy in a low tone, with his customary intensity.

Elizabeth reveled in the feeling of love she had for this man, but pushing those feelings aside, she turned to Mr. Bingley and said, "I would not wish to impose upon you so soon after you are married. And Jane deserves a large celebration when she weds."

"I do not need such trappings, Elizabeth," said Jane, taking her sister's hands in her own. "All I wish is to be married to the man I love. It matters not if Mama is allowed to spend more of Papa's money than she ought and to host a wedding breakfast to be talked of for many years to come. Those are her wishes, not mine."

"And let me dispel your other objection," said Mr. Bingley. "Jane and I have the rest of our lives to travel and share one another's company. You are concerned about imposing, but you should put such thoughts from your mind. We will be happy to facilitate your courtship with my dearest friend. After all, I shall be gaining a brother whom I have always wished to gain." A smile then fell over his features, and he continued, "Though I suppose that I shall not be gaining a brother in the manner in which at least one of my sisters has always schemed."

Though the allusion to Miss Bingley and her ambitions lightened the atmosphere slightly, there was little of mirth to be had. Elizabeth knew that the woman had not given up her fight and would not do so until Elizabeth was pronounced Mr. Darcy's wife, but Elizabeth was not concerned about Miss Bingley's actions.

"I do not think that this arrangement will be required for long," said Mr. Darcy, interrupting her thoughts. "I wish to be married as soon as possible so that I may legally bring you under my protection. Once that happens, your father will have no more control over you."

"After what happened today, I doubt that my father wishes to have anything further to do with me."

"Yet I believe it prudent to remove all doubt."

The earnestness of his gaze was such that Elizabeth felt herself become warm all over, and she could do nothing more than nod her approval.

"In that case, I believe that there is only one thing left to do," said Mr. Bingley with his typical joviality of character. When Mr. Darcy turned to him with a raised eyebrow, he laughed. "Though I might be wrong, I believe that you have not actually proposed to Miss Elizabeth. Is that not correct?"

"You are correct, Bingley," said Mr. Darcy. "And if you can give us a few moments of privacy before dinner, I shall rectify that oversight immediately."

Almost before Elizabeth was aware, Jane and Mr. Bingley had gone away, leaving her alone in the company of Mr. Darcy. Before they left, however, their pleasure and happiness was expressed amid subtle jests and mild teasing which Elizabeth roused herself to respond to in like kind. Soon, however, she was left alone with Mr. Darcy.

"Ours has been an unconventional courtship, has it not?" said he.

Elizabeth laughed, happy to finally have the ability to feel amusement. "It has indeed, Mr. Darcy. I imagine you must be asking yourself if I am worth the trouble."

"There is no doubt that you are worth any cost, Miss Elizabeth."

He strode to where Elizabeth was still sitting on the couch and knelt beside her. Elizabeth did not know what to think or how to feel. She knew that she should feel happy, but at the moment, she only knew that she was content—happiness would come after she had been able to sit back and take stock of all that had happened the past few days.

"I am not an eloquent man," began Mr. Darcy. "But I am fortunate, as I do not think you to be a woman who desires flowery statements or poetry to be induced to accept a proposal."

"Indeed, I do not."

"Then I shall simply tell you that I have grown to admire and love you. Your courage in the face of almost insurmountable difficulty, your ability to be cheerful, your indomitable will, and your determination have all impressed upon me the heights of your character. I believe you will be the perfect companion and the perfect partner in the management of my estates and life. I love you, Miss Elizabeth Bennet, and I ask you most humbly if you will honor me with your heart and your hand."

Later, Elizabeth was never able to remember exactly how she had responded. But she knew that somehow she had managed to answer, almost coherently, in the affirmative. She did remember the feel of Mr. Darcy's arms about her as he cradled her to his chest, and she remembered the feeling of utter peace and contentment. She also recalled the comforting assurance that she would never again be alone.

Chapter XXX

That evening, it was decided that until Jane and Mr. Bingley's wedding could take place, the ladies would stay in Mr. Darcy's townhouse, where his sister and her companion were currently in residence. That would satisfy the demands of propriety for the time being.

That night was therefore busy, as there was much to do to prepare for the departure. First, Jane wrote a letter to her parents, informing them of her removal to Netherfield and, subsequently, to London. It was Jane's fear that her father would object and arrive at Netherfield to return her to Longbourn, but Elizabeth said that she doubted her father would rouse himself to make such an effort. And she was proven correct, as the only response was the arrival of Mrs. Bennet, who shrilly demanded that Jane return to the family home. Mrs. Bennet was not allowed entrance to the house, however, and she eventually went away. A footman arrived a short time later with some personal effects, and while they were not all of Jane's possessions, Mr. Bingley assured her that she would be able to purchase anything she required after they were married.

The other difficulty lay with Miss Bingley, who, it appeared, was not quite ready to relinquish her argument against her brother's planned nuptials. When she was informed that they were to return to

London, she was initially ecstatic, but her countenance quickly changed to displeased when she learned that both Bennet sisters would travel with them.

"Surely you can see that Jane Bennet is not a suitable bride," said Miss Bingley as they were gathered in the sitting room before dinner. That she had deigned to descend at all spoke to her determination to extricate her brother from his engagement. Mr. and Mrs. Hurst, who had returned from a short trip to Meryton sometime earlier, could only look on their sister's lack of tact in astonishment.

A sneer in Elizabeth's direction was followed by Miss Bingley's further statement: "With no fortune and no connections, she cannot assist your advancement in society, and with a sister now boasting the singular accomplishment of an annulment, she can only be a detriment to our whole family should you wed. Surely you must see this."

"I will thank you not to impugn the honor of my betrothed in front of her," said Mr. Bingley. Elizabeth had always known him to be an amiable man, but she had wondered at his mettle. This display seemed to put that concern to rest.

"And I would think that Jane could benefit my 'advancement in society,' as you call it, very substantially. A connection to the Darcy family is not to be put aside so lightly."

"You are already connected to Mr. Darcy by virtue of your long friendship with him," snapped Miss Bingley. "Do not be obtuse, Charles."

"And I assure you that I am not being so," said Mr. Bingley. "But a connection via marriage is much more substantial than a mere friendship."

Miss Bingley appeared to be started at such a statement, but she shook her head. "If Mr. Darcy should ask for my hand, then you shall become brothers, but it shall not be due to marriage to Miss Bennet."

"And there you are wrong," said Mr. Darcy. One glace at him told Elizabeth that he was not happy with Miss Bingley's protestations or her allusion to an eventual marriage between him and Miss Bingley. "Just this day, Miss Elizabeth has done me the honor of accepting my hand in marriage. Thus, with both Bingley and I wedding sisters, we shall, in fact, become brothers."

All astonishment, Miss Bingley gaped at Mr. Darcy. Of course, such a proud woman could not accept her ambitions crumbling before her, so she chose to disbelieve what she had been told.

"I am comforted by the knowledge that you possess a fine sense of humor, sir. I know that you would never sully your name by sharing it with such . . . such a . . ."

"I caution you to consider your next words very carefully, Miss Bingley," said Darcy. Though his tone was calm, his countenance was stony. "Miss Elizabeth shall indeed be my wife as soon as may be, and I do not take kindly to *anyone* disparaging those who are close to me. If you wish to be invited to any of *our* homes in the future, I suggest you moderate your comments."

A sickly expression fell over the woman's face, and Elizabeth thought for a moment that her anger and disappointment would overcome her good judgment. But Miss Bingley managed to master her emotions, though congratulations were not forthcoming.

"That is . . . fortunate for you, Miss Eliza," managed the woman. "Now, if you will excuse me, I believe that rest will do me well, for I fear that I have a headache."

And with that, Miss Bingley quit the room. Mr. Bingley appeared embarrassed at his sister's behavior, as did Mrs. Hurst, but the lady gathered herself and approached Elizabeth.

"I extend my congratulations to you, Miss Elizabeth. I am certain you shall be very happy with Mr. Darcy."

"Thank you, Mrs. Hurst. I believe I shall."

The older lady smiled, but her eyes darted in a worried manner at the door through which her sister had just exited and betrayed her concern.

"I believe I should go to Caroline, Charles," said she, turning to her brother. "To put it indelicately, I am certain there is no one in this room who was unaware of Caroline's . . . ambitions. She is likely to be quite affected."

"Though I am sorry for your sister's disappointment," said Mr. Darcy, "I did not give her any reason to believe that I would ever offer for her."

Mrs. Hurst smiled at Mr. Darcy, indicating that she took no offense. "I believe that Caroline saw what she wished to see, Mr. Darcy. Regardless, I should go to her."

After she left, silence settled over the room for a few moments, only be to broken by Mr. Hurst. "When shall we be called in to dinner? With Caroline and Louisa away from the room, I do not know who shall act as hostess."

"I believe that we shall be able to do without one for tonight," said Mr. Bingley.

Hurst grunted and then turned to Elizabeth and Jane. "I must congratulate you both. I knew that Darcy would never propose to

Caroline."

He looked at Darcy and said with an uncharacteristic seriousness, "I recommend that you watch her. I doubt she means to go quietly into the night." After another grunt, he was back to the same Hurst that Elizabeth had always seen. "Let us go into dinner. I find that I am quite famished."

When the morning arrived, the party from Netherfield was ready to depart early. Elizabeth and Jane traveled in the Darcy carriage along with Mr. Darcy and Mr. Bingley, and though a strict interpretation could have suggested it was a breach of propriety, they decided that each couple would be a suitable chaperone for the other. Underlying that decision was the fact that none of them wished to sit with Miss Bingley, who was riding in the Bingley carriage with her sister and Mr. Hurst. That Miss Bingley was in a foul mood all morning had been evident in her posture and countenance, but for the short time they were in company together, she had said nothing. That she had *wanted* to say something was also evident in her dark looks, but she appeared unwilling to provoke Mr. Darcy further.

The journey was an easy one, and before noon, they had arrived in London and made their way into the fashionable district in which Mr. Darcy had his abode. There, they were delivered to Darcy house, where they would be staying for a few days until Mr. Bingley was able to procure the much-desired special license. When their luggage had been taken from the carriage, Mr. Bingley and Jane spent a few moments together in parting, as the Darcy carriage was to deliver him to his townhouse, which was a short distance away.

Upon entering the house, Elizabeth's breath was taken away. The interior was large and fine, and the thought of being mistress of such a place was almost enough to overwhelm her. The only other place she could really compare it to was Rosings Park, but though that estate was fine and obviously the abode of someone of wealth and consequence, the similarities were striking, though somewhat understated. Simply put, Rosings seemed to be designed with the intention of displaying the owner's wealth to all who entered. But whereas the furnishings, the floors, the wallpaper, and everything around her was very fine and obviously costly, Mr. Darcy's house in London had a more . . . comfortable feeling about it. Elizabeth had difficulty explaining even to herself exactly what she felt, but she decided after a moment's thought that Darcy house was a home rather than a trophy. It had an understated elegance about it which made it much more welcoming than Rosings' overwhelming splendor.

"Miss Elizabeth, Miss Bennet," said Mr. Darcy, startling Elizabeth from her reverie.

She turned to Mr. Darcy, noting his indulgent smile for her, and she at once realized that someone else was present. Standing before her was a tall, slender young woman of wheaten tresses and pale blue eyes who bore a startling resemblance to Mr. Darcy. It was his sister, she realized, and she wondered that she had not considered the fact that she would meet the young woman for the first time that evening.

"Georgiana, this is Miss Jane Bennet and Miss Elizabeth Bennet," said Darcy, performing the formidable introduction. "Miss Bennet is Mr. Bingley's betrothed, and Miss Elizabeth has done me the singular honor of accepting my hand."

Miss Darcy blinked in surprise and then turned a smile on her brother. "When did this happen? The last letter I had from you suggested that you had hoped that you would be able to propose. At least, the last letter I received before your mysterious express last night."

"It was yesterday, my dear, after we arrived at Netherfield." He laughed at her curious expression and said, "It is quite a story—and one which is not all pleasant. Let us get our guests situated comfortably before we proceed any further." He then turned to Jane and Elizabeth and said, "Miss Bennet, Miss Elizabeth, please allow me to introduce my sister, Georgiana Darcy, to your acquaintance."

The ladies curtseyed to one another, and Miss Darcy stepped forward and said with a shy smile, "I am so happy to make your acquaintance, and I am happy to accept you as a sister, Miss Elizabeth. My brother has had much to say about you in his letters; so much so that I almost believe I already know you."

"I hope he has been charitable," said Elizabeth with an arch smile at her fiancé.

"Oh, yes, indeed," said Miss Darcy. Then she colored, as if she had spoken out of turn, and said in a quieter tone, "We should settle you in your rooms so that you may refresh yourselves."

"I agree," said Mr. Darcy. "I shall join you later, as I believe that I have a few matters requiring my attention."

And so the ladies separated from the gentleman and made their way to their rooms. As Elizabeth walked through the house, she had to remind herself that it *was* nothing more than a house, though a fine one indeed. Mr. Darcy would not have chosen her if he did not think she was capable of being mistress of his homes.

The ensuing days passed peacefully. The sisters enjoyed their time living in Darcy house, and they quickly found a kindred spirit in Georgiana Darcy. Elizabeth found within a short time of observing the girl that though she was sweet and kind, she was also rather shy, and her outburst upon their arrival appeared to have been somewhat of an anomaly. Elizabeth's heart quickly went out to the young woman, and she endeavored to make her comfortable, thereby leading to a hastily formed friendship. Georgiana Darcy would do well for a sister, Elizabeth thought, as in character she was much like Jane, though much more shy. The young woman's companion, Mrs. Annesley, quickly impressed them as a sensible, amiable woman who benefitted her charge exceedingly. All seemed quite well among the ladies.

As for Mr. Darcy, the first day in London, he was much occupied with whatever business had built up during his absence, but on the second day, he was much more in evidence. Between brother and sister, there was a clear and strong affection, and if Mr. Darcy, being much older, naturally seemed to take on the role of a parent, he also seemed to be taking care to ensure that his sister felt comfortable in confiding in him as a brother. It was likely a natural progression, after all—he had been her guardian since she was ten, so it was only to be expected that she would look up to him as a father.

Mr. Bingley was also present several times over the ensuing days, and indeed, he appeared to prefer to spend his time at the Darcy townhouse rather than at his own. It was not surprising. After all, his own townhouse contained a young woman who was most likely in the foulest of moods, and Elizabeth did not doubt that he would prefer not to be constantly importuned by his sister about his upcoming marriage to Elizabeth's sister. Nor, she suspected, did he wish to be subjected to Miss Bingley's bitterness about Mr. Darcy's betrothed.

One subject which came up between Mr. Darcy and Elizabeth the very next day after their arrival was his desire to have her known as his affianced. Unfortunately, it was not to be, as the demands of propriety needed to be met.

"I would like nothing more than for our engagement to be known to all," said Elizabeth, "but surely you can see that it cannot be. Until Jane is settled in Mr. Bingley's townhouse, I cannot be known as your betrothed. It would not be proper for me to live here when our engagement has been publicly declared."

"I believe you know that society can go hang, for all I care," said Mr. Darcy.

Elizabeth smiled softly and put her hand on his arm. "I do

understand, Mr. Darcy. But we must live in society, and I will not have a scandal erupt over our living arrangements before the marriage actually takes place. It shall be enough of a sensation that you are marrying me at all."

Mr. Darcy was forced to give way, little though he appeared to like it. Living in close proximity did, however, have one additional benefit. It allowed her to see the man in his home in positions which she had never had the opportunity to before. She learned, for example, that Mr. Darcy preferred to eat lighter foods at breakfast, much as Elizabeth did herself, and she learned that the only reason eggs and bacon were provided at all was because Miss Darcy sometimes preferred them. Elizabeth also learned that he was fair and kind to all his servants, and she knew that such a man was to be admired. Many of his station would look down on others and treat them almost as beasts of burden and slaves to their whims.

Word arrived very soon after their arrival that Colonel Fitzwilliam had accompanied his cousin Anne de Bourgh to his parents' home. Elizabeth had been informed of the reasons why Mr. Darcy had been delayed in seeking her out after the hearing, and her heart went out to Miss de Bourgh. Eager to know the young woman outside of the stifling influence of her mother, Elizabeth insisted upon visiting her.

"I cannot vouch for my uncle and aunt's behavior, Elizabeth," said Mr. Darcy when Elizabeth had proposed her scheme.

"You think they will disapprove of me?"

Mr. Darcy sighed. "I cannot state with any certainty how they will react. I do know that though they have never expected me to marry Anne, they have always assumed I would marry a society woman who could raise my fortune and position in the world."

"And I am able to do neither of those things," said Elizabeth, the old feeling of insecurity welling up within her.

"Elizabeth, you are everything I could ever want in a wife," said Mr. Darcy as he stepped close and grasped her hand. "I care not for wealth and connections, and I have always sought something more than this in a marriage partner. These are things you will supply in abundance."

"And yet there will be many who will condemn your choice."

"Let them," said Mr. Darcy with a shrug. "I know my true friends. They will understand the jewel I have unearthed and will love you for what you bring to my life. The rest of society is of no concern to me."

"Then you must allow me to prove myself to your closest relations." Elizabeth smiled at him but held firm in her intention to visit his cousin. "Even if they do disapprove, I am certain they will be circumspect about that fact. They would not wish to offend you."

Mr. Darcy reluctantly agreed, and a short time later, she was on her way to his aunt and uncle's residence with Georgiana in tow. Jane had felt herself unequal to meeting such formidable personages, and Elizabeth did not argue with her, knowing she would be much more comfortable staying behind in Mr. Darcy's townhouse.

While Darcy admired Elizabeth's fortitude and confidence, he was not looking forward to introducing her to his relations. He had no way of determining how his uncle would react. The earl was not precisely a snob, but he also believed in the necessity of keeping to one's own sphere when considering marriage. Lady Matlock was the easier of the two to predict; as she had a longstanding feud with Lady Catherine, she would likely approve simply on the basis that his chosen was not deformed, not insipid, and, most importantly, not Anne.

The Fitzwilliam residence was close enough to Darcy house that they simply donned their outer wear and walked the short distance, and it was not long before they were announced into the earl's presence. He was accompanied in the sitting room by Colonel Fitzwilliam, Lady Matlock, and Anne.

As soon as they had entered the room, Anne rose to greet them, and though she appeared to be pale, she was also much better than she had been when Darcy had left Rosings only two days earlier. Even the mark of Lady Catherine's assault on her was largely faded.

"Darcy, Georgiana," greeted she before turning and almost throwing herself into Elizabeth's arms. "I am so glad you have come." This last, she almost whispered to Elizabeth.

"Miss de Bourgh?" said Elizabeth quietly, clearly uncertain how to take this enthusiastic greeting.

"Call me Anne, please. I hope you will give me leave to call you Elizabeth." At Elizabeth's hesitant nod, Anne smiled brightly. "Surely you must know it is because of you that I am here. It is your fine example and refusal to be intimidated by my mother which has allowed me to stand up to her. I am very grateful, I assure you."

"I am sure I did nothing," denied Elizabeth.

"So this is the young woman who, it seems, has captured our Darcy," boomed the voice of the earl, interrupting any further conversation. "You must bring her here and introduce her to us, Anne. I would make her acquaintance."

Though Elizabeth seemed to convey a sense of trepidation at the prospect, Anne guided her to her uncle and made the introductions.

Darcy thought his uncle's expression unreadable as he studied Elizabeth. He did not seem to *disapprove*, although the exact extent of his approbation was still to be determined.

"I can see that you have chosen a rather pretty sort of girl, Darcy," pronounced the earl after a moment's inspection. "She appears also to be somewhat unintimidated by meeting us, which is also well."

"Henry," chided the countess, "do not speak of the young lady as though she was not even here." And with that, the countess turned to Elizabeth and said, "We are very happy to make your acquaintance, my dear. We had begun to despair of Darcy *ever* marrying, so news of your betrothal was welcome, I assure you."

"Have I ever told you that you gossip like a society wife, Fitzwilliam?" said Darcy. Truly, he was not angry at his cousins for betraying the fact of his engagement, though he had not actually been engaged at the time!

"Just making a flanking maneuver, old boy," said Fitzwilliam with a grin. "We have been singing your Miss Elizabeth's praises since my father arrived at Rosings. We had to give my parents a good impression and all that."

Elizabeth laughed with delight. "Though I am not certain I deserve such unreserved praise, I thank you, Colonel Fitzwilliam."

"For making Darcy happy, you deserve all our praise and more," said the countess. And she took Elizabeth's arm and guided her to a couch where they could sit and talk with one another.

The conversation flowed fluidly for some time, and though the countess was all that was friendly, the earl was much more reserved. He was not unkind, but he appeared to be studying Elizabeth, likely in an attempt to divine whether she would enter their sphere and acquit herself or whether she would need to be distanced from them as an unfortunate and unsuitable connection. Darcy found himself feeling a little annoyed, but he had been aware of his uncle's character, so he said nothing.

At one point, Darcy approached his uncle and his cousin to inquire as to what had happened after the earl had arrived at Rosings.

"I have always known that Catherine was a hard and unfeeling woman, but her behavior has astonished me," growled Lord Matlock. "She would not acknowledge anything, of course, but your description, as well as the testimony of the apothecary, convicted her quite neatly. I will not countenance Anne ever returning to that house as long as her mother is in residence."

"And the state of Anne's inheritance?"

"She is Sir Lewis's heir," replied Lord Matlock. "Her mother has no say in the matter."

Darcy turned and looked significantly at Fitzwilliam, and the look was returned with a certain level of impatience.

"Give Anne some time, Darcy. She has experienced such a shock, and being free of her mother's influence has changed her life significantly. I am open to the thought of marriage with Anne, but we will not rush into it."

It was nearing the end of their visit when the subject of Anne's health arose, and she assured them that she was very well indeed.

"My uncle has arranged for me to be seen by his doctor," said Anne. "I am happy that I will finally be examined by someone who is not beholden to my mother for his livelihood."

"Anne, that is unkind," said the earl with a stern glare. "Your mother is misguided and certainly bereft of patience, but I would not have you spreading such stories. In her own singular way, I do believe that she wishes for what is best for you."

Anne rolled her eyes. "And what is best for me is whatever she decrees. She also decrees my thoughts and actions as well, so as to save me the trouble of thinking and acting for myself."

"I find that I must agree with Anne on this occasion," interjected Colonel Fitzwilliam. "When the doctor whom Lady Catherine employs was sent for, he was found to be insensible due to excessive drink. And this was in the middle of the day!"

The earl scowled. "So you informed me. Well, we shall ensure that you are given the best care now that you are with us."

The rest of the visit passed by smoothly, and when they were ready to depart, Darcy guided Elizabeth and Georgiana to the door. He was thus surprised when his uncle stepped forward and bowed to Elizabeth.

"I was concerned, I own, when I was told that Darcy was expected to offer for you." His lips lifted in the slightest of wry smiles. "Though I know Darcy to be a discerning sort of man, I wondered if you had managed to trap him. You should not be concerned that my son and niece have informed me of your trials the past few months. Though an annulment is an unfortunate thing, I think that it can be kept from general knowledge.

"Having met you, however, I am pleased. I believe that you will do well in our family and out among society in general. And if your connections are not what we would wish, Darcy here so obviously dotes on you that I believe that we can overlook them."

It was so like his uncle—genuine and respectful in general, but displaying that haughtiness which was so a part of his character. Elizabeth evidently decided to take the gesture in the manner it was intended, as she curtseyed and said:

"Thank you, Your Grace. I will do my best to be a credit to the Darcy and Fitzwilliam families."

"None of that, now," said the earl. "You must call me 'Uncle Henry,' as you will very soon be my niece in fact."

Elizabeth agreed to do so, and within moments, they had taken their leave. As they strolled back to his townhouse, Darcy walked behind his sister and his betrothed, watching as they spoke animatedly with one another. He had known that Elizabeth would charm his relations. He simply had not known how quickly it would happen.

Two days after their arrival in town, however, an event happened which astonished Elizabeth exceedingly. They were in the sitting room, both couples speaking with one another while Georgiana played the pianoforte, when the door opened and a footman entered the room, beckoning to Mr. Darcy. The master of the house rose and approached the footman, engaging in a brief conversation with him before turning to Elizabeth. She had been wondering if something was amiss, but his wide smile told a different story.

"It seems, Miss Elizabeth, that we have a surprise for you."

Before Elizabeth could respond, the footman returned, and following in his footsteps were her aunt and uncle.

Elizabeth fairly flew into the arms of her aunt, crying and laughing all at once. At the same time, her aunt's tears mingled with hers, and Mrs. Gardiner kissed her tenderly, as a mother might kiss a young child, while Uncle Gardiner engulfed them both within the comfort of his encircling arms. How much she had wanted them! Throughout the whole ordeal with her father and Mr. Collins, she had wished for their presence, knowing that her uncle would be able to make it all well again.

Elizabeth, who was trembling with emotion, found it took several moments before she was able to speak coherently, and even then, she dissolved into tears of happiness over and over again.

The sound of her uncle's voice finally penetrated through the tears and laughter when he said, "Thank you, Mr. Darcy, for caring for our dearest girl."

Mr. Darcy extended his hand, which Mr. Gardiner shook heartily, and said, "I assure you that it was my pleasure, Mr. Gardiner." He glanced at Elizabeth, and she could see his heart in his eyes as he continued. "I would do anything for Miss Elizabeth."

"You received my letter then?" asked Elizabeth as she pulled away from her aunt.

"We did," affirmed Mrs. Gardiner. "Along with a missive from Mr. Darcy promising that he would do whatever he could to ensure your safety."

"And he has," said Elizabeth, smiling at the gentleman while wiping the tears from her eyes. "I am indebted to Mr. Darcy for his kindness."

"Not at all," said Mr. Darcy. He then turned to the other members of the group, who were all standing and watching the scene with tears in their eyes. "I beg your pardon, but might I introduce the rest of the party?"

The Gardiners, of course, agreed, and soon the introductions had been completed, and the party sat down together.

"I see there have been many changes since we were last together," observed Mr. Gardiner.

Elizabeth blushed and darted a happy smile at Mr. Darcy, who returned it without reservation. "Yes, indeed, uncle. When you left me, I was a naïve young girl. Now, I am happy to say that I am free from a marriage which, according to church law, never took place, and I have been the recipient of a proper proposal. You will be happy to know that I accepted it."

The Gardiners looked at each other with knowing smiles and expressed warm and hearty congratulations. Then Mrs. Gardiner looked at Elizabeth and told her, "These tidings are not precisely shocking, Lizzy. Your uncle and I suspected that such would be the result if you could be freed from Mr. Collins."

"A young man would never do so much for a young lady unconnected to him unless he had a powerful motivation," added Mr. Gardiner. He turned to Mr. Darcy. "You were quite transparent, sir."

"Yes, I was," said Mr. Darcy. Those in the room were amused at what he did not say, but no one felt it necessary to bring up the matter any further.

"What we do not know," continued Mrs. Gardiner, "is what has happened in the interim. It sounds like quite a tale, and I would appreciate it if you would oblige us with an explanation."

And so the explanation commenced, and the entirety of the past months was disclosed to the Gardiners and to Georgiana, Jane, and Mr. Bingley, who were only aware of parts of the story. The tale was primarily told by Elizabeth, with occasional assistance from Jane and Mr. Darcy, though after the telling shifted to what happened in Kent, Jane fell silent, and Mr. Darcy's involvement grew.

Through it all, Elizabeth noticed that the others were watching her with interest, and at times, they responded verbally with sighs or exclamations. Before long, she began to feel a little self-conscious. But it was not until she fell silent that the comments began to flow in, and surprisingly, perhaps, it was Mr. Bingley who spoke first and loudest.

"I must commend you, Miss Elizabeth," said he with respect and admiration, "I do not know of many ladies who could persevere through such trials and emerge the better for them."

Elizabeth blushed and turned a further shade of red when she heard Mr. Darcy say, "And now you understand why I consider her to be a jewel I am fortunate to have found."

Looking up, Elizabeth saw Mr. Darcy regarding her with an expression of such tenderness that it almost took her breath away. He meant what he said about her, not that she had doubted him for a moment. But in that moment, it all became more real, more tangible, and she truly understood what it was to love and to be loved in turn.

"Yes, our Elizabeth does possess a resiliency that is far from the common way," said Mrs. Gardiner. She stood and approached Elizabeth, sitting beside her and engulfing her in the circle of her arms. Elizabeth felt at once safe and warm all over, though strangely enough, it did not speak to her of home as it once had. She supposed that was because of her own growth and, perhaps more importantly, because of her burgeoning feelings for Mr. Darcy. Home would now be wherever he was.

"The fact that you are safe and experienced no permanent harm from this fiasco was the only thing which kept me from striking Bennet." Elizabeth looked up from her aunt's shoulder to see the anger displayed by her uncle.

"You visited Longbourn?" asked Elizabeth.

"We did," said Mr. Gardiner. "I had thought to give Bennet a piece of my mind in addition to finding out where you were."

"But Longbourn was in an uproar," said Mrs. Gardiner, "due as much to Jane's departure as to Elizabeth's return. Mrs. Bennet was beside herself at her daughters' betrayal, as she called it, and she was incensed by your refusal to sacrifice yourself in marriage to Mr. Collins."

All Elizabeth could do was to shake her head. "It seems she has already forgotten our talk the morning that my father forced me to the altar." At the questioning looks Elizabeth received, she explained, "I warned her that she would not like it if I became the mistress of Longbourn, and I explained to her in great detail exactly what she would have to look forward to if I were to return as mistress after my father's death."

"She has indeed forgotten, Lizzy," said Mr. Gardiner. "She was ever thus, unfortunately. She tends to remember the things she wants to believe and discards the rest as unimportant."

Mr. Gardiner approached Elizabeth with gravity. "I spoke with your father, Elizabeth, and told him that I would brook no further interference in your life. He declared that he wanted nothing further to do with you and that he no longer considers you his daughter. I was quite emphatic that I am now responsible for you."

At one time in her life, hearing such a thing would have filled Elizabeth with sorrow. Two months in her father's house and all that had followed had cured her of that particular affliction, and now all she could feel was relief that Mr. Bennet could no longer interfere in her life.

"We could initiate legal action to make this an actuality, but given the situation, I think that the question has become moot."

"I would agree, Mr. Gardiner," said Mr. Darcy, "but I would like to be married as soon as may be, so that I may extend my protection in a firmly legal sense. Mr. Bennet does not seem like one who would give himself the trouble of exerting himself, but I would prefer that he does not get any other ideas concerning how to 'save his family.'"

"I agree, though we should talk further on the matter in a few moments." He turned to both Jane and Elizabeth and said, "For the nonce, I believe that it would be best for you both to return to Gracechurch Street. The arrangement as it is now strains propriety a little too much for my liking."

Elizabeth and Jane readily agreed, though Mr. Bingley did not appear to be pleased with this turn of events. Mr. Gardiner, however, noticed this, and he slapped the young man gently on the shoulder. "I will not attempt to delay your nuptials, young man. Not only has her father already given you his permission, but I also agree that both of my nieces should be removed from their father's dubious protection as soon as may be."

The expression of relief which appeared on Mr. Bingley's face brought laughter to the whole group, and even more so when he thanked Mr. Gardiner profusely.

"There is one thing I would like your opinion concerning," said Mr.

Darcy when the mirth had died down. "Miss Elizabeth and I have spoken of removing the younger sisters from the care of their mother and father, as Mr. Bennet seems to be less able a protector than ever. I would like your insight on how to go about doing this."

Mr. Gardiner nodded his head with approval. "An interesting thought, Mr. Darcy, and one of which I approve most heartily."

"Then may I have a moment of your time, sir?" Mr. Darcy turned his soft smile on Elizabeth again. "As you are now Miss Elizabeth's protector, I have a particular request to make of you."

Laughing, Mr. Gardiner indicated for Mr. Darcy to precede him from the room. "In that case, let us retire to your study, though I own that handling this matter in *your* study, where I have not the advantage of sitting behind *my* desk, will deprive me of some level of amusement."

"If it makes you feel better, Mr. Gardiner, you may sit behind *my* desk and intimidate me to your heart's content," replied Mr. Darcy. "As long as my request is granted, I care not how much you make me sweat."

Laughing, the two men retreated from the room, leaving the ladies with Mr. Bingley. The chatter in the room made it a gay party all around, and Georgiana called for tea and refreshments. By the time Mr. Gardiner and Mr. Darcy returned, talk had already turned to the weddings, and Mrs. Gardiner was eagerly plotting the dresses, wedding breakfasts, and all the sundry details which would go into making them both celebrations fitting to the occasion. It was a merry party, and Elizabeth found that she was happy, though she was a little sad that she would need to leave Mr. Darcy's house until her marriage.

When Mr. Darcy and Mr. Gardiner returned, the three men stood together speaking apart from the ladies, no doubt finding the discussions of food, lace and other finery, and similar details to be a little too feminine for them. Elizabeth had all the pleasure of watching her betrothed attempt to know her uncle, and from what she could see, he appeared pleased by what he saw of Mr. Gardiner. It was all she could have hoped for.

"You seem to have found a fine man, my dear," said Mrs. Gardiner in quiet tone. "I believe that you shall be very happy indeed."

"I believe I shall, aunt," said Elizabeth, her eyes never leaving her betrothed.

Chapter XXXI

Quite incongruously, Elizabeth felt herself to be both happy to be back with the Gardiners and wistful about the remaining time available to her in her uncle's home. Every room, every item in the house, every path in the park close to their home was familiar and comforting, imparting a sense of normalcy which had been missing for far too long. But this place was no longer where she belonged. And it was this change in perspective which caused her pensive feelings and which at times made her feel almost like a stranger in the home in which she had spent ten years of her life.

She was grateful to have Jane with her for that first period, as Elizabeth felt that she would have been in danger of becoming almost maudlin without her. Jane, with her calm serenity and ability to see the best in every situation, seemed to understand Elizabeth's feelings, and she made it her task to pull Elizabeth from her weighty thoughts when she seemed destined to fall into them.

Without the interference of her mother or her other sisters to hamper her, Elizabeth found herself drawing closer to Jane, and her suspicions of how their relationship might have been had they grown up in the same house were proven correct. Jane was everything a sister should be, and Jane appeared to treasure this time together as much as did Elizabeth herself. Many times during the course of those days,

Elizabeth found herself wondering how deep their relationship would have been, and she cursed her parents anew for what their actions had wrought. It was all that much more imperative that they use this time before marriage installed them in their own homes.

Of her aunt and uncle, Elizabeth saw much, and she cherished this time with them, even though it separated her more than she wanted from her beloved. Their conversations frequently centered on the memories they had built together, though often Elizabeth had the sense that her aunt was subtly imparting final instructions on how to be a good mistress of her own home.

Elizabeth also listened to accounts of the Gardiners' time spent in Ireland, the things they had seen, and what had been accomplished. It appeared that Mr. Gardiner's mission there had been a complete success, and he was now in a position to increase his income to a level which would rival that of most landowners.

"Then you shall find yourself in a position where you may purchase an estate, uncle," said Elizabeth in a teasing tone when she had heard the good news. "If you do, I would hope you will consider Derbyshire, as I would be very happy to have you close to me."

"That eventuality may be closer than you think, Elizabeth," said Mr. Gardiner, his amusement showing at her astonishment.

"Truly?" asked Elizabeth.

"It is something we have considered for years. As you know, I am descended from a veritable bevy of second and third sons, and it has been in my mind for some time that our family might return to its roots as a landed family.

"But nothing is certain as of yet. Even if I should purchase an estate, I have no intention of divesting my business interests, as I am convinced that business is the future of our society. I shall likely divide my time between the estate and my business in London if we should indeed decide to purchase an estate."

"How will you manage it?" asked Elizabeth. "Your business takes most of your time now—how can you manage an estate as well?"

Mr. Gardiner smiled. "A good businessman knows the value of hiring trustworthy employees and endowing them with the power to manage his interests. Yes, I am busy, but I have been gradually handing the reins off to my assistants. With a competent steward, I would be set with respect to managing an estate, too."

The thought that the Gardiners would potentially be close by brought a new sense of contentment to Elizabeth. She had been sure of her love for Mr. Darcy and her desire to be united with him for some time. But the thought of leaving the Gardiners so far behind while she went to manage Mr. Darcy's home in the country was daunting, to say the least.

Elizabeth, Jane, and the Gardiners continued comfortably for those days before the Christmas holiday, enjoying the company, decorating the house for Christmas, and preparing for the time when the two girls would leave for houses, husbands, and families of their own. And in that time, the Darcys and Mr. Bingley were much in evidence, and they also saw much of Colonel Fitzwilliam and Anne de Bourgh, whom Elizabeth was quickly coming to count as a friend.

It was two days before Christmas when Elizabeth received a most unwelcome visitor to the townhouse. The occasion was made worse by the fact that said visitor came when Jane was at Mr. Bingley's townhouse to tour it and meet with the housekeeper, as her wedding would take place in the week between Christmas and New Year's. Elizabeth had been invited to go as well, but she had begged to be excused, deciding that Jane should be allowed the opportunity to see her new home by herself. That the timing of the visit was by design was not in question, but the fact that Mrs. Gardiner had been called to the nursery to deal with some matter of the children made the situation all that much more uncomfortable.

For a moment after Miss Bingley was announced, Elizabeth watched the other woman with barely concealed curiosity, wondering what she could possibly mean in calling. Miss Bingley had not accompanied Mr. Bingley even once to Gracechurch Street, nor had she been present when Elizabeth had visited Darcy house. And though Mr. Bingley had not explicitly mentioned his sister, it was evident that she had been in a constant state of fury since their return to London. Her disgust for her surroundings was evident in the way she curled her lip, in the exasperated looks she directed at Elizabeth, and in the way she haughtily refused the offer of tea. If her feelings were thus, then Elizabeth could not imagine why she bothered to even come.

"I imagine you must congratulate yourself for this . . . *triumph* you have managed to bring about," said Miss Bingley almost as soon as she sat facing Elizabeth. The contempt fairly poured off the woman in waves, as did her bitterness of spirit and unhappiness.

But Elizabeth was not to be intimidated, and she responded, "I am uncertain of what 'triumph' you refer to, Miss Bingley. Perhaps you should come to the point of your visit."

"And I am certain you understand me perfectly, Mrs. Collins," said the other woman with a sneer.

"That is a name I did not even answer to when society deemed it belonged to me," snapped Elizabeth. "I would appreciate it if you would refrain from using it. Otherwise, I believe we have nothing further to discuss."

"Very well, then. Miss Eliza, I shall be frank. I am certain you congratulate yourself due to the *engagement* which you have managed to bring about, though by what means I am uncertain. Before he met you, Mr. Darcy was able to spot a fortune hunter without fail, but his insight seems to have deserted him when it comes to you."

The audacity of the woman knew no bounds! But Elizabeth would not respond in kind, though she was sorely tempted to do so.

"I know nothing of what you mean. Mr. Darcy and I came to our understanding by way of a mutual regard. There was nothing underhanded on either of our parts."

"There is nothing else that could have tempted him from his duty," said Miss Bingley. "The only explanation is that *you* drew him in!"

"His duty?" asked Elizabeth with an incredulous laugh. "And what do you consider his duty to be. To wed you? According to his aunt, his duty was to wed his cousin. He did not accede to her demands either."

Miss Bingley's countenance darkened to a most forbidding scowl, proving to Elizabeth—if she had not already known—the ugliness of character to which the woman could descend. She stood with an abruptness which startled Elizabeth and loomed over her in an attempt to intimidate. "Mr. Darcy's duty," hissed she, "is to wed a woman of connections and fortune, not some penniless waif who has been thrown off by her family."

"Connections!" said Elizabeth, scoffing at the woman's pretensions. "You should remember, Miss Bingley, that regardless of my current status with my family, *I* am the daughter of a gentleman, whereas you will never be more than the daughter of a *tradesman*."

By now, the woman's eyes were positively smoldering with fury, but she calmed herself with a visible effort and once again took her seat on the other sofa. But Elizabeth was not prepared to endure her presence any longer.

"I believe that it is time you left, Miss Bingley," said she. "You may take your insults elsewhere; I have neither the time nor the stomach for them."

Miss Bingley, however, did not move. She merely glared at Elizabeth in that superior manner of hers, as though she was the queen and had judged that everything before her was wanting. Elizabeth waited for a moment to see if Miss Bingley would depart peacefully, but when she saw that the woman had no intention of leaving, Elizabeth rose to summon a servant to evict her from the premises.

"I had hoped to find you reasonable," said Miss Bingley. "It was a vain hope, perhaps, but I had thought you could be persuaded to desist without having to resort to threats."

"And what could you possibly threaten me with?"

"Information concerning your past."

The two women faced each other, the tension in the air an almost living, breathing entity. Elizabeth's mind was whirling. What the woman thought she knew, Elizabeth could not fathom, but she was determined that she would not be coerced. Besides, Miss Bingley had truly underestimated their attachment to each other if she thought that Mr. Darcy would not protect her by every means possible. Miss Bingley was setting herself up for a fall in society, whether she knew it or not.

"Do not be surprised, Miss Eliza," said Miss Bingley, breaking the silence, her words accompanied by the smile of a woman who felt she held all the cards. "Your mother was a font of information once I learned how to induce her to share it. The senseless woman thought that I was commiserating with her, but in truth, I was gathering material to use to free Mr. Darcy should he succumb, as I knew what you were attempting to do. I know it all, *Miss Eliza*—your *murder* of your younger brother, your banishment from Longbourn, and your parents' attempt to persuade you to redeem yourself by marrying the current heir, not to mention your *annulment*. And I am willing to use this information, I assure you."

"To what end?" asked Elizabeth, curious as to whether Miss Bingley had thought the entire matter through.

"To see this . . . this . . . trumped-up engagement ended, of course! If you will not end the engagement of your own free will, then the details of your past will be discussed in every drawing room in London."

"And what of Mr. Darcy? Do you think that the scandal of my ending the engagement will have no effect on him?"

"Come now, Miss Eliza. It is not even announced. Whatever shred of reputation you still possess will not even be affected. It need never be known."

Elizabeth smiled slightly, though with no hint of good humor. "Therefore leaving Mr. Darcy to you?"

Miss Bingley preened and examined her fingernails. "He requires a society wife of excellent breeding, education, and accomplishments, and before he became infatuated with you, I am certain he was on the verge of making an offer to *me*. I will readily accept him, I assure you."

"And I assure *you* that he will never make you an offer." Elizabeth smiled coldly at the other woman. "Mr. Darcy has never looked at you twice, except perhaps in exasperation. He considers you a grasping, artful, mean, unfeeling woman, and he would never tie himself to you."

Her fury such that she could hardly even speak, Miss Bingley stammered and struggled for something to say, but Elizabeth continued on, discarding all pretense of amiability.

"And I think that perhaps you have not thought this matter through, Miss Bingley. A child of two can have no understanding of the concept of murder, so your claims of my being a murderer are nothing but the braying of a donkey. But even if you *were* to make such claims in the hope of ruining my reputation, you would be *ruining your own by association!* Whatever gossip taints me will also taint my family and will therefore taint you by association, given the fact that my sister will soon marry your brother."

"I shall do it before the wedding ever takes place!" snapped Miss Bingley.

"That is still no solution." By now, the angry tone of Elizabeth's voice had been replaced with an agreeable and almost friendly tone which clearly irked Miss Bingley. All the more reason to use it, in Elizabeth's estimation. "You would merely put your brother in the unenviable position of having to choose between marrying the woman he loves and protecting his family, and even then, he and you would suffer, as he would become a jilt if he ended the engagement with Jane. Your arguments make little sense, and the application you have made to me is frivolous. I must ask you to leave before I have you removed."

Miss Bingley stood, but her forbidding glare never wavered an inch. "You will end your engagement if you value your reputation."

"I will do no such unreasonable thing," said Elizabeth as she crossed to the room and rang the bell. "Mr. Darcy will not marry you. I will not give up the man I love. I suggest you find some other more interested man to sink your claws into."

The door opened, and the Gardiners' housekeeper entered. "Yes, Miss Elizabeth?"

"Miss Bingley will be leaving now. Her carriage should be waiting outside."

The housekeeper bowed and retreated, seeming to sense that more was at work here than a simple request to see that Miss Bingley's conveyance was prepared.

Elizabeth turned to Miss Bingley and gestured to the door, waiting to see if the woman would depart without being coerced. Miss Bingley sniffed with disdain and began to walk toward the door.

"Very well. I warned you, and now you will pay the price."

"I suggest you consider how to act very carefully," warned Elizabeth. "It would be unwise for a woman of your social background to make an enemy of a man of the prominence of Mr. Darcy. And you should also remember that I have been accepted by his uncle, the earl. Think of that before you spread stories concerning his future niece."

With those parting words, Elizabeth turned away. Miss Bingley did not move for several moments after Elizabeth's final words, but soon after that, Elizabeth heard the return of the housekeeper as she announced to Miss Bingley that her carriage was ready. They retreated from the room, leaving Elizabeth alone.

As it turned out, Miss Bingley's threats ended up being nothing more than a bluff. Soon after Miss Bingley had departed, Darcy arrived with his sister in tow, and when Georgiana was involved in a discussion with Elizabeth's aunt, Elizabeth took the opportunity to initiate a quiet conversation in which she explained the scene which had occurred not long before his arrival.

To say Darcy was not amused was a vast understatement. Miss Bingley had pursued him since he had had the misfortune of being introduced to her, and despite the hints he had given that he was not interested, not to mention all the times Bingley had told her straight out that he would never offer for her, she still persisted.

Darcy was a man of the world, and he had lived in that world as the master of a great estate since his father's untimely death. Though he did not as a rule enjoy society or excel at making the polite conversation which society deemed so necessary, he was aware of the fact that it was his duty to engage in society nonetheless. He was also aware that society was awash with young women seeking to marry to improve their status and wealth. However, none approached the fervor and determination of Miss Bingley. The woman was no better than a leech.

Later that evening, Darcy visited Bingley's townhouse to discuss the matter with him. Time had given him a little perspective on the matter, and he thought it unlikely that Miss Bingley actually intended to follow through with her threats. However, he could not allow the matter to go without making response, and it was a response which the woman would not like.

Ensconced in Bingley's study with the man's raptures over his angel and effusions concerning the expectations the man had concerning the marriage which would take place the following week, Darcy congratulated his friend warmly. But when there was a lull in the conversation, he took the opportunity to discuss what was on his mind, acquainting Bingley with the particulars of what Elizabeth had related to him that afternoon.

After the specifics had been imparted, Bingley sat back in his seat and sighed, his previously ebullient mood forgotten. "I *am* sorry, Darcy. I know not what to do with her. You are aware how many times I have attempted to bring her to understand the facts of the situation, but she persists despite it all."

"Unfortunately, I cannot help you there, my friend," replied Darcy with a smile, letting Bingley know that he was not upset with him.

"Of course not," said Bingley with a mirthless guffaw. "*Your* sister is the most obliging and tractable creature in existence, while *mine* happens to be the least. *Of course* you cannot empathize."

They were interrupted by a soft knock on the door, and Darcy looked at Bingley, who seemed to agree with him as to who was likely waiting to gain entrance. At Bingley's raised eyebrow, Darcy shrugged and motioned for him to open the door. It was just as well that they get the matter sorted out immediately, as Darcy would prefer not to have it hanging over Elizabeth's head and dampening her joy in this season leading up to her wedding.

When Bingley opened the door, Miss Bingley was found on the other side as expected. The woman's eyes darted to Darcy's face quickly before she turned her attention back on her brother, saying: "I had understood that Mr. Darcy was visiting. I thought I would inquire as to whether you require anything."

"So good of you to take a personal interest in our guest's comfort, Caroline," said Bingley. For the first time Darcy could remember, his friend's voice held more than a hint of a sardonic edge, a fact which Miss Bingley seemed to recognize herself, if her startled look was in any way indicative. "In fact, we had thought to send for you, as there is a particular matter we would like to discuss. If you would be so kind as to step inside, we may deal with the matter forthwith."

With a quiet acceptance, Miss Bingley stepped into the room, and Darcy was amused at how many times her eyes darted to him. Her mind was clearly warring over hope that he would finally make her an offer and fear that he had heard of her confrontation with Elizabeth.

"Yes, Charles?" asked she when she was seated. "How may I assist you?"

"You may assist me by ceasing your attentions to Darcy and refraining from attempting to threaten his betrothed." Darcy was shocked at Bingley's blunt words, and it was clear that whatever Miss Bingley had expected, she had certainly not thought her brother would speak to her in such a manner.

"I am afraid I cannot fathom your meaning, Charles," said she as she twisted a handkerchief in her hands with nervous energy. "Whatever Miss Eliza has told you, I am sure she merely misconstrued—"

"Let us be open and honest with one another," said Darcy, interrupting the woman's rambling denials. "I am well aware of your ambitions, Miss Bingley, and I have been aware of them almost since the moment we first met."

"Then why—"

"Because I do not wish you for a wife," said Darcy, looking directly at her to ensure he was not misunderstood. "I wish for something more than you can offer in the woman I marry, and though I do not doubt that you would meet some other man's requirements admirably, you and I do not suit. Regardless of the state of my relationship with any woman, I will never make you an offer of marriage."

Miss Bingley seemed to deflate at his words, and she sank into her chair, this time apparently believing him. Darcy was not of mind to break the woman's spirit, even after all she had said to Elizabeth earlier that day. And Elizabeth herself had suggested clemency, which Darcy was inclined to grant. But he would not tolerate any further attacks.

"Regarding the matter of your conversation with Elizabeth today," said Darcy, "I am prepared to allow the matter to rest. But from this time forward, I will not tolerate any untoward behavior toward my betrothed. I suggest you guard whatever you have learned of her past as your most cherished secret, for I will not be merciful should any mention of it become the fodder for London's gossips."

"Of course, Mr. Darcy," said Miss Bingley, though her tone was almost inaudible. "Not a word of it shall pass my lips."

"Thank you. I shall keep up the connection for your brother's sake and because of Elizabeth's specific request. Please use this opportunity to secure a proposal from some interested man, if that is your desire."

"I shall, Mr. Darcy." Miss Bingley took a deep breath and stood, addressing her brother: "Charles, if you will excuse me, I believe that I shall retire."

Bingley gave his approval, and Miss Bingley left the room, though without the undue haste which Darcy might have expected. When the door closed behind her, Darcy looked to his friend, seeing an unusually pensive expression staring back at him.

"Well, that appears to have done the trick."

"I should think so. Unless she has suddenly developed a talent for the theater," replied Darcy. "I apologize, Bingley. Perhaps we should have had this discussion previously to save her the mortification."

"But it was proper that *I* spoke with her, Darcy," said Bingley. "And besides, I doubt she would have even listened to *you* had she not also had your engagement staring her in the face."

"You might be correct, my friend," said Darcy. "You might be correct."

It was the day before Christmas when a second unwelcome visitor arrived at the Gardiners' townhouse, but on this occasion, the visitor asked to speak with Mr. Gardiner rather than Elizabeth, which was just as well, as Darcy was certain Elizabeth wished to see just about anyone else in the world other than this man.

Darcy and Bingley had been invited to spend Christmas Eve with the family, and they had been in the study with Gardiner sharing a glass of port. The ladies had not yet descended from their chambers; Darcy was anticipating their arrival, for he knew that Elizabeth would be even lovelier than ever that evening in her Christmas finery.

When the ponderous and sweating form of Mr. Collins was shown into Mr. Gardiner's study, Darcy prepared himself for inanities aplenty. Mr. Collins could not fail to provide amusement, even if it was a dark variety.

Mr. Collins blanched upon seeing both Darcy and Bingley present. For a moment, Darcy thought the man might flee rather than face him again, but he summoned some well of courage and entered the room, bowing before Gardiner's desk in a grandiose manner.

"Mr. Gardiner," said he, "I am pleased to make your acquaintance, for I understand that you have had Elizabeth's care these many years, though I must own that I cannot fathom the reason why she lived so many years away from Longbourn. I regret that . . . well, what I mean to say . . ." Mr. Collins paused and mopped his brow before he pressed on, saying, "That is, given my own experience with Elizabeth, I could perhaps wish that you had been more successful in instilling a sense of . . . duty and . . . respect for her betters. But I must suppose that the child proved intractable."

"Miss Elizabeth," said Mr. Gardiner.

Appearing nonplused, Mr. Collins blurted, "I beg your pardon?"

"To you, Mr. Collins, my niece should be referred to as 'Miss Elizabeth.'"

A sniff of contempt met Mr. Gardiner's words. "As you wish. I suppose I cannot be surprised that your niece's lack of manners is also exhibited in the man who raised her, though I own I had hoped for the best."

Clearly, Mr. Gardiner was enjoying the spectacle, though Darcy, who was of much longer acquaintance with the man, was already at the point of throwing him into the gutter where he belonged. Still, it was Mr. Gardiner's house, and as Mr. Gardiner still had the responsibility for protecting Elizabeth, Darcy kept his own counsel and watched the proceedings.

"Is it not evincing a lack of manners to refer to a woman by her first name?" asked Mr. Gardiner. "Elizabeth is not connected to you in any way, Mr. Collins, and I assure you that she never will be again. Now, I would ask you why you have come. I had believed that the pleasure of meeting you would be indefinitely postponed, as I rather thought you would avoid any place where my niece was in residence."

"Yes, well, I have come for a particular reason. You see, I was until lately a resident at my cousin Bennet's home after having returned Eliz . . ." Mr. Collins trailed off and swallowed thickly when he saw Darcy and Gardiner's twin glares of displeasure. "That is, after I returned Miss Elizabeth to her family. I had made the journey in the convenience of my own modest conveyance, and as the distance was long, I was forced to wait until my horse was rested before I returned to Kent. During that time, I took the opportunity to . . . confer with my cousin, though I will own that the man has used me most grievously. It was there that I discovered a piece of important information which is the reason for my visit today."

Darcy almost snorted with amusement at the man. How anyone could use so many words to say so little was beyond his comprehension.

"And what have you discovered?" asked Mr. Gardiner as he leaned back in his chair and steepled his fingers in front of him.

It was at that point when Collins suddenly seemed to become nervous. It was clear—perhaps belatedly so—that he was in enemy territory and had no friends. Darcy considered the man to be nothing more than vermin, and it likely showed on his face, while Gardiner, though he appeared to be speaking to the man congenially, gazed at

Collins with glittering eyes, bringing to mind the proverbial cat toying with the mouse. And even Bingley, who was perhaps the most even-tempered and pleasant man Darcy had ever met, was watching the parson with a disapproving scowl.

Mr. Collins was silent for several moments, clearly struggling to determine what to say—or perhaps trying to figure out how to present his case so that he had the most chance of success.

"Well, Mr. Collins?"

As if Gardiner's words had suddenly pushed him into action, Collins blurted: "I understand that you have settled a dowry on Eliz—on Miss Elizabeth."

"And if I have?" challenged Gardiner. "What is it to you?"

"I want it," said Mr. Collins.

A sardonic snort met Collins's declaration. "And why would I give it to *you*, of all people?"

"Because Miss Elizabeth was married to *me*!" said Collins, displaying a hint of temper. "As she married me, her dowry should belong to me. I demand that you release it to me."

Gardiner's eyes fixed on Collins, and the temperature of the room seemed to drop almost perceptibly. "You must be the stupidest man in England if you think that you could claim a dowry under such circumstances."

"It is mine, and I will not hesitate to bring suit against you if you do not comply." But though Collins's words were intended to be firm and threatening, Darcy could detect a hint of a petulant whine in them, and he knew that a businessman of Gardiner's acumen would hear it as well.

"Let us be very clear on the matter, sir," said Gardiner, his voice now harsh and his focus sharp on the intruder, "you have no claim to Elizabeth's dowry, and if you think you do, then it is in your imagination. You and Bennet coerced her to the altar and forced her to accept a marriage, contravened several canon laws in the process, and took her off to Kent without her permission. She has since been declared separated from you via annulment, making the marriage void, as though it had never even occurred.

"In addition to this," continued Mr. Gardiner, his voice rising to drown out whatever the man was trying to say, "I attached several provisions to her dowry, the most important of which, from your perspective, is that *I* must approve of her marriage partner before her dowry can be released. I can tell you that I would never have approved of you, no matter what had happened with respect to the annulment."

Collins gasped. "You would have withheld the dowry had she remained married to me?"

"I would have released it to her under conditions which would have resulted in you never seeing a penny of it, Mr. Collins. It would have been her money and therefore completely beyond your reach."

The room was silent for a few moments while Mr. Collins attempted to understand exactly what he was being told. Gardiner continued watching the man through narrowed eyes, though he never lost his geniality. It was clear to Darcy, however, that only the fact that he was a gentleman was preventing him from throwing Collins out himself.

"You may attempt to bring suit against me, Mr. Collins, but I assure you that your suit is doomed to failure. You will not ever see so much as a farthing from me, and if I have my way, you will never so much as lay eyes on Elizabeth again."

Shocked, Mr. Collins looked around the room wildly before he seemed to crumple in upon himself. When he spoke again, his typical pomposity was gone in favor of a wheedling sort of supplication.

"I have been relieved of my duties at Hunsford and thrown from the parsonage as if I had not obeyed her ladyship's every command and catered to her every whim. And it is all because of your niece, Mr. Gardiner. I demand restitution."

"My aunt has not the power to remove you from your position, Mr. Collins," interjected Darcy. "You may return to her and tell her such."

Mr. Collins paused and licked his lips, and when he spoke again, it was in a halting tone. "The . . . church has . . . launched an investigation against me. It is due to the . . . archbishop's decree that I am stripped of my office and . . . suspended as a member of the clergy. There is to be . . . a hearing . . . next month to determine my exact . . . status."

"Good," said Gardiner, his pitiless eyes boring into the hunched-over caricature of a man standing in front of him. "Your actions have earned you nothing less. I hope the church irrevocably casts you from the ranks of the clergy, as there is no place for one such as you within that fraternity."

If Darcy thought Collins had been shocked before, it was nothing compared to the way his face lost all color at Gardiner's pronouncement. He appeared to not know what to say, as his mouth worked, but no sound emerged. It was a peculiar sight; in the course of Darcy's acquaintance with the man, Darcy had never actually seen him at a loss for words. Typically, it was quite the reverse.

"Now, I suggest you leave, Mr. Collins, as you are not welcome here. Though I have faith in Elizabeth's ability to laugh at the absurd, I will not chance her becoming upset at the sight of you."

And depart Mr. Collins did, with a defeated air Darcy had never seen in the man before. He might have felt sorry for the man if he had displayed any sense at all or had acknowledged his own culpability in what had happened. But he remained stubbornly convinced that he was in the right.

"And that, gentlemen, is how you dispose of a fool," said Gardiner.

Darcy and Bingley both laughed.

Had the past been different and Elizabeth grown up in her father's house as a welcome member, Darcy could not know what his reaction to Mr. Bennet might have been. He could not imagine ever respecting the man, but it was possible. He could not imagine, however, having anything but the highest regard for Mr. Gardiner. That, he was certain, would never have changed.

Chapter XXXII

The next weeks were busy, as there were weddings to plan, trousseaux to purchase, details to plan, family to become acquainted with, and events to attend.

As per their original plan, Mr. Bingley and Jane were married in a small ceremony the week before Christmas, fulfilling all her hopes of happiness and contentment and his desire for a wife who would complement him in every way. From the groom's family, his sisters were present, and he had some family from his home near York who also made the journey to attend. From the bride's family, her closest sister and her uncle and aunt were the only ones in attendance. Jane had declared that she had no desire to have her parents attend, and though one could only speculate as to Mrs. Bennet's likely reaction to the news of the marriage, all were certain that Mr. Bennet had likely met the announcement with nothing more than a shrug and a demand for his wife to leave him in peace.

In Elizabeth's eyes, there had never been a more beautiful bride, and Mr. Bingley looked very well indeed as he stood grinning at the front of the church, anticipating the arrival of the bride on the arm of her uncle. Of course, Elizabeth could not say that Mr. Bingley was the most handsome of grooms, for she was sure he could not compare to Mr. Darcy, who would, after all, be marrying her within the next two weeks. In fact, that very thought was the subject of some gentle teasing the night before Jane's wedding.

"I could never imagine that I could be so fortunate," Elizabeth had mused as Mrs. Gardiner brushed her hair the night before Jane's wedding. Jane sat on the bed watching them, and Elizabeth knew from speaking with her previously that Jane had envied her sister the closeness with their aunt. This pleasant scene was something for which she had always longed.

"How so, my dear?" asked Mrs. Gardiner.

"To attract the attention of a man such as Mr. Darcy is beyond anything my imagination could ever have come up with," said Elizabeth. Her eyes were slightly unfocused as she thought of her betrothed, but that did not prevent her from seeing the amused looks which passed between her relations.

"I, on the other hand, am not surprised in the slightest," said Mrs. Gardiner. She finished her brushing and took Elizabeth's long hair in her hands and began to braid it for sleep.

"How so?" asked Elizabeth.

"You are a wonderful young woman, Elizabeth. I have always thought you would find some man who would look past society's expectations regarding dowry and connections and realize the benefits of having you for a wife."

"I am not surprised either," said Jane, though in her typical quiet and diffident way. "I must own, however, that I often feared that no young man would look past the impropriety of my mother and sisters and make me an offer. I feel blessed indeed."

Her hair braided, Elizabeth vacated the chair in front of the vanity and allowed Jane to take her place. "And I cannot imagine you remaining without a husband," said Elizabeth with a smile for her sister. "You are so sweet and obliging that you must be valued as such. My mother and younger sisters cannot overcome that which you would bring to a marriage."

Jane flushed and nodded her thanks, though her manner was slightly uneasy. Elizabeth was well aware of the reason for this reticence. Apparently, Mrs. Gardiner was as well.

"Do not fret over your decision, Jane," said she. "It is understandable that you would not wish for your mother to be here, given her behavior."

"I know," said Jane, though Elizabeth had to strain to hear her. "I simply never wished it to be this way. I tried to explain everything to my mother, but she was so set in her beliefs that she would not be moved. She would persist in blaming Elizabeth for all our family's misfortunes regardless of anything I said."

"She has been thus ever since I have known her. It is not something you can change. You are doing the best thing for your happiness. If your mother wishes to be part of your life, then she will amend her ways."

It was wise advice, though Elizabeth knew that it did not apply to her. While Elizabeth was not possessed of a temper which was disposed toward implacable resentment, there was too much between them for an accord to ever be reached, even should her mother repent her behavior. Elizabeth was quite resigned to the fact that Mrs. Bennet would never be in her life—Mr. and Mrs. Gardiner were her parents in every way that signified. She could not ask for better.

"Perhaps instead of thinking of my mother," said Elizabeth with a mischievous grin, "you should think of your husband. For you *shall* be marrying a very handsome man on the morrow. I should think that *he* would keep your attention on the night before your wedding."

"I believe that I am not the only one marrying a handsome man," countered Jane, turning Elizabeth's teasing back on her.

"Oh, heavens," exclaimed Aunt Gardiner. "He is a handsome man indeed!"

Both sisters looked on their aunt in shock, causing the older woman to laugh. "Yes, girls, I am quite happily married, but I also have eyes, and without any disrespect meant toward your excellent and handsome Mr. Bingley, Jane, I must say that Mr. Darcy is quite the most physically attractive man I have ever laid eyes upon." Mrs. Gardiner's teasing gaze turned upon Elizabeth. "Do you not agree, Lizzy, my dear?"

Cheeks aflame, Elizabeth could only nod at her aunt's assertion. Mr. Darcy was indeed a fine-looking man, and Elizabeth could hardly be insensible to that fact.

"I believe that our Lizzy is quite busy contemplating the fine features of the man to whom she will soon be married," said Mrs. Gardiner in a tone full of mirth.

"It appears to be the case," replied Jane with a giggle.

But Elizabeth did not mind their gentle teasing in the slightest. For it was nothing less than the truth, and by her reckoning, she was a very lucky young woman.

Jane's wedding was everything she had ever wanted, though Elizabeth could tell that it was tinged with sadness at the absence of the rest of the Bennets. But such a thing was for the best, and everyone in attendance was glad for the happy couple.

The weeks following were busy ones for Elizabeth. She saw Mr. Darcy almost daily, sometimes in the company of his sister or cousins—or, on occasion, his aunt and uncle—and sometimes alone. Elizabeth relished those times when she could be alone with him, whether it was when they spoke in the parlor at the Gardiners' home, when they walked in the park, or when Elizabeth visited Darcy house. And though they were not alone often, their families seemed to understand their desire for privacy and allow them a few precious moments when possible.

During that time, Elizabeth found herself gradually introduced to the close society in which Mr. Darcy inhabited. There were plenty of events, as the season was just getting under way, and Elizabeth found that she could well enjoy them, though at times it seemed that she was being suffocated. For it was not long before she began to be the object of interest to many. Mr. Darcy, being one of the most eligible men in the kingdom, was well-known, and moreover, he was known not to pay overt attention to any young woman. Thus, when he opened the first ball Elizabeth attended in the New Year dancing with her, it caused quite a stir.

As the first strains of music washed over the assembled dancers, Elizabeth, her eyes caught by Mr. Darcy's, began moving in the steps of the dance. It seemed as if all awareness of any extraneous considerations were washed away in that moment.

The instant she had stepped into the house, Elizabeth was caught by the finery displayed there, which was quite beyond anything Elizabeth had ever seen before. The ball was being given by the Marquess of Ainesbury, a man who had attended Cambridge with Mr. Darcy and who had recently been married himself. When introduced to the man, Elizabeth had been impressed by the fact that he was quite unassuming despite his high social position. His wife, the daughter of another prominent noble, was much the same, and she greeted Elizabeth—and Mr. and Mrs. Bingley—with kindness and civility, making them feel quite welcome.

To their side, Jane was dancing with Mr. Bingley, looking resplendent in her beautiful dress and as radiant as a new bride ought. The crush of the room was such as Elizabeth had never before seen in any of the events she had attended with the Gardiners in the past.

"Should I feel slighted?" the sound of her betrothed's voice broke through Elizabeth's thoughts.

She smiled at him and said, "For what, sir?"

"The fact that I do not seem to be capable of holding your attention, my dear," replied he. "We have been dancing these past fifteen minutes at least, and you have not said a word to me."

"I was merely thinking. It seems like nothing more than a dream. I had never thought I would be attending a ball such as this, sir, and I am almost having to pinch myself to ensure that I am not asleep."

Mr. Darcy smiled. "I assure you that you are not, Elizabeth. This will be your future, so you had best become accustomed to it."

"I believe that will not be a problem. Though we have spoken of my aversion to certain parts of society, there are times when I do enjoy dancing and social events."

"That is well, Miss Bennet, as I shall likely require you to socialize enough for both of us."

Elizabeth favored him with an arch glance. "I have seen you socialize, sir. Though perhaps you prefer quiet activities, you are certainly not devoid of the social graces."

"Devoid of them, no. But I certainly do not enjoy them."

Elizabeth smiled at him, and then they were separated by the steps of the dance. It was then that Elizabeth noticed that there were many people looking at her and whispering among themselves. It was disconcerting, as she was certain she had never been the object of such interest before.

By the time she had worked her way back around to Mr. Darcy, he was watching her, the slightest hint of a smile lifting up the corners of his mouth. Elizabeth attempted a bland look in response, but given the way his smile broadened, she felt that she was unsuccessful.

"This is another part of life which you will be required to become accustomed to, assuming you are still intent upon meeting me at the altar, Miss Bennet."

Raising an eyebrow, Elizabeth said, "Are you perhaps a little too impressed with your situation?"

"On the contrary," said he, "I believe that this evening's reaction is understated, if anything. Most of those in attendance tonight are either friends or people with whom I at least share a cordial acquaintance.

"Besides, the announcement of our upcoming marriage will appear in the papers tomorrow. Once it becomes common knowledge, I expect that the interest in you will become all that much more intense."

Elizabeth digested this in silence as the dance took her away from her betrothed. She had known from the start that Mr. Darcy inhabited a position of much wealth and influence in society, but she had never expected such attention. For a moment, the thought of it caused fear to well up within her, particularly due to the thought that someone might learn of her annulment and spread the story to the gossips of society.

But no sooner had the fear manifested itself than Elizabeth squared her shoulders and put it behind her. She had always prided herself in her courage, and she would not allow apprehension to have sway over her at the thought of a certain amount of attention.

"There is your courage," said Mr. Darcy with a smile when they came together again. "Do not let others bother you. We will weather whatever storms come our way."

And weather the storm, they did. As Mr. Darcy had predicted, the announcement the following day unleashed a flurry of interest which did not subside for some time. Elizabeth and Mr. Darcy attended several more events before their wedding, and as he had said, the gawkers and rumor-mongers of society were very much in evidence, and the guest lists of those events were dominated by those with whom he was not well-acquainted.

But they held up under the weight of the scrutiny with all the poise and grace they possessed, and Elizabeth had cause to notice more than one smile which Mr. Darcy attempted to hide when she made some witty comment to deflect whatever impertinent question was directed her way. She felt that she had earned a measure of respect as time passed, though she sensed that she would never be accepted by the true snobs of society.

Two additional things became apparent to her as time wore on. The first was that Mr. Darcy had, if anything, been understating his distaste for society. Many a time, she noticed a sudden clenching of his jaw or a tight-lipped smile in response to a particularly impertinent comment. He was never overtly rude or unapproachable, but he often sported a scowl, and when she mentioned it to him, he invariably was surprised, not understanding how forbidding his expression would turn when he became impatient with others.

The second item which became clear to Elizabeth very quickly was that many in society, when hearing that they were to be married so quickly, suspected a particular reason for such unseemly haste.

"I expected such a response," said Mr. Darcy after the first time it had been pointed out that there were few reasons why a couple would marry so quickly. "The gossips wish for such salacious happenings, as it gives them something to titter over with their friends."

But Elizabeth could tell that even though he had expected it, he still was not amused. Thus, she felt that it was incumbent upon her to laugh him from his irritation.

"Then we have nothing to fear, Mr. Darcy," said she in a light tone of voice.

"How so?"

"Why, when I do not show signs of increasing soon after we are wed, we shall have the pleasure of laughing at those who believe such ridiculous things."

"Perhaps," said Mr. Darcy as he stroked his chin. "But if it happens soon after our marriage, there will still be rumors."

"Then perhaps we should abstain for some time after our marriage so as to prove to all and sundry that nothing inappropriate has occurred between us."

Her words were spoken in a light and airy tone, but Elizabeth watched Mr. Darcy out of the corner of her eye, wondering how he would take this teasing. The answer was not anything she would have expected.

"In that case, Mrs. Darcy," said he, as his smoldering eyes bored into hers, "you will almost certainly be required to live at the family property in Northumberland. Otherwise, I doubt I will be able to restrain myself long enough to offer any kind of proof."

The fire in his eyes almost left Elizabeth breathless. Needless to say, she did not tease him on the subject again.

The one truly unfortunate result of the publishing of their engagement was that it drew strong attention from an unwelcome corner. The consequences of such attention were swift, and the resulting scene was one which displayed, if any doubt about such existed, that the highly born were just as capable of poor behavior as anyone else.

Two days after the engagement had been made public, Elizabeth sat in the largest sitting room in Darcy house, visiting with Georgiana and Anne, chatting as if they had known one another for many years. Anne was making great improvement under the care of the doctor that the earl had procured for her sake, and though she might never be of robust constitution, she had told Elizabeth that she was feeling much better than she had in many years.

It was nearing time for Elizabeth to return to her uncle's house when the sound of shouting could be heard from outside the closed door, followed by the sound of footsteps and the staccato tapping of a cane striking against the floor in agitation. Elizabeth only had a moment to consider who the likely intruder was when the door was forcibly wrenched open with such vigor that it crashed against the wall behind it. There in the doorway stood the large form of Mr. Darcy's least favorite aunt, her displeasure present for all to see.

"You!" exclaimed the lady, her eyes narrowing in fury. "Be gone at once and never darken the halls of this house again!"

The outright rudeness in the lady's imperious demands did far more to bolster Elizabeth's courage than anything else she could have imagined, and Elizabeth stood and glared at the lady, injecting a little imperiousness of her own into her manner.

"I shall not," decreed Elizabeth. "I was invited here by the master of the house himself, and as I shall soon be its mistress, I have every right in the world to be here."

"The right!" screeched the lady. "How dare you speak of rights when you have been the cause of such hardship and grief!"

"I know not of what you speak," replied Elizabeth, her voice chilly as a winter's breeze. "But you shall not come into this home and wail and yell your demands and expect all within hearing to fall down in obeisance."

A bitter scowl fell over the lady's face, and she stalked forward. "So it is true. You seek to impose yourself upon my nephew in a brazen manner. But I suppose, considering your performance while in Kent, that nothing better can be expected from you."

"If you refer to the incident with your parson, then you must know it was not my doing. I would never have gone to Kent if I had been given any choice in the matter."

"He is no longer my parson! And it is due to your actions that a new and much less suitable man has been forced upon me by the church. The living is mine to bestow upon whom I see fit, yet my hand has been forced due to their refusal to send me appropriate candidates. It is my right to know the doings of the parish, yet the man who is currently installed refuses to answer my questions thereon!"

From Lady Catherine's words, it was clear that Mr. Collins had been replaced by a man of some sense. Knowing some of the parishioners as Elizabeth did, she could only be glad that the yoke of Mr. Collins and Lady Catherine had been lightened to some degree.

"If he has been removed, then so much the better."

Lady Catherine gathered herself for a retort, only to be interrupted by her daughter. "You mean you are not able to meddle in their lives, mother," said Anne as she stood from where she had been seated beside Georgiana. "I believe we all must applaud that development."

"I will not be spoken to in such a manner!" snapped Lady Catherine, turning her glare upon her daughter. "You will be seated and be silent until I have dealt with this upstart. Then you will return to my brother's house and pack your belongings, as we shall be returning to Rosings forthwith."

"I will not," was Anne's determined reply. Despite Anne's blooming in the past weeks, everyone appeared surprised at her forthrightness and determination to stand up to her mother, but it was Lady Catherine who was shocked the most. That shock, however, quickly gave way to the lady's customary anger.

"I see the behavior of this woman," Lady Catherine gestured with her cane at Elizabeth, "has influenced you as well, Anne. And I suppose Georgiana, who was always meek as a mouse, has begun to emulate her as well?"

Though Elizabeth thought that Georgiana would remain silent, a spasm of a glare suddenly came over the girl's face, and she stood slowly. Elizabeth was proud of her, though her defiance was understated, as she *was* still a very young girl. A young girl faced by a relation who had terrorized her all her life.

"I am happy to emulate Elizabeth," said Georgiana, her voice shaking only slightly. "She is confident, and she is to be my sister. I am happy my brother has found someone he loves so dearly."

"Love has nothing to do with it," exclaimed Lady Catherine. "And I assure you that all my nephew feels for this trollop is a slight infatuation. He may use her and be done with her—it matters not."

Gasping, Elizabeth stared at Lady Catherine as though she had been slapped. "I wonder that a woman who is so proud of her breeding could make such disgusting statements in polite company."

"I do not consider your company polite."

"Then perhaps you should leave. I assure you that I shall not."

Lady Catherine waved her cane around furiously. "I shall not be spoken to in such a manner—and certainly not in the house of my sister's children. Miss Bennet, you shall leave immediately and not return."

"No, she shall not, mother!" A brief glance in Anne's direction showed her to be as unmovable as Lady Catherine. "Elizabeth will do no such unreasonable thing.

"You have wished for me to marry my cousin for many years," continued Anne, the emotion in her voice almost constricting

Elizabeth's heart. "And you have wanted this without heeding anything but your own selfish desires. But I will tell you once and for all that I am happy that Darcy and Elizabeth have found one another. They are 'formed for each other,' as you are so fond of saying. I can only hope that one day I might find a man who loves me as much as Darcy loves Elizabeth."

"I suggest you leave, Lady Catherine," said Elizabeth. "No one will bow to your demands here."

"No one will indeed."

The sound of a deep male voice startled each of the four women, none of whom had noticed the arrival of the master of the house, who was accompanied by his cousin the colonel. Mr. Darcy's displeasure was almost a force of nature, and Elizabeth could imagine winds whipping around him, stirred up by his great displeasure, as he stalked into the room and glared at Lady Catherine. He stopped briefly to assure for himself that the ladies were unharmed, and he came to a halt beside Elizabeth, taking her hand in his and kissing it before placing it in the crook of his arm.

In this attitude, he turned to Lady Catherine and regarded her with an upraised eyebrow, almost daring her to continue to vent her displeasure. The colonel, having followed him into the room, took his position between his two younger cousins and added his glare at his aunt. All at once, Lady Catherine seemed to realize that she had no allies in this room, as even her four relations stood united against her. Thus, when she spoke, her words were moderated by a calmness which Elizabeth was certain she did not feel.

"I could not believe the reports I heard, Darcy, so I hastened to this place to make my sentiments known. Am I to understand that you intend to marry this . . . this . . . ?"

"Be careful what you say, Lady Catherine," interjected Darcy. "I will not have my *betrothed* insulted any more than she already has been this day."

Appearing as if she had swallowed a particularly sour lemon, Lady Catherine nevertheless fixed her gaze on Darcy and said: "I am unable to account for how you have lost yourself to this woman. Even if you do not wish to marry Anne, surely there are more suitable prospective brides in society. Do you seek to betray your parents' memories in such a way?"

"I do not love any other prospective brides, Lady Catherine. And I do not believe I am betraying my parents' memories. My father might have wished for something more for me in terms of connections and dowry, but my mother would only have wished for me to be happy. *That* is the most important consideration."

"Very well, then. I shall know how to act."

And without another word, Lady Catherine turned and strode from the room, the sound of her cane echoing through the halls until the front door of the house slammed behind her.

"You know she means to go to my father," said Colonel Fitzwilliam.

"Let her," replied Darcy. "Even if she did manage to persuade him to her way of thinking, it would have no effect on me."

"As it should not," said Anne. "You are your own man, and knowing you, I would not expect you to bow to another's unreasonable demands."

As the hour was becoming late, Elizabeth declared her intention to depart, but the others would hear none of it, insisting that she stay and take some tea, which, given the events of the past few moments, she was only happy to agree to do. It was not long before the effects of the confrontation with Lady Catherine were soon dispelled, enabling everyone to agreeably enjoy their time together.

Soon, Elizabeth insisted that she must leave, and she departed, saying fond farewells to the family who would soon be her own.

Mr. Darcy accompanied her to the carriage, and she knew by his introspection that he had something to say to her. They had almost reached the front doors when he broke the silence, stopping to look at her, the concern for her evident.

"You are certain you are well?" asked he. "You stood up to my aunt admirably, but she can try the courage of anyone upon whom she turns her spleen."

"I am well, Mr. Darcy," said Elizabeth. "I had the support of beloved friends. How can I not be well?"

"I am happy to hear it." Mr. Darcy paused for a moment, seeming to search for the proper words. "What I said in the sitting room is nothing more than the truth. I love you dearly, Elizabeth, and I shall not be content until you are my wife."

"My feelings match yours in every particular, Mr. Darcy."

His eyes darted about, and seeing no one, he leaned in and brushed his lips against hers, the touch so gentle and fleeting that for a moment Elizabeth almost felt as though she had imagined it. A powerful feeling welled up in her breast, and she leaned forward, resting her head upon his shoulder, feeling a sense of safety and belonging which was so comforting that it almost brought tears to her eyes.

They stood in that attitude for some moments, each reveling in the closeness of the other, each knowing that the other was their future. It was a bright future, to be certain, and one that both anticipated with eager anticipation.

In the years to come, both would look back on that day and that memory of standing in the foyer to their London home with great fondness. And their married life was filled with much happiness and contentment, though inevitably disputes and discord did arise between them on occasion. As Elizabeth philosophically told her husband, it was only natural that two strong-willed and confident people would disagree and defend their positions with vigor.

Jane and Mr. Bingley, by contrast, seemed to have a home which practically thrummed with harmony and good cheer, and given the personalities of the two individuals themselves, it was not surprising. Elizabeth suspected that they had their disagreements, much as any other couple, but their arguments were never within sight of anyone else, and like Elizabeth and Darcy, they appeared happy in their lives. Caroline Bingley was also able to make a good match with a man of some fortune, and while Elizabeth and the former Miss Bingley never became friends and confidantes, they were at least able to meet with perfect civility — and perfect indifference.

When the Darcy and Bingley children began to arrive, they also became the closest of companions, and as the Bingleys purchased an estate in nearby Nottinghamshire within an easy distance from the Darcy estate in Derbyshire, all Elizabeth's ideals of happiness were fulfilled. As the years rolled along, the thoughts of her trials as a child began to fade into the distance of memories until she rarely thought of them again. She was able to forge a new life for herself with her family, and she was content with it.

Lady Catherine never fully reconciled with Mr. Darcy, and she kept her distance for the rest of her life, unable to endure the pollution that her sister's home had suffered with Elizabeth's presence. As Mr. Darcy did not seem to repine her obstinate stance, Elizabeth allowed herself to accept it, as she had never desired Lady Catherine's good opinion. But with her new family, her new sister, and her new cousins Anne de Bourgh and Colonel Fitzwilliam in particular, Elizabeth became very close. And when Anne's wishes for a man who would love her like Darcy loved Elizabeth were fulfilled in the good colonel, Elizabeth was able to wish them both the best in her marriage. Lady Catherine was, by all reports, not happy with the development, but in this, as in so many other things, her opinion was ignored. Darcy and Elizabeth might have wished for the Fitzwilliams to be situated closer than Kent, but they met as often as possible, though not at Rosings until after Lady Catherine's passing for obvious reasons.

As for the Bennets, Darcy and Elizabeth made good on their promise to assist Elizabeth's sisters in any way possible, and soon after their weddings, invitations were dispatched and accepted for Catherine and Mary to visit them. Under their supervision, with the assistance of the Bingleys, the younger Bennet girls saw great improvement in their manners and accomplishments and were able to make good matches of their own. Mary eventually married a parson and was situated close to her sister Jane in Nottinghamshire, while Catherine married a young man possessing a modest estate in Staffordshire.

The relationships between Catherine and Mary and their elder sister Elizabeth were repaired to a great extent, and to every other happiness, Elizabeth was able to add the closeness she shared with most of her sisters. Growing up as she had in the Gardiners' house, vilified by her parents, it was more than she had ever expected.

Unfortunately, the youngest sister persisted in her distance from Elizabeth and was, as a result, estranged from them all for the rest of her life. Catherine and Mary could never be prevailed upon to elucidate upon her reaction when the initial invitation to join them in London had arrived, but her displeasure had been loud and long, and she had apparently said things about Elizabeth which could not be repeated. Privately, Elizabeth suspected that Lydia's displeasure might not have been so acerbic had she not wished to stay in Meryton to flirt with the officers who remained in residence until the summer of that year. Elizabeth never repined the loss of Lydia's society, as by all accounts, the girl never gained a sense of propriety, and the unrestrained nature of her behavior only worsened with time.

Lydia, however, did not live in Meryton for long after her elder sisters all quit the town. For in the spring of that year, Mr. Bennet passed suddenly due to a sudden apoplexy, leaving his widow and youngest daughter without a home. Mr. Gardiner, with the assistance of Mr. Bingley—and the grudging help of Mr. Darcy—set up a small establishment in the town of Meryton for the Widow Bennet, and there, within days of her husband's passing, she was installed in the company of her youngest daughter.

Anyone who was at all acquainted with Lydia knew that such a situation could not persist. For a girl so unrestrained in behavior and high in spirits, sitting at home with a mother so lacking in sense and submitting to the strictures of mourning was a punishment of the most acute kind. It was not more than a few weeks before Lydia disappeared, eloping with one of the officers of the militia, leaving her mother alone in the house with only the servants for company. Lydia chiefly lived abroad after her elopement, and after only a few years, the sisters lost all contact with her. As for Mrs. Bennet, she reportedly became a bitter woman, railing against life and her daughters for betraying her. But as she would never recant and apologize to Elizabeth for her behavior, she was never allowed in their homes, and she would eventually pass away from one of her nervous attacks, which became worse over the years.

With the death of the previous master, Mr. Collins was quick to claim his inheritance, and he moved into Longbourn as soon as he arrived from London, where he had been staying with a relation. But as Mr. Collins had no experience in the management of an estate, the tenants he offended largely left for greener pastures, the fields soon fell into disrepair, and the annual yield fell to a fraction of what it had been previously, even under the indifferent management of its previous proprietor.

Mr. Collins, by his very character, was not one to endear himself to his neighbors, and his pompous and sometimes condescending attitude drove most of the neighborhood from him in disgust. As such, he was to receive no help in learning to operate Longbourn as he might have been able to procure had he behaved in a better manner. Thus, when Mr. Darcy offered to purchase the estate from the man, he was only happy to take the money and leave the place that he had come to blame for all his misfortunes. The Darcys were happy never to hear from Mr. Collins again. They were also happy when Longbourn was returned to a prosperous state, and coupled with the purchase of Netherfield, it became the home to the Darcys' second son.

As for Elizabeth's surrogate parents, the Gardiners did indeed purchase an estate in Derbyshire, and it was situated on the other side of Lambton, the small market town which owed much of its prosperity to the Darcy estate which abutted its borders. Elizabeth and Darcy always maintained the closest of relationships with the Gardiners, and both were sensible of the fact that Elizabeth became the woman she was due to their care and attention.

In business, Mr. Gardiner continued to prosper, and Mr. Bingley and Mr. Darcy—sometimes with the Fitzwilliams—often invested in his endeavors until they became fabulously wealthy men when their endeavors paid off handsomely. They were among the first to invest in the new railroads which soon crossed the length and breadth of England, and that investment alone secured their families' futures for generations to come.

All in all, Elizabeth was content in her life. What had begun in hardship and despair had changed to love and laughter, harmony and hope, and she could not be happier.

As her husband told her some years later, "You truly are a marvelous woman, Mrs. Darcy. You have risen above the implacable resentment of your parents and become the woman you are today. I could not be prouder."

"I believe that I have you to thank to a great extent for that, Mr. Darcy," replied Elizabeth with a fond smile. "And of course, our *implacable love*. I never thought I could be possessed of such happiness."

And happy they were.

The End

FOR READERS WHO LIKED IMPLACABLE RESENTMENT

Acting on Faith
Though Darcy has no assurances of Elizabeth's regard after her rejection of him, he nonetheless moves forward in his quest to secure her hand. Unfortunately, neither Caroline Bingley nor Elizabeth's childhood friend Samuel Lucas intends to make it easy for him.

Waiting for an Echo, Volume I: Words in the Darkness
When Mr. Darcy comes to Hertfordshire to decide between two prospective brides, he has no idea that his eye will be irrevocably caught by someone so much lower in consequence than him as Elizabeth Bennet.

Waiting for an Echo, Volume II: Echoes at Dawn
When Elizabeth travels to Kent to stay with her newly married sister, she meets Mr. Darcy's two prospective brides and is forced to deal with the consequences of a pair of tragic events. Can her feelings for Mr. Darcy conquer even the villainous machinations of a former love interest?

Open Your Eyes
Elizabeth Bennet is forced to reevaluate her opinion of Mr. Darcy when Mr. Wickham contradicts his own words. In the course of her dealings with the two men, she realizes that first impressions can sometimes be deceiving.

A Summer in Brighton
Elizabeth is invited to travel to Brighton instead of Lydia with her dear friend Mrs. Forster. But what is supposed to be a relaxing vacation turns out to be anything but. Amid intrigues and newly discovered love, Elizabeth discovers that there exists in men an evil so vile, that it will drive a man to do anything to hurt his hated enemy.

For more details, visit
http://rowlandandeye.com/

ALSO BY ONE GOOD SONNET PUBLISHING

THE SMOTHERED ROSE TRILOGY

BOOK 1: THORNY

In this retelling of "Beauty and the Beast," a spoiled boy who is forced to watch over a flock of sheep finds himself more interested in catching the eye of a girl with lovely ground-trailing tresses than he is in protecting his charges. But when he cries "wolf" twice, a determined fairy decides to teach him a lesson once and for all.

BOOK 2: UNSOILED

When Elle finds herself constantly belittled and practically enslaved by her stepmother, she scarcely has time to even clean the soot off her hands before she collapses in exhaustion. So when Thorny tries to convince her to go on a quest and leave her identity as Cinderbella behind her, she consents. Little does she know that she will face challenges such as a determined huntsman, hungry dwarves, and powerful curses . . . .

BOOK 3: ROSEBLOOD

Both Elle and Thorny are unhappy with the way their lives are going, and the revelations they have had about each other have only served to drive them apart. What is a mother to do? Reunite them, of course. Unfortunately, things are not quite so simple when a magical lettuce called "rapunzel" is involved.

About The Author

Jann Rowland is a Canadian, born and bred. Other than a two-year span in which he lived in Japan, he has been a resident of the Great White North his entire life, though he professes to still hate the winters.

Though Jann did not start writing until his mid-twenties, writing has grown from a hobby to an all-consuming passion. His interests as a child were almost exclusively centered on the exotic fantasy worlds of Tolkien and Eddings, among a host of others. As an adult, his interests have grown to include historical fiction and romance, with a particular focus on the works of Jane Austen.

When Jann is not writing, he enjoys rooting for his favorite sports teams. He is also a master musician (in his own mind) who enjoys playing piano and singing as well as moonlighting as the choir director in his church's congregation.

Jann lives in Alberta with his wife of more than twenty years, two grown sons, and one young daughter. He is convinced that whatever hair he has left will be entirely gone by the time his little girl hits her teenage years. Sadly, though he has told his daughter repeatedly that she is not allowed to grow up, she continues to ignore him.

Website: http://onegoodsonnet.com/
Facebook: https://facebook.com/OneGoodSonnetPublishing/
Twitter: @OneGoodSonnet
Mailing List: http://eepurl.com/bol2p9

Printed in Great Britain
by Amazon

49544937R00235